JOANNA

JOANNA

LISA ST. AUBIN DE TERÁN

Carroll & Graf Publishers, Inc.
New York

Copyight © 1990 by Lisa St. Aubin de Terán
All rights reserved

First Carroll & Graf edition 1991

Published by arrangement with the author.

Carroll & Graf Publishers, Inc.
260 Fifth Avenue
New York, NY 10001

Library of Congress Cataloging-in-Publication Data

St. Aubin de Terán, Lisa, 1953–
    Joanna/Lisa St. Aubin de Terán.—1st Carroll & Graf ed.
        p.   cm.
    ISBN 0-88184-690-2: $18.95
    I. Title.
PR6069.T13J6   1991
823'.914—dc20   91-4505
                                                      CIP

Manufactured in the United States of America

For Joan Mary St Aubin: Joanna

PART I

Joan

PART II

Miss Kitty

PART III

Poor Florence

PART IV

Joanna

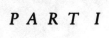

PART I

Joan

CHAPTER 1

WE are a photograph, the same photograph of every year with me a summer older, so a summer taller: lanky Joan, outgrowing the world around her. It is always Selsey Beach, a stretch of bare sand on the South Coast, and there are certain constants: myself, Granny, in her tight-bodiced dress, crocheting or gazing out to sea, and Mother with her green Antarctic eyes, cross-sectioned and sepiad by the camera. Mother, as beautiful as ever under her hat but with her cruel stare frightening even the seagulls off the beach. Or was it just empty? Out of season?

There was always someone else, sometimes two or three others, to keep my mother from getting bored. She suffered from boredom as others suffer from depression or sciatica. To qualify as a companion at Selsey you had to be a young man, well bred, well heeled, good-looking and slavishly (but not boringly) in love with Mother. Very few of them survived the summer, and they would be sent down in disgrace for gibbering or, worse still, weeping, or for falling silent and ceasing to amuse the summer queen of Selsey.

The surest way to find her disfavour was to notice me. Few dared or cared enough to try. Only Granny was immune. Granny still held a thread of control over her wayward daughter. She held the purse strings and untold secrets behind her benign gaze. So she sat still and upright like a rock among the scattered rocks of Selsey Beach. She was the silent mediator between Mother's violent bitterness and my own desire to be forgiven.

I think by the time I was twelve I had come to believe that only a miracle could make Mother love me. I have always believed in miracles. I hoped then for a new start, a new shape – to become, I suppose, as indistinguishable from the mass as any drop of water in that cold sea. In the meantime, more than anything, I wanted a reprieve. For what? For being born, for being there or anywhere. Every time the wind blew sand on to the sandwiches I felt another wave of resentment from my mother's striped deckchair. Under the sun she had managed to forget me; looking up, she'd see that I was still there. She wouldn't say anything, she didn't need to; the cold disdain of her eyes spoke for her, repeating what had come to be another creed. The destruction of her life by my birth was a story I knew by heart. I should never have been born at all, and added wilfully to this original sin by being huge and gangly, with a craven nature and red hair. Maybe all the other things could have been forgiven, but the red hair confirmed my status as a cuckoo in my family triangle. No one else had red hair – one didn't – only the Irish.

We were three women on a beach, locked in a frame, year after year, from 1928 to 1938. Sometimes I'd go there straight from the convent, and the length of my stay was the test of the current state of warfare between Mother and Granny. A long stay at Selsey meant that Granny had the upper hand. A few days were the sign of weeks of tantrums from my tired but triumphant mother.

At Selsey we'd dream of going back to Jersey. Granny would grow nostalgic for Claremont and her gardens there, and even Mother would allow herself to drift into memories of balls and summer nights and tiaras of emeralds as brilliant as her eyes. I grew to love Jersey with the kind of fervour I learnt from the nuns. At the convent they fought to make me inconspicuous, and to control my every thought. They knew enough about me to hold me in contempt, and they knew that if they needed a scapegoat, I would do. My mother would never write and complain. But I had Jersey in my mind, secret from them and all their prying.

At Selsey even I could share in the family stories, by listening. And I could sit near Granny, so long as I kept away from Mother, and I could sift the fine sand through my fingers like all the time past and yet to come that Mother couldn't keep me from. I'd sit for hours under my hat (which failed to stop my freckles, but covered my hair) running that sand through my hands.

It was at Selsey that I first discovered something in me that Mother could not control. She could read my thoughts. She could read most people's, so I don't think she often bothered with mine.

Whenever I was with her I felt as though I were singing my responses out of turn in chapel, but as soon as I was away from her I wanted only to be able to sing them again. I used to feel that I was the disguised heroine of a story book that she kept closing before the end. So I kept growing out of my costumes, like a snake shedding its skin, hoping each time to be released from the spell.

By the time I was twelve I was five foot nine, and I looked eighteen years old. I'd lie on the beach in my bathing dress and wait for the summer's heat to make rivulets on my skin. The touch of sand on my legs and back felt as sweet as sugar, and as sticky. Once in a while a passing man would stop and look at me with the same attention Granny lavished on her rarest blooms. It was not the way she peered for greenfly; more the way she inhaled the scent of her first azaleas. Whatever it was, even the nuns could sense it. Sister Marie had my gymslip recut to cover my chest in pleats, and Sister Thérèse warned me that I had the devil growing in me. She said it would possess me unless I gave myself up to prayer. Sister Thérèse never knew if she was coming or going, with her chronically red eyes and her ready tears, so she didn't know that Mother had already told me of the devil in me years before and that I had been praying since I was five, praying and begging for the devil to go.

Between the hours of Matins and the Angelus, Mother Superior controlled all the girls of Les Filles de la Croix with her cobweb of piety. She ruled from the centre of her web, drawing in pupils and nuns alike on her righteous silken thread. Like the beads of her black rosary, she told us endlessly, passing her trembling prey through her sharp blue-veined fingers. Her office, at the end of the dark corridor beyond the refectory, seemed to palpitate with broken wings. The corridor itself was lined with creaking linoleum, brown paint and a gallery of paraffin-stained martyrs. On winter evenings, the oil lamps flickered with the draught from under the Mother Superior's door.

She wore the black butterfly of the Order of the Daughters of the Cross on her head as though the stiffened cloth could transform her into a death's-head hawk moth. In her high-backed chair she would sit under the sullen gaze of an oleograph of Saint Teresa the Virgin and wait for tears. On a low shelf behind her was a collection of pinned butterflies mounted over pressed flowers that appeared desperate to escape from their desiccation and ether death, where the last tears had been pressed from them. Mother Superior insisted on tears before she would release anyone from her office. Whenever I was summoned there, the size of my hands made me cry. She was small and bird-boned. She seemed to me to be a heartless jackdaw whose quick beak would tear the soiled lace from my hands. My fingers used to struggle inside my gloves as though they were growing visibly. All through the Junior School I would bang my fists against the square of wall below the crucifix over my bed and bruise my palms until they refused to stay within the confines of the regulation lace. White gloves for visitors, Mass and Mother Superior; white gloves and tears, those were the rules.

On feast days and holidays my hands were no less bruised. They were permanently mauve and blue. Mother thought she had killed all my pleasure and all my thoughts; but out there, on the hot sands of our holidays, I felt my body rebel slowly. I made my fists into hourglasses and I filtered the yellow grains through them, a trickle of hope at a time.

Granny told me to wait. From the age of twelve I waited with a new prayer in my head: to be strong enough to survive Mother's bitterness until such time as I could go and find some comfort in the eyes of a man, any man, who'd admire me. Meanwhile I was still lanky Joan, the human giraffe, ungainly in the photograph beside her beautiful, diminutive, clairvoyant mother, who might, in a different century, have been burnt as a witch.

Perhaps, though, those times were strangest of all for Granny, coming as she did from another century. Her clothes and mine were a miracle of mending and cutting down. She wore every shade of charcoal without so much as a hint of colour and she never would tell me why. I think it might have been a penance of some kind. The only times she ever seemed completely at her ease were in the garden tending to her arum lilies or picking her azaleas or just pottering about surrounded by bright flowers. After four decades of Catholicism, Granny still felt the inner stigma of being a convert. She was feverishly devout. I used to think she was atoning for Mother's cruelty with her kindness. Mother and I must have been sent to try her faith. She carried our misdemeanours on her shoulders, crocheting them into her silkwork with her prayers. Each stitch made up a little for what our wilfulness had undone.

At Selsey, Mother would sit seething in her canvas cradle. It angered her to see the tides recede without her approval. It angered her not to be rich and to find that she couldn't spin gold. Sometimes Granny would glance across at Mother's restless figure over the finger-spinning of her own hands and it looked as though she wanted to reach out and touch her daughter but didn't dare. Granny seemed to know and accept that her Kitty would never spin or exert herself; her idea of work was to flash her eyes. She even seemed to know that Kitty had little religion beyond her own vanity – just as she understood that I had no real understanding of Mother or myself beyond the imagery of fairy tales and half-remembered prayers.

Mother got obsessive about things. Sometimes she'd come home and start to pick dog's hairs off her clothes as though she were covered in a canine thistledown. Once she tore the silk suit she was wearing into shreds and made her arms bleed, snatching at air. The more she picked, the more hairs she said were there, on her, in her tea, over her chair. Granny kept Rufus, her own special dog, out of the sitting-room, but Mother refused to believe this.

'Why do you let him soil this house? Tell me! Tell me!'

But Granny sat mutely and sadly out of the way while Mother wound herself up and snapped, 'Where's Rufus? Bring him here!' She rang the bell and shouted at the mumbling maid, then slapped her. When no culprit appeared, no imaginarily balding dog, she turned on me, and left the cowering maid alone. Mother could slap harder than any nun, and that day she tore at my hair. Its very thickness exasperated her and when only tufts came out in her hands, she pushed me under Granny's frail sewing table and kicked at me, missing half the time but still making my nose bleed over the Chinese carpet. Then it was Granny's turn to restore the house to calm merely by saying, 'Kitty, remember!' Those two words were enough to reduce Mother's rage to silent spite. She went upstairs to change; the rips in her clothes were scattered with my hairs. They looked like scratches and I wished they were. I used to lie in bed at night and wonder: remember what? What had Mother done that Granny could blackmail her so into submission?

When I was little, in Jersey, Mother refused to speak to me or let me be in the same room as her. It was only in London that I was allowed to see her, and even there, not very often. I used to hide on the stairs and spy on her and wait behind doors to glimpse her through the gaps in the hinges.

'When you think how she suffered,' Granny would tell Agnes or whoever else had inadvertently witnessed Mother's studied neglect of me, 'no wonder it is hard for her to see the child. One of them should have died that night. It is a miracle that they both survived.'

It was small consolation to be half a miracle. When I was little, I saw my quest as regaining what I had lost through Mother's ordeal in Jersey. It took me years and years to accept the unpalatable truth: there was nothing to win back. I was unwanted, and therefore always unloved. Nothing I could do would ever restore that natural balance of affection that I saw between other girls and their mothers. I tried for a time, on my brief devout visits home from the convent, to win her forgiveness. But Mother despised kindness, she saw it as a form of weakness. My willing-ness to please was more irritating to her than my previous tearful pleading.

'She cloys the house,' she would tell Granny. 'Send her back to school, then at least she can learn some self-respect. There is something servile about her.'

I knew there was. I was being taught to serve Our Lady, but I wanted to serve Mother instead. I substituted my catechism with a heretical passion for her. I transposed the Scriptures to fit my triangular family. We were the acrobats from the circus that came to Hendon Green one autumn. I was the base that supported the climbers. The weight of their feet on my shoulders crushed me down. I longed to support them without so much pain. I don't think Mother really wanted me to be strong, though; she just didn't want to be annoyed by my lack of strength.

At night, in the convent, draped in the coarse gown that protected us from the evils of our flesh, I would lie awake and think. What had I done wrong? I prayed until my prayers turned to bullying. My '*Miserere mei, Deus, miserere mei: quoniam in te confidit anima mea*' turned first to a wheedling bargain and then the 'have mercies' began to contain more and more veiled threats until the 'Have mercy on me, O Lord' came to be weighted with 'or else I won't trust in Thee ever again'. My frustration grew apace with me. Every week before the sacrament we used to sing:

'*O salutaris hostia*
Our foes press on
From every side,
Thine aid supply
Thy strength bestow.'

And by some strange emotional osmosis, I did grow strong. Mother loathed me, and I grew to thrive on her disdain. I courted it. I gloated at her cruelty, I was proud of her hardness. I had survived fourteen years of her regime. I had borne what no man could. I was her target. Other people were just peripheral, but she aimed at me, set me in her sights and fired over and over again. I was the position she could not take. I apprenticed myself in her ways, studying how most to infuriate her. I knew how to electrify her eyes and defy her stare.

She was small and as fragile as the tendril of a new vine. But she was resilient. Her skin was like the alabaster madonna in our chapel. She had a small mouth which she held tightly pursed as though to hold in all her disappointments. Life itself was a disappointment, and I was the leader of a world conspiracy to let her down. Everything about her shape was perfect, perfect but small, like a rare poison, a concentrate of perverse powers. I saw all that she was, and gradually I saw that I was bigger than she was. For years she had slapped and pinched me until I wept. It was a seemingly endless flow of tears, provoked as by a recurring tide. Then I noticed how she had to reach up to me, or catch me sitting down. I noticed how she was forever on her toes. And as I looked down, ten inches down, below me, at her bobbing enraged miniature figure, I felt I could knock her down with one blow of my fist. I could swat her like a fly, the way boys did on the bus when the summer flies buzzed and hovered over the windows. I could hurt her. I could break her bones.

At school, the girls used to chant, 'Sticks and stones may break my bones but names can never hurt me.' I always remembered that, because it was back to front. A stone is only ever a stone; it cuts and bruises and then the wound heals. But names, words, have a life of their own. They grow in your bloodstream, they lodge in your brain. Her words have never left me. Her blows, now, down the distance of decades, are nothing. At fourteen I hadn't mastered the art of maiming with names, but the old playground lore was on my side. I was bigger than she was, I stood up to her. I threatened to break her arms if she raised them to me. I thought, as I said the words, that she'd go berserk, but she just looked away and shrugged.

'Don't be such a fool, Joan,' she said. 'Where will it get you?'

Then it was my turn to shrug, but I kept my fist clenched over her head. I wasn't going anywhere, but I didn't tell her that. I was just biding my time until I could get away from her. So anything meanwhile that undermined her power had to be good. I was surviving, and my little mother was beginning to lose ground.

CHAPTER 2

GRANNY moved through the house with a serenity that was in itself disturbing. She limped very slightly from one hip, and her tall thin figure always sloped a little to one side. She had silvery grey hair arranged in a loose bun, and enquiring grey eyes that I had inherited. She seemed not to register either Mother's tantrums or my own grief. Yet she comforted me, moving closer with her calm. Even in her reprimands, there was a tenderness that made her smallest order a pleasure to obey. We played solitaire together on neighbouring tables inlaid with birds and flowers. Sometimes we played bezique or cribbage, but mostly we had our own games, separate yet shared.

In Jersey she had ridden a bicycle and taken her four dogs (three English setters and a Yorkshire terrier) running behind her on their leads. It was her one eccentricity. She wandered all over the countryside around St Helier, and knew all the lanes that linked the different farms and parcels of lands. In her riding habit, hat and gloves, sitting bolt upright in the seat, she combed through the Longuevilles, and Grand Vintaine, Mont à L'Abbé and Mont au Prêtre, and Mont Cochon and Coin Tourgis, touring the parishes with her canine escort. She knew all the different farmers and their wives, and the market gardeners, and the carters and labourers. Half French and half English by descent, she had found in Jersey, through her marriage, the perfect place to be. The sound of Jersiaise clung like a childhood lullaby to her ear. Despite her broad sunhat, or through it, she used to catch the sun. Each summer found her thus, with a deep tan on her face, glowing with an unfashionable vigour that all her friends and neighbours lacked. She used to smile in a way that gave me a glimpse of my own mouth in hers, when she told me how she'd get jagged oil stains on her clothes sometimes from the chain. No amount of disapproval could dissuade her from these rides; with the seed of her daughter's future stubbornness, Granny stuck to her cycling, celebrating the island she loved by pedalling over it yard by yard.

Agnes, the maid, was like the family chronicler. She had left her own family in Ireland so long before that she had almost entirely lost touch with them. Then, somehow, after amassing a handsome dowry, trousseau and all the necessary skills of a wife while working under Granny's rule, she had let the marriageable time pass. An excess of prudence and raw memories of her own childhood in the bogs of County Cork had prompted her to turn down her early suitors, while a sense of her own importance, wealth and superiority scrimped and gleaned from Granny made her loath to mix her lot with a vulgar fortune-hunter after she passed her middle age. Agnes was convinced that the world was full of people who had learnt of her savings and the many presents Granny had given to her and would, upon the slightest encouragement, be down on their knees making sly proposals to her, if she were to drop her own guard for so much as a second.

With her own passions reserved for the polishing of her mahogany and rosewood pieces and dusting of the porcelain trinkets that had been her ritual Christmas presents now for nearly thirty years, Agnes lived our family passions vicariously. She never tired of describing my grandfather's death scene, and assured me that she suffered 'continually' for the poor man. My birth was her favourite topic, and she could keep her narration of that tormented night going for almost as long as the actual events. So Mother's long hours of labour were saved for a reluctant posterity by Agnes's histrionic rendition of the cries and moans and her more than graphic descriptions to all concerned. Not surprisingly, after the first few months nobody really wanted to hear the saga repeated for the umpteenth time. It was only as I rounded the corner into concentration that she got her perfect listener. I was enthralled by the gore, the detail, the suspense and the whole idea that I had ever actually touched my mother.

So Agnes and I grew close, albeit behind the kitchen doors out of Mother's earshot, or in the garden, sheltered by the high raspberry frames. Mother not only didn't want to see or speak to me herself, she didn't want anyone else to either. Agnes would, I think, have given up her life to Mother, but she could not resist the temptation of repeating her stories, so she risked her displeasure by gossiping to me.

I didn't meet my father until I was eighteen, but Agnes told me that Mother left him in Canada only six months after their marriage. She sailed home, alone, with her bitterness, to have the abortion that is me. She was delayed overland, and then a freak storm hijacked the ship. She never saw or spoke to my father again. I don't know exactly what happened out there in those winter months of 1920, or what she did to him, but in eighteen years he never came to see me. He must have offended Mother in the worst way he could. He must have bored her, and Mother suffered from boredom as from a disease.

Even if she had come home without me to disfigure her, she would have arrived too late to see her own father alive and just in time to see his estate auctioned. As his only heir apart from Granny, she stood to inherit a mansion and a park, a farm and his money. Instead, she inherited his debts. Her daddy, to whom she was running home from the Arctic cold of Canada and the monotony of married life in the outback, had gambled her birthright away behind her back. Her father, the ageing, debonair, slightly eccentric pillar of Jersey society, had bet away hundreds of years of accumulated wealth, leaving a widow and a reluctantly pregnant daughter to fend off his creditors while the shocking affair of his gambling debts was sorted out. So the land and the house and the cottages and the silver and the paintings were all sold, while the bewildered and defrauded heirs – Granny and Mother – stayed in a hotel in St Helier. Mother's delusions grew apace with the unwanted baby in her womb.

By April her discomfort was such that she refused to stay in the hotel any longer, and they removed themselves to Agnes's own house in St Aubin, and it was there that I was born.

'Your granny used to ship maids from Ireland to Jersey to work at Claremont in the same way that Captain Bouvard used to ship kippers and gentleman's relish to India. They arrived in batches but they went off after two years, like the kippers.' Agnes herself had worked at Claremont for over twenty years. She had watched Mother grow up, and Granny said once at Selsey that she was one of the few Islanders who didn't seem to rejoice secretly in her downfall.

But for my birth, Mother need not have stayed in Jersey, need not have watched her possessions fall under the hammer and scatter among her friends. But for my birth she would never have had to humiliate herself by staying with a former maid. She had not the heart to face her friends penniless and runaway and pregnant, so they hid on the other side of the Island – Granny, Mother, and her thwarted mortal sin.

My unborn self became the focus of her malaise. Then my birth came, like the removal of a tumour. I left a wound which was stitched and cauterised, but the cancer had already seeded.

Agnes said that whatever there was in Mother which was potentially maternal, whatever dregs of goodness or forgiveness to a child, were scraped out of her in childbirth. And her screams that night in Jersey took the place of whatever words there might have been for me in the next five years. I came, pulled by a drunken doctor like the bad sediment of her marriage, to live in the shadow of her warped silence.

'Your poor dear mother is five foot and one inch tall, and so slight,' Agnes would whisper, 'while you were never natural. You weighed fourteen pounds newborn – twice the weight of an average baby. I never saw nor heard the likes of it, Joan.'

Agnes said the mattress turned into a crimson sponge. She showed me the bloodstain on her pantry ceiling, dripped through from the night when I was born.

'Miss Kitty bit through all my wooden spoons, you know, suffering. It was said that the sailors could hear her screaming, right out at sea!' Mother kept the scars, no doubt, and I kept the blame. *Mea culpa. Mea culpa.* It was always *mea culpa.* Mother never took any blame.

I had my own scars too from that first night. I have deep dents in my skull where the forceps crushed me out. I learnt so much about it that I almost ceased to be the huge wide-boned baby ripped from between my mother's thighs and came to be more of an Agnes, the hovering maid, the helpless onlooker. I saw the scene as from behind the jugs of hot water and the piles of linen swabs that Agnes relayed into Mother's room, her own guest bedroom with its shutters painted in new white and green like the shutters of the sewing room at Claremont, where she'd spent so many years. The furniture had mostly come from Claremont too, bits and pieces that Granny had given her when she retired. There was a bow-fronted chest, a card table and an inlaid wardrobe, all gathered from the attics and polished and cleaned to make a home for Agnes, to recompense her years of loyalty.

After we left Agnes's house, Granny rented a terraced house nearby, directly overlooking the Bay, on the harbour front. It was close enough for Agnes to run up and down and wait on Mother, who seemed to find her loss of status easier to bear so long as she could treat the willing Agnes as a slave.

We lived there for the next year, and although I remember nothing of that time for myself, Agnes filled in the months for me so clearly that I almost feel I do remember them. She put the scraps of my past into one of her own porcelain jelly moulds and turned out a distinct, if wobbly, shape. For instance, the arrival of the remnants of Granny's furniture from the warehouse where it had been stored since the auction seems like a really vivid memory. I can still imagine Granny stroking the writing-box that was one of her wedding presents and pursing her lips slightly, realising for the first time how very little had been salvaged from the financial wreck. And Mother coming to the doorway, still frail from her ordeal of having me five months before, looking down impatiently at Granny's sudden grief.

'Is there something wrong with the box, Maman?'

Granny didn't answer, she just stood, leaning and looking at the bands of silver and mother-of-pearl inlaid in the dusty wooden top.

'Is there?'

Mother could never bear to be ignored, and the sharp edge had come into her voice now, the slight shrillness that foretold trouble.

'Well?'

'I suppose it brings home to me that your father has really died.'

'Hmmm,' Mother said, and then smiled her scalpel smile. 'Yes, Maman, and he lied and lied and lied, which is why we are here, with the filthy sea at our feet and that thing in the attic. We're all women now, Maman. No men at all.' Having said her bit, Mother turned back to the little morning room where she was sitting doing a jigsaw puzzle with her back to the September sea. Agnes, the silent witness of all their scenes, went back to the attic to calm down the screaming 'thing' there, which was me. For Agnes and a daily nurse and a set of glass bottles were struggling to be a mother to me. But though I grew and grew, gaining weight as quickly on that island as the potatoes and cabbages that were force-bred for shows, I screamed night and day, and even from the banishment of the attic my cries crept down and drove my mother mad.

Granny had some money of her own, pin money which had once bought jaunts to St Helier and theatres and presents for maids; it now formed our only income. Granny called it her pittance. In fact it was enough to rent a house of some size, to feed and clothe us, and also to keep at least one maid. Looking back, it seems strange when I recall how Mother raged against our so-called poverty; while Granny often mourned, I know, the power to provide which she had lost, and regretted the inadequacy of her 'pittance'.

I grew up during the Depression. There wasn't much sign of it on the harbour front or in the shops or on the promenade or the Royal Square in Jersey. And there wasn't much sign of it in Golders Green, where we went to live in exile in that social no-man's-land peopled, increasingly, by affluent Jews. There wasn't much sign of the Depression either at Selsey, on our three annual pilgrimages to the sand and the sea. But sometimes a flash of life beyond our parish pushed itself into view. The queue for soup outside the Town Hall in Camden, for instance, and the occasional group of men standing around in that special way of people who have nothing to do and are ashamed of it, but are still proud under their shame. And other groups, of those who have swallowed their pride so many times that it has broken something in their chests. Those were the signs of the Depression for me, glimpsed from the top of an omnibus as I travelled backwards and forwards on my Sundays at home, from Golders Green to the River Thames; to St Thomas' Hospital to visit a friend.

After our decampment to London, Granny dropped most of her friends. I suppose our circumstances were too changed for her to feel comfortable with her old set. Or maybe she just wanted to hide away the irregularities of our home, or maybe she just felt tired, or merely knew that by not entertaining we could survive better on what we had. There were a few exceptions. One of these was an old, close friend from Jersey whom I knew as Mrs de Gruchy, who lived in a suite of rooms at St Thomas' Hospital surrounded by her own furniture and a circle of Jersey friends. Granny visited her every Sunday afternoon, and when I was at home, I did too.

Mrs de Gruchy seemed very grand and very old and she smelt of lavender water and Penhaligon's lily of the valley blended together with a strange, musty smell which seemed to be her own. At the end of each visit she took her leave of us and retired into her bedroom, implying that she might never rise from her brass four-poster again. Her illness was of an extremely mysterious nature, and its symptoms were hinted at and whispered about but never openly mentioned. Apart from the musty smell, Mrs de Gruchy always looked extremely healthy, but her presence in the hospital, and the attentions of the two nurses fussing around her apartment, belied appearances. Granny would never hear of any suggestion that her dear friend was an arch hypochondriac who enjoyed the attention and the privileged view of the Thames.

Mrs de Gruchy showed no signs of recognising the existence of a Depression – or, indeed, of any form of life other than the one inside 'her' hospital. Beyond the convent and home, there was only Mrs de Gruchy in her cocoon, so from an early age I came to love my visits there, if only for their diversionary value. Granny was gratified that I enjoyed visiting her friend so much. It pleased her that I had this taste for Jersey talk and Jersey news. And it pleased me that Mrs de Gruchy served afternoon tea with an abundance that satisfied even my enormous appetite. To avoid embarrassing Granny on these occasions I was given five thick rounds of bread and butter after my lunch and before setting out so that I would not appear to pounce on the food at St Thomas' as though I had not eaten all week.

Second helpings were considered vulgar everywhere except for St Thomas'. I spent the hours between meals wondering constantly about what would be on the menu and how much of it I would be able to eat before it was whisked off the table by our long-suffering maid. Before I went to school, I thought it was just another of Mother's torments that she half-starved me. Later, though, I discovered that most of the girls at the convent actually went to great lengths not to eat their meals. My early popularity there stemmed from relieving the other girls of their greens and puddings. None of them could swallow tapioca, my favourite, without feeling sick. Mrs de Gruchy was fat and unashamedly fond of cakes and sweetmeats, and she took a perverse delight in plying me with them so that she could watch someone indulge herself to an even greater extent than she. When Granny remonstrated, which she did every week, Mrs de Gruchy would say, 'Let her be, Florence, poor girl, she hasn't much to look forward to with her looks.'

To which evident truth Granny, crocheting away, could only tacitly agree.

Once, I remember, during an Easter holiday, Mother accompanied us to the hospital. We passed a group of jobless men preparing to march. They were gathered on the Strand in huddles around the slip street beside Charing Cross Station. From my position on the bus I could see their furrowed features and wilted clothes as they waited, like weeds in a discarded flowerbed, at the edge of the road. As our bus crawled along, their faded faces were mostly turned away from the slow traffic. It was in the early days of our time in London and, newly arrived from St Helier, I was unaccustomed to seeing such numbers of motorcars and shops and people, and vaguely embarrassed by the city itself in which we were so alien and apparently ostracised.

I remember looking up and out that day, and catching the eye of a dark-haired, battered man. The bus stopped at that moment, and he stared at me staring out at him. There was a fierce look on his shadowed face, a resentment of my look. I was seven and used to the politely pitying or openly curious looks of my mother's friends or passers-by in Jersey. I was already used to the mocking stares of London children, and the incredulous glances of tradesmen who dealt with Mother and found it hard to believe that such a delicate lady could have produced such a huge and ungainly scion. But no stranger had ever given me such an openly hostile look as the one which then confronted me through the glass of my window seat. We were downstairs for once, and so there were only inches between me and the marcher. I suppose, looking into his face, I saw poverty for the first time. It was not the genteel scraping of my home but something that pinched the bones and sapped the marrow, and marked a face more clearly than a rubber stamp.

I was fascinated by his desperation – so much so that mine seemed to diminish beside his own wilder sorrows. It couldn't have been for more than a few seconds that I saw him, glowering through the brass-rimmed window, but it was long enough to convulse my whole view of the world, the enclosed world of Granny, Mother and me. Beside the sudden knowledge of his piercing presence, I felt myself freed for the first time from my own immediate concerns. I looked into his eyes and at his disdainful face, and I smiled.

It wasn't just a polite smile, or a compromise. It wasn't a smile I'd ever known before. I thought later, as the bus rolled on past Westminster, that it was rude of me to have smiled in his face with only the glass and a few feet of kerb between us. I watched his drawn silhouette as we left, light-headed and happy to discover that there was more to the world than our uneasy triangle and an occasional genteel Agnes in the background, or a Mrs de Gruchy wallowing in a wheelchair.

'Who are those people?' I asked Granny. She turned her eyes only to the receding figures and shuddered.

'They're vagrants.'

'What are vagrants?'

'Dogs!' Mother interjected, and Granny bristled, thinking, I'm sure, of her own three dogs: the English setters, left behind in Jersey, and Rufus, her one remaining companion. Mother disliked Rufus with an intensity that seemed almost wasted on such a small animal. Rufus was Granny's last legacy from the Island, brought in a wicker basket on the ferry. He had to make up to her for the loss of everything from the Gulf Stream to the lighthouse she loved. She sublimated her memories in the cultivation of exotic plants in the green belt around North London. Every year, from 1927 until her death, she seemed to dwindle in direct proportion to the flourishing of her shrubs in the garden behind our newly built and rather cramped house. This was the stage for the drama Mother made of every moment of her life.

Golders Green was like Dante's Inferno to Mother, or at best a nationless place for the dispossessed to grapple with or fall from. The Jews from all over Europe settled there – that is, the ones who had the money to buy the villas with the mock Tudor beams that would house their exiled dream. It was a place, so my paternal uncle Frank said, that any self-respecting person would be ashamed to live in. Not surprisingly, it suited Mother and me. We made our home to one side of the gaudy affluence of the salvaged Germans and Viennese. 'They' lived on the far side of the High Street in their new and abundant four-bedroomed ghetto while we, the fallen gentry, lived on the Hendon side of town.

Mother was one of the few Hendonites who was indifferent to the Jews as an issue, and she refused to join in the anti-Semitism of our neighbourhood. She disliked most people on principle, and when it came to comparing them to herself, they all fell short of her rigorous standards. The only nation she was prepared to discriminate against wholeheartedly were the Canadians, and we never met any. Canadians and all members of the male sex evoked her scorn, together with the weak and witless.

Even Granny, otherwise so mild and generous, feared and shunned the Jews with a deep-set antipathy. It wasn't just that 'they didn't come out of the top drawer', they didn't seem to come out of the same piece of furniture at all. But Mother even made friends with a Mrs Goldman and insisted on inviting her round to tea, and she had some of her clothes made by a Mrs Müller, a Viennese modiste. All Mother's loathing in Golders Green was banked up for me and Rufus. Granny often tried to incite her daughter to feel the kind of decent prejudice a well-born Jersey girl should feel to outsiders. It was no use. Mother liked those Middle Europeans. She liked their cooking and their sewing and she liked the way one or two of them, notably a Miss Cohen and Mrs Müller, always tried to outstare her. I expect she would have made rissoles out of a genuine refugee, but these well-to-do Israelites had a flair and a love of glitter that mirrored itself in her empty heart, and she championed their cosmopolitan charm.

She despised only the whining, cringing Rufus, dragging his hind legs towards her in abject appeal; and me, servile to a degree. Later, if she had pinned a yellow star to my forehead I would have worn it; and later still, I would have put her eyes out with it. Mother was no one without her eyes. Without her stare she was just a diminutive, bossy, slightly hysterical woman with dark brown hair and an unnaturally pale complexion. She managed to be fashionable in what she called her sackcloth chic, and her story appealed to the popular fantasy of high society. She rarely accepted any of the invitations she received, and so her presence became the more prized. The most entertaining men of a house would be sent round to beg her to come to this or that dinner, this or that dance.

Mother liked to be begged sometimes, so long as there was never any need for charity. People said she had psychic powers. She could frighten people just by looking at them, and she could make people do what she wanted. Her eyes were like the stylus of a wind-up gramophone. She could make her world play her tune in endless repetition. She could wear out the grooves of anyone's life until it was smooth and black. She tired quickly of songs and friends and then discarded them.

Granny and I could gauge Mother's moods by her turntable. We were the uninvited guests at each recital. I can still remember those thirties songs which catch in my throat like sentimental tapioca.

> I'm sitting on top of the world,
> Just sailing along . . .

drifted across the landing for weeks before the inevitable crash and splinter. For years Mother's temper passed as fascinating: only Granny knew there was more to it than that. I don't think she was afraid of Mother, she was afraid for her. She protected her daughter, covered up for her; and she protected me, as best she could, without ever admitting that Mother's anger went beyond the bounds of normality. Whatever lacked at home in the way of kindness on the one side was balanced by Granny's quiet generosity. So, Mother would beat me, and Granny would tend my wounds. Or, far more often, Mother would ignore me, and Granny would make up for it by reminiscing to me as I went to bed, filling my head with Jersey stories. It was always the Jersey before the crash – the island that had seemed to her to disappear back into the English Channel, with all its cliffs and villages, at the time when her own dreams and expectations crumbled to nought.

At bedtimes, when Granny came to me, and smoothed my nightie and my bordered pillowcase, and sat beside my bed, sometimes for hours, talking, certain subjects were taboo. For instance, I was never allowed to ask why Mother treated me as she did — or, indeed, why she behaved as she did. But my other worries were allowed to surface and be smoothed as Granny crocheted beside me.

After she had heard my prayers, she stayed with me a while. In those moments, in the darkness, I felt safe, and I fought off sleep so that I could listen longer to the muffled crick of Granny's arthritic finger crooking around her thread as she darted her crochet hook backwards and forwards. I imagined that she was knitting red hoods to save me from the wolves. I felt my own hair on my pillow and I loved the touch and smell of it on my face, like hot sand and soft soap. Even the jobless people on the street, the hungry wolves of Westminster, couldn't get past my granny there.

CHAPTER 3

LONDON was a maze of greyness that I never belonged to. After six years of Jersey with its soft southern ways, I found London an astonishing and unsightly invention. I had grown to know first the sands of St Aubin and then, to the far side of the Bay, St Helier itself, which was all a town should ever be, filled with familiar shops and faces and garlanded by the sea on one side and countryside behind. I used to pick the sea columbines with their striped trumpets to take home to Granny, and wait by the stalls of subtropical flowers in the hope of fallen orchids. And there were seagulls on the beach and over the harbour, and palm trees with their furry detritus. There were the fishing boats with their bleached planks opened like a gutted fish, smelling of seaweed and hot rope, shells to collect, sea anemones to poke and fishermen to talk to who didn't care about the colour of my hair or the size of my feet. By contrast, London looked like an utterly unnecessary growth blotting out an already unattractive landscape.

It was all very well for Mother to ignore me. But in London, not only in Hendon and Golders Green but even in the West End where people like Mother and Granny lived, they themselves were ignored. We queued for buses with indifferent strangers, and we shopped in places that didn't even know who Granny was. She could give her name, and it seemed to make no impression on the shop girls at all. Our exile was hardest for Granny; not only had she lost so much but here in London, nobody even knew she had lost it. We were reduced to what we were in ourselves, in our outward appearance. So Granny, dressed in her old-fashioned charcoal grey, moved like a shadow through our north-western suburb, having no pew of her own in St Joseph's church. As the years passed, she shifted slightly further over to her right hip, as though the inhospitable pavements of Hendon were softening under her laboured tread and gradually swallowing her up. And the little finger of her right hand crooked in a permanent bend, where the thread of her crochet silk had kept it stiff and swollen on the joint.

Entrenched in the religion she had embraced, together with her favourite sister, Violet (the painter of miniatures and watercolours, the pianist of the family), she refused to find fault with her lot. Violet had died, aged only twenty-two, but she had died happy in the visual richness of her new faith. Granny remembered her, this younger sister, whose beauty – but not height – had been reproduced in her own recalcitrant daughter. The emerald eyes, the pale skin, made paler in her last years by consumption, they were all Violet's. As were the gaiety and the grace; but the sweetness and generosity of her sister had been warped into a monstrous reverse caricature. Granny wore a locket of Violet around her neck. Her dead sister's angelic features were painted in miniature and mounted on white gold and seed pearls, with a locket of hair twined in the back into a delicate V.

From April to October Granny sat in the window of her oval sewing room crocheting her sorrows into intricate designs, exorcising her fears in fine borders, with her faithful, contentious Rufus ageing at her feet, while she gazed out on to her garden of camellias and cinerarias and hibiscuses that struggled in the grey climate of the sunless city. She tended the garden herself, wearing galoshes and gauntlet leather gloves, and she had, behind the vernacular revival of our house, a small botanical miracle as a reminder of the Gulf Stream she had left and never had the heart to return to.

The rules of the house varied by an unspoken code, depending on Mother's presence or her absence. When she was in I was banished, except at meal times, to my room. When she was out I was invited into the sewing room and even the sitting-room, and Rufus and I had the run of the garden.

Agnes came to visit us twice a year and her gossip, together with a daily scrutiny of the Births, Deaths and Marriages columns of *The Times*, kept Granny abreast of the Island. She made very few new friends, and those she made she kept at a distance. She seemed to be locked irretrievably in the past, with only the ritual of her religion to hold her to the present. Like me she hated the dull light, and the incessant rain and the dampness that seemed to emanate from her own bones. From October to April she would be driven from her window seat to the fireside, to pine in the heat. It was only when I started boarding school that I realised she was actually ill and not just sadly missing Jersey.

Watching her day by day, the changes in her limp and the greyness of her face increased almost imperceptibly. Later, coming home for exeats after weeks and often months of absence, I would notice her eggshell frailty corseted into her rigid bodice more clearly. Sitting in the palm house at Kew Gardens, breathing in the warm, peaty air, I sometimes thought her willpower alone kept her living – that, and an undefined fear. I realised that Granny had sent me away for my own protection, and that she was staying alive for as long as she could so that I might grow up unbattered by Mother's fury. I knew she wasn't doing it just for me. It was for her daughter too, to save her from herself, and for the family and for her own innate sense of decorum. For, side by side with my elephantine growth and Granny's ailing health, Mother herself was becoming ill: her girlish temper and mounting bitterness were accumulating out of all proportion.

Granny saw the signs, but she couldn't openly accept them. Meanwhile I spent my first ten years consumed by guilt and remorse. I wanted to be forgiven, and loved, in that order. Later I became an imaginary Cinderella, a misunderstood waif in the clutches of a wicked witch. She was worse than the traditionally cruel stepmother, because she was my real mother. But I never was able to see her as a real woman, I couldn't see past my self-righteous innocence. She was in the wrong, and I condemned her out of hand, gradually gaining ground at her own game. I studied her weak points, then goaded her. All through my adolescence I exploited her wrath, revenging myself on her for the hours of tears, and the anguish, and the cracked ribs, bruises, nosebleeds and cuts.

Granny tried to protect me from the truth as she saw it. Regardless of what happened, she assumed that my age placed me in a statutory state of bliss. She equated childhood and innocence without reckoning with the strange nature of the warfare between

Mother and me. The lethal bite was always there in each other's throat, so my only hope of Eden seemed to be whenever I became old enough to leave home. I had heard Granny whisper to Mrs de Gruchy that our only hope of escaping our cruel fate was by jettisoning our past. But the present was so disturbing, and the Island beckoned continually like a lighthouse beacon guiding its lost souls back across the treacherous sea. Sometimes it was as though we were shipwrecked on a raft in that city of fog and strangers. The slightest jolt could have drowned us. Our survival was miraculous. We hid our wounds. Granny hid her grievous sadness in grey bandages, and I hid mine, instinctively covering up the bumps and scars that Granny could not explain, not even to Mrs de Gruchy. Only Mother seemed unaware of our precarious situation. I had to pretend not to see things, but Mother was blind. We were bound together like shotgun brides for ever by Granny's will. I needed my mother's forgiveness so that I could be free to live, and she needed my death. And between us and our apparently insoluble dilemma we wore Granny down, like two unequal bits of pumice stone grinding each other to death in a silken crocket sieve.

In Hendon, when the crises came, as they did every three months or so, I would lie in bed with the scent of lavender on my pillowcase and a pattern of daylight shuddering through the lace curtains. I used to dream of running away to Canada. Since that country had proved such a nightmare to my mother, I imagined that it would be like terrestrial bliss to me. My father had chosen to live there and I was constantly accused of being like him, of taking after him, of threatening to 'be an Allen'.

When I read the stories of 'Grey Owl' and followed his Indian footprints in my sleep, from Golders Green to Alaska, I could see that Mother could never have found such a place anywhere as near to her taste as the Café de Paris or the Ritz. And yet, beside the otters and the Indians, my father, who was a full blood brother to my Uncle Frank and could not, therefore, be entirely savage, had found somewhere to live. From time to time, I addressed SOS letters from the convent to 'Arthur Nelson Allen, Esq., Canada', begging him to kidnap me from my mother. Not surprisingly, I never had any reply, not least because all our letters were censored by Mother Superior. For years, I didn't know whether he was still alive. I fuelled the forests of my night-time reading with scenes of my younger mother murdering him in the wild outback.

I had too few illusions about myself simply to run away. My father showed no signs of interest in me, and from what I could gather, the people who took in mistreated runaway children would not be keen on a huge voracious redhead like myself. Eventually it was the war that brought my father back to me, just as it was the war that finally released me from the purgatory of home.

While we were in Jersey, I spent so little time with my mother that she never really had a chance to batter me. I know, because Agnes once told me at Selsey, that one of the reasons we left the Island was that Mother had kicked me down a flight of stairs, and Granny had had to call the doctor in to stitch up my head. I wish I had been old enough to have told Granny then that I would never tell on her, or on Mother. There was always a limit to the scope of damage available there, whereas later, in London, we had to hide Mother's tantrums from everyone, even the doctors. I don't know if Granny ever saw the harm she caused by making us all stay together. Sometimes I thought she did, and that was what made her so sad. We were her world, the world as it was left after the Great War. Maybe she saw us as an indivisible unit and feared, before her time, the splitting of the atom. Sometimes, though, it just looked like a self-inflicted blindness. If Mother hit me in our own house, Granny could mop up and then pretend it hadn't happened. If I had lived away – boarded out, say with Agnes – what could stop Mother from going to find me and causing a scandal?

The shrubs in the garden covered the downstairs windows. Our house was camouflaged with leaves. The music from Mother's Grafonola, topped up by Granny's wireless, disguised our shouts. Not that there was such a great deal of noise. I tried hard not to scream. It was quicker and better not to. In my first year in London, I said Hail Marys in my head, as Granny had taught me to in times of stress:

'Hail Mary, full of Grace, the Lord is with you.'

Every time Mother became 'headstrong', the first sting of her assault came as a surprise. When the lower half of her jaw set in a certain way, I knew a tantrum would inevitably follow. Lots of times I could have run upstairs and locked myself in the bathroom, or dashed for the garden, but I would just sit or stand where I was, waiting. Then the first slap would feel different and I would feel cheated – disappointed, because there was no security, even in her violence.

I am what nurses call a 'bleeder'. A slap on the cheek can make my nose pour; give me a punch on the nose, and I can soak an entire carpet. So I had a double goad for Mother. My presence infuriated her and then the sight of my blood drove her to a frenzy.

Mother had a mole on the side of her right hand: a single chestnut blemish on her orange-flower skin. After the first few slaps she would tire and clench her fists tightly, using her right hand as a hammer to pound into my skull. I would watch the red-brown mole, fascinated by what seemed to be its power to hurt me. I used to fantasise about nailing Mother down to a board and cutting out that mole; when she sat by the fire I wanted to burn it off her hand. When she was 'headstrong', I was frightened of her eyes. She could make me wet my pants as I stood before her. But it was the sunken rusty nail-head on her hand – the misplaced stigmata – which battered into my own rust-covered head, that caused the harm. It traced a record of Mother's state of mind on my scalp; a path of blue scars buried under my hair. It was maternal graffiti, subtly coded now, if brutally written at the time. The scars read, 'Mother was here'. At the time they just spelt out plasters and compresses and days in bed or banished to my room.

There was always time to heal one lot of cuts before the next batch came – that is, until the end of our first year in Hendon, when Mother ricocheted from Rufus to me twice in one week and landed me in the children's ward of the Royal Free Hospital. She gave me a detached retina and a fractured skull. They gave me seven stitches in my head. It was the only time an ambulance came for me. All along the hilly way to Hampstead, Granny wept silently into a handkerchief so tiny that it dripped tears on to my wrist. I was carried in a red blanket out of that ether cabin. I could smell the ambulanceman's breath on my face: hot tea and apples. I liked his holding me.

'What happened?' the registrar asked.

'I fell downstairs,' I lied, and I saw Granny sigh, torn between relief for Kitty and grief at my lie.

I went straight from hospital two weeks later to a Dame School on Primrose Hill, where I lived as a sporadic boarder until I was eight. Granny kept taking me home to sit with her in her sewing room. It wore the colours of the room where I was born, the Gulf Stream colours of white villas with warm green shutters. She imbued me with Island tales there, and a due sense of pride at being Jersey born.

'We might be living in England, Joan, but we are not English. This is foreign soil.'

Although Granny delighted in our own foreignness, she continued to be unhappy about other people's. She said, 'To be French is honourable, to be Italian is acceptable but rather unfortunate. It is all very well to be English but it just isn't the same as Channel Island.' To be anything else was declared a terrible shame.

My months at the Dame School were a bewildering interlude. Starting mid term, as I did, I was behind the other children in my class, and quickly branded as stupid. I found myself unable to concentrate. I missed Granny and I feared for Rufus's life without me, and for Granny's happiness without him.

Miss Sidebottom (seedy-bothome), the headmistress of this small establishment, was a surprisingly benign lady. She had silvery white hair arranged in Shirley Temple curls in a bid for youth so blatant as to be quite touching, even to the eyes of a child. Miss Sidebottom was as bland as the very pale strawberry blancmange that she served as a mainstay of our diet. She was plump and a powdery pink. She smelled of soap and baby talc and artificially softened wool. There were eleven pupils in her school. Lessons consisted of reciting passages of *Chambers' Encyclopaedia*, which we copied out during prep. Meals were tasteless and based on cornflour. The flagship of her menu was always the blancmange, shaped like either a rabbit or a fish, depending on the day of the week. I was linked to the other girls there by shared misfortune. We were all disturbed in one way or another, and unwanted at our respective homes. Most of the girls were younger than I, and most of them were only temporarily in their family's way. Our rootlessness bred a form of cruelty. I held my own there through the advantage of sheer size. But I was unversed in playground lore, and no matter how often Miss Sidebottom warbled that she had seen worse heads than mine change colour, I knew mine was there to stay.

It was in the early autumn that Mother scored a point and got me sent right away from home. I had spent most of the preceding summer holiday on my own with Miss Sidebottom and a catatonic, anaemic girl called Caroline. I had been taken down to Selsey twice, and twice been escorted back to Primrose Hill in disgrace. Mother managed to evict me with a minimum of violence and the force she did use was channelled and disguised as discipline. The charge of spying was dropped, temporarily, and replaced by one of ignorance.

'It's heathen, Maman. Unless you organise a convent it will be quite savage.'

So I spent my eighth birthday as a Fille de la Croix at the French convent I was to attend for the next four years. It was a maze of brown corridors hung with pale martyrs, and the nuns, with their black butterfly heads, kept us all under constant surveillance. We were supposed to speak French in all our lessons. Only religious books were allowed, so the fairy tales and adventure stories from home were confiscated and banished to my trunk. Our mistakes were monitored and magnified into sins in such a way that some of the girls lived in a state of continual anguish.

Granny looked so sad as she limped away from the main entrance to her waiting taxi on my first day that I wanted to run after her and tell her I'd be fine inside that high convent wall. But the Mother Superior was holding my wrist, so I could only watch her go. She looked worn and worried as she walked, straight-backed and lopsided, to the car. I was seeing her in defeat. Sending me away meant a battle lost. It was as though she knew the rout must inevitably follow.

My peers regarded each term as a prison sentence, yet for me it was the nicest place I'd been to since St Aubin's Bay. Even the French had the soft, slurred lilt of Jersiaise words of my infanthood. I was the scapegoat of the nuns, but their discipline was benign after Mother's. I made both enemies and friends. I was a promising strategist at the art of warfare, so the former didn't disturb me much, while each new friendship filled me with the ecstatic euphoria of falling in love. My hours were filled by thinking of the softness of another hand in mine, the rub of a cheek. I waited dizzily for whispered messages and forbidden trysts. The first moments, before the doubts set in, were always so sweet, I just had to keep repeating them. I entered into these relationships with such passion that the victim of my latest crush would become overwhelmed by the sheer volume of my affection and sink into a cloying closeness that became the envy of the other girls. An epidemic of romance swept across the austere environment of our suburban convent. We were garrisoned away from any contact with a village or town, like a quarantined ship anchored outside a port. Yet I never felt lonely or isolated there. I had never had a real friend before, and the new pleasure of my whispered endearments and extravagant promises came like a miraculous balm to my aching nerves.

My first love was called Louise Hunter. She had the most angelic face I had ever seen. Her carmine lips curved into a natural kiss and left a dimple with gossamer down that could catch shadows and play with them like a pale kaleidoscope. We swore undying friendship in spit, blood and calamine lotion, and the pact lasted for the first five weeks of term. After this, I found Louise's insistence on calling me 'Mummy' when we alone more than I could bear. I couldn't bring myself to break off what had virtually become our formal engagement, but I transferred the bulk of my affection to first one girl and then another until, after my first year, I had come almost full circle. We shared some of our most indiscreet secrets and, on occasion, blackmailed each other with them. Louise Hunter's mother kept a bottle of whisky by her bed in a box marked Private, and her brother smoked cigarettes. Edith had an aunt who suffered from wind. Adelaide Parker dreamt extraordinary things about horses and had a brother who lived in a clinic. Genevieve's family hadn't paid their butcher's bill for two years, and Lisette's parents argued at night, and her father said things that he had to pay penance for at confession.

It quickly emerged, though, that nobody else had parents who were divorced, so I killed my father off in a heroic battle fighting the elements and the Indians somewhere to the north of Toronto.

I felt that with the handicap of my unladylike size and my undisguisable red hair and harvest of freckles, I would have enough to put up with if the wheel of playground fortune were to turn and crush me, without the scandal of an unknown father and an actual divorce. Roman Catholics never got divorced; the Pope did not allow it except by annulment. Thus my own father must have been a Protestant, a baiter of Saints. Mother Superior and even my friends would have cast me out, had they known the truth.

This was by no means the only untruth I told at the convent, nor was I the only girl to resort to fantasy on the home front. But maybe, when I described my mother and the idyllic love we shared; the hours I spent cuddled in her lap, and the hundred brush-strokes she gave my treasured locks each night before she tucked me up in bed, I was the most brazen of the liars.

It was inexplicable, and even embarrassing, that I actually and actively missed Mother. And although I didn't and couldn't understand her myself, I couldn't bear it if any of the other girls were to think badly of her, particularly for anything she had done to me.

I knew perfectly well that on her first appearance at the school my lies would be uncovered. I didn't care at first. I prayed with such fervour that even the nuns, who distrusted me instinctively for the base nature lurking inside every redhead, approved. Did not Judas Iscariot have red hair? We were not meant to think of our appearance or ever see ourselves in a looking-glass. Vanity was a sin. But redheads were what Mother Superior called 'given to lust', tinted by the Devil himself. So I saw myself mirrored in the nuns' vigilance to save me from the nastiness of my flesh. By the time I had been there a year, I was truly terrified of the consequences of a maternal visit. I wished I had kept my counsel and neither maligned Mother nor beatified her. Unable to bear the burden of my other lies, I had, gradually, admitted that my father lived in Canada, and even that my family actually didn't like red hair either. All these admissions had been accepted, and I was still friends with the girls I had formerly tricked. However, I had waded in far too deep to retreat where Mother's imaginary love for me was concerned.

It was June, and my ninth birthday had come and gone, and the whole school was convulsed in its preparations for the Feast of Saints Peter and Paul, its annual Open Day. The parents would gather from all over London and the Home Counties, and everyone would see that Mother hated me. I migrated from the chapel to the sanatorium, and then back to the chapel. The nuns hitched up their black habits and climbed the precarious wooden apple ladders to pin paper flowers on the wisteria growing on the southern façade of the school building. The real flowers hung like depleted bunches of grapes. It was always a battle to get them to flower on the 29th of June, falling as it did between their first and second blooming. The washed mauve of wisteria petals smelt of holidays and big breakfasts and sun. Beside them, the rustling clusters of paper flowers seemed to cheat.

The activity of the other girls and the nuns only served to thrust me further down into the quagmire of my own invention. The large storerooms were opened, and the dormitories were hung with the special Normandy lace curtains, the beds covered with the counterpanes that were reserved for Open Day and the beginning of term only. These had Sister Thérèse's intricate chain-stitch mends tucked against the walls. Chairs, cushions and carpets that served the same decorative ephemeral function were also dragged out, to make the convent as attractive as its prospectus.

Not even the unusually large and nutritious supper served on the night before could rally my spirits. Nor the porridge, bacon and eggs the next day. These meals were generously designed so that if a concerned parent asked, 'What did you have to eat this morning?' the reply would be reassuring. The dinner was thrown in for thorough mothers and aunts, so that everyone could enjoy the Open Day with their minds at rest.

The excitement was contagious. The older girls and prefects had been up since half-past five in the morning, tidying up last-minute eyesores and chivvying us younger girls. With the exception of a handful of parents who lived abroad, we had all seen everyone else's 'people'. So the highlight of this particular Open Day, in the infant school at least, was that everyone was going to get to see Joan Allen's wonderful mother at last. I had shown them all photographs, mostly snapshots taken at Selsey Beach, and they had seen for themselves how extraordinarily beautiful she was. And now they all wanted to meet her. One or two of them had even prepared little speeches.

I woke up that morning, and after the noise in the dormitory had reached unignorable proportions, and at least five girls had tried to kiss me awake, I opened one frightened eye. I had asked Our Lord to take me to Him in the night, in such a way as to not inflict too much grief on my granny. Eventually, I slept in order to give God and *l'enfant Jésu* time to carry out this arrangement. I was unable to dress myself that morning, but Louise Hunter buttoned my liberty bodice for me, and tied the sash and straightened the ungainly black pleats of my white muslin dress, reaching up to do so, since she was a good head and shoulders shorter than I. There was a ritual covering of flesh in our dormitory. Our skins were never bared, even to bathe. Layer upon layer of regulation cloth was artfully applied to conceal as much flesh as possible from ourselves and each other. We were as though mummified by layers of volcanic dust, petrified by our swathes of convent muslin. On holidays and feast days even our uniforms were white. I had to slit the lace on my gloves that morning to get into them. Some of the girls wore coloured ribbons on their dresses as tokens of exceptionally good behaviour, study or piety. I was once one point away from a yellow ribbon, but only once, so I wore none.

At exactly eleven o'clock, as the gates opened, we were to wait on the granite steps in front of the school and then to proceed down the gravel drive, two by two, to greet our parents and guardians in an orderly fashion and escort them to Mass. I was paired with Adelaide Parker, who dreamt about horses and lived in Kent. When it was my turn to walk along the wide gravel path towards the main lawn and the gate, I felt so sick and dizzy I could hardly see. I tried one last desperate treaty with the Powers above, promising my entire life in exchange for a last-minute reprieve.

I didn't know what Mother would do. I couldn't concentrate enough on the actual disaster to imagine exactly how it would be. I had been too busy praying to avert it. I just sensed that it would disgrace not only me in front of my friends (a humiliation that I felt I deserved) but also Mother herself and my sweet, long-suffering Granny. This disgrace would be so public that we would then have nowhere to hide, not even Golders Green, not even among other transient refugees.

I was awoken from my cold sweat by the artificially sweetened voice of my Mother saying, 'Hello, darling' to me.

I looked behind me in alarm. For there was Granny in her charcoal elegance, accompanied by Mother, veiled and gloved but totally noticeable in a mauve sheath that reached from her chin to her ankles in the most alarming way, glinting its silken creases in the sunlight. Her words formed an indistinct echo in my head. I found myself unable to speak or move. My eyes told me that Mother was resting on the arm of a strange, smiling man, but he too seemed unreal. She moved one foot and her dress rustled like dead petals.

Never once had Mother called me darling, nor had she ever addressed me with any kind of friendship in her voice.

'Hello, old man,' her companion said, filling my silence. 'I'm Robert Peel, I expect we'll be chums in no time at all.'

I looked down at Mother's tiny buttoned shoes, expecting one of them to kick him or me. But she merely said, 'Peter', in a matter-of-fact way, and opened her silk parasol against the very sunshine the nuns had prayed for. Adelaide was enchanted, curtseyed, forgot her speech, spotted her own parents and left us alone. This new apparition of a friendly mamma was just what I had prayed for, yet I was more frightened by her sudden change than if she'd proved true to pattern. At Les Filles de la Croix I had invented a heresy, with Mother and not the Devil as the source of all evil. Granny was Our Lady of Sorrows, and I was the innocent victim of Mother's wickedness. I used the props of the Church to support me. Each day, the chapel bells tolled out my deceit. I had a life built on lies. I was sure Mother Superior could smell out my heretical beliefs as surely as the Saints could smell the evil odour of sin. I believed in God Himself, but the remainder of my doctrine was my own. Only Mother's nastiness made my blasphemy viable. My sabotage was a mask to save me from Mother's mustard gas. I had been so sure of my crusade until that Open Day that I hoped God would understand my plight and forgive me.

Mother's sudden kindness made me feel unworthy to walk on the grass beside her. I vowed never to think ill of her again, or skulk around her or take advantage of her temper. She moved towards the chapel in her wisteria silk, sounding at every step like a flurry of brittle autumn leaves being blown across a marble corridor. *Mea culpa, mea maxima culpa.* I would say a million Hail Marys for her.

It was Granny's soft voice that drew me out of my reverie. 'Robert and your mother are getting married, Joan.' The long line of her upper lip trembled slightly as she said this; it always did when she was pleased.

'Peter', Mother repeated.

Her jovial fiancé leant down, took my hand and led me in the direction of the main building with its bunches of real and paper wisteria dangling down in the sunlight.

'Your sweet mamma insists on calling me Peter,' he whispered in a conspiratorial fashion, then turned back to call the ladies on.

'Are you ready, Kitty?'

Whereupon my 'sweet mamma' joined us, together with Granny, while I thanked God for my deliverance and felt as proud of my new family as the Maid of Orleans, my namesake, had once felt of her troops.

CHAPTER 4

MOTHER went to Paris for her honeymoon, and then to Nice, while Granny and I went to Selsey with Agnes. Mother sent them postcards of the Promenade des Anglais from the Negresco Hotel, which Granny carried around in her crochet bag. She traced the palm trees there with such nostalgia that I thought she might actually return to Jersey that year. Agnes saw this as well, and tried hard to tempt her back.

'If you could see the size of the cineraria you put in by that side wall, now. It fair cascades on to the road, you know. And the Carterets took a cutting from it and every time I see one of them they will stop and ask me when you'll be back on the Island, you and Miss Kitty, back home.'

Other days would be spent openly yearning.

'Do you remember the pinkness of the rocks at La Corbière when the sun set over our teas, and the scent of jasmine? Do you remember the first asparagus every year, bundled round with grass and lying in the trees by the kitchen door, and Cook always left it a little so as you could see it piled up in the sun. You'll be reminded, I'm sure, with the Peels.'

We had been invited, after the honeymoon, to accompany the newlyweds to the Peels' country seat in Yorkshire, and Granny was looking forward to that. We could have gone to Jersey, though, during the month we spent at Selsey, but I think an old, inbred streak of puritanical reserve had risen in Granny's blood; the Huguenot of her ancestry cautioned her to avoid counting her blessings lest an avenging cleaver fall.

Mother had married and settled, by what seemed like a miracle, into the eminently tractable personage of the Honourable Mrs Peel. She had fallen in with her new husband's jovial policing of her character. Her rages had subsided to mere ripples of discontent whenever she was crossed. Strangest of all, to my eyes, was that her husband liked children, and liked me. He had twice taken me out for a spin in his gunmetal SS Jaguar, once with Mother and Granny, and once all on my own. The ice of Mother's eyes had melted away from the summer's heat into a premature hibernation. Though I didn't dare do it more than once or twice I had looked into them, and seen only their emerald glisten. She looked at her most beautiful during the months of her engagement and her early marriage. And Peter, irrevocably name-changed, bought her an emerald necklace with silver claws for a clasp. She treasured emeralds and used them, like the magic mirror in 'Snow White', as a touchstone for her own peerless eyes.

Agnes arrived at Waterloo Station, laden with baskets, carpet-bags and a trunk. She had made the crossing many times but had a superstitious view of leaving the Island, so she prepared each journey as though it were her last, taking her dearest possessions for burial with her, as in an Egyptian tomb. She was younger than Granny by some years but had aged early, having the kind of wide-boned fleshy face that seems to fall spontaneously into old age without any encouragement from its wearer.

Agnes, in her fifty-second year, took as poor a view of travel as she ever had. At the age of fourteen she had crossed the Irish Sea during a storm on her way to Jersey and had never, she claimed, suffered so severely, not even at the hands of her irascible and drunken father. After crossing the Home Counties by train and taking the much milder ferry to the Channel Islands, she arrived in a state of trauma, determined never to travel again. She had kept to this early vow right up until our decampment to Hendon, whereupon she sacrificed her own fears and scruples to visit us regularly in the midst of our 'heathen neighbours'. From under the grey urban smog she would grimly survey our suburb, horrified that her dear mistress suffered such grisly surroundings instead of the Elysian fields around Claremont that were hers by right.

Agnes herself felt very proprietorial towards Jersey; she felt that by her service to the Island she had practically come to own it. She was as proud of her position there, on the harbour front overlooking the turquoise bay, as any of the Carterets or the Le

Hardys or the de Gruchys. She had arrived, still pale from her crossing, having sicked up the little pride she had for her own County Cork over the side of the Irish ferry.

She was the youngest of seven children, born near the Bally-houra Mountains. Her family was Catholic and poor. When her father was in his cups, he occasionally boasted of a dispossessed ancestor who could once have laid claim to all the lands around them. Her mother, who was tall and had arms like a circus wrestler from her prowess as a laundress and expert wringer, still remembered the Black '47 of her childhood when famine had swept across Ireland, devastating County Cork and decimating her own family. So she boasted of nothing, and laid claim to no more than a full pot of stew on the hearth every day. When the winters were bad, and times were hard, Agnes's mother wept in her sleep for fear of what might follow. She wrung her clothes with a near demonic energy, determined to stave off any chance of starvation. It was this fear that bade her surrender her sons and daughters as they came to working age, to cross the seas rather than stay under the cloud of hunger.

Granny had an Irish cousin by marriage, a Lady Pitsligo, who treated her County Cork estate more as a breeding ground for maids and gardeners than an agricultural concern. Lady Pitsligo was a Protestant and a great entertainer, who liked her friends to think of her as a philanthropist with the risqué leanings of an intellectual. During her winters in Dublin she occasionally attended lectures, one of which had suggested that the poverty of the 'mere Irish', the natives of that Isle, was due not to the oppressive wealth of the Anglo-Irish like herself but to the over-population of the Catholic homes.

It didn't take a wise mind like Lady Pitsligo's long to see the truth of this assertion, for indeed, while all her friends lived in spacious mansions, the mere Irish huddled together as many as fifteen or twenty to a hovel. Never one to avoid her duty once she had seen the path whereon it lay, Granny's cousin set about weeding out the local peasantry, thinning out the sons and daughters of the Catholic families around her, and transporting them to the (often baffling) drudgery of the households of her English friends and relatives. From April to June she would harvest the girls in droves, and personally supervise the packaging and labelling of her latest batch. In September, when her own harvest was in and safely baled and stooked, she would then single out the boys, the young men to be shipped across the Irish Sea, who would be, like their sisters, either too glad to have got away to want to leave, or too terrified to return – or sometimes just too bewildered by the foreign land to do anything but drift with the mass of other evacuees of unemployment from one town to the next. Whatever the other chosen ones of her experiment felt, Lady Pitsligo herself wore a tiara of virtuous fulfilment, and Agnes regarded her as the patron saint of her own happiness.

Granny, at the time of Agnes's arrival, had just entered into her household duties with all the enthusiasm of a new bride, and the two of them loved Claremont. Agnes, raw from her homeland of drizzling rain and sporadic want, quickly blossomed in the warmer climates of kindness and plenty, where the potato was grown as an art and not a sour necessity. The brogue she spoke soon became lost and replaced by Granny's own clipped diction. She modelled herself on her new mistress with the devotion of an understudy. The young Agnes was determined to outshine her three slightly older compatriots who travelled across from Cork to Claremont with her. She had made up her mind to graft on to the Island, and transform herself into a local lass. She bided her time patiently, waiting for the three girls from her previous life to marry or run away.

This chrysalis phase took two years. By the time she was seventeen the witnesses to her passage from Eire had gone, the irritating evidence was erased, and Agnes spread her wings as the most diligent maid on the Island. She was Granny's 'treasure'. When new girls came to be trained by Claremont's demanding housekeeper, it was Agnes who taught them how to be civilised.

She stayed loyally by Granny's side, from the afternoons spent in the sewing room to the days spent crocheting the world back into place. She nursed her through her pregnancy, and held her hand during the long birth of Kitty. After Mother was born she worshipped both of her 'young ladies', cloning her devotion to do so. Although Agnes attributed her own spinsterhood to a reluctance to share her good fortune with an outsider, she seems to have loved Granny so much that she couldn't bear to leave her. In later years she would tell me how Granny referred to her as her treasure, and it pleased Agnes to remember that although Granny had lost her wealth, she would never lose her. Agnes's only thoughts of death were the very detailed descriptions of other people's relayed to a select number of listeners in an order of precedence as strict as Debrett's. Granny, needless to say, was the first lady: the female equivalent of the Duke of Norfolk, the first peer of the realm.

At Selsey, in that summer after Mother's remarriage, Agnes found fault with the landscape, the beach, the sand itself, the turn of the waves, the colour of the sea, the paucity of the vegetation, the quality of the visitors — in fact with everything except her beloved Mrs Roberts herself (whom she called 'dear Florence' in her dreams). Our holiday consisted of sitting on the beach under wide straw hats, me sifting sand through my hands while Granny hooked silk through hers, and reminiscing about Jersey. Agnes's holiday consisted of supplying the myriad details of every change in St Aubin and St Helier, and in keeping house for us, and making endless pots of tea, and picnics that spoilt in the wind-swept sand.

I had never been to Selsey without Mother, nor had I been anywhere without a daily surveillance and a reckoning at nightfall for the inevitable shortcomings of the day. Suddenly I found myself free to play whatever I wanted and, within reason, wherever I wanted, without the arbitrary caprice of Mother's rules and shifting dislikes, or the petty discipline of the nuns. I filled my days exploring the beach and its immediate hinterland. It reminded me a lot of the days of my earliest memories when Agnes would be instructed to take me 'right away' from the house. This would mean not to the curve of beach in front of the house with its harbour and its rows of fishing boats — where we might be seen from the windows, thus ruining Mother's day — and not even to the beaches of St Helier, where we could be glimpsed from the esplanade. My vivid colouring was like a torch, the sight of which could taunt Mother to despair. On her bad days, I had to disappear. So Agnes would take me on the bus to Portelet Bay, through the lattice shadows of palm trees and hibiscus bushes to the sea.

At low tide we could walk across the sucking sands from our

harbour to the cliffs and follow the jagged footpath above Belcroute Bay, and on past Normoint Manor and round to Normoint Point with its lighthouse tower stabbing its warning finger towards Pigonet Beacon. The cliffs themselves were pitted with gannets' and gulls' nests, and once a boy from my dancing class dared me to scramble down and bring back a gannet's egg, for which feat he promised me sixpence. The incident proved to be the end of my early dancing career, with Granny bewailing our fall in station and the necessity of mixing with such rough children, and Mother, no doubt, regretting that I hadn't accepted the challenge and broken my neck. From the Point we went cross-country to the quarry, coming out into the spiky grass and the gorse of Portelet Beach.

There were dead men's bones not far out to sea, buried on a mound that moved right on to the sand at low tide. The continual washing of the waves over this grassy rock made me think that bits of the body dug into it would get swept away, just as my sand castles did with each new tide. I had a horror of seeing uncovered bones. The only ones I had ever seen were sheep skulls and fish bones, and the shin bones that Agnes brewed up for Rufus's midweek broth, but my own bones were so large, and their proportions so often discussed, that I feared to go anywhere near the water, dreading to see a whitened boiled-up version of my own anatomy rocking under the waves.

Whenever we went to this beach, wedged between its two headlands and catching the sun even in winter, it was strictly to be out of the way. Yet those visits, spent endlessly digging in the sand or collecting water zoos among the rocks, were some of my favourite Jersey days.

By the time I left Jersey I knew the names of St Helier and St Aubin and a few of the shops, and a few of the towers or beaches that fell to my lot. Maybe I didn't even know that much. What I know has been learnt abroad, here in England, the only country I really know. Jersey is a jigsaw, reconstructed second-hand. I learnt the litany of Jersey's saints together with my creed.

I grew up to 'believe in one God, the Father Almighty, Maker of heaven and earth, and all things visible and invisible'. And I grew up to believe in the charm-like powers of Saint Ouen, Saint Mary, Saint John; Trinity, Saint Martin, Saint Peter, Saint Saviour and Grouville – only Trinity and Grouville uncanonised, but all parishes of the Island whose nostalgia was drip-fed into my upbringing like an antidotal poison.

It was all preserved, as for posterity, unchanged and magical in Granny's tangible fantasy. In all my life, I never had the courage to return. Long after Granny died, and I had ceased to see my mother, my vicarious knowledge of Jersey was the knot that still held us together. To return there would break its spell. To return would have been as a tourist, a mere voyeur. I could never know the Island as well, however long I went for, as Granny with her half a century of memories.

It seems built into my system to keep falling in love. It isn't so much a fickleness in my case as an excess of loyalty, a constant discovery of greater faith. Every man I have ever loved I have loved truly, and I have thought each time, in the arms of one, that I could never love another. It is as much of a revelation for me as it is for them that I keep discovering a greater love inside me. My unfaithfulness is a kind of truth. To go back to Jersey would seem like unfaithfulness to Granny. Since she never returned, why should I? It would be like doubting her word. And I do fear to find a missed stitch in her remembered pattern, to fail to find the mystery of her descriptions in an Island that has seen the changes of decades, and the occupation of the German army, since the time when Granny sat and remade it in the image of her recollection on Selsey Beach.

While I dug waist-deep traps in the sand, covering them over with sticks and leaves, or hung about around the fishing boats, hoping to be asked to stroke a dead fish, or wandered along the sands gathering shells and driftwood, Granny and Agnes gossiped retrospectively. They sat in their deckchairs, intermittently talking and staring out to sea, while Granny wielded her ivory hook through the sandy balls of thread. Sometimes I would sit and join them. Whenever there was a lull in the nostalgia, we would all sit in a line looking out to sea, to a particular area of the horizon, as though waiting for news of Mother to arrive there as on the captions of a silent film. With an almost pagan wish not to put the mockers on her marriage, by tacit agreement, none of us mentioned either our hopes or fears for the future.

1930, for me, was the strangest year of my childhood. It held, stitched into its seams, the miraculous convent Open Day and a protracted Selsey Beach. It was lined by the homecoming of a transformed mother and her husband, and a stay in Yorkshire. And it contained not only the five months of her marriage but also the landslide into a nightmare at the end of which Mother and I were actually to share a bed.

If it wasn't for the snapshots I might think I had imagined the interlude of that marriage, it passed so swiftly from the idyllic to the melodramatic.

Granny was waiting for a telegram to recall us to London. Nothing arrived, and she grew restless knitting sand, so we returned to Hendon. Agnes stayed with us for a week and then departed, considerably less laden than she had come. We saw her off at Waterloo. Agnes always brought hampers filled with Island delicacies: potted meats, smoked fish, fruits and flowers and cheeses. She so scorned all the English products available that she refused to take anything back except for one of Granny's silken tablecloths; she had dozens but she declared they were the only things worth carrying back to her Garden of Eden.

It was another week after her departure before Peter himself arrived, this time in a navy-blue Bentley, to escort us to his wife in Eaton Square. He had a large, rather dilapidated house there which Granny admired enormously, not so much for its heavy scratched mahogany furniture or its row of lugubrious portraits lining the stairs as for the fact that it was within walking distance of Harrods.

Granny came from a generation that distrusted the motorcar. In her youth she had driven a phaeton and she saw the motorcar as a vastly inferior mode of transport, even though the ridiculous man with the red flag had long since been removed from the road in front of them. God, she maintained, had invented feet for the express purpose of walking, and when this proved impracticable, He had invented horses. She regarded motoring as a silly fad. Cycling, on the other hand, she deemed to be a genteel necessity.

When we arrived at Peter's house we were given afternoon tea in his drawing-room. Despite the name, it looked less like a drawing-room than anything I had ever seen. There was no chintz, and a great deal of leather and hunting magazines. We were informed, in his by now customary cheerful way, that Mother was unwell. She had been unwell for the last week. He had been hoping she would get better quickly so as to surprise us on their return.

'But there you are,' he announced. 'We've been gathering grime here for a week, and the old lady can't get up. So I thought I'd pop down and get you, and just let you know we're all off to Hadders at the weekend. You're both expected from Friday. The aunts are dying to look you over. My chariot is at your disposal. I could call for you at noon if that suits. Lunch *en route*, as they say.'

He paused here to smile at Granny, who was racing along with her crochet, trying to keep up with events. I kicked the leg of the leather chesterfield, praying that Granny would accept the offer of a car ride down to Yorkshire, but wasn't surprised when she refused.

'We would both love to visit Haddersly,' she said, 'but as Joan is rather delicate, I think it would be wiser to take the train.'

Nobody, in their most fevered moments, could have thought of me as delicate. At nine I was the size of a hefty adolescent, with broad boyish shoulders and long strong limbs. However, Peter smiled equably and proceeded to supply a rather too explicit sample of the Great Midland Railways timetable. Granny listened patiently and then, finally, interrupted to ask to see her daughter.

'Kitty's a bit off colour, Mrs Roberts. The doctor can't make head or tail of what she's got. They think a month in the country will do her good, though. So we'll make a bit of a party of it, us lot, and the aunts, and see if she doesn't get her gumption back.'

He didn't seem unduly worried by Mother's malaise, he just seemed genuinely puzzled. He showed us both up the long staircase, past the portraits of his ancestors, which were grimly unlike him but still recognisably related.

'A dour lot, aren't they?' he whispered to me as we climbed the stairs, dawdling behind Granny's limp. At the landing Peter passed in front of us, leading the way to one of the many rooms that fanned off it. Outside a deeply panelled door he stopped, and knocked, and without waiting for a reply he went in, ushering Granny and me behind him. Granny made a signal to me that I knew of old meant 'Wait here', so I did, while she walked into the room.

It was a large room with a high ceiling, decorated with a number of armchairs, occasional tables and a collection of hunting prints on the walls. On a wide, scroll-end sofa Mother was lying, looking even paler than usual. I waited at the crack of the door, watching Granny tend to her ailing daughter. Peter hovered around for a moment and then left them alone. Seeing me still outside, he signalled me to go in, but I refused. He shrugged and proceeded downstairs. I followed him. We passed the ancestors in silence, then went back into the tea-room, where he offered me the remainder of the plate of cake and the biscuits.

'Tuck in,' he said. He threw himself back into an armchair and pulled out a gold cigarette case and then spent some seconds extracting and lighting a cigarette, while I ate his cake as inconspicuously as I could.

'I'm blowed if I know what's the matter with her!' he muttered, more to himself than to me.

I continued to eat the cake, scooping up the walnut crumbs and studiously avoiding any reply. I had seen her through the half-open crack of the door, and I knew what was the matter with Mother: she was bored, and Mother suffered from boredom.

CHAPTER 5

GRANNY and I caught the train to Halifax, then changed on to a branch line which took us away from the grimy mill towns with their tenements and back-to-back cottages into a landscape of hills and dales covered in brackens and oaks and heather. We travelled third class from London so as to economise, and then first class for the last leg of the journey to keep up appearances when we arrived. We were met by a rather breathless chauffeur who escorted us into his Jaguar without stopping talking once, from the moment he saw us standing forlornly on the platform to the moment we arrived at the pillared portico of Haddersly Hall. His confidential chatter was underscored by an almost silent whistle which he emitted at regular intervals.

Because we were now, by marriage, part of the family, he assumed that we knew all its business; with his deep asthmatic wheezing, and his broad Yorkshire accent, he endeavoured to supply us with the last-minute arrangements of the entire household. Peter, it emerged, had not yet arrived with his lady. Sir Thomas, his father, was in his room. Sir Thomas, we later discovered, had been in his room for the last six years since he had had a riding accident and broken his neck and injured so many other of his bones that the remainder of his life was spent in a wheelchair. And the three aunts, who were referred to by all and sundry as 'the Graces', had fallen out over the menu, but had made it up over tea and were looking forward to playing charades with us. They had been practising all week.

Granny met these snippets of information with mixed feelings, none of which she displayed on her face, which was fixed into a slight smile of the kind that exempted her from having to give any verbal reply.

Haddersly Hall was a large stone house with three layers of sash windows along the front and gardens that seemed to be planted entirely with laurels, and rhododendrons, tiger lilies and statues. The latter had sunk into decades of mud and grown so much lichen and moss around their feet that they seemed to metamorphose from vegetable to stone somewhere around the knees. There were stables behind the house, with high arched windows where the grooms and gardeners lived, and eleven stalls for the horses, and espaliered pear trees with sweet stunted pears. Peter had bought a Dartmoor pony for me to ride, which I know he thought would be what I most wanted. When I discovered that I was too terrified to mount it, not least because I felt almost bigger than the shuddering little horse, I went and hid in the kitchen garden. This was vaguely out of bounds, and beyond it there was a long range of kennels where Peter and his father kept their hounds.

Sir Thomas, in his invalidhood, still kept a keen interest in his pack of hounds, and his red-nosed groom carried one of the dogs in in the morning and one in the evening to sit with the old man for a few minutes at a time. There was an enormous pair of rubber galoshes kept by a side door for this purpose. The groom was of an indiscernible age well over seventy, and when he hobbled up the back stairs with a squirming foxhound struggling in his arms it was always a matter of luck as to whether he would reach the landing with his reluctant visitor, or whether the dog would escape and rampage through the bedrooms before being caught by the inside staff, who rallied to the old man's hunting cry. Sir Thomas enjoyed this slight rumpus of the hunt in his house.

I was taken to meet him on the evening of our arrival. He had two rooms at his disposal upstairs, a bedroom and a games room. The latter was furnished with a number of wheeled tables set out with jigsaws and war games of one kind or another, but mostly reconstructions of naval battles which Sir Thomas had either witnessed or visited the sites of during his early naval career. He had spent three years in the West Indies and certain areas of the house, most notably his own chambers, had a faintly piratical, Caribbean air about them.

I was very struck by the eccentricity of the old man and his rooms, with his miniature palm trees lining a toy coastline surrounded by exquisitely painted lead ships complete with their masts and flags. Sir Thomas had three parrots and a white cockatoo in his room and he seemed to love these as much as, or more than, his hounds. He peppered his rather hearty, abrupt conversation with endearments to one or the other of them without pausing for a second, so that he appeared to be unnaturally fond of me on our first meeting. Later, when I discovered that the sweet nothings were for his birds, it made no difference; my first impression was the one I kept.

Lady Thomas, his wife, had died at some earlier date, from another hunting accident. Her vaulted grave was shown to me in the cemetery. Someone had put used horseshoes around it, and where the neighbouring graves had stone angels, Lady Thomas's had a black marble hound with a fox in its mouth. The Peels were not a Catholic family, which was Granny's only regret about them. Mother subsequently declared that they were scarcely Protestant either, existing in a neo-heathen state in the rumbustious isolation of their rambling grandeur.

Peter had three aunts, 'the Graces'. These were so called not for their charms, but for their mutual middle names. Although they were sisters, and similar in their looks, presenting a united front of uncorseted plumpness, with the same very bright blue eyes and the same over-ruddy complexion, they could not have been more different in their characters. Aunt Amy Grace was their spokeswoman. She had the manners and voice of a man. She reminded me of Peter, with the same boarding-school jargon and the same enforced chumminess. She rode with the hunt regularly, and thought anyone who fell from their horse was a 'muff'. She regarded her brother, Sir Thomas, as more of a spoilsport than anything else, and the deceased Lady Thomas as scarcely worth mentioning. Fortunately she never discovered that I was too much of a wimp to mount the pony provided for me. Granny vetoed my riding with the hounds, finding the track record of the household rather alarming. Aunt Amy assumed I could ride – all decent people did – so she merely commiserated with me for not being able to tally-ho with her. She assured me that by next year she would have won Granny over.

At some point in her strident career Amy Grace had been married, but since she never mentioned her husband I assumed that he had disgraced himself in the field. Her next sister was Aunt Laura Grace, who appeared to exist merely to shadow her sister and simper at her remarks. Aunt Laura Grace was a giggler. She giggled whenever she spoke, and she giggled whenever anyone else did. It wasn't a loud giggle, but it was quite perceptible. From time to time, her older sister would say, 'That's enough, Laura,' and the other would hold her breath and go very red in the face before subsiding into a wobbling silence. Aunt Laura, so I was told, was a spinster.

'I used to have so many suitors, but I've never wanted to leave home. I went away, once, to accompany Lady Heavestone – do you know her? – No, she died and apparently she was too long for her coffin . . . or was it her dress? I declare, I can't remember, but I know I've always wanted to stay at home. Wait there.'

Such long speeches half choked Aunt Laura Grace. She had a habit of asking me to 'wait there' and then disappearing. Aunt Amy Grace described her sister as 'a bit silly in the house, but a wizard at a fence'.

Their third sister was quite unlike either of them, except in her obesity. She wore horn-rimmed spectacles at all times and read novels in French and German, which she carried around with her in an embroidered sack slung around her ample waist. She was very quiet and uncommunicative. She rarely spoke at all, and when she did it was at meal times and only to ask for something to be passed down the table. It was impossible to tell what she made of the noisy household she lived in – or, indeed, what the others thought of her. She, too, rode with the hounds, but no judgement was passed on Aunt Mary Grace's merits, or lack of them, in the saddle.

I was given a bedroom adjoining Granny's on the first floor, and the luxury of my apartment was a recurrent source of pleasure to me. Peter and Mother did not arrive until long after my bedtime on that first night. Their room was a long way from ours, somewhere on the other side of the house and further upstairs, I think, because I never saw it. I thought that when Mother arrived the wonderfully relaxed atmosphere of the house would change, but by some miracle she had rallied from her morose silence and became unrecognisably jolly.

I suppose that must have been how she always was when I

wasn't around. I myself was reduced to a mere nothing in her life. We saw each other rarely and when we did meet, the tension seemed to have been drawn out of our relationship. Perhaps the sheer size of the Hall helped, as I know the boisterous heartiness of Aunt Amy Grace did. Mother gave herself up to the prevalent girlishness of the household. She spent very little time with Peter, who spent a great deal of time with me.

Granny spent her days sitting in the morning room or pottering around the garden. She often borrowed one of Aunt Mary Grace's books in French, and then she would sit reading, for once allowing her crochet hook to relax in her fingers. I don't think she made more than one tablecloth in all the three weeks we spent at Haddersly Hall. Aunt Mary Grace was obviously thrilled by this elderly polyglot ally, and although they scarcely talked, preferring their studious silence as they read side by side, Peter declared that he had never seen her smile as much as she had since Granny and I had arrived. Peter had a genius for including me in everything he said. He even took a lot of photographs of me, claiming that I had started to grow pretty, and we needed to record the time of its beginning. I knew he was lying, but I appreciated his intentions. Nobody had ever called me anything more flattering than plain. Plain was almost a compliment, and infinitely preferable to ugly.

Under his almost ruthless jollity, Peter had a great deal of instinctive tact. For instance, he would call any of his aunts to be photographed with me, and sometimes even Granny. But he never even asked Mother, sensing that she saw me as rust tarnishing the setting of her own beauty. Up until the time I met him, there had been no men in my life. I discovered that I preferred his attentions even to the whispered kindnesses of Granny, and with a fickleness that I later regretted I abandoned my one real ally to bask in the company and the embraces of my stepfather.

Having grown up with an aunt with the androgynous qualities of Amy Grace, he seemed almost immune to my complete lack of femininity and my gangly size.

'I get all the delicacy I need and to spare,' he told me, 'with the little lady. You'll grow out of your boyishness, don't worry.'

I wasn't worried by my boyishness myself, but I was alarmed by my growing. My month by the seaside, and now these weeks of immense breakfasts and huge dinners, were taking their toll on my height. I was bursting the buttons on my frocks, making them look even more unflattering than they usually did, and the hemlines were rising. It was Granny who grieved for my charmlessness. Every night she curled my hair into rags and papers, making me sleep with my thick red hair nearly pulled out of my head in the hope of curling it into a semblance of grace on the next day. Ringlets were what little girls wore, even if the little girls were threatening to be giantesses, like me. Every morning, within minutes of removing the curling rags, my hair would have fallen down into the same straight lank locks as before.

By the end of our three weeks Mother had begun to tire of the holiday, and we packed our trunks ready to return to London. Granny had made friends with Sir Thomas upstairs. He had found my lack of military and naval skills too enormous to correct, so I proved a disappointment as a partner in his games. I had sat with him for a while helping with his jigsaw puzzle, but just as he was nearing the completion of his two-thousand-piece ship I caught my sleeve in one of the wooden pieces, and knocked a whole heap of it on to the floor. I apologised to him, and quickly got down on my knees to retrieve the scattered pieces, but when I looked up into his silence I saw that he was crying. Not knowing what to do, I put the bits back on his table and left him.

I had always been clumsy. I was at home. It was I who dropped the last remnants of our more stylish past. I broke the Waterford crystal, and one of Granny's Venetian sherry glasses. The gaps in our dinner service were my doing. So the Meissen and the Wedgwood, and even the Coalport breakfast service, were all missing plates or had chips and mends where they had slipped wilfully through my fingers. It panicked me when things broke or spilled. I hated my clumsiness. I didn't admit to anyone about dropping the jigsaw for some days, and I didn't dare return to the old man's room with the mocking parrots and the weeping invalid. Eventually, though, I told Granny, and she went up to see Sir Thomas. She fared far better than I. She had been married into a naval family and knew the jargon of the decks and the ranks of all the sailors from admiral to hand. She knew the principal battles of the English Navy, and the names of the towns they had besieged and overthrown. So she sat for an hour or so a day, crocheting while Sir Thomas manoeuvred his pieces with the help of a number of wire gadgets that hung ingeniously over his chair.

It seemed, as we were driven back to the station, that our visit had been one of many, and that our dreary days in Hendon were about to end. We travelled home first class all the way to King's Cross – I with a new sailor suit Peter had bought me, and a new crop of freckles, and Granny with a hint of a smile relaxing her features.

The autumn term began, and I picked up my friendships where I had left them. Some of the girls had been abroad, others had been to the country. They all had stories to tell of their holidays, to which I added the glamorously eccentric stock of mine. Everyone was impressed. The nuns, with their bat-like social radar, sensed that my status in the family had changed. My position in the class as general culprit was taken away from me and given to another girl whose family were known to have lost a lot of money in America the year before. Derogatory references to my colouring ceased in the light of the occasional visits of my new swell stepfather. And then it was Christmas and the end of term.

Everyone in the convent was excited. We were not supposed to give presents or cards to each other but we did, smuggling missal markers and other tokens through the network of vigilance. Signs of affection were signs of the Devil. Our school trunks were packed and already stacked on the top landing ready to be let down on the luggage lift after breakfast. Sister Marie, who had swallowed her gall for the entire autumn, watching my reverse of fortune with ill-disguised disgust, had just finished inspecting our dormitory. Her toque was so immaculately starched that it rubbed a red line down the side of her cheek, a mark that she wore as proudly as if it had been a new form of stigmata. In her scrubbed hands, clasped just below her rosary, she was carrying the secret of bad news. She twiddled her thumbs with a repressed glee that we knew of old. I watched her and my heart went out with a spasm of pity to Janet, the girl with the American losses, thinking perhaps that her fees still remained unpaid, and she was to be publicly dismissed. Together with the pity, I felt a warm glow of contentment that the misfortune was about to fall upon little Janet's head and not on mine. I was musing on my own generosity in having given her the blood-blister marbles that Peter had given me, when through the mists of my self-praise I heard my own name being spoken.

'Joan Allen.'

We were standing in two lines by our beds. The slurred French 'J' of 'Joan' was so similar to the 'J' of 'Janette' that I managed to twist the name into the other girl's.

'Joan Allen,' Sister Marie repeated, clicking her thumb nail against her jet rosary in a way that spelt out trouble in her own convent morse. She had walked past my bed, and she had said nothing. She had inspected my overcoat together with that of the girls next to me, and she had said nothing. She had waited until she reached the door so that she could shout out whatever mishap had befallen me.

'Joan Allen,' she repeated, and I stepped out into the abyss of linoleum in the middle of the room. I curtseyed and answered, '*Oui, Soeur Marie.*'

Then she told me the news, in French, and I heard the words twist from her mouth to my head and out again somewhere on the swallowing darkness of the floor. I made no response at all so she repeated her message, adding to it this time: I would be staying at school for Christmas. The Mother Superior would see me shortly. Turning in the black tent of her habit, she left. The other girls crowded round me; someone must be ill, someone must have died. Who could it be? What could have happened?

But I half-knew already. Death was holy. Had there been a death, there would have been the customary respect. No one had died. If there was an illness, the convent would be supposed to feel sympathy. This was something else, something different that communicated itself telepathically from one party to the next. For reasons I didn't understand, I had fallen back to my former status. I was unwanted again. And this time it was worse: I had lost what little ground was mine by right. Not even Granny had come for me, nor Peter. No car had been sent to take me back alone. This had to be Mother's doing. It was Mother as I'd known her before the reprieve; but now with an increased power.

I wanted the girls to leave me alone. I wanted my friends to abandon me to the frustration in my chest. I wanted to bang my fists against the wall and cry. I wanted to die. But like a martyr I spent my ten days of Christmas holiday with the nuns, bearing their barbed instructions with a studied indifference. Sister Marie personally supervised every minute of my days, wearing me down. She sensed some scandalous calamity and she wanted to know what it could be. I behaved like the stupid oaf she had so often accused me of being. I refused to speculate with her as to what could be the precise cause of my internment. I steadied my nerves by surreptitiously watching the red line on the side of her face. Whenever she caught me staring thus, she rapped my knuckles with a brass ruler which she kept about her person for that purpose. I further infuriated her by not asking when I might be allowed home. She tormented me by dwelling on the possibilities of staying at school through all my holidays for the next eight years, so long as my fees were paid regularly. Twice a day I dragged my feet down the long corridor to Mother Superior's room. I saw her nun's headdress flap in the draught from her propped-open window. There was snow on the sill which blew in sometimes and melted on the floor. I concentrated on that snow, making it substitute its own water for mine. I refused to weep and she refused to enlighten me as to my plight.

During Mass, morning and evening, I prayed to be delivered. I called on Granny to forgive me for preferring Peter at Haddersly Hall, and I called on Peter to remember me, as he had promised he always would. I knew I was unworthy, but I believed in a Church that welcomed even the unworthy through the communion of sins.

Granny came for me on Christmas Eve. She arrived unannounced, looking haggard and old. She came in a hackney cab and took me away with instructions for my trunk to follow. She told me very little about what was happening at home, except that Mother had been to stay and had left that morning for Haddersly Hall.

'Are we going there?' I asked her, having recovered quickly from my recent fall and hoping against hope for a return to our previous happy way.

'No, Joan, we'll be in Hendon for Christmas this year.'

'When will we be going back to Yorkshire?'

'There's no point asking questions, Joan, when you're too young to understand the answers.'

The rest of the journey took place in silence while Granny stared at the back of the driver's neck and crocheted her silk. Her fingers were moving as fast as I'd ever seen them.

We spent a very quiet Christmas. A new maid had come in my absence, but after preparing the Christmas dinner and putting the turkey in the oven she had the day off, leaving us to our own resources. We finished the cooking and served our dinner in the cramped dining-room. The coal fire was smoking with the wet coals I had carried in for it, and the steam from the turkey filled the room with a stifling gravy-laden heat. The cranberry jelly spread in a red gash across Granny's slice of uneaten meat. All the rest of the turkey and stuffing could have been mine, but there was a claustrophobic pall over the table. The presence of the red ribbon, holly and mistletoe made the room seem more gloomy than festive.

Peter had not forgotten us, nor had his aunts. I received a coral necklace from the three Graces together with cards and an enormous carved rocking horse with a real leather saddle and horsehair mane and tail from Peter. Granny received a beaded crochet bag and some tortoiseshell combs. A live green and grey parrot with a red forehead and horny beak also arrived, together with its own brass cage. Granny was rather taken aback by this parrot. She thought it was one of Sir Thomas's own, and she confessed to me that she wished she had not admired them quite so openly when she was staying with him. After lunch, while we were playing bezique, the parrot began to flap about inside its cage, bobbing its head up and down in an excited spasm. It then calmed down, and turning its orange-circled eye to Granny, pronounced, 'Now's the time', in exactly the same strident tone as Aunt Amy Grace. Granny blushed at this, wondering, no doubt, what else the parrot would say.

'Parrots can live for a hundred years, you know,' she told me, and then fell silent, brooding, it seemed, on the number of blasphemies a bird could learn in a hundred years from as many sailors.

Her particular parrot, which arrived with its name, 'Hanno', engraved on its cage, said nothing more unseemly than 'Now's the time'. Notwithstanding, it didn't add to the ease of our Christmas. Granny was unusually nervous, expecting, I now realise, an impending disaster. The sibyllic 'Now's the time' must only have served to increase her fears.

On Boxing Day we went to visit Mrs de Gruchy in her hospital home. It was bitterly cold on the streets, so cold that Granny's limp seemed to freeze her hip solid and almost stop her from walking. Mrs de Gruchy had a party, with over a dozen of her family gathered around. The adults drank hot cider punch instead of tea, and there were liqueurs with the cake. I spilt Granny's cherry brandy on the floor and dropped the almond icing off my cake. Mrs de Gruchy said she didn't mind, but I could see that Granny did.

'And Kitty?' her friend asked.

'She's up at Haddersly Hall.'

'Thank goodness for that. You see, it's not as bad as you feared,' Mrs de Gruchy whispered with the authority of one who knows much of illness but has never suffered one. 'Girls don't change overnight, she was bound to . . .'

Here, seeing that I was listening, Mrs de Gruchy raised her eyes in my direction and made a significant nod. Granny sent me away to the back of the room to talk to a scowling seven-year-old who was sitting there. The last I heard was a whispered 'Joan doesn't know anything about it.'

I sat on a carved ottoman with the small unfriendly boy, musing over what I had heard. I didn't know why Mother had married Peter as opposed to one of her other beaux. Personally, I would have married him like a flash, but he seemed more my type than Mother's. She must have really cared for him, though, to have dried her spite for all the months of their time together. Then I remembered her face on the day we had seen her at Eaton Square, just after the honeymoon. She had been bored then, I was sure of it. The more I thought of it, the more it seemed that spite could not be buried for long; it would worm its way back to the surface. You couldn't drown it either, because even dead fish rose and rotted on top of the sea. If someone was as violently allergic to boredom as Mother was, that too would putrefy any amount of love.

I refused to believe that Peter had done anything wrong. He was an innocent victim, like me. I hoped she hadn't hurt him, that she didn't pinch him or kick him. Most of all I hoped she hadn't said things to him that would eat away at his insides. He told me that Mother had cast a spell over him with the magic green of her eyes. I knew he had never seen them flash. He had never felt the malign power that could paralyse a man like him. He hadn't seen any of that at the time he talked to me, in the walled garden at Haddersly Hall. But what had happened in between? I just didn't know. I would never know. Granny had hinted that I was too young. Yet even now, so many decades on, it's still a mystery.

It was very dark when we left St Thomas'. We went by taxi through the lamplit streets, and frost was forming on the windows. There were a great many people trudging about in the iced-up sludge. Granny said she thought it was too cold to snow. There were people curled up under Waterloo Bridge, whom Granny told me not to look at. When I asked her why, she replied, 'However hard our life may seem, there are always others whose lives are harder. Remember that, Joan.'

I nodded. 'Yes, Granny.'

'Promise me,' she insisted, 'promise me. There are always harder.'

I had never seen Granny so upset. Usually when we passed any signs of hardship beyond her immediate control, she looked away and tried to pretend it wasn't happening. I couldn't understand how she should be moved almost to tears so suddenly by the very vagrants she had always seemed to despise. Looking back, I think she must have had an inkling of what was to come, a thread of Mother's own clairvoyance.

By the time we reached Hendon, we were both tired. Susan, the maid, prepared us some Horlicks and with that and some bread and butter we went to bed. I'm not sure how long I had been asleep when I heard Mother arrive. She had travelled from Yorkshire and she was numb with cold. I heard Granny ministering to her downstairs.

'You'd better go to bed, Maman,' I heard Mother say, 'Peter may arrive at any moment.'

'Oh, Kitty, what have you done?'

'Don't be silly, Maman, go to bed.'

After that there was a long silence, and I dozed off to sleep again. It must have been long past midnight when Peter arrived. I didn't hear his car. I was awoken by his shouting downstairs in the sitting-room. Mother didn't seem to be saying much, but Peter was very angry. I had never imagined that he could shout and say cruel things. It wasn't that what he said was untrue, yet it was crueller in its accuracy. I knew it was evil to eavesdrop, but I couldn't help it. The combination of the noise and the revelations was too much for me.

Between the hinges of my door I watched Mother climb the stairs like a priestess approaching an altar, trailing in her wake Peter's accusations like an acolyte's chant.

'You're evil,' Peter called after her, 'evil.'

Mother reached the landing, her head twisted and she laughed. The anger was sucked out of Peter's voice and he slumped at the curve of the stair, emptied of strength.

'You're not like other people.'

'Thank God!'

'You're evil . . . too evil . . .'

The last word fading away like candle smoke in a church.

Mother went into her room, and I heard her at her dresssing-table fiddling with her bottles and potions. Peter was pacing downstairs and the parrot, awakened from its sleep, was goading him with its 'Now's the time'. After some minutes our front door slammed, then a car accelerated away.

I was asleep again when Mother crept into my room. I pretended not to wake up when she pushed her way into my narrow brass bed. Mother had never touched me, except with violence. It made me feel sick with emotion when she crawled in beside me and laid her cold scented limbs beside mine, making my head swim with the incense of her nearness. It was still dark when Peter came into my room. I hadn't heard him return, but I saw him clearly silhouetted against the crack of the door by the bright light of the hall. He looked tired and ill, and out of a skin the colour of bandages his eyes shone with fever. He stood in the doorway for some seconds, then he moved to the foot of my bed.

In one hand he was holding a gun, carried before him as an offering aimed at Mother; his other hand shook at his side. I moved a little and under the bedclothes Mother gripped my hand, digging her long nails into my wrist to keep me still.

Peter switched his gaze from Mother's face to mine, then

lowered the gun slowly, like a coffin cord. He muttered something like, 'It would have helped you too, old chum,' and then he left.

We never saw him again and his name, like my father's, was erased from the family roll. Within seconds of the front door slamming, Mother left my bed, and without saying a word she went to her own room and locked the door.

CHAPTER 6

IT seemed that the whole world would change because our life had. I thought, after Peter's dramatic farewell, everything would begin to shrivel and fade. Our garden was already bare and the plane trees on our street were stripped for winter, holding their scarred grey branches up to the sky in hopeless supplication. It snowed, and the road outside became an umbered stretch of sludge. The park at the end of the crossroads had a forlorn wind-battered look to it, with its iron railings ready to impale whatever was set adrift in that strangely transient part of the metropolis. Leaves and litter and dropped gloves were left on the spikes like messages from a lost world where remnants of colour still existed, faded but flapping on.

On the morning after Peter left, Granny went down to breakfast and sat with me over my grape nuts and her coffee, then carried on with her life and her crochet as though nothing had happened. When I tried to tell her some of what had occurred the night before, she merely said, 'Yes, dear,' and 'No, dear,' and 'Perhaps if you ate less you would have nicer dreams,' closing the subject for evermore. Mother stayed in her room for twenty-four hours, ringing her bell sporadically for Susan, her maid. This was how Mother thought of Susan and all the other girls who came before her. They were her maids. The fact that they were also the only help we had at home, and had to be cook, cleaner and general drudge as well, made no difference. Mother would shake her hand bell with the urgency of a fire alarm at any time of the day or night. It was silly in itself to have a bell at all in a small bungalow in Hendon Green, but to ring it with Mother's insistence, as though to make herself heard through the long corridors of a country house, seemed like a constant mockery.

The sage-green partition walls of the dining-room were as thin as screens, and one could hear whispers through the ceilings. Mother's tunes could make the four arms of the small chandelier dance in the sitting-room below her. One could hear the tap of her heels on the stair rug and the swish of the brush-strokes through her hair. A call would have sufficed to summon anyone from anywhere in that narrowly partitioned house, but Mother made it rattle and shake with her imperious bell. The succession of Susans and Nancys had to learn to go and curtsey to Miss Kitty, in her royal-blue bedroom with the short Chinese drapes, as though running to a vast *piano nobile* from an ancient distant servants' hall.

Mother excelled herself with her bell on the morning after Peter left. She rang for Susan to draw her curtains, and then to close them, to find her robe and her rings. To bring up her Grafonola and then her new needles. To find the Trix Sisters, and Jelly Roll, Caruso, Martinez, tangos and waltzes, foxtrots and lullabies. She tried them all, cranking up the ebony handle of her Grafonola on such a medley of bands and songs that she seemed, while searching for a new tune, to be looking for a new mask with which to face this new scandal. We heard her tentative steps over our heads as single minutes of dance routines punctuated by the bell and the weary pounding of Susan on the stairs. At last Mother settled on a charleston with a novel twist. Then she danced through the afternoon, 'da da, da da,' touch-typing the rhythm above the already cracked ceiling. Having satisfied herself with her technique, she called a taxi and left, telling Granny that she would be staying with some friends in Paris.

That night I went back to my friends, back to the convent where I stayed for the next three years with only the short exeats that were the results of Granny's long tugs of war. She won me my few days at Selsey, or my afternoons out with her, while I grew so used to being a Daughter of the Cross that I failed to see Granny's own limp to Calvary. My life rotated around the convent routine while I was there. Granny and Mother regained their pre-eminence in my thoughts only on my rare visits home. I allowed myself to drop a lot of stitches during those years of apparent peace. I realise now that poor Granny never got a rest. While I was relaxing inside the convent walls, she must have been constantly mending and making good.

When Mother went to Biarritz for a month, Granny smuggled me back to Hendon for ten days over Easter. It had all been arranged so that I would be back at school before Mother returned, and if she didn't ask, Granny told me not to tell her. It was one of those bleak Easters when the sun cannot decide whether to shine or retreat back into the winter mists, so it compromises, hovering in a pale simulacrum of itself. Granny loved the sun; she used to follow it around the house, catching its warmth now through an east window, now to the south, culling the comforting rays through the thick glass of our suburban home.

We were sitting in the conservatory, with Rufus lying twitching between our feet. I was holding a skein of silk on my two upheld hands, while Granny wound it into one of her tight crochet balls. She had the air of a convalescent about her. Her daughter was safely away across the English Channel, her cinerarias in the garden had survived yet another vicious winter without succumbing to the frost, and her two banks of camellias were already in bud with their tightly furled flowers waiting to blossom later in the year.

I was ten years old, and growing with the speed of a flick cartoon. I had outgrown my school uniform three times in the last year. I knew a number of the senior girls through the humiliating process of having to buy their old uniforms second-hand. I could arm wrestle with Marguerite le Blanc, the school bully, and beat her, and I could win a fight with any girl in the school. It was far easier to fall out than to be friends there. Closeness was the real crime. Talking in twos was punishable. Walking arm in arm, even liking each other, was frowned upon. It encouraged the cult of 'self', and Catholic girls had to be selfless. But the malicious Sister Marie was forever watching me, and she reported back my rough ways to the Mother Superior, who wrote to Granny twice. Granny was so distressed that I began to pay Louise Hunter half my pocket money on a regular basis so that she would keep watch for me in future when I found myself forced to indulge in these unchristian feats. However, I had fasted and made my confession and been to many daily Matins with Granny, and I was forgiven. We had made pancakes and Easter buns, and been shriven by Mrs de Gruchy. I had promised to be good in future, and my case was neatly packed and ready for my return to school.

Neither of us was expecting to see Mother at all. I was due back at the convent immediately after supper. We had a fire burning in the miniature grate in the sitting-room nearby, and Granny had sprinkled sugar on the coals to brighten the flame. The room smelt of caramel. The house was silent. There had been a number of new maids who had come and gone since Mother had reinstalled herself in her rooms. Agnes said that now the days of kitchen tyranny were drawing to an end, it was only the rising unemployment that kept any of these girls with us in Hendon. They would put up with Mother's tantrums and insults for as long as they could, and then, when her abuse finally outweighed the counterbalance of the soup queues in the streets, they would leave. Some of them would sneak out in the night with their cardboard suitcases and never be seen again. The more daring would smuggle their belongings out of our house before they left, and then leave a piece of their minds to Mother, who would avenge herself on Rufus and, whenever she could, on me.

On this particular occasion, there was no maid in the house. The last one had left, weeping, just before Mother left for France, and a new one was due to start on the following Monday. Granny told me that it seemed safer to have no one in the house to witness my presence, and I had helped her with the chores. She had been cooking the supper herself – fish, because it was Friday. There was a faint smell of it from the kitchen wafting into the conservatory and making Rufus twitch in his sleep as he sprawled out in front of the toadstool of electric heat at Granny's feet.

As there was no maid, there was no warning. No one to answer the door. So Mother arrived, together with a pair of young men, for a whirlwind refuelling of her wardrobe and a change of gramophone records, and caught us trapped in Granny's silk.

'Afternoon, Mrs Roberts, how do you do?' the first young man said, lifting his early boater to show a mop of sandy hair. His companion nodded and bowed with a mock servility to Granny and myself.

'I'll . . . um . . . wait here with young Hamish while you sort out the records and your strings of pearls and whatnot, Kitty. Perhaps your maid could fetch us a glass of something to keep the wheels lubricated, and ... um ... give you a hand with your stuff. Would you?' he said, turning to me. I sat very still with my hands up in the air, while Granny flushed slightly and pursed her lips ready to speak. Mother was standing in the doorway watching Rufus crawl towards her from his recent sleep. She didn't look at me, so I looked at her as her face changed from its usual features to an even paler plaster of Paris set.

'You'd better choose the records yourself,' she said, 'they're upstairs.'

As they trooped out and up into Kitty's room, Granny continued to wind her ball of thread. Her movements had altered to a deliberate slow motion. I felt the blood drain from my upturned hands. It seemed she would never finish. Through the ceiling we heard the two men's playful appeals to Mother.

'But Kitty, it was you who made us get the wretched flight to Croydon, you can't miss the plane back. You know we're all expected at Le Touquet tonight.'

'Come on, Kitty, what's bitten you?'

'I've changed my mind.'

'It's not good enough. I daren't go back and tell the mob we left you here?'

'Kitty?'

'What is it? You look so strange.'

'She's only joking, can't you see?'

The silk continued to twine thread by thread around the ball. The sounds of merriment died out and then the voices re-emerged, backing down the stairs.

'Honestly, Kitty, of course if you've really changed your mind. It's up to you. I . . .'

Granny continued to increase her ball, twisting it this way and that, dextrously criss-crossing the silk so that there would be no slackness in the end. The two men took their leave, with puzzled startled looks on their faces, as Granny sighed.

Mother was still upstairs, but we didn't need to see her to know that she had switched on her eyes and the tight ball of her spite had made her friends retreat, feeling her ice burn inside them. Once out of its range they would shrug and laugh, and race their motorcar back to Croydon and the waiting evening plane. They lived by a chivalrous code that made them the willing slaves of their women friends, the potential lovers and slightly less-potential wives of their set. They pretended to be afraid of upsetting or offending these 'girls'. It didn't do, though, actually to feel fear, so they would shrug it off as a misinterpreted moment. Girls were damned difficult to understand, particularly the capricious ones like Kitty.

Eventually the skein of yarn came to an end and the last yard of it slipped from my numb wrists. Granny stood up, tall and veering on her lame side. She knocked the empty parrot cage as she did so, and then made her way slowly, painfully, to the glass-panelled door.

'Go to your room, Joan,' she said. 'You can have supper upstairs tonight.'

I sat looking after her as she left. I wanted to get up and take her hand and tell her it was my fault. I didn't want her to get into trouble for me. I didn't want her to suffer just because I looked like the maid, an Irish maid, big-boned and coarse, and not like her family at all. I sensed that she felt in the wrong. It was wrong not to have kept Rufus from the conservatory, and wrong to have brought me home against Mother's express wishes, and it was wrong not to have corrected the slightly drunk young man when he thought I was her servant. When her presence had limped out of my sight I looked at the parrot's cage, with 'Hanno' engraved under the empty perch. 'Parrots live for a hundred years,' Granny had said, but that was elsewhere. They didn't live long in our house, not when they were presents from the families of ex-husbands. This Hanno hadn't lived to campaign across the Alps or to pillage any of Spain or Italy or even Hendon. This Hanno had died the day after Peter had walked out of our house, and he was buried under a camellia bush in Granny's pretty garden.

She was waiting for me at the top of the stairs. She didn't call my name. I wanted her to. Even when she punished me, I wanted her to say my name. She never said it. When I was born, Agnes told me that not only did Mother refuse to see me, she refused to name me either. She had wanted me to have no name at all. Granny, of course, had insisted, and eventually Mother had said, then you name it. So I was called Joan, because Joan of Arc had been canonised in 1920 and it was fashionable to call girls after

66

her. Most of the Joans I've ever met were born, like me, in 1921. Mother, however, continued to rebel against my name, any name, and she refused to pronounce the one Granny had chosen. I used to dream about it. I'd dream that Mother would call me: 'Joan, Joan, I need you,' or just 'Joan . . . Joan'. It would have had a sweetness to it. Sometimes I would contrive to twist things so that my name could come forward. But it never did.

She drew me to her with her eyes, and I sank in the green undercurrent of her hatred. I felt the numbness of my wrists spread along my veins until it lodged like a ball of yarn, with no looseness, in the pit of my stomach. I felt sick. I tried to keep walking straight. I knew it was better not to antagonise her further, but I couldn't help it, and I cringed against the wall. I climbed towards her, feeling the raised chrysanthemums of the Lycra dado pressing against my hip. I knew she was going to hit me, but I wanted it to be over soon so that she would take her scorching gaze off me. She was holding something black in her hand. It was a thin discus, one of her gramophone records. As I reached the landing, it flashed through the air and came down on the side of my face.

It was not what I had expected, and in my surprise I whispered, 'Mother.'

Then I hated myself for having said it. It only made her worse. It only ever made her worse to call her that. I was not meant to call her anything in her presence. I was supposed to weave my words as carefully as she so as to avoid any mention of our relationship. I never stood a chance with her in battle. I had learnt to stand my ground and no more. To keep to my feet and not to scream or plead. And now I had called her name, summoning up her rage, concentrating it on me. I felt the record come at me again, slashing into my face above the ear so that it burned. I sank to my knees, while my assailant lashed at me. The record broke and thick wedges of Bakelite dropped to the carpet.

Mother was headstrong. With the jagged edge of her broken charleston she continued to flail into me, catching now my head, now my shoulder, and finally my arms as they rose up against my will to protect me. I forced myself not to shout so that it would stop sooner. Mother herself made no sound except for a swallowed howl and the occasional crack as she missed her target and hit the wall behind me.

That night I ate my supper, as Granny had foretold, in my room. The fish was tasteless and overcooked. Granny herself said she had no appetite. She sat with me a long time, telling me stories about Claremont. She kept dozing beside my bed. She had dried all the blood from my hair and dabbed my swollen arm and shoulder with tincture of arnica. Where my cuts were deepest, she had put butterfly sutures of sticking plaster to join the edges. She told me they were better than stitches and they left less of a scar. She told me that at least three times, and she told me I had better stay at home until I felt better, and then I must stay at the convent and not come home for a while.

Out of those wounds, I gained nine days of sick leave. I spent them hiding behind *Bleak House* in my room. 'Fog everywhere. Fog up the river, where it flows among green aits and meadows; fog down the river, where it rolls defiled among the tiers of shipping, and the waterwide pollution of a great (and dirty) city.'

The new maid started after a couple of days. She was very sympathetic about my injuries. She assured me that I'd been lucky to come out alive from the accident.

'It must have been really nasty. Poor Miss Kitty's got her hand all bandaged too.'

Like Agnes, the new maid had a taste for gory details and she was sorry not to be furnished with a full account of our accident – so sorry, in fact, that she left before I recovered. She told me she didn't like leaving just when she'd started, and Mrs Roberts so kind, but Miss Kitty seemed to have had a nasty shock and sometimes when she looked at her it gave her the jitters, and her own nerves had never been strong, not since a dog bit her in the street.

My other, much longer stay at home was when I came out one Christmas and went down with measles and was quarantined to my bed for three weeks after the fever and the unsightly blotches left me. It was after the measles – or rather, during them – that my legs stretched to their giraffe-like length. I had always been tall for my age and, indeed, looked several years older. But while I lay in bed, sweating out the infection, my legs alone grew and grew while the rest of my body stayed the same size, with the exception of my bust, which developed simultaneously.

I lay down as an oversized child and I got up, three weeks later, as an over-generously formed adult. It was six weeks before I returned to the convent, and the girls and the nuns scarcely recognised me. The effect was mutual, for despite the darkened sick room Granny had insisted on, my eyesight had diminished to a mere haze. I never, without the help of my spectacles, saw anything clearly again. By squinting, I could even diminish Mother's vitriolic gaze. The large glasses I wore from the early summer onwards didn't enhance my looks. Not that I really minded; I could hide behind them, and I had long since stopped praying for a fairy-tale conversion from ugly duckling to swan. My legs and newly formed breasts met with a very mixed reaction. The girls at school were deeply envious of the latter; the nuns were incensed by them and considered their sudden appearance as a wanton and wilful incubation. But the tradesmen and the occasional beachcomber at Selsey were definitely attracted by my new and exaggerated shape. Granny made me a linen band to wrap around my chest to flatten it, and told me I was the unluckiest child she had ever come across, while Mother, to my chagrin, didn't even deign to criticise.

More astonishing, though, to me, than any other aspect of my illness or its aftermath, was the sudden appearance of my Uncle Frank. I knew he existed, this brother of my father's, because years before, when my parents' divorce was going through the courts, my Uncle Frank's name had occasionally been mentioned at home. And once, when I was nine, I had actually seen him in our front garden – a visit that resulted in Mother's being head-strong for a week. I remember, at the time, being surprised to see, via the back of his retreating head and his half-profile, that he looked perfectly normal, if not a little distinguished. I had previously imagined my father and his family to be of the cloven-footed variety, with misshapen heads and horns and an enormous bonfire of blazing red hair topping their giant bodies.

After that one fleeting prospective visit, nothing more was heard of or from my uncle. He left, on that occasion, the sum of five pounds for me to spend on myself. Mother had handed it to Granny, who had handed it to me together with the injunction that I was to put it in the collection after Mass on Sunday. The five pounds was duly donated, although Uncle Frank remained in my memory as a hero and a keen understander of children. But the flags of my religious devotion retreated and entrenched at this loss of my short-lived fortune. For months afterwards, as I sat in church, or more often in the school chapel, my mind wandered from the prayers and the droning sermon to calculate exactly how many Swiss buns I could have bought with the fiver. I could have bought one thousand two hundred white iced buns, or eight hundred Danish pastries, or two thousand four hundred of the small doughy sweetmeats they sold in the Polish delicatessen on the High Street. It was the only time I recall having an interest in mathematics. I sat in my pew, squeezed in between my classmates, and stared at Father Gregory over my red leather missal, wondering resentfully how many doughnuts he had eaten out of my money, and hoping they would choke him.

Uncle Frank, however, returned after my measles and, scorning my quarantine, he came right into my room to visit me. Granny was horrified by his insistence on ignoring the contagiousness of my disease, but he insisted that an illness was contagious only during its incubation and not after, and that it was a misguided formality that kept one housebound after such a bout. I don't know what had changed in the years between his first tentative visit and his second successful one. Whatever it was, to Mother's disgust, Granny sided with Uncle Frank in believing that it was important for me to have some contact with the other side of my family. Perhaps she could feel the progress of her own disease, and was worried about what would happen to me if she ceased to be there to umpire my existence.

The first visit took place in my room, with Granny chaperoning me, not so much from my uncle as from what I might say to him in a moment of indiscretion about my life with Mother. However, when she saw that I had rewritten my childhood in such a way as to erase all the embarrassing moments, she trusted me to see him again and even to be taken out for treats from school over the next two years.

Mother and Uncle Frank never exchanged so much as a greeting. My uncle, who alternated between moments of what he called 'man-to-man talk' and moments of bemused silence, told me they didn't have anything in common. Yet it seemed to me that they shared quite a lot. Neither of them felt at their ease in the presence of children, and both of them were easily bored. He took me out to do the museums. We would arrive in South Kensington by cab, and then proceed under his enthusiastic guidance to visit the enormous Natural History Museum, or the Science or Geology buildings, where he would begin to tell me about his travels, particularly in the Argentine.

Uncle Frank had spent many years in the Argentine, designing railways there, tracing their lines and waiting to reap the profits. Another uncle (it emerged that I had six) had become a millionaire on the Argentine railways, and Frank had followed him out. Frank would pace his way around the exhibits, rejoicing now in an ostrich egg, now in an early engine, explaining how his transatlantic adventures had fared.

'I never had a head for business or whatever. Charlie never seemed to move much from his office, and there he was amassing a fortune. By the time I got there, he was well into packing his trunks with bullion and sailing home. He left me an enormous list of connections, of course, but I didn't know what to do with them, or whatever.'

He would wheel me around the mahogany display cases, particularly in the Natural History Museum, which always seemed more to his taste than the others. By the cases of stuffed humming-birds and the huge splayed feet of the emus and ostriches he would pause for long stretches of time, saying, 'I never could get over those . . . birds, all of them . . . extraordinary when you think of it . . . all so different, and all laying eggs.'

After a while of walking between them, with the minuscule eggs of the colibri and the huge opaque eggs of the ostrich, he would start to dwell on the discrepancy between his own meagre gains in South America and his brother's enormous nest egg, and his interest in the rest of nature – be it long since stuffed or still alive – would wane visibly, and he would take me instead to tea at one of the London hotels.

Personally, I was far more interested in tea than in resuscitating

Patagonia, so while he drank gin cobblers in the foyer of the rather grand but seedy Russell Hotel I would eat to my heart's content, listening to the snippets of information that he let fall about my other uncles and, most fascinating of all, about my father.

Uncle Frank was very vague about his family. He would look into his tall glass of gin, staring into the vacuous liquid with his own rather vacuous pale blue eyes, and pulling at his Cupid's bow moustache, he would mutter, 'Nelson was always a bit of a dark horse.'

Nelson was my father, and I would slow down my eating to an absolute minimum to concentrate on his disclosures.

'And impulsive . . . married your mother, just like that. Mater didn't like it at all, Kitty being Catholic.'

He looked from his drink to me and then back at his drink again. 'I expect you're a bit of a Catholic yourself. No harm in it really, I suppose. A lot of fuss for a religion or whatever. I've known some perfectly good Catholics. Why, I met one out in Buenos Aires, he was a very decent chap, very decent. Died of typhoid.'

He dropped into one of his characteristic silences and then mused on: 'The main thing I'd say about your mother, is that she's not the sort of woman a man wants to spend too much time with. I expect you've noticed.'

Uncle Frank, like Peter, always referred to me as a man.

'Haven't heard from Nelson in years, not since the . . . er . . . divorce business, and before that he just disappeared. Never did know what happened between him and Kitty. Didn't know about you until you were nine. None of us did. Funny, isn't it?' Uncle Frank found it so funny that it made him uneasy when I spoke about his brother as my father, so I started calling him Nelson.

'Does Nelson have red hair?'

My uncle seemed quite taken aback, and shook his head.

'Does any of your brothers?'

'No, never gone in for that sort of thing. One of Charlie's brood has a club foot, though. You'd think with all that money they could avoid that, or whatever, but no, it twists right in.'

Uncle Frank receded back into his brooding, casting a quick glance at my own large feet to make sure neither of them was twisting in. Relieved, he settled back into his drink and ordered another. After some long pauses of this kind, he would say, 'Your Uncle Frank has got work to do.' And he would settle the bill and order the cab and escort me home, tipping me half a crown each time as we approached the dreary miles of mock Tudor mansions and smaller terraces that heralded Hendon and home. His last words to me as I stepped out of the taxi would be, 'Remember now, you can always count on your Uncle Frank; just call me if you need me.'

Since he never left an address or telephone number this was not a possible option, but we both enjoyed the sort of imaginary pact we had between us.

It often occurred to me that Frank was like a guide dog that knew its way along certain routes and instinctively avoided others. After he left me at the gate, and disappeared back to West London in the taxi, I would hover around on the street, praying that no one would see me. I was not an inconspicuous person. Often as not, I was not meant to be there. Frank would usually pick me up from my convent, but he had such a great distaste for schools in general and convents in particular that he would contrive to take me home instead of back to school. Sometimes, because he would tire of our outings earlier than the allotted time of my exeat, I could get another taxi and get back to school before any harm was done. This involved breaking into my half-crown tip, but was infinitely preferable to bumping into Mother or even Granny.

The one time Granny caught me, deposited in Hendon thus, she bustled me into the house, saying, 'Well, that's nonsense. Frank hasn't done a day's work in his life. I shall speak to him about this; he has no business leaving you here. What if Kitty were to come home?'

For some reason, though, she never did speak to Frank about his dropping-off arrangements, and I continued to be collected from school and dumped outside our garden gate. And once Kitty was at home, but she was in one of her strangely quiet phases when she drifted about in a kind of trance. So she merely asked, 'What's she doing here?'

'She's on her way to the convent,' Granny told her.

'Oh, good,' Mother said, and trailed away to the side of the house with the skirt of her embroidered silk dress flapping behind her, following the graceful swish of her hips.

CHAPTER 7

GRANNY said nothing was ever the same after World War I. The old order had rotted with the soldiers' feet in the trenches, spreading like gangrene through the blood of the country until everyone felt hurt and cheated by the present, and ached for the past, and mistrusted their leaders. There was institutionalised nostalgia. Life had been perfect before the war, people claimed; the strawberries had tasted better, girls were prettier, men were more romantic and parties had been more fun. Even among the jobless a fantasy of romance grew up around their stolen pasts. The drudgery of farm work became idolised, and long-forgotten factory shifts from the days of few regulations and interminable hours were hankered for with watery eyes by jobless queues. Those were the days, though, those days gone by. Perhaps it was the order of things that people missed, rather than the things themselves.

Whatever it was, this 'thirties malaise', it was endemic. Only Mother, and to some extent Granny and I, believed it to be unique to our family. Because of the peculiar circumstances surrounding our flight from the Island, and our relative social isolation afterwards, we were unable to see that the whole country was altering its way of life, or having it altered. When ends didn't meet, and the butcher's bill was hard to pay, Mother blamed me rather than the cost of living. And when Granny went shopping and a shop girl lacked respect, Granny blamed our situation: our fall from grace. If a tradesman was overfamiliar, Mother believed it was because the culprit knew of our plight, and not because times had changed. If her life was less pleasurable than it had been before, it was my fault.

Agnes said the change between the wars was atmospheric; she

said it sat like the uncomfortable closeness of an oncoming storm. Mother and Granny began to monitor each other's behaviour in ways they had not done hitherto. Mother was pleased when the Stock Market crashed in New York: she told Mrs Müller that the wealthy had been chastened. It upset her, though, when the feathered, sequined glamour of the previous fashions dulled into more conventional lines. Where once her young beaux had tried to stand out, now they found it more prudent to stay firmly within the confines of a group, with no risk of losing it by being too obvious. One of her friends went to Spain to fight and she never forgave him. Agnes told me that Mother thought all the daredevils should find their thrills hovering around the knife-edge of her ephemeral passions, pitting their strength against her spite and winning or losing, as luck would have it.

I was removed from the care of the Filles de la Croix at the age of twelve, and placed in the far more disciplined environment of German nuns. I left my French convent 'under a cloud'. From the time it settled over me until the time I left home, six years later, it never quite lifted again.

I attacked a child in our local park, and her mother claimed that I had tried to kill the girl. Granny was appalled, and although she maintained that I had no murderous intent she immediately moved me to the guaranteed strictures of a Prussian upbringing. Mother, it seemed, had been lobbying for such a move for years and had already visited the borstal-type establishment in Hertford-shire. As for myself, I was sorry to leave my friends, and lose my exeats, and my Uncle Frank, and sad to have upset my Granny and sad, too, not to have actually killed the battered girl in question.

Although there had been many fights before, in the convent, carried out in our dormitory or behind the tennis sheds, they were just fights to settle old scores and readjust petty quarrels. My first and only public fight was far more serious. I wanted to kill the girl. I knocked her to the ground and then sat on her and, holding her hair in my fists, I beat her head against the tarmacked path. I banged it as hard as I could, and if she did not die as a result that just went to show how difficult it is to finish someone off. I was bigger than her, too – not older, but bigger. No wonder Mother had such haphazard results with me, thrashing out with her tiny size at my much larger frame.

I had met this girl intermittently for several years. It was one of those cases when two people loathe each other at first sight – except that, as in love, the loathing was uneven. For she took an instant and active dislike to me, while I became aware of her presence more slowly, and always through her own sly little sleights. When I went shopping with Granny, this girl, whose name I cannot even remember, used to walk behind us, or across the road, mimicking Granny's limp, undermining her position in the neighbourhood. I always pretended not to notice, and this fanned her dislike. We were too stuck up for her, too secretive, too unusual with the relays of glimmering cars pulling up to our gate. That was part of the problem. The other part was simply that she didn't like me. She teased me about my hair and my freckles, and she taunted me about my family. Years passed, and we both grew older, and I ignored her.

By the time of our final contretemps, I had almost forgotten about her. She was just a shadow from other times. I was too involved in my school and my introspection, too rarely at home even to see her. Mother had visitors that day: two sisters and a man called Denny. They were all dressed up in hats and veils, including Denny, playing a very noisy game in the sitting-room. I can't recall why I was out of school, but I was. Granny went into town, which consisted of a short walk to the High Street and a stint at the local shops. She took me with her, but left me at the park with instructions to wait for her on 'our' bench. This was a black iron affair sheltered by an enormous oak tree. We spent hours there, staring at the other trees and the grey-green vista towards the railings, with only the shuffling of my feet and the silent twitching of Granny's fingers to disturb the stillness of the solitary gardens. Occasionally a stranger would stroll or hurry past us, and occasionally my unnamed enemy would dawdle by, splashing if there was a puddle to splash, or just pulling a face when she could get away with it.

On that particular afternoon I went and sat on the bench alone, staring out across the sodden grass unevenly quilted with fallen leaves. It was a bleak day, with its ashen face turned to the wind. I felt the damp chill begin to creep along my fingers and my nose while rusty oak leaves rocked themselves to the ground, landing in jagged patches on the mud-splattered path. I compared the dull day outside to the colourful romping of Mother and her friends within, and a transitory glow hovered around her image in my mind. I loved seeing her with her friends. It was like seeing a beautiful stranger from a distance. Being with other people transformed her from the witch I held her to be, with all the evil connotations of that profession, into something glamorous and unreal. I often wished she lived next door so that I could spy on her and see her always at her best, unaware of my intrusion yet still near to me. Instead, two singers called the Trix Sisters lived next door, and although Mother had often played one of their songs, 'I'm sitting on top of the world', she declared them to be boring and without an ounce of brain between them, so she rarely, if ever, visited them. Notwithstanding our – by now – mutual dislike, mine was sometimes tinged by other more complex emotions, as on that afternoon, sitting in the park and musing on Mother as a pocket of colour in an otherwise grey world.

On to this soft mood of filial affection stepped my enemy. She sat down on the bench beside me, at a distance of some feet, and began to hum. She hummed 'John Brown's body lies a-mouldering in his grave', while tapping out the rhythm with her hands. It was never my favourite song, but it was a public park, so I ignored her. And I continued to ignore her despite the fact that she could hardly hum out the tune for her smirking. She stopped abruptly, and said, 'Do you know what a slut is, Joan Allen?'

I did know what a slut was. I had frequently been called one myself, and at school we discussed the connotations of all the insults we could cull into our dormitory. She managed to pronounce my name as though it, too, were an insult. I ignored her.

'Well, do you?'

I continued to ignore her.

'Everyone says your mother's a slut. Everyone says she does it with half the men in London. Everyone says . . .'

I punched her very hard in the arm, and then stood up to punch her again, but she had run off and was standing now on the wet grass.

I was actually more interested in her words than in her, so I didn't follow her, but sat down. Was it possible that everyone said that? And was it possible that Mother did 'do it' with all those men? And what did it mean if she did? And who was everyone, and why were they talking about my mother? I had the monopoly of hatred on my mother. I owned all the ill thoughts about her. I had earned the right to think bad things about her, but I was her daughter, and even I didn't say what I thought. The more I thought about it, the more incensed I became about this slanderous girl. I decided that she was a guttersnipe (another name I had frequently been called by Mother) and that it wasn't so much what she said as her actual mouth that was to blame. I felt a wave of hot blood rise up my face. Through the dizziness it brought, I heard this obnoxious gossiper singing; it was the same tune, the 'John Brown' of before, but now the words were changed to:

'Joan Allen's mother is the slut of Hendon town,
Joan Allen's mother is the slut of Hendon town,
Joan Allen's mother is the slut of Hendon town,
And everybody says she is.
Dah-dah.'

She was enjoying her taunt, stomping like an insipid soldier on the grass verge while she swung her arms and took her breath for the next verse:

'Joan Allen's mother . . .'

That was when I jumped on her. She was half in the grass and half over the edge, with her head in the path. I heard the crack of her skull as it hit the tarmac, and a shiver of pleasure ran through me. That was what I wanted to hear, not her singing but the back of her head hitting the ground until it went all soft in my hands.

I hadn't seen her own mother sitting knitting on the next bench along, just as I didn't see Granny limping towards her with her carpetbagful of thread. I didn't see anything except my victim's bulging eyes and the top of her head; her head that was usurping mine, trying to take my place insulting my mother. My mother. She was mine, whether anyone liked it or not she was *mine*! I had lived through twelve years of her neglect, twelve years of her torment, and no one was going to share her.

My victim must have felt relatively safe, with her mother within calling distance. She must have known a fight would start, and have reckoned to win it by parental intervention. I was only vaguely aware of the screaming that very quickly gathered around my attack, just as I was only vaguely aware of being pulled and hit myself. I was headstrong and I had turned the colour of her head to the colour of my own. There was quite a little crowd by the time I was eventually hauled off the bleeding girl. Granny was there, silently ashamed, and looking at me with Mother's eyes. I looked down in disgust at the battered heap at my feet, with the red ribbon I had tied in her hair. She was moaning, and my nose was bleeding. I went home under the cloud that was to hover over me like a demonic halo for years. We were followed for the first few paces by an unknown woman who thought I should be locked up, and shouted as much to Granny's retreating limp.

And I was locked up. I was smuggled back into the house and hurried upstairs, where Granny locked me in my room. There was no tea, and no supper as a punishment, but since the sounds of romping continued to drift upstairs for some hours, changing now into the clink of drinks and now into the soft slur of conversation peppered with laughter, I guessed that Granny hadn't told Mother about my disgrace.

Perhaps there had been tantrums at home before about the Prussian school, because the speed with which I began there belied any sudden decisions. I never went back to the French convent, even to collect my things. They were forwarded to me. I had always felt relatively safe with my friendships at school because I knew that a term's notice was necessary in order to leave, and our straitened finances could not have risen to a term's worth of wasted fees. So Mother must have given my notice long before-hand. Perhaps she gave it every term, and then thought up some excuse to put me back there. However she managed it, I started two days later with the Germans and it felt as I imagine a straitjacket must feel.

It was total constriction. Even the dormitories were supervised by spies. Wherever I went, be it in the grounds or in the school buildings themselves, the nuns were there. They usually went around in groups of two, patrolling and punishing. They called it grooming us, but it was the grooming of brass and leather on our bare skins. Next to their rosaries they carried a leather thong which they flicked as often as they could across our wrists.

Whatever their intentions, the team spirit in the school was strong. Apart from a group of wimps whose fear had got the better of them, most of the girls stuck together, united by a common front. The only way to survive was to learn the rules. The only way to rebel was within their framework. To me the nuns seemed, at times, as cruel as Mother, but ultimately less powerful. The hardest thing about them was their language. I had never heard German spoken before, except for the odd word in Hendon or Golders Green when the German Jews met in the street and gabbled their greetings. From the day I arrived until the day I left, German became my language. I learnt it, and I spat it out, not just for what it stood for but for its sound. I had been dealing in French and in English, with the odd remembered word of Jersiaise; I wasn't prepared for the guttural choking of their barked Deutsch.

Just as the nuns kept us girls in an almost militarised regime in which the slightest infraction was pounced on and punished, so they themselves lived within the strictures of a harshly disciplinarian order. I grew to know them better than most of the other pupils, because I spent the bulk of my holidays locked inside the granite blocks of the convent. I noticed how they cringed to their Mother Superior, even more abjectly than the girls did to them. After my first years there, I felt vastly their superior. They were interned for life, while we were interned only until our matriculation, or sooner if a parent or guardian could be made to believe the deprivations that prevailed.

I was about fourteen when I began to notice the escalation of surveillance and severity that had started to invade the convent. Girls had always been encouraged to inform on each other, but suddenly there were exaggerated rewards for these petty betrayals; the punishments themselves became harsher. Mother Superior, in her pristine white robes, was riddling the convent with a fanatical poker. Detentions that used to be spent memorising passages from *The Lives of the Saints* were now spent repeating nationalistic slogans. There was only one nation: Germany, to which, if Sister Gudrun was to be believed, God the Father Almighty and His only-begotten Son belonged. The refectory which had once been panelled with holy paintings showed grazes in its stained oak where all the brown-eyed Saints had ceased to hang. Gaudy prints of Our Lord and Our Lady with blonde tresses were nailed to the walls to replace them.

Every month, our books were tampered with. Even our Bibles and missals had cuts in their pages where the lay sisters had snipped out certain sentences. Yolanda de Leon had her plait of black hair cut off and burnt and had to sit at the back of the class and sleep in a cubicle far away from the rest of us. She became the keenest follower of the nuns and knew more about the Social Democratic Party in Germany than any of us, but she was dark and foreign and tainted with sin. Her father was a diplomat. Every term I watched the Embassy car that brought her to the convent door with relief. I was safer with Yolanda than without her. We all knew that Judas the Jew had red hair. The nuns were looking for scapegoats and converts. It was far easier to be the latter.

The nuns themselves – who had until then shown only a fear of the Mother Superior seconded by a fear of God and a zealousness in both – suddenly altered in their attitude to us. Before, we had been treated as a species of trainable maggots whose fees financed the convent and, therefore, whose profane presence was unavoidable. Now, we all rose as potential missionaries for their Fatherland.

A large part of our curriculum already consisted of German language lessons, and German history and German geography, with a small but unavoidable slot for German literature. To this diet was added the daily adulatory accounts of the miracle of Germany's new leader and the country's inevitable rise to glory and world power. The cult of the Führer hit our convent like an inexplicable reprieve. Any lesson could be diverted by skilfully bringing up Hitler questions. Innocently murmured praises of the Leader, and carefully stage-whispered desires to flee to the enthralling new order in Berlin, were greeted with indulgence.

When called upon to do so, we could arrange ourselves into a human formation of the swastika. We regularly used *Heil Hitler* as a greeting. Even on the playing fields, we were taught to use our hockey sticks to give the Nazi salute. Mother Superior was adamant: we English girls were decadent and doomed, only the purity of Germany had a future. She offered us salvation so long as we 'distinguished our cause from the nation that is not holy'.

On my very rare visits home – visits that usually involved a trip to Selsey Beach – I would try to explain to Granny that the whole of Europe was about to change.

'There's going to be an alliance between England and Germany. We'll be the Führer's junior partner. It's all going to happen quite soon, you know,' I would tell her.

'Yes, dear,' she'd say, without ceasing to gaze at the horizon as if expecting some more interesting message to arrive by ship. She seemed prepared to wait interminably there. In her latter days nothing appeared to interest her beyond her nostalgia for Jersey, her crochet, and my assurances that I believed in her faith, the strictly rigorous faith that she interpreted with her own benign charity.

I wanted Granny to deny my news. I wanted her to contradict me, and tell me no such alliance would take place. I hoped she would assure me that England's future would not be overrun by German zeal. For although we absorbed the militarism of our school, school was a transitory place, a temporary purgatory from which we all planned to escape. We might live there in a holocaust of 'Heil Hitlers', but most of us hated the German nuns gloating in their sackcloth and ashes. We resented their way of life and their insistence on inflicting it on us. Hitler himself was their one hero we liked because he alone had given us whatever respite we had there. His obsession was our one relaxation.

I wanted Granny to snap the tenuous spell of the nuns' predictions, but Granny was too busy putting her life in order, hour by hour, clawing back her past and packaging it in the camphor of her memory while the cancer in her hip gnawed away her future.

CHAPTER 8

SOMETIMES, when I look back, it seems that I was born in 1939. It was the year I became a painted lady, not because I used any rouge or make-up but because I hatched my wings and turned into what others saw as a butterfly, a huge and startlingly coloured decoration, and I fell in love. And my body, which had always worked against me with only an undertow of something pulling admirers towards me like a gathering tide, began to work for me. It was finally on my side. It became everything. I lived through the next decade, feeling my way along its sensual corridors. I fell in love then, just before the war, and then I fell in love again and again, sating my appetite for touch and affection, slaking my need for love with an ardour that some might interpret as revenge. But my passions were genuine. I was no longer an alien. Sex became my family, my country. The exile seemed to be over. My long limbs dropped their package of guilt, and wrapped themselves around a series of lovers.

I began to be known as a beauty. It was my passport to parties, and the key to my growing power. I had been branded as ugly for too long ever truly to believe this new label. The only times I felt anywhere near it were in the arms of a lover. I hungered for embraces; for near-lethal closeness. The minute there was a separation, a physical distance between me and my current love, the old doubts set in again. It was as though a few cells from Granny's hip had transplanted themselves in my heart and grew there, cancerous cells, subdividing inside me until the warmth of someone's kisses could drive them back in a passionate chemotherapy.

Granny must have kept her cancer at bay for at least eight years. Her limp went back that long. Her illness gradually turned her face from the dry ivory of her younger days to the bleached frailty of paper. It was the same thin paper that she used for writing letters to Agnes. Held up to the light, it was transparent, with only the immaculate characters of her blue-inked copperplate spidering over the surface like the blue veins of her face, punctuated by lines of pain. She limped, but she never complained.

I thought she had arthritis, as many people did. One day, while she was out shopping, a gypsy came to our house. She was a woman of an indiscernible age with a skin tanned to the colour of congealed gravy that looked quite out of place in a London winter. She carried an air of fields and hedges about her. People did sometimes come to the house to sell things, but this woman appeared to carry nothing in her arms – no basket, or pegs, or trinkets. I answered the door myself and was confused at the sight of her, in her long flared skirt and thin cotton top. It was cold outside. It was winter.

'I have come for the lady of the house,' she said.

'My mother's out,' I told her.

'No, not her, the lady. The lady.'

And she pushed past me into the hall, brushing the marble-topped credenza and nearly knocking over Granny's Chinese vase with the long copper beech twigs in it. Every year, in the spring, Granny gathered these leaves as their colour was rising and then, with a glycerine mixture, she would keep them all year, fading very slowly, until the sap began to rise again in the whole trees outside.

I was frightened that the woman would steal if she came in. Gypsies were thieves. They had stolen the nails from Christ's cross. Gypsies stole children, too. But I was sixteen and no child at all. It was Granny's things I thought she had come for. I had been told by Sister Gudrun that gypsies were pollution. Once Europe was cleansed, all the gypsies would be swept off the map. The convent world was as flat as the earth before Columbus and the lay sisters were ready with their brooms to push all the tainted tribes over the edge. Seeing this woman so close to me, I felt guilty in this knowledge. So I let her barge on past me, and limited my efforts to following her.

'The lady, I've come for the lady,' she kept saying, and she took to the stairs, limping painfully up them as Granny did, lopsided on the polished banister and carrying an imaginary bundle. It was exactly like Granny herself, smuggling Rufus under her arm. Rufus had been dead for over a year. When she reached the landing she smiled regretfully and climbed back down, limping again in an imitation of my grandmother, accentuating her steps as she neared the hall.

'That's the one, isn't it?' she said, staring right into my face.

'She's not here,' I mumbled. It had upset me to see Granny's innate elegance caricatured in this way. There seemed suddenly to be so little difference between the two women.

'The cancer's killing her,' she said. 'Did you know?' I shook my head.

'It's killing her. I came to take some away with me, but since she's not here . . .' She looked around her, fixing her dark hooded eyes on everything in the hall. After a moment she rested her stare on the copper beech leaves, and the tension around her seemed to drain away. She tore a side branch off the arrangement and held it in her tortoiseshell hand.

'Give me this,' she told me, and I nodded.

'Not stealing, mind, giving, these leaves. There'll be no more jugs of them. Did you know that?'

Again I shook my head. The front door had remained ajar, letting in its bitter draught of January cold. Without any other explanation, the gypsy woman left. She walked along our garden path, lurching slightly as she went. At the gate she limped again, for a step or two, then turned back to look at me once more. I shut the door, bolted it top and bottom, and then went round the house locking everything.

I didn't tell Granny that this strange visitor had 'come for her', nor did she ever come again. Her prediction about the leaves was wrong, for the next spring Granny gathered and treated them again. However, on my eighteenth birthday she told me she had arranged to go into a nursing home in Chislehurst, and she went there shortly afterwards. It was only then that I was officially told she had cancer. She lived to see the first bombs fall over London, but died before her beloved Island was invaded and then occupied by the Germans. After she went into the nursing home she ceased to hold on to her life any more, and it slipped away visibly. I replaced my visits to the still hale Mrs de Gruchy with regular weekly visits to Chislehurst in Kent. From Sunday to Sunday I could see her fade, shrinking into a thinness that seemed to be pushing her bones outside her body like an ark.

When she talked, I could see the hinges of her jaw. She talked less about Jersey in her latter months, concentrating her frail energies on Mother. She tried to explain to me how different Mother really was. She told me about instances of her kindness, about her loyalty and her difficulties. She tried very hard to make her human for me. It brought tears to my eyes sometimes, explaining away her daughter's cruelty. I wanted to graft my own flesh to cover her, to wrap her up and protect her mummified frame. I hadn't realised how much I loved her until then, dying as she was, dislocated by the burden of her family. She begged me to look after Mother.

'She's so alone,' she kept saying, 'so alone.'

I listened to all she had to say, and out of respect for her I didn't disagree with what she had to tell me. I just sat and nodded, and held her throbbing parchment hand, and watched the leaves falling from the trees.

I think she died believing that I understood Mother and her rages a little better. I think she died believing that some of her own spirit of forgiveness and understanding had passed on to me. I hope she did. I hope she didn't realise how hard I felt to Mother, how I gloated on the prospect of her decline; and that her prophecy of Mother being 'so alone' had a sweet ring to my ears. I wanted my mother to suffer. It has taken me another thirty years to understand even a fraction of what Granny was trying to tell me. I had to live my own life first, and burn it out, before I could see even a glimpse of what Mother really felt. I never wanted to understand her before: I wanted to hate her. I had decided years ago that Mother was a witch. I had grown used to the idea, grown up with it. The fact that she stayed in the back of my mind, like Hanno's empty parrot cage in the conservatory, was something I chose to ignore. I thought I could exorcise her power by merely telling people from time to time that I had hated her. For even her powers shrivelled in my memory, and she shrank back to nothing more than her diminutive height and was pushed backstage, out of sight. Bigger, more important things were happening, like the war and my own love life. Everything seemed to happen in 1939.

In that one year I left home, married, met my father for the first time, the phoney war began, and last, but not least, Granny died. I had matriculated and left school in the early summer, and I was as sick of politics as all my friends. Hitler's and Chamberlain's every whisper had been relayed to us at the convent with an awed excitement that none of us girls shared. The Nazi boasts and threats had been pumped out for so many years by then that none of us took them seriously any more.

One of my friends was spending the summer in Kent with her family. There was to be a house party and she invited me. I accepted gratefully, and arranged to travel there four days after the end of term. Granny gave me permission to go. I didn't realise at the time that it was to be her own last summer. The gypsy had prophesied one year for her, and since she had long since outlived it I had come to think that she was delicate but immortal. So I abandoned her to Selsey and went off with my friends.

It turned out that with all the talk of war that had been circulating during the preceding months, my father had returned to England to join his old regiment should the need arise. He had been in touch with Granny and sent an intriguing, typewritten piece of paper with his address on it for me. He was living in Chelsea, in a borrowed flat, and would, he had written, be interested to see me, if I had the time. I spent most of the next four days traipsing backwards and forwards to Chelsea without once managing to find him at home. After eighteen years of total absence, I did not find this as alarming as I might otherwise have done. He had said in his letter to Granny, 'Tell Joanna . . .' That was me. Converted by a mere sweep of his pen from Joan, the surrogate Maid of Orleans, the young martyr, into this new transatlantic entity, the future *femme fatale*. I liked it. I never called myself Joan again.

Agnes arrived from Jersey to keep Granny company for the summer. She had put on a great deal of weight that seemed to hang in folds around her chin, hips and waist, with minor tucks on her face. I saw them both to the railway station and on to their train, while resenting the time it took me away from the vigil outside my father's door. Granny had told me she would be moving into the nursing home on her return, but I didn't associate this with dying. I felt that it was merely a logical move connected more to my leaving school and having a nursing job lined up than anything to do with her own state of health. I had grown too used to her frailty and to the idea that she existed solely to keep Mother and me apart from each other and off each other's throats.

It was Granny's idea that I go into nursing. I agreed gladly, as it meant liberation from the German nuns and the capricious tyranny of Mother herself. Also, I was going to train as a Nightingale, one of the nurses attached to St Thomas' Hospital, and Tommy's held fond memories for me, not to mention the familiar presence of Mrs de Gruchy. After Granny and Agnes left, there were just two days until I was due to arrive in Kent. I had never been to a grown-up party before. My social knowledge was limited to children's parties and the vicarious pleasures of watching Mother leave for and return from parties of her own.

Sheltering from a shower in the china department of Peter Jones, I bumped into a girl from school. After a quick '*Heil Hitler*' she told me her brother was having a party that very night in Cadogan Square and was short of girls, and that I absolutely had to go. Simultaneously I promised her I would, and myself that I wouldn't, and then made my way back to the increasingly familiar address my father had left. Sitting on the red, threadbare carpet of his hall stairs, I worked out a number of alternative stratagems. The first was to meet Nelson and bask in his paternal welcome – whatever that might be, and I admitted that I had no idea. The second was to trail back to Hendon on the Northern Line of the underground and stay in until my already agreed escape to Kent was due. The third was to telephone home and ask Mother's permission to go to the party that night. It was several hours before I could effectively word in my own mind how to make this request. By the time I had found a public telephone there was no reply anyway, so I decided to call it a day, and just go home. Once there, though, a mote of rebellion began to bathe and dress me for a night out.

I had never been out in the evening, so I had no official curfew time. I argued that since I had not been forbidden to go out, there was always a possibility that it was actually allowed. I was eighteen and I would be earning my own pittance by the end of the summer. My willpower extended to resist the temptation of borrowing Mother's clothes. I sunk my hand into a drawerful of her silk lingerie; it felt like trailing my fingers through water. I longed for silk on my skin, and the soothing motion of river punts and young men in blazers to steer me away from noisy crowds. Mother's doll-like things couldn't help me, though. The adrenaline of my daring dressed me that night.

No other party was ever as good as that. I drank gin and champagne and I danced and laughed and flirted and flaunted myself. I must have looked terrible, but I really didn't care. I met about fifteen potential boyfriends who between them called me 'a card', 'a brick', 'a sport', and dozens of other near-endearments that filled my head more than the gin itself. I got drunk, and was sick in my friend's bathroom, and hid a towel behind the lavatory, and then went out and danced again.

Before setting out I had, in lieu of any higher authority, given myself strict Cinderella instructions. Mother would scarcely mind, I argued, if I was back by twelve; and there was also the real chance that she wouldn't return before then herself. On lots of nights she didn't get back until the early hours of the morning.

One minute the room seemed to be full and spinning round with people in coloured flares that reflected in the long gilt mirrors beside the fireplace, and then it just seemed to be spinning. The next thing I remember is touching my way along the shrubbery to our front door, pulling leaves off Granny's precious camellias. It took me a long time to find the lock, which inexplicably had moved. Once inside I stumbled towards the kitchen, forcing my mind to articulate the names of foods I would eat: bread, and meat paste, cheese and rice pudding and . . . I found the light switch, again with difficulty, but before I could turn it on I became aware of two bright cat's eyes glaring at me from the middle of the room. Mother was sitting at the bare kitchen table like a little jar of potted evil. I switched on the light and saw she was holding a carving knife in her hand.

I don't know what would have happened without the help of the gin and champagne that were gurgling inside me. Had I cringed or shrunk away, she might have sprung at me. As it was, years of nervous tension surged up and got the better of me, and I laughed. It took her aback, and gave me just enough time to grab one of the stick-back chairs and hold it in front of me as a lion tamer would.

Her arms were shaking so much that they looked like puppets which she was making dance. I found the light and she blinked at me. Blinking was out, I had never managed to make her do it before. A nerve in her left cheek began to twitch, forcing her upper lip into a rhythmic grimace.

'Slut,' she shouted.

I said absolutely nothing. I had overcome a wave of gin nausea and felt exultant at this feat.

'Slut.'

Again I said nothing but I thought, knowing that she would pick it up, 'Yes, I am, and I like it. I like being touched.' She stood up and stabbed the carving knife deep into the old pine of the table, pulling it out again as though the wood were butter. Then she edged towards me. Her voice began to rise:

'I have been cursed with you. You feed on blood. I've watched you, you're destroying her. You subhuman slut. Spying, creeping slut. I would have cut you out before you were born. Our Lord will forgive me now; He understands.'

As she said these last words she jerked an arm and a leg across the remaining distance between us, rising like a ballerina suspended in midair. The knife slashed the back of my hand. My flesh looked wet and white like meat fat. Then it started to bleed, splattering the kitchen floor. Mother's whole body began to tremble, and she thrashed both her arms about. One still held the carving knife, the other was groping to catch my blood.

'Red is the colour of the Devil. Red is degenerate. Red is wrong. You are red inside and out. You are dead.'

Her lips tightened to a pale line. The sweat glistened and rolled on to her shoulders. She aimed again and again, flailing the empty air or whittling splinters from the chair. Her pallor was relieved by my blood streaked like war paint on her face.

'You are mad, bad mad, red.'

A low crackle was coming from high in her chest. It sounded like a fire starting, or the crossing of electrical wires. As by a signal, both her hands dropped by her sides, and she stood rigid but apparently lifeless in a pool of bloody shavings on the floor. I waited to see if this was a trick, then tentatively I moved towards the door. Mother's arm, the one with the hammer mole, rose in a spasm. I pushed the ruined chair towards her and saw it fall with her to the ground.

Upstairs, my bedroom was in tatters. My clothes had been cut into patchwork squares. My crocheted counterpane was torn and unravelled, my books were ripped and my collection of sea shells was shattered and trampled into the carpet. My room was reduced to a parody of Selsey Beach. My suitcase, when I left, was correspondingly empty. I bandaged my cut hand with a strip of linen from my sheets. I had two pounds and four shillings saved up from my years in the convent; and Granny had given me a pound to take to Kent to tip the maids there. As I left, I spied on Mother, as I so often had before. Her shoulders were as white as litmus paper, but where her hands and forearms had touched my blood, her skin had turned an acid red. She was on all fours, moaning like a wounded beast.

The street lamps dropped long gallows shadows around me. All the curtains of our street were tightly drawn. The privet hedges had grown into thicket barricades. Even the High Street had the metal shutters of its shops portcullised down. The darkness was winding itself around my feet, weighing down my belongings in their black crocodile-skin suitcase to stones. I tried to say 'Hail Marys' to the night, but my mouth was shapeless and too thick to move. I wanted to sleep and wake up believing in one of Granny's dreams. I wanted the gash in my hand to be a sword wound that rose to my armpit. The park gates were closed and there was nowhere to sit, so I walked on, drunk with the mixture of gin and tears. I hadn't cried for a long time, longer than I could remember, and I found some companionship in my weeping. I sat on a low wall, out of earshot of any of the sleeping bungalows, and I forced myself to cry as hard as I could. The pink light of morning silhouetted the rows of chimneys against the sky when I woke up gasping for air.

I walked from where I was to Golders Green through the busy twittering of sparrows, interrupting their song with occasional convulsive gulping. My eyes ached, and my hand ached, and so did my head. It was all Mother's fault. Everything was. I determined then and there never to see her again. I told myself that I would never deal in her petty spites and snobberies, either. I would renounce all the things she had stood for, even to the point of my hair; I would grow it long and wave it as I walked, and mix with only people like myself, vulgar people and sluts and drunks. I made a million resolutions as I tramped along. I had nine hours to go before my train to Kent. I resolved to live entirely off Swiss buns and thoughts of future revenge during that time.

I cleaned myself up at the ladies' lavatory at Victoria Station, dabbing my swollen face with cold water until the whole of my blouse was soaked and sticking to me. Then I walked in the sunshine by the taxi rank trying to dry off while half-watching the bustle of holidaymakers on their way to the coast and the Continent. There was a family of children standing guard over a pile of scuffed luggage, taking it in turns to chant a line of the skipping song that we used to like at Les Filles de la Croix:

> 'Nelson Nelson lost one arm
> Nelson Nelson lost the other arm.'

I stood for some minutes watching them, mesmerised by the name:

> 'Nelson Nelson lost one eye,
> Nelson Nelson lost the other eye.'

It wasn't until the youngest of the children, a small girl with virtually no teeth, stopped and returned my stare that I realised I still hadn't seen my Nelson. I determined to find him, even if it meant postponing my journey to Kent. I would wait for him on his Chelsea stairs.

I didn't really expect him to be in. It was enough to believe in his existence. The mere idea of him was as exotic to me as the multicoloured creatures of the Natural History Museum. Perhaps the nearest I came to imagining him as a man was to see him as a hybrid between my Uncle Frank and a Red Indian. He would be someone who wore a suit and moccasins, a tie and a feather headdress. Instead, the man who opened the door to me and momentarily failed to recognise me as his daughter was calm and smelt of woodsmoke. He looked immune to worry.

I studied him from his black velvet slippers to his clipped

moustache, scanning his smooth unlined brow, his arched sandy eyebrows, his large, slightly surprised grey eyes, while his own mouth moved into a smile.

'Joanna?'

'You've got my nose as well . . . my eyes, nearly, but my nose.'

'Joanna! I have to hand it to you, you're absolutely huge. Congratulations. I seem to have miscalculated your size somehow. I laid down a crate of ginger pop against your turning up, but I think we'd do better with a bottle of champagne . . . come in, come in,' he told me, backing into his cluttered sitting-room and almost tripping over the corner of one of his half-unpacked trunks as he did so.

'Joanna, you see, you've been a good daughter to me already. You've turned up to keep an old man company in his drinks.'

I sat down in a big leather armchair and helped to ease the stuffing of horsehair out of its arm through an already existing tear. Nelson busied himself uncorking a bottle of champagne, which he spilt into two glasses.

'Here's to us Allens,' he said, tipping the whole of his drink down his throat. I followed suit, feeling the same dive into foaming surf of the party the night before: an undercurrent of bubbles shot up my nose and I spluttered.

'That's the stuff, I hate to think of any girl of mine trying to struggle through her life without a drink or two.'

Then he paused and took in the redness of my hair.

'Can't imagine your mother having been too keen on your colouring . . . lucky, really, that you're twice her size.'

He paused and looked around him, resting his eyes on the untidy contents of his trunk as though hoping to hide some unpleasant memory in it.

'So, how is your mother?'

I tried to explain how much she hated me and how we'd fought, and how I'd never see her again, but Nelson's attention seemed to wander, and I stopped.

'By the way, *you've* got *my* nose, you know; other way round, isn't it? I'm the senior partner.'

A sudden silence fell between us and we both watched the fern pattern on the carpet for a while until Nelson stood up and rummaged in his trunk for a pair of brogues which he put on, burying his head in his knees to do so.

'I feel a bit strange, actually, I think I could do with a stroll; can I walk you anywhere?'

We walked all the way back to Victoria Station. Nelson did most of the talking; I was too afraid of losing him to risk losing his attention again; so I basked in his proximity to me and in the deep lull of his voice, taking in only snatches of what he said. I was so excited to be with him that the emotion suffused my brain with an overall sense of well-being that drowned out the specific meaning of his words. My footsoreness of the early morning was all forgotten. I was walking with a handsome man. I was walking with my father. I belonged on the pavement under the plane trees with him. I wanted to live with him. I hoped he would offer to take me in, but he didn't. Instead, he offered me a port in the storm. A freshwater stop only.

'It's a bit late for me to be a father to you, Joanna, but I'd like to be your friend. You can count on me whenever you need someone to pour you a drink or hold your hand for a moment. We'll talk about good times, and we'll have some good times together, you and I.'

He took my hand and held it in his own as tightly as Granny's twine when she used to ball her skeins from my imprisoned fingers.

'I'll always be there for you. Track me down at White's. I move around a bit. I never can decide whether to pack or unpack my trunks, but you'll find me. So look me up again when you're next in town.' Then he pressed something into the pocket of my jacket and was gone. I watched him merge into the crowded street, following his broad shoulders until they disappeared. I wanted to follow him but I didn't dare intrude on his enforced calm.

My height and my nose and my eyes were all his, but my turbulence was Mother's. It was alien to him. He couldn't cope with anguish of any kind. I believed he didn't want any disruptions in his life because he had seen too much of it in the trenches. I always liked to romanticise Nelson. But I know he was a propper-upper and not a man to pick up anyone off the ground. I loved him from the moment he opened his Chelsea door to me to the moment nearly ten years later when I kissed him goodbye on the station as he left for the boat train to Paris that crashed in the night.

This time I was back at Victoria Station with as much right to be there as anyone else. It was nearly time for my train. I felt hungover from the jostling emotions and the champagne. I was bemused, confused, relieved and abandoned, homeless and tatty and free. Granny and Selsey and Agnes were all forgotten for the time being. Even Mother had temporarily lost her monopoly on my thoughts. I was travelling alone on a train to the See of Canterbury with a five-pound note in my pocket and a crushed camellia, both presents from the man I loved. As the carriage rattled along its tracks, I tried out all the different endearments I might use if Nelson ever proposed to me. I wondered if he had noticed how rounded my figure was, how ample my breasts. I decided he had. I conducted a retrospective autopsy on his grey gaze. Had he winced at the sight of my hair? I fancied that it had made him smile. I ran through all the different lines I could use when I returned from Canterbury, older and wiser. They were sweet words, all of them, killed in their prime by a jolt of the train that stopped and hissed what sounded like 'Slut'.

As the hops and the apple trees flitted by, I tried not to remember Hendon and not to cry. I was still practising what line to use on Nelson when we next met, but I had decided not to marry him. I'd marry someone else instead, and be a kind person amd make a man happy and not be like Mother at all. I wanted a marriage that would last for ever and fill my house with children of my own. I was suffused with tenderness by the time I reached the station, and it was only as I grabbed my small suitcase from the luggage rack that I began to worry about whether Mother would have rung ahead and told my hosts that I was now disgraced and turned out from my house to be a streetwalker. As it happened, nobody there at my girlfriend's house knew anything about me. The general assembly was amused by my complete lack of any presentable wardrobe, but they clubbed together and kitted me out with donations of clothes which far surpassed in fashion any that Mother had torn.

While I was there in the country, I started off by talking a great deal about Nelson, inventing exploits for him and boasting about everything he owned and was, from his velvet slippers to his mustard gas. I adopted as many of his ways and mannerisms as I could remember from our one brief meeting. I made a habit of swilling down my cocktails, just as I made a point of packing and repacking my newly acquired clothes. Every time I found myself alone, I relived the scene of the carving knife and my last minutes at home. Gradually, the feeling that I was more welcome in that rambling red-brick house than I had ever been with my own family eclipsed the drama of losing one parent and gaining another.

Within ten days these episodes had faded into the background of a new love affair, as everything would fade from thereafter, as time after time I gave my heart to whoever would promise me their undying devotion.

CHAPTER 9

'JOANNA . . . Joanna!'
I loved hearing my new name called, just as I loved that summer before the war. Everybody's nerves seemed to be keyed up to the same pitch as mine, and they praised me for the very defects that the nuns had tried so hard to stifle.

I met a number of boys, and I learnt how to tease them. We stayed up until late into every night, and after the dancing finished a group of us girls would lie in a heap on one of the canopied beds and discuss love and sex – when were we going to launch ourselves into it all and who with. At my last convent we had often whispered sexual discoveries to each other on our walks to and from chapel, two by two, relaying the news backwards and forwards along the eager crocodile. We had also defied the ban on nudity of any kind to monitor the progress of our breasts and nipples and body hair. Yet all the excitement was suppressed there like container-grown roses that spread and bloom as soon as their roots feel the freedom of real soil. One of the girls in the year below us was rumoured to have some sinister relationship with Sister Gudrun, but when interrogated under mild torture the girl in question insisted that all she ever did was kiss the German nun's thin moustache.

Each night, as we lay in bed, we paired each other off with one or other of the brothers or friends. Some of the boys were men, which gave them an extra appeal. They came down to breakfast with small white blotches on their chins where they had cut themselves shaving. They would not be free for tennis because of work they had to see to. Work was like magic and uniforms of any kind were admired. Soldiers and sailors were said to 'do it' with prostitutes and they could wink without twisting the corner of their mouths and they would say rude things while dancing. My own secret favourite was a naval officer called Dickie. He was twenty-three, and he smoked a carved amber pipe which he used to tap out over his forearm on the drawing-room terrace. Then he'd rub his sleeve with his long ivory fingers, caressing the cotton or the tweed in such a way that I wanted him to touch me. The other girls were unsure. One said he was boring, another too shy, another that he always smelt of old tobacco and was too interested in looking interesting. The more we talked about him by night, the more I noticed him by day. Soon Dickie began to notice me, too. He would single me out from the other girls, calling my name.

'Joanna.'

I would run to his stale tobacco scent, wanting to push my hair, my face, my whole body into its marine odour. Behind the rhododendron bushes not far from Caterham, I found my vocation.

At the end of the month we travelled back to London together, pledged for eternity. We parted at Victoria Station in the tea-room of the Grosvenor Hotel. Dickie had to spend some time with his mother and I had to start my training at St Thomas' Hospital. According to my ward Sister, I proved to be the clumsiest, laziest, least attentive nurse in my year. It didn't matter to me, I scarcely heard her or the staff nurses raving: I was in love. Even without the quicksilver activity in my pulse and brain and the dizzy effervescence of my blood, I would have made a terrible nurse. My first few months consisted almost entirely of sluicing and bedpans, with the mere promise of ward work later. The sight of sick people gives me the shivers; I could think of nothing worse than having to tend them. I had gone into nursing because it was a way out of Hendon. It was the one kind of work that Granny approved of. She was proud of my striped uniform and starched cap. Having once started, though, I found that the possibilities of marriage were far more enticing.

In the wide disinfected corridors that sutured the theatres and wards together I would forget my errands, aware only of my thighs touching over my thick stocking-tops. When war was finally declared in the autumn, after a great deal of yes-ing and no-ing, we nurses were all told how vital we would be to our country. Dickie was extremely patriotic, and I think I found extra favour in his eyes by standing to do my bit in such a traditional role. I didn't care for all the fervour myself, I had heard enough of patriotism in the convent to last me for life. As I emptied the bedpans day after day, it was a tiny consolation to know that the nuns would all be interned.

Dickie was impatient for action. His father had died in the Great War and he seemed determined to equal this heroism in some appropriate way. Granny was in her nursing home and, even to my unskilled professional eye, was preparing to die. Mother had ceased to feature in my life. The war was happening, or supposed to be. Sandbags were being stacked all over London, and ARP wardens began to appear at nights. A lot of the boys I knew were being called up or were already off on training. Dickie proposed to me regularly, it was part of his romantic manner. He gave me flowers and chocolates and lavish dinners at an Italian restaurant called Roman's. Occasionally he spent days away, doing things at the Admiralty and 'sorting stuff out'. We both wanted to get married, but his mother was unhappy about the match; the combination of my Catholicism and Mother's divorce had set her against me.

So we married in secret at the Kensington Registry Office in the November after we met. Dickie thought I should carry on nursing 'for the time being', which I did. It meant that I had to live in at the hospital annex and had only my evenings and Sundays off. I also had to get back by ten o'clock. I was working on Dickie, and getting halfway to winning about leaving my job, when he was called up for active service. He was so thrilled by this that he seemed to forget it would mean leaving me. He stood on the Charing Cross Embankment, cupping my hand in the porcelain saucer of his own. I heard his deep apologetic voice telling me, 'It won't be for long, Joanna darling, and then we can be together for always.'

He had lovely eyes, hazel brown with a soft, sad expression in them, as though he continually felt regrets. His long clean-shaven face tapered down into a square chin. He was handsome. All the student nurses thought he was, and he was even handsomer in his uniform. He came to say goodbye at the hospital, calling me off duty to do so, his first of many acts of daring.

'I'll write to you every day, no matter what. I love you, Joanna, believe me, and as soon as I can I'll be back to take you away from here. I promise you.' I didn't realise it then, but Dickie was like the Fry's Turkish Delight Bars that I kept in my apron pocket and ate in the sluicing room; he was full of promise.

I've often wondered how things would have been if he hadn't gone away. All I know is that I loved him, and I wanted to love him, and I tried to believe in his 'always'. He didn't come back for six months – six long months that I spent nursing under conditions which were scarcely better than school. He sent me an allowance, but he didn't tell anyone we were married. He thought it might harm his career in some way. He wrote to me, as he had promised he would, every day. As the months passed, though, his letters became more and more descriptions of his life inside the Navy and less and less the love letters of a newly married husband. I couldn't bear to admit any kind of failure in this marriage. I remembered Mother's short-lived forays into the field and determined to do better, to make marriage work even if it meant waiting through the long winter on my own.

Granny died just before Christmas. The telegram Matron handed me in her office said she had died. 'We regret that Mrs Roberts passed away last night' was quite clear. But the blocked letters didn't spell Granny to me. I went straight to Mrs de Gruchy, who held her chest tightly and cried in swallowed hiccups. I couldn't cry. I felt that beyond the coded message Granny would be sitting somewhere staring out to sea. It appeared that if I waited another weekend I could catch a train and go and see her. I cabled the news to Dickie on his ship. He telegrammed me back with 'all his love' but he didn't come. As he explained later, because he was still officially 'single' he wasn't allowed any compassionate leave on my behalf. The funeral took place at Chislehurst. No one was there except for Agnes and the nurses from her home, Nelson and me. Mother, Agnes told me, had flu, and so she had stayed away. After Granny died, I missed her more deeply even than I missed Dickie. I was sorry I had neglected her in those last months. My hours at the hospital didn't allow me to travel to Chislehurst more than once a fortnight.

Despite Dickie's qualms, I had told her I was married and she was pleased. I took Dickie to meet her, and he too was relieved. I suppose after some of the things he'd heard about my family it was good to meet such a presentable member of it.

Dickie came back on his first leave, just after my nineteenth birthday. It was late spring, and already warm. I took a week off work, and we booked into a hotel as husband and wife. I had never loved him more than I did then. I didn't ask him how long he was home for, not wanting to spoil my first week. On the fourth day I went out to buy some violets and a bottle of champagne. When I got back to the hotel, Dickie was gone. He had left a letter for me saying he only had a four-day pass. He would come back soon, he promised, and he knew his 'poor darling Joanna' would understand that this war thing had to come first, before everything.

I felt ashamed for both of us, and for the first time I felt afraid of the war. The bombs had started to fall and I had no one to hold me, no one to hold. I stayed in the hotel for the rest of my week, unable to face an early return to the hospital. I had told too many of my fellow nurses about my secret marriage and passionate reunion, and I couldn't bear to go back and tell them that my dashing young husband had dashed back to his beloved ship.

My first loathing of the Germans was born in the convent, my second was born there in the empty hotel room. I resented them for stealing my husband. But I knew from the exploits of my girlfriends' soldier-lovers that they managed to get away far more often than mine. His letters continued to arrive: short impersonal bulletins of his progress, rounded out at the beginning and the end by his stock professions of love. As the months wore on and the war escalated, I wanted someone to love me as I loved them. I wanted to recapture the wild euphoria of my first party, to replace the loss of my Granny inside my head, and I wanted to cut up my nurse's uniform into even more useless scraps than the ones Mother had made of my previous wardrobe.

When Dickie started putting little clauses in his letters about how extremely long it might be before he could get home again, and how he felt like a cad for having forced me to marry him and how he would absolutely understand if I felt I had to have my freedom, I realised I had made a stupid mistake. His dutiful letters continued to arrive, each one dated and timed precisely, but I stopped reading them after a while. Instead, I brooded on how I needed to find myself someone who wasn't shy or sad but knew how to enjoy themselves to the full, someone who would dislike the idea of my working as much as I did, and would love me with a physical passion equal only to my own.

I started going out to parties again, truanting from the hospital on some nights and climbing in late on others. My dismissal as a nurse coincided almost perfectly with my meeting Thierry de Gastonville. Thierry was the complete opposite of my absent errant husband. Thierry was debonair and French, sophisticated and reputedly debauched. He spent his nights gambling in expensive clubs, drinking and talking scandal. All this was a far and welcome cry from Dickie's obstinate patriotism.

Despite my long hours of nursing, I had still not seen such a thing as a wounded soldier. So, sympathies that would later rise and bind us Londoners into an elite club of survivors had not yet begun. The cascading buildings were not a part of our daily rationed life. London was a city of clubs and pubs. Sandwiched between the river and the unravelling suburbs, its rich filling flaunted itself. We lived off drink and sandwiches so as to stay as close to the gaming tables as possible. London was its own croupier, spinning its wheel where every number was a winner. The politicians' talk of war seemed as far-fetched as the nuns' unsubtle propaganda. I belonged to a generation of would-be pacifists. Millions of young men had died in the last war, culled by the insanities of their leaders, of governments who used boys as cannon fodder in trumped-up fights and 'causes' that were lies. We were not gullible tools to be thrown into a war at a government's whim. People like Dickie were rare among us. We gave him no credit for his keenness. We put his zeal down to a fear of disappointing his mother and a complex about his father.

Later, lovers would separate for years and their love would survive that gap. But later, we could all see what we were up against. We could see the fragility of our lives. Not only the soldiers and the sailors and the pilots, but we too, the civilians, could be dead by morning. So every night became a farewell celebration. And every morning, picking our way through streets reduced to crumbled biscuits, we gave thanks to whatever gods we believed in for the privilege of breathing in that brickdust, if only for another day. All that came later, together with the platforms of leaving trains where soldiers leaning out of windows to snatch a last goodbye would look like lines of hunting trophies shunted into smoke. There was gentle elbowing to get at the casualty lists to know the worst. These were the names of the maimed and burnt who would later merge with the still unharmed in larger and larger numbers so that the general mixture of our accumulated blood swelled with its injuries. Our world became an unreal place. Its parameters shifted and disappeared, landmarks ceased to be.

By the time the bombing really began, and half of Europe was occupied by the Germans, and refugees began to creep through our ports with horror stories of atrocities in Germany itself and Poland – well, by then I was doing war work too. Everyone was. It wasn't patriotism as such for me, it was a common need to survive. And although I may not have loved England as I should, I felt for Jersey with its Gestapo invaders and its Nazi laws and its swastikas flying over the Island. There were rumours that over a thousand Jersey men and women had been transported. There were rumours of Gestapo methods, there were rumours of spies among us, of landings along the Channel coast. I knew nothing first-hand about the Gestapo, but I did know a little about German methods; I had served my time with their nuns. I knew them to be thorough and cold, and I was willing to put on any uniform to help prevent them from marching into London with their greyness that surpassed any natural greyness the city held. Their jackboots and their 'Heil Hitlers' had long since ceased to be a schoolgirl's joke.

At the time when Dickie was first serving, though, and the time when Thierry was scorning to fight, only the phoney war was taking place. Nothing much happened except waiting. The bombs that fell over London were few and far between and seemed to drop more by accident than by design. So we remembered the propaganda that had survived from the so-called Great War and saw the old posters which claimed that German soldiers spiked babies on their bayonets. And we remembered that then, only twenty-four years before, it had all been lies. To us, the bravest of the men were the Conchies, the ones who refused to kill, refused to fight. They were our heroes in that first year, the men who were brave enough to speak out against the rising panic. Of all those men, Thierry seemed to have a symbolic Victoria Cross for nonchalance. He lived as if there were no war at all. He never spoke of any danger to his own country. He treated politics like a joke. It would all be over in a few months, he claimed; treaties would be signed, and life would go on regardless.

Meanwhile, I moved into a flat he owned in the Edgware Road and lived like a kept woman in the kind of luxury I had never known. We were engaged to be married and, unlike Dickie, he flaunted this engagement, telling all his friends. For all the debauchery of his behaviour, his drinking and spending and the violent passion of his embraces, we never actually made love. Sometimes we spent a whole night together, but never as often as I wanted. Thierry used to kiss me very roughly, and this would excite me into telling him that I was quite happy to go the whole way. At these moments, instead of undressing me he would address me as though I were a public meeting.

'You are a young maid asleep, you must be woken slowly,' he would say, stroking his fingernails and occasionally slipping his forefinger along to his crested signet ring. 'You have been chosen by a Frenchman who will call your body to be crushed like its grapes. But not yet, my blood-head, you are too young to understand the complexities of love.'

It was as if in his mind he were leaving the bed and stepping on to a balcony. With hindsight I can see the absurdity of those announcements. At the time, though, I believed that there was some secret sensual world to which Thierry had the key. I lived in a state of permanent arousal. I spent hours studying and worshipping his face. I thought that after he guided me into a life of passion I would never get a proper chance to see him again. My eyes would be naked and my vision blurred by continual orgasms. He had blue-black hair which he greased back like Valentino, and almond eyes of a brown so intense Sister Gudrun would have branded it satanic. When he was tired, his lids made hoods that turned his challenging bovine stare into something reptilian. He scorned all my life until the moment I met him.

'That is not married, Joanna,' he'd say, at any reference to Dickie. 'When you and I are married, then you will know what real sex is like. First, you must learn to be chic, to have style, to live. You are a hermit crab, in your shell, with only your head sticking out. You see life, but you don't know yet how to live it. Why, you didn't even know how to kiss. You meet my friends, you like them, you listen to their talk of art, the painters, the poets. But kissing is an art, too.' The last word was said with a purse of his lips as if he were giving a performance for his own benefit. 'Making love is an art. Do you think Louis learned to write just like that – no! It all takes time. You are very impatient. I like that, though, it is better. You have passion, not like all these English girls.'

Thierry had a way of implying that he had personally made love to 'all these English girls'. He also had the reputation of a rake. Sometimes he would disappear for a night, sometimes for two, and return mysteriously silent about his exploits.

'Only you English like to tell the details about their sex. In France, we just do it, we don't have to discuss it.'

I loved it. I loved him. And I had French blood in my veins. I wanted him to touch their blue traces across my breasts. After the war we would go back to Thierry's château in the Champagne valley, out there to the south of Reims. Meanwhile, I worked on my image, cutting my hair in a new way, learning to dress and wear the jewels Thierry bought for me. They were jade and amethysts and antique silver. He liked me to show off, and he liked me to flirt with his friends. He was proud to be the co-respondent in my divorce.

We travelled down to Brighton and spent a dirty weekend under the tutelage of a private detective so that I could say, 'On June the sixth, seventh and eighth 1940, in the Metropole Hotel in Brighton, I did commit adultery on more than three occasions with Thierry de Gastonville.' It felt so daring, and sounded so scandalous. In fact it sounded more scandalous than it was, for on those nights we locked ourselves into our hotel room as Mr and Mrs Gaston and lay in our double bed and kissed while Thierry talked, stroked my hair and ran his nails along my freckled arms, leaving long scratch marks that I wore proudly outside my short-sleeved dress the next day at breakfast.

I basked in the notoriety my new liaison brought me. I was tantalised and captive, but free to roam among the Bohemian backwaters of London and the percolating cafés. I made friends over the bar of The Wheatsheaf and The George. I grew close, most of all, to the poets who could write down public things and make them private, while Thierry, in private, made everything sound as though it were intended for a public. The boozing writers were an antidote for my lack of intimacy with Thierry. I found surrogate sex in their banter. After I left Thierry, there was nothing surrogate in my affairs and liaisons. Yet I always liked poets best, with their gossip and scandal and the continual crochet of words. Eliot was reported as having said of Pound: 'he doesn't come round here talking like Westminster Abbey'. I always liked that phrase. I had my own Abbey in the Edgware Road. I laid myself at its altar. Once spurned, I too became an Abbey, more fragile and ephemeral than Westminster but still a place where great poets lay down to die in my own aisle. Long after my marriage to Thierry was over, those friendships remained; they saw me through the war and on into the fifties. Whatever spirit dictated the frenzied euphoria of these war nights, it was my spirit too. Every minute had to be crammed full, all the wildness had to be squeezed out and enjoyed before it was too late. We danced on the ashes, and buoyed our fears with hilarity. We sang in the packed tunnels of the underground shelters and brewed 90 per cent proof alcohol with laboratory equipment in a room of Guy's Hospital medical school.

The war brought out in my contemporaries the very things I had always felt myself, the symptoms of manic depression. It was in me to swing from one extreme to another. So I swung, as London burned, together with my friends. And the whole of that metropolis was a potential friend. The barriers had been smashed down. The formal introductions of my childhood were gone. There was no time to waste over such things. Every second counted and had to be used to stop anyone from actually counting them.

In between these good times, a hovering sadness set in. Friends died or disappeared, favourite places were bombed. The stretcher-bearers, stumbling as though walking on hot sand, then digging and poking in the brickdust and debris, reminded me of my days at Selsey when I used to build mantraps on the beach. The undamaged houses stood proudly like so many successful sand castles until the next wave of bombs would come and sweep them away. It was important not to see too many impaled limbs on the sites. It was better to look away and not hear the underground muttering. Civilians weren't allowed inside the corridors anyway, but voices from inside the anthills could burst through the bubble of our excitement. I understood these pendulum emotions because they were always mine. The war would end after seven long years, and those who survived would try to move into a new era. I was never able to do that. The euphoria and the despair were deep inside me. It wasn't the bombs that had made me so, or a fear of the Nazis. It was Mother. It's quite funny, really, to live through history welding our times into such drastic and different shapes, and to be so irrevocably locked into a microcosm of the past. But so it was. I was moulded by the recurring tides of my loves.

Thierry's ideas about passion were so grandiose that they never translated themselves into practice. We married in the spring of 1941. It took me yet another year to realise that Thierry was a homosexual and I was a mere front to ward off scandal of a more serious kind. I determined that it was all my fault, *mea culpa*, determined to stand by him. Alas, my gesture was lost, he didn't want me and he was irked by my acceptance.

The marriage was annulled three years later. It was never consummated. As Thierry himself had so often told me: I was an innocent as far as sex was concerned.

In a form of mute patriotism, his luck turned with that of his country, monitoring the grip that the invading forces had over France with his own luck as a gambler. He began to lose so heavily in the early days of our marriage that all my jewels were pawned and later sold. He peeled the onion of all my possessions right back to the soft bud of the centre – all, that is, but my own soft core which remained as chaste as my first absentee husband had left it. I was not, technically, a virgin; my few weeks with Dickie had seen to that; but neither was I the scarlet woman of my reputation. Only my hair, the emblem of my unfurling notoriety, was true to my image. It was red with the redness of cherry brandy and the added, darker but still natural sheen of conkers newly burst from their spiked cases.

After Thierry there were two more husbands, a succession of lovers, four children and thirty years of misunderstanding that have led me here, on my back again, but this time in a hospital bed. The only man who ever really lived up to my ideal of what a man should be was Nelson, my father, who emerged out of the unease of wartime London and gave me the place in his life that I had always wanted to occupy. When Nelson went away to fight, I was proud of him, and waiting at Victoria Station for him each time he returned.

Down all the years, he alone survived as more than just a photograph. The others became snapshots located in time, but Nelson meant more to me than his good looks, more than his blond moustache streaked with grey. Nelson managed to have a slight look of surprise on his face, which gave him an almost childish appearance. I used to imagine the waves of mustard gas wafting across the poppy fields into his trench and then smothering him in its sickness as he choked out his argument to the fumes of the gas itself, and to the Powers that be: 'There must be some mistake, it's not for me'. Yet it was, and it clawed its way into his life, keeping that first look of dawning amazement on his face, stamped for ever into an endearing expression of misunderstood innocence. It was the one face to survive my tangled misunderstanding of love.

I went from Cinderella to Princess without the intervening need to squeeze my ample feet into my glass slippers. After the virtual incarceration of my childhood I loved the big world I moved into, with such a passion that it seemed to possess fairy-tale qualities. Perhaps that was what moved me to test every love that was ever mine. I was the Snow Queen's daughter, and when anyone came to my gates and told me they loved me, no matter how much I loved them, they had to prove their love. If they passed the initial statutory three tests: the slaying of the dragon, the gathering of magic stone and the like, I was never able to settle down and live happily ever after. I just could not believe that anyone loved me. So I would continue to plague them with idle and often impossible requests, driving out all the goodwill with my caprice, until one or other of us could bear it no longer. That is an exaggeration, but it was also a pattern I could clearly trace. I could feel myself doing it. Forcing things. Making my prophecy come true. I used to believe that no one loved me – that I was ultimately unworthy, and my beauty a myth.

Eventually, each time, after months or even years of guerrilla warfare, and sniping and laying traps, I would tell myself, 'There, I knew he didn't really love me!' Mother always used to see into the future; perhaps I hankered after that too. Though, I don't know. I was caught up on a carousel of marrying. Some people are bolters and some are stayers, and I was a marrier. The first two husbands should never have been more than affairs, the last two were different, but in between I was engaged to so many people I can't even remember their names now, not even the ones who broke my heart.

I used to think my heart was like one of Granny's most precious pieces of porcelain and that it would shatter when I mishandled it. Then I realised that it didn't break, my heart just stretched and stretched until everything ached and hurt and was permanently ready to ache and hurt again. I had a rubber heart, like a rubber stamp, making the same statement over and over again. Looking for the same tenuous ecstasy while being irresistibly drawn towards failure. My daughters call them my lame ducks. And it's true that I do have a soft spot for emotional cripples. They change the message on my rubber stamp to a temporary headline, I become the redeemer. I become the curer of impotence, the homosexual's first proper love, the neurotic's stabiliser, the neurasthenic's moment of peace, and finally, almost inevitably, the resenter of flaws. The heartbreaker in my own right. And through all the traumas, I have never loved a man as much as I have loved a child, my child.

I have four daughters of my own. For nearly thirty years I have funnelled my life into theirs. I guided them through squalor and luxury. I steered them through their illnesses and through the minefields of their potential delinquency. I have four girls, four women, each one completely different from the other. They are the four poles of the world bound together by me, their mother, who loved them in their fatherless childhoods. No courtiers were allowed to stay at my scarlet court for long. If the children didn't drive them away, I did. Sometimes there were deserters who baled out of the mad shambles of my bedroom before I was ready or prepared for their loss.

Sometimes the pills I take to make me forget whatever failures are past repairing now don't work. Sometimes the greyness that

Granny chose for our exile climbs inside my head and I want to weep until my entrails spill through my eyes. And I still get angry, so angry that waves of rage sweep over me and I can't breathe. I walk these off. It doesn't happen so often now. But when it does, I walk through the city night, pounding my feet on the grey pavements, asking myself, 'Why am I so alone? What am I doing with my life, and what have I done? Where are my old friends? Where did they go? The entertainers who used to invite me to lunch, or the real friends like Louis and William? And David, and Roger, and the once glamorous Nancy, even Nancy who was so morose that she used to make us laugh watching her sway over her drink, propping up the bar in the French Pub, brooding on the last dregs of her life. We didn't see ourselves in her. It's easy to mock at tarnished glitter.'

I spent twenty years in Bohemia, and then retired. Twenty years of constantly changing my name. That became more than a habit to me. It was as though I couldn't survive without it; couldn't accept myself. I made my friends and welded myself very close to them, living with some, sleeping with some, and sometimes just nursing others. I was a terrible nurse at St Thomas' but when it came to the emotionally sick, I liked nursing people through their crises. It gave me courage, I think, to nurse myself through mine.

Why everyone called Soho and Chelsea Bohemia, I don't know. Sometimes it just seemed like wishful thinking. Whatever the reason, it didn't matter much. I moved and moved from one address to the next, slaking my restlessness by constantly rearranging rooms. People travelled backwards and forwards, to Paris, to America, to Italy, but those friendships were as near I got to a real marriage as any I had known. They were till death do us part, and for better and for worse, in sickness and in health. I had a great strength in me all through the forties. It was my time. I didn't think anything could take that away from me. I knew that no man could, no lover or husband could dig in and destroy my carapace. My headlong escapades amused our crowd. I had found a way of working (as a journalist on the *Kensington Post*) and keeping my social life afloat, while having three daughters and a fourth in my womb. Everything was in place. Until, out of my own motherhood, I grew curious about Mother. It was 1953, and I didn't know if she was dead or alive. I had never heard from her again. I had never wanted to. I had told so many people I hated her that the words themselves had become hollow, and I discovered that I still hankered for her forgiveness, or understanding, or something – perhaps just a sign from her.

PART II

Miss Kitty

CHAPTER 10

THE best beaches are the killing fields, the coves and rocks where ships have floundered, the frayed shores where soldiers have landed and smugglers have unloaded their contraband. If I were a man, I'd be a sailor like Daddy and Grandpapa. And I'd build a house like theirs, with terraced decks for roofs and porthole windows. I was born on a battleship, on the grey granite landlocked ship, on Claremont, with her masts and flags, run aground in the long shadow of La Corbière lighthouse. Claremont was a retired admiral's folly; a wounded seaman's dream anchored in the gardens of unruly bushes and ornamental trees with its views across the cliffs and rocks to Corbière Point, and beyond it the solitary lighthouse.

Claremont was furnished with nostalgia; it was a naval reliquary, with the inherent restlessness that entailed, papered into all its many rooms. There were redwoods from Canada, and jacaranda from Brazil, and Chinese papers and chinoiserie, and Indian tables and Japanese screens and carved wooden angels from Veracruz. All geography and history seemed to be distilled there in the house, as all the world was in the Island. Between the two great nations of England and France it sat in its own thermal waters, culling the best from both, like the delicacies salvaged from a wreck, while leaving all the tedious aspects of life to drift like flotsam into other seas.

I was born already linked to the sea. It was my heritage. Grandpapa knew it, and it made him proud.

'Would you just look at Miss Kitty here,' he'd tell our visitors. 'Only just turned six and she knows all the tides to the inch and the minute. It's as though the little minx could foresee them. I'm up till all hours over my charts watching for storms and this mere child can always tell you when the sea will be rough.'

Then he'd turn to me, creasing all the small scars on his face.

'And you pretend you can feel them, but I know what you're up to. You watch La Corbière from your room at night. I'll wager that beacon signals to you and tells you all the information your grandfather likes to find out for himself.'

And he was right. The long light of the lighthouse used to flash into my room where I would play, staring into its beam to see if I could hold it with my eyes. I could never keep it from swinging back out to sea, but I could feel its secrets flowing into me.

It told me when a fishing boat was lost and it told me what the sailors said as they sank through the waves. It told me words I'd never heard. It told me ladies' names called out by fathers and sweethearts. Once it even told me my own name, Kitty, in a gurgling whisper. But I knew it was another Kitty, and I knew she must be different, taller and less pretty and without such a clever grandpapa or handsome father or smart mamma, and without the friendship of the moon or the tropical waters of my eyes. People called them emerald eyes, but I liked the men who said they were like the sea. Cartier, the jeweller's in St Helier, sold emeralds, and Maman had a brooch with one. But they were only stones. Water is better than stones; it wraps itself around the stones every day, twice a day, and drags them out to sea.

I was born lucky. I wanted to be born in a great year, though, so that people would say, 'Ah yes, 1406, the year of Kitty Roberts' birth and of course the invasion of Pontbriand and Pero Nino. That was a great year, a victory for Jersey.' Or looking out to sea from over the cliffs, a group of men would murmur, 'I'll never forget 1781, what a year! The Battle of Jersey, and the birth of Kitty Roberts.' Or, '1766: Admiral Philippe de Carteret circumnavigated the world, and as though to celebrate, a star was born here on the Island: little Kitty Roberts.' Yet it was my only disappointment, as a child, that I was born in 1899 when nothing more remarkable than an extension of the railway from St Aubin to La Corbière was opened, and one of Daddy's setters had a litter of fourteen pups.

It would have been so appropriate to have been born together with some great event, twinned to posterity. Agnes didn't think so.

'Why, just think of it, Miss Kitty,' she used to tell me, 'you might have been born in the wake of a great invention, or trumpeting in some calamity, and then who would have had so much time for you? You couldn't have been so unique if the Island were under siege or a famine had set in. At best you'd have had to share your honours, like sharing with a sister. As it is, you've everything for yourself.'

But Agnes didn't understand. It was her way. She said the things she thought would please Maman and me, but she couldn't see the world very clearly. She thought she could, because she'd come from Ireland in a ferry boat and crossed a piece of England on a train. She'd seen the inside of Waterloo Station, and made the crossing from Weymouth to St Helier, and she had learnt to embroider and crochet and to speak in Jersiaise downstairs. Agnes had large feet and plump hands and when she combed it out, her hair came down almost to her waist.

'Whenever anybody asks me – which they have no business to, but men are forever interfering – I say it does come down to my waist, and that is because, if I were to wear my dresses any higher at all, it would, so you've no need to contradict me, Miss Kitty, no need at all,' she used to explain.

But it was all part of her not understanding, because sometimes I did need to say things, the words would burn their own path in my throat. When the sun shone in a certain way, or when the candlelight caught her, Agnes's face was covered by a very fine down, almost as thick as the lamb's-tongue leaves in the south garden. She called it a peach complexion. I never liked peach skins, but I liked Agnes. The fur on her face was thickest on her upper lip. When I told anyone about the real length of her hair, or when I told her I didn't love her, Agnes's lip would twitch and the fair hairs would seem to dance. It was the only dance she could do, apart from a strange hopping thing she showed me once and called an Irish jig. I didn't like Ireland, it sounded as different to our Island as anywhere could be. Agnes was always so pleased to be with us that she acted like a limpet. Sometimes she just had to be pulled off. It didn't seem to make a great deal of difference to her except fractionally to weaken her grip.

The sea lights of La Corbière were like a recurring spotlight making sure everything was in order in our house. It was my light. It kept the shadows of our life moving. It tired me when things were still. I suppose I was allergic to any sameness. I liked life best when faces changed around me. I liked all the staff to come and go – all, that is, except Agnes. We had a gardener once who didn't like me. He never said so, of course, but I could tell. When I walked past him I could hear him thinking, and sometimes I used to answer the words out of his head. It got so that he used to hide if he saw me coming, but I could find him anywhere. He didn't stay very long. Before he left, he changed and stopped shuffling away from me; instead, he called me to him.

'You're fond of the lighthouse aren't you, Miss Kitty?' he said, pointing to the white tower of La Corbière. 'They say its name comes from the carrion crows, and do you know what they be?'

I shook my head, digging the toe of my white kid shoes into the edge of his flower bed in a way I knew would annoy him. He ignored my inroad on his turf.

'Well, it's a bird of ill omen . . . Do you know what an ill omen is then, Miss Kitty?'

I didn't and it irritated me that this man was suddenly so sure of himself, gloating over his work.

'You will, you will, and so will everyone around you.'

I didn't want anyone to know more about the lighthouse than me. I was its keeper as much as the old man who climbed up its steps and swung its beams around the black spiked waters. I had watched the waves making their patterns as they crashed and fell, and I had watched them as they beat calmly against the shore. I knew their rhythm, I could have danced to it from the memory of it in my veins as well as I danced any of the polkas or waltzes Maman played on the piano.

That night, as Agnes brushed out my hair, I asked her what the lighthouse meant.

'I don't really know, Miss Kitty. Unless it means that the ships are safe. I don't believe lighthouses have to mean anything.'

After I was ready for bed, Maman herself came up, as she did every night, to say my prayers with me. Maman and I were Catholics, Daddy and Grandpapa weren't. We had two embroidered velvet hassocks which lived in a cupboard by my chest of drawers, and these would sit side by side on the floor, one for each of us as we knelt while Maman listened to my prayers. In the early years she had said them with me, prompting me over the hardest parts. It didn't take me long, though, to know them all off by heart, but Maman still joined in, even with the children's parts. She said it mattered to her so much.

After prayers, Maman would sit on my bed for a few minutes and tell me how happy I made her just by being myself. I didn't want her always to be in such a sentimental mood at bedtime; I preferred her as she was normally. Besides, it struck me as silly. How could I have made her happy by being somebody else? I tried not to listen, just as I tried not to listen to myself as I responded to her endearments. They didn't last long, and afterwards there was a time for questions.

'What does La Corbière, mean, Maman?'

'It's Jersey for *corbeau*, a crow,' she told me, hardly noticing how much her confirmation of the gardener's words hurt me.

'Why?'

'It just is, Kitty, there's no "why" about it.' I didn't sleep that night for a long while. I knelt at the window, watching through its roundness to the roundness of the moon outside. It was in the third phase of its cycle, waning to a crescent again. Its thin white light merged with the broader light of the beacon, casting its long beam across the sea. Grandpapa said it could be seen for eighteen miles on a clear day. It could be seen in France. It could be seen on ships all over the Channel and on all the fishing boats. I had wanted to ask Maman what an ill omen was, but I didn't because I knew from the gardener's voice that it was bad, and she didn't like bad things. She liked to avoid them whenever she could. When the slugs came into the garden, she would make the gardener's head boy lay out the arsenic-baited orange skins, and then she would inspect them after they were laid, but she never went round in the morning with me to see the heaps of dead slugs in the silvery winding sheets of their own glare. Maman had to be protected from bad things. The church protected her a bit, but at other times it was up to Agnes and me to keep them from her.

Grandpapa was in his study for all of the next day. He had gout. I wasn't supposed to disturb him in his study, but usually he liked it when I did. I waited all morning for Father, but he had gone out riding and left word that he would be at the de Gruchys' for lunch, and although I sat on the roof terrace for a whole hour concentrating hard inland to draw him back home early, it didn't work. I ate my lunch in the nursery and then went to find Grandpapa. He pretended to be annoyed at my arrival, so I pretended to leave, but he called me back from the door: 'Come on in then, Miss Kitty; since you've already disturbed your grandfather, you may as well stay.'

I went and stood beside him, resting my own arm on the carved lion arm of his chair. 'How's your gout today, Grandpapa?'

He looked morosely down at his swollen bandaged foot, and sighed. 'It's an old man's penance.'

'I think it will be a bit better tomorrow, the rain will lift, you'll see.'

'I hope you're right again, Miss Kitty, with your predictions.'

'What is an ill omen, Grandpapa?'

He looked at me strangely, almost with fear, and he leant over and stroked my hair. 'Why do you want to know?'

'I was wondering if the carrion crow was an ill omen.'

He moved sharply in his chair, grimacing with pain as he remembered to keep still. 'One of the servants has been filling your head with rubbish. They're a superstitious lot, they'd still be burning witches if they could. Don't you pay them any heed, Miss Kitty. Ill omens indeed!'

'But then why . . .?'

'Crows feed on dead things, they eat them, it keeps them alive, there's nothing wrong in that if it's their nature.'

He was cross, crosser than he wanted to be, remembering, it seemed, some incident from his past. He shook his head as though to make it go away, then he held his leg and sighed again.

'I won't be up on the top deck tonight; it'll just be shadows of La Corbière for me.' He paused and then said, more brightly, 'La Corbière, there's another crow for you. Been there since 1874. First concrete lighthouse in Britain, I'll bet you didn't know that.'

I kissed him on the dark side of his head, feeling a strange closeness to his hair, as though the silvery strands mixed with the few remaining brown hairs were wrapping themselves around my lips.

I was seven years old. I had never been away from Claremont, except to children's parties elsewhere on the Island, and to the puppet shows in the summer and to St Helier to see the shops at Christmas, and occasionally to accompany Maman when she went to visit her friends. Mostly, though, people came to us. The children especially loved our house. No one else lived in a house that was a ship or had their own lighthouse to guide them down to the cliffs and the sea. On Wednesdays and Saturdays our dancing teacher came to Claremont and, together with five other boys and girls, we danced in the parquet clearing between the dust covers of the ballroom. Sometimes Grandpapa came down and watched us there. He used to tell me he had wanted Daddy to have a son so that he could follow the family into the Navy, but I had been born instead, and now he didn't want any other grandchildren, he was happy to heap all his treasures in the one casket.

I found it hard to imagine any other child coming to sully the perfection of my family. All my friends had brothers or sisters or both. Sometimes Agnes or Maman, and once even Papa, had asked me if I wanted another child to play with all the time. I would tell them 'No'. My friends were good to be with because they came and went. Sometimes even my close friends, like Harry de Gruchy and Emily Carteret, used to get on my nerves if they stayed longer than an afternoon. I've always liked to be entertained. When people run out of interesting things to do or to tell me, I don't want them hanging around for a moment longer. The idea of a sibling appalled me. Sometimes Maman would answer me mysteriously, implying that I would get used to the event and even grow to like it. I assured her I wouldn't, but she'd just smile and tell me, 'You'll see.'

At times like these my parents would seem to grow closer together, drawing a net around themselves into which they would keep inviting me. I didn't like it. At other times I was already at the centre of their circle, I didn't need any invitations. It was I who drew them together, I who invited Grandpapa to be so close, I whose every whim was catered for. Later, Maman told me she had been pregnant five times after my birth, and each time she had miscarried at exactly five months and two weeks. She told me she had tried everything to save her babies. She had been seen by the specialists on the Island, and had even travelled to London to be seen by an eminent gynaecologist. However, they never found anything wrong. Clinically, she was perfectly healthy and so, it seemed, were the fetuses.

She told me that on the last three occasions she had taken to her bed almost as soon as she knew she was expecting, and a day bed had been added to the drawing-room, and Daddy had carried her everywhere, and she had seen no visitors but her family who used to sit with her quietly while she crocheted or talked and I sat beside her, resting my head on her side. I was never told that she was actually expecting a baby. I knew nothing about such things. Just the possibilities of another addition to the nursery were broached, and the four-month vigil would occur, followed by the inevitable tears.

Grandpapa was closer than anyone to me during those months of hushed upheaval. He showed me his telescope and how to work it, and what the different rocks were called along that southwest coast. He told me of his days at sea, his years of combing the oceans. He gave me an ivory fan from China with its fins filled with painted silk, and he told me that Jersey was like a fan, ribbed by its roads spreading out of St Helier. He told me about the battles of our Island and about other battles he had seen himself far away where there were more palm trees than on our promenade. He was always calling for me, sending for me throughout the autumn of 1906 and through to the spring. His gout was growing worse, pinning him to his chair and footstool.

I was allowed out of the schoolroom and the nervous instruction of Mademoiselle Bazin to attend to my grandfather's demands. He had been ill in the winter, with more than his gout, and he was a reluctant invalid. He wanted to go down to the Point, to take his daily constitutional, ending up with its customary scramble across the jagged grey rocks that led their precarious path to the sea.

'It's only Claremont and you that are keeping me going, Miss Kitty. The two of you are a ship afloat on a pair of clear water eyes. I can't bring myself to leave you.'

'But you're not leaving me, Grandpapa.'

'No, of course not,' he'd say, almost abruptly, and then sink back into the cushions of his chair. His energy was ebbing away. He had had pleurisy over Christmas, water on the lung. Agnes told me he had complained, in his fever, that he was drowning. Later, he spoke of it a lot.

'It's a terrible comfort, to feel the waves dragging you down, and to fight them and choke and feel that your lungs will explode and then to feel the sweetness of surrender into something that was always you. I never needed that Darwin to tell me we came out of the sea. It's a wonderful strange feeling being taken back into it – what do you say, Miss Kitty, huh? Do you feel like a mermaid? Do you know what I mean?'

'Father, what on earth are you telling Kitty?'

My own father had crept in unnoticed on his rubber shoes. He insisted on wearing rubber shoes. He loved them. Everyone else in the world wore leather except Daddy, who had an unexplained affinity with rubber soles and canvas tops and refused to wear anything but plimsolls.

'Come on, Kitty, run along,' he said to me, gesturing towards the door and himself to hurry my departure.

'No, Dickie,' Grandpapa explained, 'you don't know your own daughter, she understands things as well as you or I.'

'She's seven years old!' Daddy reminded him in a half-whisper as though to keep this information from me, as though it were something I didn't already know.

'Well, say what you like, but I tell you, she's quite bewitched me, and it's sweeter than drowning. Try it yourself, remember I said so. Can't you see she's unique?'

My father turned full towards me now and looked hard at me, assessing the greenness of my eyes, the whiteness of my skin, my curls, my hands, the organdie dress and sash I was wearing, and he smiled. The smile spread slowly across his face, distorting it from his own face into a version of Grandpapa's, adding creases where there had been none, lighting his eyes as though by some unseen flame. He put his arms out to me, and bent his knees very low. I was shorter than all the other children of my age – so short, in fact, that I looked like a china doll.

'Kitty's stunning,' he said, over my shoulder, 'I can see that.'

In reply, Grandpapa merely nodded, nodding himself into one of the sudden sleeps that seemed to overtake him now, stealing him away for seconds or minutes at a time into an impenetrable slumber. We left him marooned in his armchair.

March turned to April and April to May, and the Gulf Stream swept its warm waters around the coast, interceding as it always did with the climate so that the otherwise northerly air stayed warm and subtropical plants could grow. Grandpapa continued to ail, gathering a kind of grey dust along the scattered hairline scars on his face, and his eyes grew watery, as though anticipating his desire to return to the stranglehold embrace of the waves. All through the spring, he kept on calling. His voice echoed through the house: 'Miss Kitty, Miss Kitty.' By June he had grown too weak to sit up any more and he was cashiered to his bed, where he lay under the heavy canopies of his carved four-poster, muttering to himself.

I wanted to stay with him, but Maman wouldn't let me; she claimed that it would be too distressing for me to witness his by now certain death. Occasionally I was allowed to tiptoe in and see him, sunk in the linen spume of his restless sick bed, but this was only when, out of the unintelligible mumblings he made, my name could clearly be deciphered. At other times I did my lessons, and pottered around the gardens with Maman, learning all the names of the flowers, or danced with the other children, or danced with my friends, or watched my other friends, the lighthouse and the moon, signalling to me.

The moon waxed and waned its silent code, there was a sailor in distress, and this time he was calling my own name and calling it for me. There was Kitty streaked into the clouds in the sky and Kitty in the lighthouse beam. Miss Kitty was strung in light from the treacherous rocks of La Corbière across the causeway in both high tide and low, reaching out for me, clawing with its long silvery fingers, just as Grandpapa was dying and calling my name. I had him on my mind all through the month of June. He was so clearly in my head that it was scarcely possible to be me any more. By the middle of the month, his desperate whispers and his unspoken anxieties were so crushing my brain that I was no longer in possession of my own body. I felt his flesh in mine, and it was all in pain. I couldn't tell Maman, of course, it would have hurt her, and Agnes was far too earthly to understand; so I too took to my bed, and lay in my barred nursery, tossing in the restless wake of Grandpapa's fever, following his slow descent, his rise and fall until he finally drowned in the uncured pleurisy of his lungs. I felt the water weighing on his chest. I felt the pain and every twist of his struggle to stay afloat, and then, on June the 25th, Saint William's Day, he found the sweetness he had been scared to go to, releasing all the strings in my head.

CHAPTER 11

WHEN we were children, we played soldiers. It was our favourite game. Sometimes we were Customs and Excise men ferreting out smugglers from behind the shrubberies in our gardens or from the caves of the beach. Sometimes we were the smugglers themselves, rolling bits of driftwood into hiding places. We were never French or English, we were always Jerseymen defending our Island against attack and invasion. We dealt with the girls who didn't like playing these games by taking them prisoner or making them stand at the day-nursery window, waiting for their menfolk to return. Claremont was perfect for playing naval games, and since several of the other children also came from naval families it became a point of even greater pride. It was my house, a dream house preparing to fall into the ready hands of its fourth generation.

Harry de Gruchy was my best friend. I liked almost everything about him. Sometimes, he would get on my nerves, but he was quick to see it and always found a way of stopping the effervescence that seemed to rise from my knees and up through my body into a full-blown rage before it could disrupt us. We were quite similar in some ways; we liked to tease. When he wanted to annoy me, he would find a way of mentioning that he 'rode with the century'. He was a year younger than me, born in 1900, and he was inordinately proud of it.

'The whole of the twentieth century is harnessed to me,' he'd say, 'so if great things are to happen, I'll be part of them. It's quite exciting, really, when you think about it.'

He got it from his mother. She used to weave his birth into the most casual conversation, so Maman and I had heard at least a hundred times that Harry rode with the century. I was jealous of it. 1900 hadn't, in itself, been a remarkable year, according to Agnes, so why be so proud? And yet he was, all through our growing up. Had we not been secretly engaged to be married since 1910, I couldn't have borne his arrogance. When the war began and his brothers went off to fight, together with all the young men of the Island, he hated his birthday. He was only fourteen, and too young for anything, and then fifteen and sixteen and still too much of a boy to join the Army. He could have joined the Navy then, as a cadet, but he wanted to fight, to wear khaki, and go to France, and write letters home full of nonchalance and camou-flaged *savoir-faire*. Instead, he finished his studies at Victoria College, coming to Claremont occasionally for weekends, but mostly in his holidays.

Harry used to say he didn't know whom he loved more, me or Claremont, and that pleased me. I never wanted to marry a man who would try to take me away to his own house. There were no other houses built like ships, and if there were, they were not mine, and filled with the ghostly traces of my Grandpapa, or standing so near to cliffs, or bathed in the bright lights of their own beacon.

The war made Harry sad, it took him away from me. Even in 1914, when the Royal Jersey Militia was mobilised to defend the Island, he resented not being able to take part. We had played the game so many times, watching the breaking sea through the old telescope on the roof and making our plans, carrying them out, fighting so bravely, with Harry in the lead. When we were children we never felt the handicap of our size or the unreality of our games, it was only the real war that brought them home to us. It dashed Harry's hopes, and it spoilt our past.

In 1915, when the Overseas Contingent left for war service, the sight of the ships departing did something to him. He had always been restless, and impulsive, and strange in his way. After the men had gone, though, taking his two elder brothers with them and leaving nothing but the old and young and the girls and the perennial palm trees and the warm-water flowers and the beaches littered with the white feathers of the circling gulls, he grew withdrawn. He began to stay away from me for weeks on end, turning up at odd times of the evening or before dawn and whistling me down from my room. He had grown wilder than he'd ever been, and some of his usual high spirits had turned to a kind of roughness in their frustration. He discussed the war in great detail with me, going over battle after battle, running through the men and the guns and the strategy of each side as could best be gleaned from censored letters and the local newspaper. He was desperate for the war to last long enough for him to join in, fight it, win it. Sitting on the rough grass at the clifftop overlooking the Point, Harry would uproot the short tufts and scatter them down the steep rocks.

'You know what I mean, Kitty. I can't live my life with something like this that I've been kept away from. I feel like a coward. I'll always feel like one if I don't manage to get out there ... Mater keeps saying the war's nearly over, she wants it to end before I get a chance to go. She's determined to keep me back ...'

Harry had large cornflower-blue eyes with a small grey spot in each one, a perfectly symmetrical flaw that would catch the light and seem to change his whole expression sometimes. They were very slightly hooded, which gave him a mysterious look with a hint of mockery about it. He had black wavy hair and high colouring, and when he got angry he used to blush. His mouth was small and Cupid-plump. He came from a good-looking family but he was, without a doubt, the best-looking of them all.

When Maman was a girl, she had gone to Florence with my Aunt Violet and she had been so overcome by the beauty of the paintings in the Santa Croce, and by the feel of the city and the church itself, that she had embraced the Catholic faith. Harry's mother, who had also been to Italy, said she could quite understand such an emotion since she, too, had spent days in the old Renaissance churches looking at the frescoes and feeling quite overwhelmed.

'I didn't know it then but I was carrying Harry at the time, and it has always amazed me how very like a Botticelli angel he's turned out. I sometimes think it must have had something to do with my gazing at so many there.'

No one else in our family was Roman Catholic, just Maman and me. It was as though the men humoured us in this, treating it as a passing whim or, perhaps, more like a strange aberration. Some people caught cholera when they travelled, and some people caught typhoid, and some people caught religion. Daddy was a very tolerant man, he didn't mind what people did so long as it was civilised. It didn't seem to bother him that out of his own staunch line of Protestantism his only child should grow up a Catholic. He feared for other things. Both my maternal grandfather and aunt had died of consumption, and his own sister had succumbed to it too. Right by the cliffs of Claremont, she had died as a child. He viewed my unnatural pallor with alarm. When others praised my alabaster complexion, he would wince: was it a sign of the illness lying inside me? He supervised my health himself, which was eccentric at the time, but I was small and apparently frail. Every time he saw me his hand went out almost involuntarily to my forehead, to touch my brow and see if the telltale fever had begun.

He would have been appalled to know that I sat out in the dew and talked to Harry with the early wind from the sea blowing right in my face, dampening my dress. I expect he would have been appalled, too, to see his seventeen-year-old Kitty being kissed so passionately on the cliffs. Harry grew up very quickly from the time the war began; he wanted to be a man, he needed to be. He wanted to leave school and marry me in 1916. He talked about running away to Gretna Green and then enlisting as an ordinary private and sailing to France on a troop ship and writing me letters of his own.

'I know it's stupid, but you know what I mean, Kitty, we've got to start living our life . . . I simply must represent this time, this now, whatever it is. I have to go.'

There were bald patches all along the edge of the clifftop, where Harry had thrown down handfuls of grass and dirt.

'You can see things, Kitty, that other people can't see, and I know you understand the future. I don't just want you to tell me a lot of bumf, I want to know the truth. When you look out into the waves, what do they tell you? Will I get to France? Will I? Will I get a chance to fight?'

And I would tell him what I already knew: that he would go. He would go later, and something about his going made me feel bad, so bad that I couldn't bear to contemplate the sea for long.

'It makes you sad, Kitty, because we'll be apart, but when I come back, we'll get married, and we'll make all the decks and terraces of Claremont glitter with light, and we'll throw parties every night, and dance till the sun comes up. And you'll always be the best dancer, you always were.'

Harry believed in me, so it made him happy when I told him he would get his chance, but it made me sad. After he left, he too would grow morose, and as the months moved so slowly through the summer of 1916 and on into 1917 with nothing but stalemate and carnage and terrible stories that circulated about the Hun, the waiting made him ill.

I have never liked illness, even in Harry. I hated standing by his bed and watching his sickly features stretch into a smile. I liked him to be well; everybody to be well. Illness is a weakness, it seems dishonourable. The only weakness we can allow is one that leads us into strength. Last illnesses are all right, but Harry couldn't have a last illness, he was my fiancé, we were going to be married, the ballroom was waiting under its dust covers.

His family lived in the parish of St Peter, it was only a short ride away from our own St Brelade, along the coast around St Ouen's Bay. He and his brothers all had rooms on the top floor, with sloping attic roofs and Gothic windows carved into the grey granite. His wasn't a pretty room, it was too thin and full of junk. We had chosen Grandpapa's room at Claremont to use as our bedroom, and Harry had picked the library to use as his personal study. We had known each other since we were babies. We had pinched and fought and played with each other for so long that it seemed quite natural to our parents that we should climb into each other's nurseries and later, into each other's rooms to visit when we were ill. They thought of us as honorary brother and sister, and far too young for any thoughts of romance. There had been no shyness between us, no detectable attraction of an adult kind to warn for the need of a belated chaperone. Our engagement was a secret, although our love was well known. Both families referred to us as 'the children', and we were often left alone.

Harry was lying stretched out on his bed. He had grown. He was already tall, but now he was even taller, stretching out some of the ruddy plumpness from his face into a more serious drawn-out length. His arms, resting on the coverlet, were also thinner. He had very long, very thin beautiful hands marred only by the stumps of his chewed fingernails. I campaigned for him to leave these alone. I found it inelegant in him – in anybody, but especially in him. He saw me looking disdainfully down at his gnawed fingers.

'Hmm, I've been at it again.'

I said nothing, but sat on his bed, trying not to look at his thinned face or his eager eyes. Instead, I counted the tiny hexagonal pieces of his patchwork quilt.

'You don't like me like this, do you?'

'No,' I said, without looking up.

'Did you go to the dance at the Carterets' last night?'

I nodded. I didn't have to see his face to know that he was jealous.

'And did anyone there dance better than me?'

'Reginald is very good.'

He stretched his hand out to hold my own.

'Kitty, come on, don't be cross with me,' he said, too gently for his own voice. I took his hand and pinched the skin above his wrist. I pinched it so hard that he cried out in surprise and pulled his arm away and raised it to hit me back, but I was already out of his way.

'Kitty Roberts, you are the most vicious child in the whole world.'

He often called me a child, even though I was a year older than him. I was at the foot of his bed, staring at him, defying him to get up, to be well enough to get his own back.

'I'm not supposed to get up,' he said weakly.

'And you're not supposed to swear, or leave your house at night, or ride your father's horse or load his guns without him, but you do.'

He didn't move except to shift himself into a sitting position. I could see he was dizzy, but I didn't care. I wanted him to be strong. After a while he looked away from me.

'I love you, Kitty; even though you are a vixen, I love you. You should have red hair like a fox and then everyone would know how nasty you really are. You don't frighten me with your stare, so you can take it off me . . . Pass me that book, and then run along, they'll be waiting for you downstairs.'

Harry was the only person in the world who could trick me. I think he really was immune to my eyes. He loved them, but they couldn't control him. When I got angry, he laughed. So I passed him his book, a heavy naval tome, and as I put it down beside him he lunged out at my arm, dragging me down to his lap. With one hand he twisted my arm, and with the other he pulled my hair.

'How does that feel, Miss Kitty?'

He had my head bent at an angle that felt as though my neck would break, while his eyes were mocking me. Then he kissed me in the way he had started to kiss me the year before. He had said it was how men were supposed to kiss a girl. He had learnt it from spying on his father, who regularly kissed their upstairs maid that way when his mother was absent.

'So,' he asked breathlessly, 'do you still love me?'

I whispered my answer: 'Yes'.

'Then stop pretending to be so horrid. I know what you're like, and I'm stronger than you, so there's no point acting the little madam with me. You can treat the rest of the world as your slave, but you and I are equal. You can't drown me with your eyes.'

He let me go, and I straightened out my dress. The sleeves were all rumpled, and I could feel the bruises forming on my arm where he had held it.

'You've bruised my arm.'

'You asked for it.'

I didn't mind that Harry had hurt me, he was himself again. I needed him, and he was right, it was I who made him spiteful. It was five months until his birthday. Five months until 1918.

I've never understood why it is that I can look into the future and see what will happen to other people. I can see their lives and their deaths mapped out as clearly as the rocks and islets on one of my grandfather's charts. I have never wanted to foresee the deaths of strangers, or to feel the more piercing strain of old friends dying or mere acquaintances invading my brain with their alien anguish. There were eight hundred and sixty-two deaths of Jerseymen in the Great War, of which at least a dozen flashed through my mind and held their last days or hours there before their names ever appeared on the bulletins posted in St Helier and St Aubin.

There were mothers and sweethearts and wives waiting all over the Island to hear of the fate of their men. The casualties had swollen to reach proportions that none of the civilians could understand. There were rumours that hundreds of thousands of men had died on certain battlefields, massacred in the space of a few hours and the space of a few hundred yards. There had been rationing for two years, and certain things had grown scarce in the town. This didn't affect us on the whole; we had very well-stocked gardens at Claremont, and in the fields beyond the deep ha-ha we had our own cows and sheep. It was the stables that suffered most, as our horses were requisitioned to the Front.

Daddy served in the militia, wearing his uniform more than was necessary as did many of his friends. There were constant patrols of the beaches, and the old telescope on the roof came back into its own, searching out for enemy boats and submarines or platoons of invading men. On still nights, some of the Islanders claimed that they could hear the guns across the sea in France. Over six thousand men left from the Island – six thousand boys and men marching so proudly to the beat of the drums, and then waving so happily from the decks of the departing ships.

I had finished my schooling. It was finished by the time I was sixteen. Lessons had taken place at Claremont, with the occasional foray into town for more specialised classes. Daddy didn't want me to go to school away from home; I think he was afraid I would come into contact with a tubercular child and succumb to the family blight. Maman was greatly in favour of a good education, but preferred Catholic governesses to Protestant teachers. I continued to study music and French and Italian conversation, and I had a drawing master who came in once a week and taught me how to paint passable watercolours. I liked drawing and would have liked to go to art school, not to use watercolours, but to learn to use oils. Maman, however, decided that it would be unladylike for me to do so, despite the fact that her favourite sister, the consumptive Violet, had been a successful miniature-painter in her own right.

I brought up my Aunt Violet in my defence many times. I imagined how my life could be, painting the sea in great rough oils tamed only by my hand. I had a constant view of it at Claremont, I would never need to go further afield than the roof or the cliffs. Harry liked the idea of my painting, and he encouraged me. Maman was unmoveable.

'But Aunt Violet was a painter, and she was respectable.'

'Aunt Violet lived in London, my dear,' she would reply, as though this somehow clarified the whole situation.

'All I want is to learn to draw, and then come back to Claremont.'

'But you are learning to draw, Kitty. Mr Anselm says your sketching is very nice, and we're all pleased with the watercolours.'

'Mr Anselm is an idiot, Maman. I don't want to paint streams and flowers, I want to paint the sea.'

'Well, why don't you then?'

Yes, why? I didn't know how to. It was beyond me, I felt it so infuriatingly inside me yet always beyond. I made several feeble attempts at using oils, but I found them impossible. Mr Anselm said they were not genteel and refused to help me unfathom their mysteries.

Meanwhile the months passed by, and our neighbours' sons kept dying, flitting through my head and fixing there. Maman began to find my clairvoyance unnerving and too far at loggerheads with the tenets of our faith to cope with. So I ceased to name all the faces that besieged my mind, telling only Agnes, who had known a seer in Ireland when she was a girl and understood that it was a rare but possible gift to sense when the hour of someone's death had arrived, even if they were in France. It was not until those war years that I myself fully appreciated this dubious 'gift' of mine. The cries and whispers of drowning sailors had been such an integral part of my childhood that there seemed to be nothing strange about them. Again, when Grandpapa died, it seemed only natural that he should call his favourite child to him. The war was very different, though. Both the recognisable and the unrecognisable were clawing at the condemned cell of my brain. They were on my mind until the moment of their execution. In times of peace, only a few people can grapple and control my head like that; during the war I felt their cries were killing something inside me, inch by inch, as surely as they dragged their bleeding bodies across the mud. And behind the ones I knew, there were two armies filling the waves with unrest.

I knew all this, and I knew that there was something more

unique about me than the astonishing greenness of my eyes and the fashionable whiteness of my skin and my inexplicably small stature. I saw so much, and so little. Every time Harry came to me and begged me to look into the waves for him, I did so, drawing out the sadness and failing to translate it into a premonition of his own death and the birth of my own loneliness. We interpreted this sadness as a token of our love. He rode the year again, and was eighteen, and eligible to serve his country, his Island. He trained, sticking his fixed bayonet into a dummy sack with more energy than he had ever shown before, illustrating his prowess with a sack of straw hung from the belvedere in my garden. He wore his uniform with an almost savage pride. Our last talks before he went away were full of childish dreams of how our life would be after he came back, after the war was won, for he had no doubts that he, Harry de Gruchy who rode with the century, would be the catalyst necessary to end the war with honour and a fine hail of glory.

He had won a scholarship to New College, which would be waiting for him on his return. He was going to study Greats, immersing himself in the deeds of the old Greek warriors. Meanwhile he would be a warrior himself, the rest would have to wait. While he was to be at Oxford, I would study painting, and then ... there was so much to follow that we could scarcely decide which bits of our future to gloat over.

It was June when he left; the camellias were in flower, and he came round to Claremont early in the morning, bringing me a white camellia which I recognised as one of Maman's from her south garden. Harry always brought me flowers, and he always picked them from our beds. Maman had a theory that the plants at Claremont would suffer if touched, in blossom, by any hands but her own. Harry's romantic offerings were a running battle between them.

I had felt him coming towards the house, and I'd seen him riding along the gravel drive, but I was too excited to go downstairs right away. It was Agnes who came to tell me, 'Captain de Gruchy is here to see you, Miss Kitty.'

'Captain de Gruchy' – it sounded so strange. He had served in his army corps at school, and done his few months of training, but it was hard to imagine Harry as a Captain. Promotion was very fast, though, during the last year of the war. Some people said it was because there were no men left out there, so they gave the command to boys. Harry, of course, believed it was because of his innate powers of leadership alone that he could now rank so proudly ahead of his men. He had come to say goodbye and to tell me 'his men' would be embarking from the Victoria Pier in St Helier that same morning.

He had asked me so many times, as we sat on the cliffs overlooking La Corbière, 'When you look out into waves, what do they tell you? Will I get to France? Will I?' But I, the precocious child, the wonder of Claremont with my clairvoyant eyes, failed to see that yes, Harry would go to France, but he would never return, not even to be buried. His cross would stand at Versailles in the War Cemetery with the tens of thousands of other white crosses, each with its name and date of birth and death. I could not see that then, as I looked into his own eager eyes and stood a step above him on the granite porch to hug myself closer into his embrace.

There was never any sentimental nonsense between us – no tush, as Harry called it. So he didn't say 'Wait for me' or 'Remember me'. We were sweethearts. We had been since he was ten and first decided he wanted to live in Claremont for ever.

'What will you wear to come down to the quay?' he asked. I told him I would wear my watered-silk dress with the faded poppies painted on its skirt and the pretty lace insets. I knew he liked that dress best, particularly when I could promenade it with a small lace parasol that it pleased him to fidget with. So he winked and untethered his horse and rode away, back to St Peter and to his own family there.

Maman came with me to the quay; Daddy was already there doing something with his militiamen to keep the crowd back as the last of our soldiers sailed away. It was a new battalion, entirely formed of raw recruits and freshly trained officers, so they sailed without the reluctance of older soldiers catching the ferries. They had heard of the casualties, and wanted only to do their bit. Some of the men looked much younger than eighteen as they leant over the railings on the side of the ship. The crowd around me cheered, and I cheered too, and then went home to wait with all the other separated lovers who grew to know what fear was far away from the cannon and smoke of the battlefields. I came to understand what women felt like as they crowded round the bulletins to see the lists of dead and wounded.

I had no fears that Harry would be killed; he was too brave and too sure of himself, and the war would end soon – everybody said so. But I thought he might get wounded, and a morbid curiosity led me to keep looking at the lists. There were men in St Helier who had lost their legs, and men who had lost an arm; there were blind men and many who had the rather unmentionable shell shock and wandered around looking dazed and lost and jumped when one said hello.

I couldn't imagine Harry losing a bit of himself, not even the tip of one of his bitten fingers. He was too clever. One had to be careless to lose a limb. It wasn't the light of La Corbière that told me of his death, not the bird of ill omen, nor its disciple, my own knowing thought. It was Agnes who heard the news first, and came to tell me, knowing of our friendship but not of our love. It was Agnes who burst into my room and blurted out, 'Captain de Gruchy's been killed, Miss Kitty, in France.'

I should have known, I should have seen enough at least to have told him the truth. I should have predicted the mine that was to blow him apart, and warned him that if he felt himself to be the envoy of his time, his whole generation's ambassador, it was precisely because he was going to die the grim, anonymous death of so many of his peers. Destined to rot into the mud and be nothing more than a memory, engraved in wood and stone, with all his dreams shattered in front of him, and only a short adolescence behind him, and a bundle of letters from the trenches, a few photographs and a posthumous DSO.

Two weeks later the war was over, fulfilling his prophecy that it was his presence there that was needed to end the show. Out of the heaps of War Office slips announcing the deaths in action, a kind of hilarity grew in place of grief. I wanted to cry for Harry, it is the only time in my life that I have ever wanted to cry. But I didn't know how to. Crying was what other people did inside my head. I had never made any other plans for the future. Harry was the future. I hadn't liked him ill, now I hated him dead.

CHAPTER 12

IT was Daddy who kept me going after the war – Richard (Dickie) Seymour Philippe Roberts; he was fifty-eight when the Armistice came. He told me, 'I'm a typical Islander, Kitty, with their typically insular mentality. It comes from the security of being cut off from the rest of the world by the sea. We get to taste the world from the quayside, from the traders from Newfoundland and Canada and all the exotic ports across the Americas.'

He liked to analyse himself; like all Jerseymen he was caught in the crossfire of cultures between England and France. He had been educated at Victoria College, on the Island, and then, like his father and his grandfather before him, he joined the Navy. I don't think he was ever really happy with the Navy; he missed his own ship back at home, the still newly furnished Claremont, erected forty years before his birth on his illustrious grandfather's retirement.

Daddy loved Jersey with the same devotion that Granny gave to God. His family had come, originally, from England, from the West Country. But his grandfather, the admiral, had visited Jersey in the line of his business and fallen in love with a pretty widow there. When he retired, battle-scarred and prematurely aged, he married his young bride and built himself a replica of a ship on the south-west tip of the Island that he swore was as near to paradise as any he had known from the South Seas to the Caribbean. But other families had been there far longer and had their names and their blood mixed with the history of Jersey: the de Gruchys themselves, and the Carterets and the Cabots and the Granvilles, were all good Jersey stock. My great-grandfather was not content to be the second son of a fine family back in England, he wanted his scions to be fine Islanders. To this end he married a pure Jersey widow, and later he urged his own son to do likewise. However many times Grandpapa told this story, he always managed to get in the fact that his young bride was a first-timer. He used to say, 'Your Grandmaman's blood was Jersey, but there were no dead husbands in her trousseau.' Then, just as the family was gaining its island pedigree, Daddy broke the pattern by marrying Maman. She was a newcomer and English-born, although to hear her talk one would never believe it. Perhaps she's right in thinking of herself as an honorary citizen because she has French blood – Huguenot – and that was always a passport to favour.

The different generations came to overlap at Claremont, gathering like accumulated tides. The women were the worst, lasting on past their natural span like living skeletons in cupboards, locking themselves away from the draughts in smaller and smaller rooms, fossilising their ideas and multiplying their prejudices. One such old lady hovered over poor Maman's early years at Claremont like an ancient spider spinning a Calvinistic web to discredit the new Catholic bride. This old lady regarded Maman's religion as a taint on the page of *Burke's Landed Gentry*. She considered Papist synonymous with witch. Having failed to prevent the marriage, she retired to a tiny sick room in the south wing and, despite her ninety-nine years and a severe case of jaundice, she insisted that she was dying at the hands of a Papist plot.

The men of the family seemed immune to this fanaticism, despite having lived in its tyrannous wake for so many years. Daddy himself might have been warped by such intolerance, were it not that those were times when a woman's wrath was rendered ineffectual by the prevailing male authority. Besides which, my grandfather was the most intelligent of men. When Maman joined the Roberts family, he reminded them:

'On my travels, I have come across breeds as far apart as the natives of Fiji and the Indians of North America, the Russians and the Chinese, and I tell you, I found gentlemen among them all. And once, in New Zealand, recovering from a bout of fever, I was nursed by Maoris with naked bodies and painted faces, and I found them a damn sight more civilised than some of my fellow officers, and a lot more hospitable than a certain family down at Red Houses to boot.'

It was one of his favourite stories, and although he told it in Maman's defence, I think she was one of the people most shocked by it. The fact that he ended up by saying, 'So you see, we are all God's children, whatever our religion, and I'll have nothing said in this house against Catholics or totem poles,' used to strike her as tantamount to blasphemy.

By the time I was born, all the old ladies had died, which is probably just as well, for I don't think I would have liked them in my house. They always sounded to me as though they had too much or too little spirit unevenly distributed between them, and for all their etiquette, I don't think any of them had the sense of place that Maman and I feel. I don't even think Daddy did, not really. He'd learnt such a strange mixture of things from his schoolmasters and his family. More than anything else, he had a fascination for numbers. This was a passion to which he converted several of his friends. Daddy believed in numbers. He used to explain all sorts of things by translating them into numerical codes.

With hindsight, I can see that roulette and poker must have had an almost fatal magic about them. To be able to place all he owned on a mere number and see it win or lose, double or break him, must have been the ultimate thrill for a man like him, immersed in the doctrines of Francis Galton, the apostle of quantification. Daddy had read every word Galton had published; he found Galton's cousin, Charles Darwin, much less interesting. My father was a keen, anonymous disciple of the pioneer of modern statistics.

For instance, Galton's concept of a 'beauty map' amused him more than anything else he'd ever seen. The master had compiled, from across the length and breadth of the British Isles, a series of beauty data classifying the girls he passed in streets or elsewhere as 'attractive, indifferent or repellent'. Galton found that London ranked highest for beauty, and Aberdeen lowest. Daddy, on the other hand, rated St Helier highest; London came second, and a large number of lesser places made an enormous joint last.

Galton also claimed that he could quantify boredom, but when I read what Daddy had to show me on the subject I realised that neither of them understood it at all. Boredom is a disease. It is one of the most dangerous conditions in the world. Those who have never suffered from it cannot comprehend its gravity. People say that what a man does under the influence of drink or rage can mitigate his guilt for any crime, but they can't see what boredom drives a person to do.

Although Daddy used to talk for hours about his number hero, he had a way of making all the ideas fascinating. The nearest he ever came to being boring himself was when he insisted on reading a chapter of *Hereditary Genius* out loud at dinner for a week. Even then I didn't really mind, because Daddy felt himself privileged to proselytise (as indeed he was), having had his own head and body measured by the great Francis Galton in person at the International Exposition when he was only twenty-four. It had cost Daddy threepence, so he often retold, to illustrate the absurdity of relative prices.

'And that, Miss Kitty,' he'd say, 'was, without a doubt, my finest hour.'

In his library, Daddy had works by everyone who had published anything on the subject of human measurement. He spent whole evenings poring over papers in English and French and American, written by the likes of Morton, Broca and Bean. One of his favourites was the Italian, Lombroso. A book that we were particularly fond of was, I recall, called *Criminal Man*. The cover was a collage of criminals. When I was still a little girl he explained to me all Lombroso's theories: the stigmata of the lesser types. There are certain signs that mark a person as a criminal regardless of what they do in their lives. Big ears, big feet, thick skulls, large jaws and too much hair were all clear signs of criminality, as were dark skins and tattoos.

Grandpapa would argue with Daddy for hours and hours about these new theories. The ultimate challenge would always be another account of his own experiences at the dark tattooed hands of the Maoris.

'Surely, Dickie, you can see that's a bit of definite proof that at least some of this Lombroso fellow's ideas have to be wrong. Dark as the stain on this floor, Dickie, and jumping with boats and butterflies tattooed into their skin, but wonderful people . . . wonderful!'

The debate was forever unwon, but the liberal and the elitist causes were batted across Claremont like an endlessly protracted game of shuttlecock until Daddy won by default when Grandpapa died. Meanwhile, I was measured every week. Maman didn't allow him to measure me every day, and my chart was compared to those of Lombroso to make sure that Daddy's one and only heir should measure up to all his ideals. He loved the whiteness of my skin, despite Grandpapa's injunctions as to the merits of darkness, and he often told me that I was a perfect dolicho-cephalic, which pleased me; it sounded much more grown-up than the usual epithet, 'china doll'. His only worry – and it disturbed him – was my lack of height. All the family were tall, and tallness was one of the necessary attributes for his charts. He supervised my diet, selecting delicacies that no nursery would normally be allowed. I was encouraged to breakfast on oysters, and then to lunch on rare meat and dine on fish. I had a quota of milk to get through every day, and the orchid house was pressed into service to grow tropical fruits. This last was on the advice of Grandpapa, who was fond of saying:

'All this fuss about eating and indigestion and gout is brought on ourselves, I suppose. In the South Seas they eat nothing but tropical fruits, and I've never seen a healthier or better-grown race of beauties.'

So I was force-fed pineapples while Daddy struggled in the old conservatory to make a breadfruit grow.

As well as my diet, Daddy personally supervised my physical education, taking me riding and walking or just standing in my nursery jumping up and down while swinging my arms in circles so that I would grow. For a time, there was dissent at Claremont. Daddy's obsession with criminal types reached its peak simul-taneously with his own father's loss of patience. They bickered until a compromise was reached:

'Some of those newfangled ideas are fine, Dickie, but, given that a tattooed man can be a gentleman, then so can a short one. And ladies' – so Grandpapa decreed – 'are more elegant when they are petite. It's a feminine attribute. Doesn't the whole of literature praise the delicacy of girls – the fragility of their bodies. For goodness' sake, Dickie, Kitty is a beautiful child, and what's more she's intelligent; stop torturing the girl.'

Gradually, Daddy became convinced that this was so. He still held firmly to certain of his ideas, and he had a lifelong prejudice against red hair, large feet and big ears, and a permanent soft spot for dolichocephalics, but he let much of the rest sink back into a more theoretical study of numbers.

By the time the war ended, his studies had shrunk to the use of an occasional quotation and the continued construction of his beauty map. Apart from his insistence on wearing rubber-soled shoes, his most noticeable eccentricity was muttering one or other of the categories upon being introduced to – or, more often, on passing – a member of the opposite sex. It was odd, but not particularly so, that he should murmur 'Attractive' on passing an attractive woman in the street. It was slightly less excusable when the murmur was 'Indifferent', but when the bottom grade was reached, and his indictment of 'Repellent' was uttered, it was often cause for embarrassment. Maman was quite brilliant at turning his comments into other things.

Daddy's concern for numbers reached its climax during the war. He followed the Fronts and their exploits with a single-minded concentration. He knew just how many officers, men, horses and guns there were for each battalion. He followed the course of their battles and the calamity of their losses. His love of statistics must have brought home to him more of the tragedy and the terrible waste of that war. Even on the Island, of the six thousand two hundred and ninety-two men who served, only five thousand four hundred and thirty returned. He became obsessed by the war dead, by the missing figures. And his grief mulled with my own, more personal grief for Harry de Gruchy, and together we painted the town red, first St Helier and then London. Numbers one and two on the beauty map became our party ground.

Daddy had always been sociable. He liked to ride over, however far, for a lunch or a dinner, and he enjoyed evenings at his club, or evenings at home, entertaining his friends at Claremont. He and Maman had a great many friends between them and they seemed to take turns for their fun, like riders on a carousel.

And then, quite suddenly, their way of life changed. The carousel stopped, their country houses began to run down. People said it was worse in England, lots of the great houses had been wrecked and used for troops and hospitals. There was a servant problem, where there had been none before. Girls wanted to work in proper jobs with proper wages. They didn't want to be servants any more. Pankhurst and her mob were inciting all the women to violence. The men who returned were shocked either into a dullness or into living every second of their borrowed lives carousing. After the trenches they wanted more than the luxurious gentility of their country houses; they were not prepared to 'settle down'. There was something unleashed about them which Daddy shared. Although he was much their senior in years, he began to outdo the returning soldiers in their wildness, and for some reason he took me with him. Maman saw his change as a passing phase. A lifetime of values had been lost in France, and a whole generation had been maimed. She too felt disorientated. Her friends had lost their sons. Jersey had lost its immunity. The mail ships had been sunk, our ships, like the *Roebuck* and the *South Western*, the Island threatened, its people depleted and its morale shaken. The old order was changing and nobody seemed to know into what. In the ensuing confusion, she sought solace in her religion and in her garden, and in her friendship with Mrs de Gruchy (Harry's mother), who had taken to her bed at the news of her youngest son's death and who might, it seemed, never recover.

At first we stayed in Jersey, and then, in the summer of 1919, we moved to London for a season. Daddy said it would do me good to get away from the Island so that I could forget. He told me he had always hoped I would fall in love with Harry and marry him.

'I never mentioned it before, what with your mamma being such a stickler for religion. But there's nothing wrong with us lot, as you know, and he was such a well-proportioned boy.'

Well-proportioned was his highest term of praise. We stayed at Claridge's, in adjoining rooms with a sitting-room between them. He wanted to go to London, it was very much his idea. I see now that he was in the grip of his gambling and didn't want any of his close friends to see. I expect he didn't want to gamble away the house he loved while he was so near to it. London was a neutral territory. He used to call it the lost city that we had found. In it he discovered old friends from his naval days, and a number of new friends who, like me, basked in his extravagant generosity.

Never before had I had such beautiful dresses or jewels. Some days he would get up looking flushed and excited, and take me to Bond Street, to Cartier, and buy me exquisite things. He bought me an emerald necklace, my first, and a brooch with a giant ruby surrounded by garnets. When we went on one of these binges, he always bought something for Maman. I noticed how strangely he would choose these presents, taking as much as an hour to pick something out of the jeweller's cases, and then when he was told how much he would sweep it aside, saying 'That's not enough, I want something that's worth a lot of money.'

I didn't know it at the time, but he must already have been gambling heavily then. His spending sprees were his winnings, the intermittent days of his depressions must have been the hangovers of his losses. His presents to Maman, too, must have been his only way to salve his conscience, for he was gambling her fortune away as well. Every night, after he had escorted me back to our hotel, he would go out again and not return until the small hours. Sometimes he didn't come back till after dawn. We would always have a late breakfast. I was drinking heavily with him, everyone was, it was a sign of our time. Harry would have been drinking too, since he rode with the century, but Harry was gone and his small-jawed body had been scattered carelessly somewhere across the Channel. For all his claims, I rode near to the century as well, I was one year out of time, one year out of step. I tried to keep up but I knew, as a dancer, that one step is everything when it's out.

I missed the sea, I missed La Corbière, I missed my future and, perhaps more than anything, I missed Claremont. I had never been away before. Daddy contrived our season for my benefit, but it was he who needed or wanted it, not I. Despite all that, I grew to like it. I made friends, a whole circle of friends, all survivors from the war and the decimation of the influenza epidemic that had followed it. We were bereaved, young and rich and at a loose end, and there was a new music coming in from America and new songs every week and we loved dancing, and, as Harry said, I was the best dancer.

Twice Father had to return to Jersey, and both times he insisted that I stay behind. Again, it never occurred to me that he was selling my legacy behind my back. Over our hangover breakfasts he would say, 'Have you found a husband yet, Kitty?'

'You know I want a Jerseyman, isn't that best?'

'What with this war, the numbers are down, there aren't many left, and those there are will take time to get to know. Why not grab one of these rich earls while you can?'

I thought he was joking at first, then realised he really did consider any of the young men I was using as my dancing partners as marriageable propositions. He didn't even seem concerned with measuring their heads, he'd just give them a cursory look-over and decide on the Lombroso principle: small jaws, small ears and no hair on their chests, no red hair even in their beards, and they would do. He added one last criterion, which I had never heard him mention before our trip to London: they must have big wallets.

Each morning as our eleven o'clock breakfast arrived, ferried in on silver trolleys with our trays of grape nuts and scrambled eggs, haddock and devilled kidneys, he would pick at his food and ask, 'Well, is there a husband on the horizon yet, Kitty?'

But there never was – never, that is, until I met Nelson Allen, who could describe the sea as though I were looking out at it, and had grey eyes like the rough waters around La Corbière Point. He had just come back from Canada. He had fought all through the war and survived it. He danced with me at the Café de Paris, and he understood about Claremont and the sea.

After a week, he brought me an emerald engagement ring which I wore for a joke. I showed it to Daddy. 'Don't you think it's funny, Daddy, I hardly know him!'

It was one of his sullen days which he would spend in his room jotting calculations on slips of paper and then throwing them into the bin.

'Do it, Kitty,' he said, 'if you love him. The numbers are down. I want you to know that. The numbers are down.'

I didn't know, though. I liked being with Nelson. I waited for his flowers and his calls. I loved dancing with him. I liked him to kiss me and talk about Claremont. I didn't like him telling me about his own family much, but then he didn't like them much; he called them boring, which seemed like a good sign – most people are boring. Everyone around me was falling in love. It was the craze. I suppose I followed it, because we became officially engaged.

It was a short engagement. Nelson said life was short, and we had to get back to Canada and then see what we would do. I was unsure from the first about Canada, but Nelson said I would love the sea. There would be days and days of sea with no land to hinder it, and nothing but our voices to merge with the rising waves. Maman was very unhappy about the suddenness of it all, and more so because Nelson was not a Catholic, but Daddy talked her round. Sometimes it sounded as though he was the one in love. Agnes was thrilled, even though Nelson was English, and she threw herself into the preparations for the wedding as though it were going to take place the next day.

I spent the Christmas of 1919 at Claremont. Nelson came for three days and then sailed for France. I went down with a kind of flu, and I lay in bed feeling as though all my nerve ends had been grated. Daddy was extremely restless and then went down with flu as well. I was bored. Nelson wrote to me from France; his letters were like Harry's letters, they were in the same copperplate and had the same slightly bewildered illogical air about them.

Maman adopted her crochet during that time. She gave up the pretence of making lacy edges in her spare moments, and began to weave and loop her silk continually. Despite what Daddy said about my marrying away from her Church, she saw it only as a sin. The crochet was her penance and her defence. She knotted her excuses into her work, unravelling herself in the process. She bowed to Daddy's will, but the bowing broke her.

The ceremony took place at Claremont, in the morning room, conducted by a vicar whom Daddy had dragged up from London. The Reverend Ellis he was called, Percy Ellis. He loved cricket, and poetry, I remember, and good port wine. Maman decked the house out with so many flowers from her borders and conservatories that it seemed like a funeral parlour. We could hardly move for vases of forced lilies and pots of flowering currant.

We were married in February, on Saint Valentine's Day. The first ten days of our honeymoon were spent in London. It was snowing when we set sail. I didn't like the other passengers on the ship; I didn't like them and their gangly children. Nelson hadn't mentioned that the crossing would entail being locked on board with their inanities for eight days. The sea itself, it is true, was wonderful, but once I had it in front of me, I didn't want Nelson's voice forever interfering with the waves.

CHAPTER 13

So the whole world fornicates, so what! Even Queen Elizabeth, she was a spiteful monarch to her men. Only fools and liars dare compare me to her. Why must there be a sameness in how a woman feels? We are not all sluts, whatever Nelson and his degenerate friends may say. She had red hair. She may have been queen of England, but so was Anne Boleyn with her extra finger. It was bred in her, the red hair of her harlotry. Only her loyal subjects called her the Virgin Queen, the French called her the heretic whore. I remember that. I never had a taint like hers. There was no such baseness in my blood until it mixed with Nelson's.

He was an impostor, pretending to be so fine with his knowledge of the sea and his understanding of its greyness. After we married, he told me none of the girls he knew was a virgin. Why should I be subjected to his filthy harlotry?

'What about your dear Maman?' he said. 'What about her? How do you think you were born if she didn't do just that with your father? You came out naked from between her thighs. Like an animal . . . There's nothing wrong with it. Everybody does it.

'What goes on in Jersey? You may be Catholic, Kitty, but you're not a nun. This is what marriage is. You're twenty years old, for God's sake!'

We fought in London. After the first two nights, we fought, and I won. Harry never said anything about it. He never tried to hurt me on the cliffs. Never; if that was how things were to be, he could have tried in his bedroom, or in mine, but he never did, and we were going to be married. I had known Harry all my life, while Nelson was just a stranger. We were surrounded by friends there, and celebrations. I won, though, because Nelson changed. He said it didn't matter and dismissed it as a joke. He seemed to understand, then, that whatever other girls did, I was different. Harry had always been able to see that I was different, that was why he had asked me to look into the waves for him, that was why he wanted to marry me – that, and Claremont.

All through the months to come, a little part of me hated Nelson for trying to break me. I began to notice all the defects that had been hidden before. He seemed blind to the world, blind to unpleasantness. He would just shrug off any situation that was hard to cope with. Out of his gassing or his shell shock he had developed an immunity to all that is dreary in life. He saw only the good, and he managed to redefine goodness and good fun in ways that were invisible to me.

More than anything else about him, though, I hated his feet. I found them so repellent that had I seen them before, I would never have married him. They could have been used to illustrate the foot page of *Criminal Man*. I first saw them on board, on our voyage. Nelson was asleep after a bath. He had covered his nakedness, so he thought he was protected from my scorn. But he had forgotten his feet, and I saw them. They were prehensile, with the long separated toes that mark a man as animal for life. For all his good looks and his grey eyes and his titled relatives, Nelson was hiding things in his blood.

On the voyage, I couldn't escape from the silly prattle of the other passengers. Later, it was the immensity of North America that I couldn't escape from, the monotonous vastness of Canada. We spent three days in Toronto, the first and only place of any interest there. I was surprised to see how much bigger than St Helier it was, and full of English shops and names. There were virtually no Red Indians to be seen, but I think I saw one. What impressed me most was the grandeur of the furs. Just as we began to get invitations, and could have made something of our visit, Nelson insisted on dragging our trunks inland, into the interminable negative of the provinces. He told me we would return to Toronto later. So we left the Cosmopolitan Hotel with its halls that were a gayer foretaste of the country's huge interior. It was, so I was told at least a dozen times, the largest hotel in the British Empire.

As I drank my champagne in the dining saloon of the train,

seeing the outline of the city pass by me, I didn't realise I was seeing the last of any recognisable civilisation for nearly a year. The rest would be the long trek to the ludicrously isolated Lethbridge in the aptly unheard of South Alberta. For reasons I shall never understand, Nelson loved that place. He knew the town and the lands around it, and had done since he was a mere boy. He had been here before the war. He thought of it like a haven in all the years he had spent prospecting for the Union Pacific Railway Line. His post as surveyor with the company was still open for him. He had told me a little about it before, glamorising the whole affair in the most underhand way. He was a measurer, but somehow he managed to convert even the gathering of his data and statistics to utter dreariness.

He had left a slot in Lethbridge into which he fitted back with perfect ease. There was a group of people there, mostly men, all English or Scots, all with their hidden boxes of ribbons and medals from the war. They lived like truant schoolboys, indulging in their boorishly wild habits and their drinking, throwing themselves around room after ill-furnished room, turning life's pleasures into something vile. Nelson's elegant high spirits became a caricature of those of his oafish friends.

For the first month there was snow. Deep unvarying snow like a photograph. Everything was black and white, trees and snow with no end and no hope, just a vast prairie of sameness. Out of that numbing coldness, Nelson pulled furs: beaver and white fox that he'd been keeping since the year before when he had spent a winter in the Arctic north. I had capes and muffs and hats made up for me. My trips to the fitters were the only touch of colour in those weeks of bleakness. When I complained or even commented on the wretchedness of the weather, Nelson would bring up the infinitely worse winters of the far north and call me lucky. He might as well have excused our tasteless dinners on the grounds that they were preferable to the thin porridge our neighbour threw to his dogs.

From snow the landscape seemed to turn to swamp, and the people who had battened themselves into the coffin-like boxes of their houses emerged to swell the ranks of what was laughingly called Lethbridge Society. They called me their queen. My life was filling with vicarious royalty. If I was to rule there, it would have been like Bloody Mary. It would have been as a scourge. The stakes would have been up in the market square, and instead of the logs and the price of logs and the quality of logs I would have had the townspeople gather twigs to tinder the pyres and burn their boring ways out of them. Only the furriers would have survived my purge. For the furriers, without a doubt, could cut the most beautiful lines I had ever seen in a coat. They could work miracles with pelts, even in Lethbridge.

I used to sit brooding on these things, looking out of my bay window on to the dark thaw of the tail of that Canadian winter. I used to think, too, about Harry and Claremont, the man and the house I had swapped for that dismal brick chicken coop with its small rooms and its wire netting at the windows. People who live in such places begin to cluck, like hens.

The war was over now, and we were supposed to be celebrating. Instead we had found new enemies, the climate and geography of that perverse place. I told Nelson we would have to leave as soon as it was safe enough to recross the country through the surrounding floods. He took scarcely any notice of my plans.

'It always takes time to get used to a place, things'll seem very different later on, you'll see.'

I didn't want to see, and the last thing I wanted was to get used to such a stultifying place. Sometimes, when I made this clear, he'd just shrug and say, 'Well, I married you, but you're still not my wife, so before you start demanding this and that, perhaps you should think again about giving me my due.'

He had changed, he had lost his debonair charm, and ceased to be the English gentleman I had married, and become instead a half-breed lumberjack. Nelson gloried in the woods. He treated them like secret gods. He would drag me to them all through that mosquito-ridden spring to be chewed to blazes while he gathered his pathetic clumps of primroses and violets. How could he think those flowers could disguise the bile that was rising in me? And they were Jersey flowers, what right had they to grow in that half-colonised wasteland?

Into the sweltering heat of the summer Nelson kept up his fantasy that I would 'come round'. He liked to be right about things. When he was, he had a way of closing his big grey eyes with a slow blink. He was infuriatingly patient, despite his bursts of impulsiveness. If a season was bad, he would just wait for the next one. If a town was ghastly, he would wait for it to improve. So he insisted that I would come round, and come round I did, as from a dead faint, to find myself in Canada with him. It was 1920, the beginning of the mad hilarity that followed the war, the beginning of a new era. Chaperoning was dead along with all the heroes in France. In every great city of the world there were dances that lasted all night and the most stunning clothes ever seen; and I was in South Alberta with a husband I no longer loved.

We had known each other for nine months, and we had reached a point where we were strangers. When I first met Nelson I thought I loved him. It had seemed so. But I came round, and what began as a creeping indifference grew to loathing. His words choked in my head. The sight of his feet, even inside his brogues, sickened me. When he mentioned the sea, it was like sacrilege. The name of my own house and Island became defiled on his tongue. I shuddered when he was near. I found myself wasting away in the boredom of his company. I began to use spite to keep him from me, and to lock my bedroom and sitting-room doors.

He tried to get me to socialise with him: to drink the raw whisky and smell the raw stench of his drunken friends, or to sip the abominable wine with which the local ladies addled their blood. There were a fair number of old soldiers there, even in Lethbridge, not just the band of shell-shocked hooligans from our armies, but born Canadians who had served as well. These particular ex-servicemen seemed to think that their war records created some kind of special relationship between them and me. They sought me out to tell me so. They mistook my snubs for coquetry and were unabashed. The numbers were down, they had been down for years. Why had one of their numbers not been drawn when Harry's had? Why had he died while they survived, and Nelson – why?

I could redefine purgatory. Maman, for all her praying, didn't know: purgatory was watching Nelson and his gang clomp through dances, with their wild and noisy stamping. In their sums, fun equalled noise plus a wild assertion of enjoyment. Fun, for them, was breaking things, smashing records (which took months to replace) and glasses. I thought of the glass at Claremont with its filigree silverwork and it seemed so far away that my spirit perished during the insane heat of the summer that followed.

Sensing my distaste for the place and my longing to escape, some of Nelson's so-called friends offered to elope with me. I desperately wanted to leave, to go home, but I didn't know how to go about it ... yet. Nevertheless I dared not accept their treacherous offers. I had begun to feel so angry I was afraid of myself. I didn't trust myself not to kill one of those men *en route*. The temperature surpassed any I had known. The tarmacadam on the High Street melted. Nelson's canary died and baked in its cage.

Letters from Maman filtered through with an unreal slowness. Her sympathy and advice were never enough to deal with the escalating venom of my feelings. There was a lapse in time across the Atlantic and another, greater one, like the lapse between two civilisations, between Toronto, where the mail came in, and South Alberta, where it finally arrived. Daddy was a little bit run-down, she supposed he was missing me. The hibiscuses were going to flower soon, and the white ones seemed to have a blight. A child drowned off St Ouen's Bay; Mrs de Gruchy was still not recovered. Agnes was retiring to her own house by the sea and Maman was fishing out some of the junk from the attic for her. Claremont was missing me, and so was she. And in between the lines, crocheted as skilfully as only her lacemaker's fingers could, were hints about subjugation and submission and the doing of one's duty and the suffering of pain. That was when she told me of her own many miscarriages, and her suffering at the time, each time, with a list of all the things she had and had not done in order to retain her lost babies. Her letters didn't help me much then; for all that I loved Maman, I loved her best when I was with her. And I knew that she needed me to protect her: she was like one of her own hibiscuses, she needed shielding from the harsher things of life.

It was in May, when the town was hovering between winter and summer, crouching between two inevitable excesses, that I met Arabella Lintock who, apart from my beautiful, unusable furs, was the one good thing that ever came out of Canada for me. I thought she was Scottish when I first met her, she spoke with a definite Highland lilt, and she had a certain style and subtle wit that seemed to come only with the newly arrived people. She had very light-brown eyes that conveyed much of what she was saying, as did her hands, which weaved a strange mime of her words as she spoke, as though she were accustomed to making herself understood by a deaf relative. She was of medium height, with brown bobbed hair and a slim graceful figure. I discovered her through the window of our upstairs landing. She was standing under a huge sycamore tree at the end of a garden, dancing alone to the music of her phonograph. I had heard of her before; her bobbed hair was the local scandal, such was the level of excitement there. But I had heard that she lived outside the town. The house whose garden she was dancing in was her uncle's.

Arabella hated Lethbridge nearly as much as I did. Her family had come to Canada three generations before. Her grandmother was what was known as one of the Red River Women, which meant, I gathered, that she had had an even worse time of it somewhere along the Red River than we were having then. Her father had been an official of the Hudson Bay Company, and was now retired. It was he who was deaf, after an accident on one of the ships he was inspecting. So the family had moved, and was pining.

I began to meet her family. Her father was a splendid-looking old man, but I wasn't keen on him because he was deaf. Her brother, David, was nearly as pleasant to be with as she, and between the three of us we made some gnat-bitten outings and many less harassed gatherings at her uncle's house. Arabella was nineteen and a widow; I envied her the latter situation, although she told me she missed her dead husband all the time. During the one year of her marriage, she had lived in Toronto. She spoke of that city as of the Garden of Eden, and she was continually scheming how to get back there. I told her how much I loathed not only Lethbridge but my marriage to Nelson, and how much I wanted to go home.

Somehow, I hated Nelson less once I discovered how to run away from him. I almost completely forgot he was there, with his room a mere stumble from my own. I had been out with Arabella and got back late. It must have been after midnight when I reached home. Nelson was in the cramped drawing-room, sitting over a collection of empty glasses. He had obviously had some friends round. The house, which was his house that he had shared in his bachelor days with his unruly comrades, still retained its masculine look despite our five months of marriage. There were a great number of skins and trophies and stuffed birds, and the furniture was mostly covered in dark leather.

As I went past the opened door to the room where he was sitting, he looked up angrily. Nelson never got angry. He never bothered, but his eyes were angry then.

'This is a fine time for a chap's wife to get in,' he said. I ignored him and went on up to my room. He followed me up the stairs.

'I'm talking to you, Miss High and Mighty. Where have you been?'

I had nearly reached my room, and I couldn't be bothered to answer him. I was on my way home, climbing those stairs was a step on the way back to Claremont. I didn't care.

'Just tell me one thing. Were you with David Lintock?'

I turned round then. I didn't even like him to name my friends. They were mine, he stole something when he said their names.

'Yes, I was,' I said, 'and it's none of your business.'

He came up behind me, until he was close enough for me to smell the traces of whisky on his breath. He didn't seem drunk, though, just angry.

'I can't say you forget you are my wife, because I've never made you that, Kitty . . . I've seen enough violence . . . I don't want any more . . . But we have been married a long time, and while you were so afraid, I respected you, but now you're making me the laughing stock of Lethbridge with your precious Scottish boy, we can waive the delicacies. So there'll be no more locking of your doors.'

He was in my room now, and he took the key from the brass plate of the lock and pocketed it, then turned on his heel and left me.

All that I own I own in emeralds, the stones I have gathered to repay my wrongs and the soft stones of my own eyes. Why are they blind for me? Why must I foresee what will become of others when I cannot even see what is happening to me? It was always the same. Whatever instinct works to warn more normal people failed to warn me. I had a greater foresight chained to a treacherous myopia. I felt no fear that night – on the contrary, I would soon be leaving, so I undressed and went to sleep without so much as a notion that I would never be myself again. Nelson destroyed me.

CHAPTER 14

MAMAN said that Nelson had a right to do what he did to me. She said every husband had that right by law. If I hadn't been asleep I would have clawed the grey sea eyes out of his face, I would have killed him, or let him kill me before he ever had the chance to tear my insides out with his wicked bony flesh. But I was dreaming. I thought I was on the grass verge by the cliff with the thin wind of La Corbière blowing over me, and Harry lying by my side. I dreamt it was Harry who rolled on to me, Harry who never hurt, not Nelson who filled my room with screams and my bed with blood. Maman said it must always hurt the first time, God willed it so. Either I don't believe it, or I don't believe in God. For only Nelson and his repellent daughter have torn those gashes in my body, and both of them left their scars.

At first I didn't realise what it was, I felt only the pain and the darkness and his great smothering weight crushing me. He covered my mouth with his hand to strangle my screams and I bit him, I remember the taste of his blood in the back of my throat. And I remember that he kept whispering my name, and through my own cries I heard him cry out, 'Darling, I love you!'

After he was done torturing me, I screamed for as long as I had strength left in me, while he stood at the door wiping the running blood from his nakedness with the towel of my washing bowl. Every time he tried to come near me, I screamed my loudest, so he stood in the doorway, saying, 'Kitty, forgive me. I swear I didn't know it would be like this.'

He was gibbering, crying and stuttering words I couldn't hear except for all the times he said, 'Forgive me.'

Never. I have never forgiven him. Not in the eight days it took for the torn flesh to heal until I could stand again, not in the weeks that followed when my own rage and frustration shook my body with screams, not when I left him three weeks later, not in Toronto or Jersey or London, not ever. I thought then that he had destroyed me but I didn't know destruction until it came, because he planted his huge tainted seed in me and it grew, in secret, inside me like a fungus in my womb.

During the eight days while my cuts sutured, he tried to come near me again and again. He said it was to explain. But out of his lust I drew my only strength. The scorn I felt for him fixed in my eyes, and when I flashed them he was afraid to come near me, even as I lay helpless in my bed. I could make him back away from me. I could make him flinch and weep. The sins of the fathers are visited on their children. He filled my eyes with their bitter fire and just as I burnt him, I burnt his nasty daughter.

When I sent for Arabella and told her I was going to leave as soon as I could rise up from my bed and pack my things, I didn't know there was anyone else going with me but my friend. I didn't know about the thing inside me then. We left, with all our trunks, before the three weeks were out, and took the long trail back across the Union Pacific line to Toronto. Nelson didn't try to stop me once he saw what I was doing. He even helped the carter to lift my trunks downstairs, carrying them with his unbandaged hand. I told him that if he ever tried to follow me, or see me, or contact me again in any way, I would kill him. He cried, silent sickening tears that dropped on to the floor over his feet.

There was a fever in Lethbridge in the weeks before we left; people were sickening with it all over the town. After our first week in Toronto I seemed to have it too, with its strange sporadic sickness that kept me feeling low for several weeks. Arabella wanted me to stay with her, to take a house and share it and make up for our months of captive dreariness, but I wanted to go home. I had a place that could cure my wounds. I waited in Toronto, though, trying to persuade her to come back to Claremont with me. She used to say,

'I just can't imagine ever loving anywhere more than I do this city. I belong here. From the first time I came here and walked under its elm trees and breathed its air, and found myself so much a part of it, I've never wanted to be anywhere else. I think I'd pine, like you did when you left Claremont, if I were to go away.

This is my home. I wasn't born here, Kitty, but I want to die here; in about a hundred years, after I've walked up and down Young Street at least a million times. Don't you see, I couldn't leave it, not even for you?'

And when I'd try to say something to make her change her mind, she'd say, 'It's not fair if you try to persuade me. You know you can make people do things. But I'd get halfway across the Atlantic and then I'd start to cry, and you know you hate crying, even in close friends like me.'

So I booked my passage for the 15th of October and we spent the three weeks between then and my departure enjoying all the elegance Toronto had to offer.

A week before I was due to sail, I was ill again. It was Arabella who first broached the possibility of a pregnancy. I fell into such a rage when she suggested it that she called a doctor to sedate me. Never having seen the violence of my newly acquired tantrums, she was afraid for me and called for professional help. A week later, the same doctor confirmed her guess: I was possessed.

I would rather have died than bear a child, any child. But Nelson's tarred monster planted inside me was almost too horrible a thought for me to grasp. During the next few days, Arabella kept me alive. It must have been seeing the extent of my rage and fear, and the extent of her own love for me, that made her help me as she did. She talked me through that first phase of my anger and she told me there were ways, unknown to her, of halting a pregnancy. She said they were illegal and she knew people often died in the attempt. I didn't care. I was going to die anyway by my own hand, mortal sin or no, if the thing inside me were not taken out.

While she was finding out, I had my trunks sent back from the Port Authorities and I unpacked them to find Maman's letters about her miscarriages. Then, like recipes in reverse, I followed through her dos and don'ts hoping to produce the same result as she inevitably came to . . . I ran and rode and lifted, danced and drank and smoked. I took scalding baths and late nights, violent exercise and sudden frights, and nothing happened except a slight rounding of my waistline. I was in my eleventh week of contamination. Arabella found a Chinawoman on Lower Elizabeth Street who sold us a concoction of bitter leaves that she swore would take a week to work. Every night, amid Arabella's tears, I took the poisonous brew. It made me sick in all my bones. It made me sweat and shake and cry out in my sleep. It gave me cramps deep inside me that made me grit my teeth so as not to faint. But nothing happened.

Then Arabella found, through the help of an old friend, the address of a nameless doctor on Brewer Street who worked his practice under the guise of a small upstairs office, and would be prepared to perform an operation so long as there was absolute secrecy. By this time, my friend was beginning to lose her nerve. It wasn't the crime against the Church she feared – she was not a Catholic like me – it was the crime itself, and the risk of discovery. We moved to a house in the suburbs, vacated by another, absent, friend, and the doctor came and dug his knives in me. That is the only time I ever voluntarily opened my legs. He said I would begin to bleed at any time in the next few days, and when I did, I must never contact him again, and I must find my own way to dispose of what he called 'the debris'.

We had been warned of these arrangements and I was ready to sail. The debris would be tipped into the sea, and there would be no chance of discovery. I took brown paper and string with me for the purpose, and a piece of sacking too, for extra security. He told me that under no circumstances was I to let myself be examined by another doctor or I would go to prison. Arabella saw me off. I felt my first real excitement then, about going home, since I had heard my bad news. I was unrepentant, I was free and soon I would be able to forget the whole affair. I could not forgive it, but for the sake of my sanity I would forget it.

That night, as the ship steered its course into the Atlantic, the first trickle of blood stained my cabin sheets. I celebrated by ordering a bottle of Bollinger and drinking it in bed. In the course of the crossing there was a storm, a wedding, a theft and a great deal of discussion about a furrier's wife who had run off with her politician lover to live in sin in Quebec. Some said New York and some maintained that the two adulterers were hiding on our ship. There was a London financier who had gone bankrupt. There were rumours of an engagement to a Rothschild. Every aspect of life was dissected and judged on board, but there was no debris at all. By the time we docked at Liverpool most of my clothes were unwearable.

I dared not go to a doctor yet. I had no alternative but to go home. At Claremont I would force Daddy to help me. Maman must not know. Her religion would never tolerate what I was determined to do. But if I told Daddy that I was never going back to Nelson and that he must either help to arrange a proper abortion or see me die cutting the thing out myself, then surely he would understand. And even if he didn't understand, I felt sure he would help me. I took the train to Weymouth, and from there I took the ferry back to the Island. My luggage was to follow. I had virtually run out of funds since I'd left Lethbridge, but it didn't matter because I was going home. I was wearing a dress that disguised my pregnancy with its cut, and one of my wonderful furs over it. I had telegrammed to Maman from the ship to tell her I was on my way. As the ferry neared the English Harbour at St Helier I looked out for my parents, knowing they would both be there, Maman in her finery and Daddy in his suit and plimsolls.

But Maman was on the quay alone, dressed in black, in such full mourning that it should have shrunk my heart. Was I heartless, or did I just believe still in an order of things? I thought immediately of Mrs de Gruchy; she had been ailing when I left and I knew Maman loved her with a friendship that bordered on devotion. I thought the fullness of her mourning a little absurd. It never occurred to me that it could be Daddy. Daddy was only fifty-seven. He was the one man I could depend on. I needed him; unlike Harry, even, he had never let me down. She broke the news to me in the carriage going home. I could hardly take it in. The carriage itself looked different; it wasn't even driven by the groom, the reins were in the hands of a roughly dressed boy.

She didn't tell me the whole news there. She just said Daddy had died, and was buried in the cemetery at St Brelade's, and there hadn't been time to call us back for the funeral. Us. She thought of me as half of a couple. With the thing pressing inside me under the white warmth of my coat, it seemed that she had divined my condition. It was still warm on the Island. After the cold of the Atlantic crossing and the windy autumn of Toronto, it seemed deceptively familiar.

The carriage rattled along the esplanade and on down Victoria

Avenue, passing the long sands of St Aubin's Bay. I was so happy to be home, I wanted to talk, to show Maman how nice everything would be. She sat in the far corner of her seat, squeezing the navy-blue leather to its limits. She was shrouded in silence, and could scarcely respond to anything I said to her. The death had sunk into her and swallowed her up, leaving only a thin upright shadow. The road followed the coast all the way to St Aubin itself, sweeping past the gardens and gates of our friends, before turning sharply inland after its passage through the harbour town and on towards Red Houses.

Despite what Maman had told me, that Daddy was dead, I don't think I believed her as we rode home. I think I expected to see him wandering somewhere in the garden, waiting for the sound of hooves and wheels to greet us. Or I expected him to wait until we were having tea in the drawing-room, and to walk in noiselessly on his rubber soles and put his arms on my shoulders and welcome me back.

Maman kept mouthing something and then pursing her lips. She was trying to phrase the kindest way to tell me that she was ruined, before we reached Claremont and I saw for myself the auctioneer's board on the gate: '. . . an outstanding country house and grounds, for sale by auction November 28th', followed by the name and address of an estate agent. As we drove into the flat lands of La Moye before reaching the ruins and the cliff and our own gates, she said, in a voice which seemed to come from somewhere other than her mouth, 'I am ruined, Kitty, ruined.'

I thought she meant that to be a widow would ruin her life, and I reached out and took her hand, realising for the first time some of the truth of Daddy's nonexistence.

'Dickie, your father, was seriously in debt. There is nothing left. He has left me – us – nothing. Just debts.'

I pulled my hand away from hers as though it were burnt.

'Don't be silly, Maman, we'll just settle the debts and manage on the rest. There's always Claremont and you have your own money, that must be safe, whatever else. Don't worry.'

'I'm so sorry, Kitty, so sorry.'

She didn't say any more, there were tears in her eyes and her face had a strange mildewed patina with a whiteness around the lips. We sat there with nothing more to say – I had no real knowledge of her calamity, nor she of mine. As the carriage jolted, the thing inside me jolted with my body and I remembered that Daddy had been going to help me. If he wasn't there, I would cry. Then I saw the wooden board staked beside the high cast-iron gates: 'Claremont, an outstanding country house and grounds, for sale by auction'. The blood in my knees began to fizz, and a bitter liquid began to effervesce with it and then to rise like molten poison through all my veins, into my head. My blood was smothering me, choking me to death, strangling me somehow from inside.

When Harry uprooted the tufts of green grass from the cliff edge over the Point, he would throw them down and they would bump and scatter on the rocks, breaking and bruising over and over. It always seemed so far to fall, such a hard transition from the safe edge to the sea. I was uprooted too: Daddy had died. The flu that had been plaguing the Island since the end of the war had clawed back another victim and taken his life with only three days of illness as a warning. There had been no time to tell me. It was all too sudden.

So Maman, too, began her spiralling descent. First the death, then the lawyers, then the loss. The shock of discovering that all his wealth was gone, gambled secretly away, and Claremont mortgaged to a London bank with all its land. There were creditors from all over England who put in their claims when the time came and the statutory announcements were made in the press. Daddy had run into debt immediately after the war, and he had been sinking lower and lower. Everything had to go, even the furniture and the silver and the glass. Even Maman's best jewels. He had ruined us. Maman's dowry was all gone in the final reckoning; only a tiny legacy from her own mother saved us from the poorhouse that year.

She must have thought, 'Thank goodness Kitty was safely married before this disgrace, thank goodness she, at least, is secure.' And then I returned to add the last straw to her burdens. Poor Maman, her world had become lopsided, she saw her misfortune as a judgement on herself. I think she believed that had she prayed harder, catechised her daughter more, married a good Catholic, given more to the poor, none of it would have happened. She accepted our plight as a penance, bearing the shame as proudly as she could. After all her years as mistress of Claremont it must have been galling for her to have to be no one, and more galling still after I returned to turn her sudden enforced anonymity into notoriety. Girls didn't run away from their husbands.

I always say, when I retell the tale to scandalise and amuse my new friends, that when I returned from Canada, Daddy was dead, Claremont was sold, the Roberts were ruined, and Maman was living in the cottage of one of her Irish maids. It is easier and more dramatic to telescope events.

There were five weeks of dust covers and tantrums and strange men labelling and numbering our furniture. Everything was catalogued, everything was to be sold, from the boule cabinets in the drawing-room to the rocking horse in my old nursery. The pine tables in the kitchens would fall under the hammer, and the paintings in the hall, the chinoiserie; my vases from Grandpapa, the library, the beds, the Turkey rugs – they would all go. Outside, people were talking. They were talking in St Helier and in St Aubin. They were talking in Red Houses, muttering and whispering all over the Island. The skeleton staff were talking in the kitchens. The greedy prospective buyers with their prying eyes were talking as they touched our things. 'Daddy was a gambler', 'Daddy was a cad', 'Dickie Roberts was a gambler', 'Dickie Roberts has left his poor wife in the streets, left her poor, who would have believed it?' 'What would his father have said?' 'And all in secret, all underhand, mortgaging and selling in secret, cheating his heirs. His poor heirs.' His poor heirs didn't want their pity.

Claremont, my dream house, my house, was circled in shame. I thought Maman was going to die. She was so thin and pale during those weeks, wasting away as the days neared the auction. Agnes was with her. Agnes helped her and coddled her, trying to nurse her back out of the silent trance she was disappearing into. It was Agnes who did her best as well to calm my grief and fury, bandaging the cuts that came as I flayed the condemned furniture, screaming out my anger at the forthcoming sale and at Daddy's desertion. It must have been Agnes who told Maman I was pregnant.

I was never going to tell her. My body was stretching and deforming around the huge thing inside me. I beat it with my fists, I threw myself on to the ground, I jumped down the stairs, watering my knees and twisting my ankles. I took all the pills and potions in the medicine cabinet. I starved myself, but the fungus inside me had grown hard, as hard as pumice stone, and it was growing and growing and nothing seemed able to stop it. No matter how much blood I spilled or how much bruising I brought up, it was inside me with its evil stranglehold. It had a power of its own, a loathsome power that set itself up in defiance of my will. It dragged Maman back from the borders of whatever decline she had chosen for herself. It brought her to my room one night. To my bed. It made her pull back my blankets to uncover its mound, it turned her against me – my own Maman, who had never threatened me in my life. It gave her a strength she had never had. So then the whole world was against me.

'Kitty, Kitty, why didn't you tell me you were with child?' she said.

'I'm not.'

'Kitty, darling, you know you are. I can see you are.'

She pulled my nightdress back, and I felt frozen with revulsion. I so didn't want her to see, I was unable to stay her bony hand. She saw the bruises and the gashes and something in her stiffened, stiffer than any corset she ever wore. Something hardened in Maman and she told me, 'Kitty. It is God's will that you bear that child. What you are doing is a mortal sin.'

'I want an abortion.'

When I said the word, she gasped and then I felt the hardness of her hand against my face. Maman had never slapped me, ever. It made me angry, almost as angry as she.

'I'm going to have an abortion. I'm going to and you can't stop me. Daddy would have helped me. I hate him for dying. I hate him, he would have helped me to kill this thing.'

Maman had stepped back from me as I spoke. She was looking at me with a strange mixture of love and revulsion. What had been anger had distilled in those few seconds into a firmness that came out in her voice.

'I have lost everything, Kitty, everything I had or could have. I cannot hold my head up in St Helier ever again. The rest of my life will be spent in poverty. I had hoped that you were safe from this crash. I had hoped to protect you as much as possible from its pain. I prayed that I might follow your father and thus cause you as little embarrassment as possible. But now I swear on my own mother's grave, and by all that I hold sacred, that I shall live to see you bear that child and I shall live to see it grow decently in this world. You have dared to speak of an obscene operation here, knowing that it is a mortal sin. I am your mother, Kitty, and I love you, but I will denounce you and see you in prison unless you cease to harm that baby. Do you understand?'

I was staring at her, gathering the anger that I felt rising into my eyes. Once it was there, I threw it at her through the candlelight. Instead of backing away from me she stared straight back, filling her own eyes with a granite anger.

'Do you understand?' she repeated, coming as near to shouting as she ever had. I nodded, but she was relentless.

'Answer me!' she demanded.

So I said 'Yes', and she left me. I understood: the whole world was against me and siding with the unborn thing. I had never known such bitterness.

CHAPTER 15

SHAME shaves away one's friends like unwanted hair. Some of our friends were too embarrassed to know what to do, so they stayed away. We carried too much calamity with us when we left Claremont. It was disturbing. People didn't know how to respond. A death alone makes people back off for a while, but with all the rest, the spoken and the unspoken, the seen and the suspected, we moved through the Island like germs of a contagious disease. Other friends stayed loyal, and wanted to help. The de Gruchys, for instance, offered us the hospitality of their house for as long as we should need it, knowing full well that might have been for ever. Another branch of the same family offered Maman financial help. Several of Daddy's friends offered houses on their estates. There was a dower house here, a manager's house, rent free and gladly given.

I was proud of Maman for turning them down, and preferring her own pittance to charity. Daddy had always had his poor relations, his hangers-on; I didn't want to be one. I think perhaps we should have left the Island then and there, as soon as the auction was over and the debts were paid. Staying for the next five years was like panning the salt out of the sea and rubbing it in our wounds. I said as much to Maman, but she just said salt was the best healer. I don't know. Maybe she knew best in that, at least. The sea was the most healing thing about the Island. I would have gone mad if I hadn't been able to stare into its waves.

Poor Maman, she had blackmailed me, and she thought she was so right, so in the right, and then, when the ordeal came, she knew that however evil my first plan had been, it was I who was right: the thing shouldn't have been allowed to live. It destroyed all that was good in us. It was a cancer in our house. Maman died of cancer, it was in her hip. The doctors said it was too late, it should have been cut out sooner. Tumours have to be destroyed or they destroy you. They grow until they burst.

Mine grew. We moved to the North of the Island. We stayed outside Rozel, in the parish of St Martin, overlooking the sea at Rozel Bay. Maman chose the place, she must have had her reasons. It was five miles from St Helier and thirteen from Claremont, and that felt like a long way away. It was about as far as we could have gone without leaving Jersey, so it seemed like exile, the first of many. The landlady and her sister knew who we were, though, despite Maman's refusal to discuss our affairs. It was a small private hotel which kept what Maman claimed to be a reasonable kitchen. We had three large rooms on the first floor, two bedrooms and a communal sitting-room. It was a mockery of London to me.

Maman had brought her bicycle, Agnes had taken in her dogs, and there were the patience cards and her books and the rough winter sea followed by the murderous spring tides. We were far apart from each other during those months, despite our proximity. I resented Maman's tyranny. She thought that by reading to me and sitting with me she could make me forget what I carried inside me. I could hardly walk. I looked like a huge spider with its repellent body bulging out in the light. We had the mirrors removed. I was grotesque, swelling with my affliction that was like an infection. Maman tried to take me to church with her, but there was no way. I stayed hidden in my room. No one was going to get the pleasure of seeing me in that state. Every Wednesday and Sunday Maman attended Mass. She told me I would feel better if I went too. She wanted me to confess, I know, to regain my state of grace. But she didn't insist, she could see that I prayed. I prayed through the day and in my sleep as well. I prayed that the Lord would take away my scourge and rid me of my growth. Prayers are private, mine had been for years, so Maman didn't know of my daily sacrilege (as it would have been in her eyes).

As to confession, I didn't go again until after the ordeal, when Maman herself confessed to me that although she could never condone what I had wanted to do, she at least understood why I had wanted to do it. She said she knew I could see into the future and I must have foreseen the agony that lay ahead. That was when I returned into the folds of the Church, but only because she had climbed down; had I really known what I was to go through, I would have thrown myself over the cliffs or dropped over the edge of the ship, with my emerald engagement ring, midway across the Atlantic. Maman leant more and more on her faith, it was all she had. She had a forgiving nature; when our troubles came she believed she was to blame. I couldn't do that, so I couldn't lean on the God who had stolen everything from me, leaving me only with my huge unwanted legacy. If He was such a jealous God, then let him have the thing. I vowed as I watched it grow that I would find a way to make it die, but if Maman outwitted me and it was born, then it would suffer all the strictures of the Church, the harder the better. The Church had cosseted me as a child, but now that times had changed, what was it doing for me?

I have tried to forget the remainder of my time in Jersey. Why savour bile? We moved from one establishment to the next, from north to south and back again, fleeing my temper, Maman said. But it was a part of me, it accompanied our every move, disrupting boarding houses and scandalising otherwise quiet hotels. Maman explained my behaviour away to the various landladies as grief, and they pretended to understand. I know that from the coming of spring I felt nothing but lethargy. I shunned all my friends, as I had since my return. I couldn't find the face to wear for them, I was too used to being one of them to know how to be anything else. I felt the gap between us to be unbridgeable. Perhaps, after the thing was gone, I would be able to deal with them again. Meanwhile, I just hid in hired darkened rooms. By April my discomfort was such that we moved into Agnes's house so that she could nurse me. It was a relief to be able to sleep there without having to pretend to strange maids that I was still living. I was virtually catatonic for the last few weeks. Only the sea was any solace; the sea hadn't changed.

I should have Agnes here. Agnes with her tedious repetitions of my ordeal. Agnes with her squeamish fixation with pain sobbing over the torture to which Nelson and his child subjected me. The rest is all voices. All the doctors talked about voices, they seemed to be obsessed by them.

'Do you hear voices, Mrs Allen, what do they say?'

They were so boring; doctors are boring. Of course I hear voices, I'm not deaf!

'But do you hear voices inside your head?'

They are such absurd creatures. What do they want? I have a memory. We all have memories, and memories speak. Just as Agnes's did, retelling my trials until the very sound of her voice made me sick and she had to be banished, in her own house, from my room. And Maman telling me how nearly I died, as though I didn't know. Maman telling me that the doctor said I should never have had a child. I wasn't built for giving birth, and at least one of us should have died. Why couldn't it have been the thing? Where did all its disgusting health come from? And then the nurse's voice, not the spying nurses they have in squalid hospitals but a real nurse with a clean uniform and cap and properly brushed hair. I heard her words to me and her whispers to Maman. She said the doctor must have been mad to have done what he did. The cuts and tears took sixty stitches. Sixty stitches, and an hour of forceps to tear the fourteen-pound monster from inside.

So how dared anyone be surprised that I couldn't abide my daughter? That's what Maman used to call her when she remonstrated with me. But not even Maman could deny that the degenerate thing the doctor ripped out that night was ugly. It was the law that made me have it, but there is no law to decree that a mother must love her child. As Maman kept telling me, over the years, there were laws that could force me to keep her, but none to tell me how.

I know we wouldn't have lost Claremont if it hadn't been for my marriage. I can measure the steps from London to Lethbridge. It was in London that everything started to go wrong. We shouldn't have gone. We should never have left the Island. It was leaving it then that lost it to us later. How different everything would have been!

How different I would have been if I hadn't lost Maman's love over the abortion I wanted! She came to care more for her grandchild than for me. She always said she didn't, but it wasn't true. If it were true she would have understood me again, and she wouldn't have left me like she did, just as the war was about to begin.

I don't want to remember Jersey any more, not as it was then, in the twenties, when we were poor. Thank God nothing ever came to steal my memories of La Corbière. Nothing has sullied its beacon. Far from being a bird of ill omen, it is the one thing left to me unspoilt. Later, I used to look out to sea at Selsey and imagine its shafts of light, my light. Everything else was tainted by the time we left, but La Corbière stayed intact. And as the years passed, the Island itself became more whole, until it could be set in any balance and outweigh, in memory, whatever dreariness ensued.

I never went back. I belonged to Claremont and Claremont belonged to me. The thought of other hands clutching its railings to look out to sea makes me feel ill. It makes me so angry. In the olden days, Grandpapa told me, there used to be sanctuary paths across the Island. They called them the perquage and they were very wide and winding, and they all led to the sea. Any Jersey man who committed a crime, however bad, could follow one of these paths and escape, and as long as he stuck to the wide confines of the perquage he could not be arrested. His friends were allowed to meet him at the water's edge with a boat and take him away from the Island. All his goods were confiscated by his Seigneur and the felon could never return. Was that what we did?

I thought Maman would go back sometimes. She had kept more friends there, and she missed it so much. On the day we left, though, she told me she would never return. I remember, as we took the ferry, she and I and Agnes with the redhead by the hand, that she climbed on to the upper deck and stood staring at St Helier until it was out of sight. She seemed to be breathing in its image, trying to drag a part of it away with her. She looked so strange, I asked her what she was doing, and she said, 'I'm memorising it, Kitty, for I shall never see it again.'

At the time, I had no plans to quit the Island for ever. We were merely making a change which she hoped would be for the better. Maybe Grandpapa had told her the legend of the perquage too. Maybe she knew it was the mercy of the Church which the law allowed. Maybe she thought that by leaving, never to return, with all our goods confiscated and lost, we would wipe clean the slate of our sins, and annul our shame.

I don't know why she chose London as a place to settle in — except, perhaps, that it was London that had punctured our own insularity. Claremont had been mortgaged to a London bank. Our wealth was there, somewhere in the city, circulating in the hands of gamblers with more luck or sense than Daddy. I had friends there from the time before my marriage, and now Maman had a friend there too. Mrs de Gruchy, the mainstay of her social life, had left the Island before us to be treated at St Thomas' Hospital, and she had stayed there to convalesce. She was in the second year of her convalescence and showed every sign of staying on in her suite over the Thames until she followed her favourite son. And last, but not least, it was second on Daddy's beauty map.

I can't think of any reason why she chose Hendon. It was not in our nature to live in the suburbs, yet we decided to. We took the house unseen. It was hideous. She had said earlier, after we moved from Agnes's cramped hospitality into our own horrid little terrace over the Bay, 'If we do move to London, I must have a garden. I don't think I really need anything else.'

I nodded my approval, knowing that a garden on our pittance would mean a poky uninteresting thing. She seemed pleased with my consent, which was absurd, considering the only pennies we had were held by her purse strings. But Maman had grown *nerveuse* in many ways, most strikingly in her addiction to crochet. She did it all the time without even noticing. It was turning into a nervous tic. She never went anywhere without her ball of silk and her hook.

We had had some very disagreeable discussions about money since my so-called recovery from the ordeal. Maman was convinced that I should write to Nelson (whom she stubbornly insisted on referring to as my husband) asking him to support me and his child. I refused. After the first year she reluctantly accepted that I take nothing for myself, but she continued to lobby for maintenance for the redhead right up until the divorce. Not only would I rather have starved than taken a single shilling from him, I was determined that he should not know of its existence. The thought that he and I were joined for ever was totally abhorrent to me and I was determined that he should never know.

Maman was the only person I couldn't control. She actually

wrote to Nelson behind my back and told him he had a daughter. Fortunately he had moved from Lethbridge by then, and the letter was returned, months later, with 'Address Unknown' stamped on the envelope. I nearly choked when I saw it in the mailbox, with his address written in Maman's beautiful hand. I didn't speak to her for about a month after that, and I threatened to leave. It was an idle threat, and she probably knew it. Where could I have gone? The only things I had of any value were the emeralds Daddy had bought me and my furs, and I sold the emeralds in the winter of 1922 so that I could buy some of the Paris fashions, and nothing on earth could have made me sell my furs. I thought of them as lined not so much with the blood of the poor animals who had been trapped for them, as with my own. They covered my scars.

I never thought, till after Maman died and left me her pittance, how much better she could have lived on her money on her own. The taste of Canada was too sour then for me to consider the more practical considerations of my pride. But for me, she wouldn't have had to leave the Island at all. She could have lived in a good hotel and stayed there with her friends as the widow she was. Nobody thought it was her fault that Daddy had gambled away everything else she owned. It would have been hard for her, but never as hard as Hendon and her long years of exile. It wasn't my fault, though, it was the child's. If it hadn't been for the redhead, Maman need not have died.

CHAPTER 16

SUBURBIA suited me, in its way. It kept the redhead reasonably out of sight, and it allowed me to embroider our exile and poverty with some of the more traditional attributes that our actual condition lacked. It added a definite air of mystery to our story. Maman was able to tend her atrophied garden, planting it out with the grand, temperate bushes of the Island. Occasionally she would overreach herself, as when she tried to get the first mimosa tree to live through a winter in Golders Green, or when she attempted to train a bougainvillea over the front of the house. But as long as she stuck to her wisterias and camellias and the like, her protégées flourished and could almost bring back the smell of Claremont's garden on a summer day. Almost, but never quite, for the profusion was lacking, the mixture of whole banks of philadelphus and azaleas fusing with the distant tang of the sea.

From the time we first reached Hendon, right up until the end, Maman was strangely monastic in her ways. It was she who had chosen the place, but she was never able to accept it. On the Island, during the days of her glory, when she had entertained and been entertained by the first families on Jersey, there hadn't been a single Islander, however lowly, with whom she wouldn't pass the time of day. She used to cycle on her huge-wheeled bicycle through whole parishes, and she knew all the cottagers by name. She was always stopping to admire their babies and cauliflowers and early Royals. In those days, she was not above taking a glass of lemonade at anybody's house. She seemed to love company, and she was popular. I always found it odd how she'd take off with her slavering dogs in tow and tour the country lanes and the coast road, mixing with people one wouldn't otherwise have known existed. She seemed to needle them out of nowhere.

When the gardens were in their peak months, and there was soft fruit and salads enough for an army growing at Claremont, she had always encouraged her entourage of poor admirers to come round to the kitchens with their baskets and carry away some of the surplus which would otherwise have been 'wasted'. It was a habit the gardener particularly disliked, since even I could see that far from tipping hundreds of pounds of raspberries and tomatoes on to the compost heaps, he was selling them at Red Houses and St Helier at a fair profit to himself. Maman, for all her brilliance as a housekeeper, had a certain naivety about her.

Once we reached Hendon, though, Maman cocooned herself in her solitude. Not, of course, that I would have wanted her to become intimate with most of the sort of people who were living around us, but even in her shopping she was aloof and haughty in a way she had never been before. She never trusted our succession of moronic maids to hand her lists over to the shopkeepers and bring back what she wanted; particularly when the chemist or the haberdasher was involved, she would insist on going herself. Yet in all the years of her stay, she never managed to muster so much as a fraction of her friendliness for any of them. The milkman, the postman and the delivery boys were all banished from her former kindnesses, thus excluding her from any reciprocal attentions of the kind she so missed and needed.

We never spoke of these things, and I don't expect she imagined that I noticed. At Claremont she had been used to eight smartly dressed, doting members of indoor staff; at Hendon she had to make shift with one slovenly maid after another. For after the first months there, when Agnes returned to the Island, we had a succession of girls to work for us, each under her separate cloud and either giving her notice or getting it when her behaviour became too insufferable to bear, or her sullen temperament too stubborn to accept the rebukes she so justly deserved.

We should have kept Agnes, we could easily have made her stay, and then the tedious domestic side of our lives would at least have been solved. Agnes had pined for the Island. She declared she had never seen anywhere as nasty and foreign and dirty as London.

'It's a wonder anyone survives here,' she'd say tearfully, after running the gauntlet of the local High Street on her shopping day, 'and look how many people there are. They look like insects. If the Good Lord had wanted so many people in one place, He would have said so in the Bible.'

Agnes knew exactly what God intended and thought, and she was always fond of interpreting His will to other people.

'Do you know that those buses can travel for hours through all the dirty streets and still not reach the sea? It's scarcely decent. I don't know how Londoners put up with it!'

If Maman was less than popular locally, and thought to be stuck up, she was excused on the grounds that she was so obviously a lady. Agnes, however, with her outspoken disgust for everything English, was almost a menace in the local shops. She could have been kept in the house, though, and somebody else could have shopped. The main thing was that she pampered Maman, and made her her cinnamon toasts and her hibiscus tisanes and laid her breakfast tray just as it should be, and changed the water in the endless vases of flowers. Agnes would never have soaked my sequined dress from Paris, the Worth one that had such a beautiful thistle and gold on the back and streaks of opal and the same green as my eyes. She would never have left it in a tub of suds and dissolved it in a huge bowl of multicoloured unset jelly caught round a slip of net.

God knows, I nearly killed the girl for doing that. I can't remember her name, it was Susan or Sally or something like it, and she had a very poor complexion. I told Maman, as soon as she hired her, that anyone with skin in that condition had to be a bad choice: 'Food should not be prepared by someone in such an obviously septic state.'

Maman just said she had excellent references, and she was the sort of girl who might stay for some time instead of disappearing after a few weeks. She said she had 'stoic qualities'. Why one had to choose servants for the qualities of soldiers was an absurdity Maman did not choose to explain.

I had bought that dress with the last of my garnets. The emeralds had gone to boost my morale. Daddy had bought me a great deal of jewellery on the mornings after his flutters when we were doing our season in London together. But as the years passed by, I had to sell it all. It was the only way to stay presentable. Maman's pittance didn't rise to a decent dress allowance.

Before the crash, I had to worry only about which dresses to wear, and which new ones to buy. Later, it was always what could I buy them with? How could I afford the shoes I wanted if I took the suit as well? Not having money is a nightmare. It was all very well to be reduced to poverty, but if one was going to have any kind of social life one had to dress well, look stunning, and then admit to being a beggar.

Maman's spotty new recruit was so keen at her job that she took it upon herself to do not only all that she was asked but much that she was not ... I never could get used to not having Agnes or an inferior equivalent of her following me around and tidying up my clothes. I had picked up with the same set of friends that I left when I met Nelson. Anyone who had known him, of course, I avoided, but that still left a great many to keep me amused on my circuit of dances and house parties. I made a point of belonging to several different sets, so that I should not tire of any one particular group too soon. Sameness can be very boring.

The Mosleys used to entertain regularly and I was always invited to stay with Lady Mosley, who came to be one of my closest friends. I had been staying with her, I remember, for a long weekend, and I'd rushed back to Hendon late one Monday evening for a dinner in Holland Park at nine. I only just had time to bath and change, and I threw the contents of my suitcase over the floor of my bedroom, looking for all the bits and pieces I needed to get ready while Freddie Palliser, my chauffeur of the month, waited for me. After I left, it seems, the halfwitted skivvy tidied up my room, and decided to surprise me by washing my favourite dress.

When I emerged for luncheon the next day, feeling the usual irritability that one feels after a pleasant evening, I mentioned that I couldn't see the dress in question in my wardrobe. She had the effrontery to simper as she told me she had washed it. Maman exaggerated terribly when she said, afterwards, that I was trying to kill the simpleton. After all the tribulations I had gone through, I was scarcely going to hang for the likes of that. I was merely trying to maim her in the interests of fashion and *haute couture*. I still feel my blood curdle when I think about it. What with her, and the one who ironed – ironed, if you please – my Fortuny grey silk!

I expect both of them are somewhere now, manhandling their way through life, breeding scores of insensate children to destroy other people's dreams. I don't suppose the war will have wiped them out – not that it was particularly selective – but it would be too much to hope for, and I'm sure I would have remembered if either of them had come clawing through my head on the way to their muddy graves.

I loved London sometimes, it allowed me to forget all my misfortunes and I made the best of our life. There was no other way. I realised that Daddy, for all the wrong he had done us, was right about one thing: breeding and beauty were the most important things in life. They were all I had, yet they were enough to tide me over the awfulness of losing Claremont; they kept me sane. I might have really forgotten how much it ached to be robbed of my inheritance if it hadn't been for the presence of the redhead. It grew like an enormous maggot, its proportions were truly alarming and to make matters worse, as soon as it could, it tormented me with its existence and its size. It hovered, if anything as ungainly as that can hover. It waited in corners and behind doors. It had Nelson's eyes, and even Nelson's voice. When it said, 'I'm sorry, Mother, I'm sorry,' it made me feel as though I would burst with disgust.

And it was slow and stupid. What little had been salvaged from Claremont for our own use it contrived to spoil or destroy. I knew it did that on purpose. It was so near to having taken everything away from me, from us, and still it wanted to cheat us of our last little souvenirs. It took me years to establish that it was never to call me 'Mother'. I could feel its presence in the house. I could hear its revoltingly servile thoughts; it was just like its father, but with all his inward faults daubed over it to warn of their treachery. It was sorry, always sorry, sorry it had been born, and just because of that it pretended to deserve forgiveness. It honestly believed that being sorry atoned for all it had destroyed and was destroying still! Thank God there are other things in the world to talk about and other people to see.

And I managed. I lived through the twenty years of London life and made my mark. It was not an anonymous passage. Poor Maman, though, didn't seem able to cope with our move. She lost her spirit, and her clarity of judgement. She began to imagine things and lived a prey to quite ludicrous fears. She confused her own disordered thoughts for mine. She fancied that it was I who was at risk, not herself. She became almost afraid of strangers, even of our maids. She thought the world was spying on us and whispering about us, and it disturbed her badly. Of course, the simple explanation was that the world of our neighbours was spying on us, and inevitably they speculated and gossiped about us.

We were different. Maman was a lady, how could they help but notice how incongruous it was for her to be living there in our little modern shoebox? We were three females hidden behind the camellias. They wanted to know – where were the husbands, were there husbands, how did we live, what on? Maman grew so paranoid, poor thing. Whenever I so much as rebuked the skivvy or the redhead, she would grow tense with fright. What would the neighbours say? I'm afraid the dreadfully middle-class values of the neighbours were contaminating her. Her condition was quite pronounced at times; she would even talk about it openly, telling me about her fears as though they were real.

By the time she died, Hendon had come to be like a sprawling condemned cell for her, and every day was just a stay of execution. She told me the same words so many times that I can quote our conversations on the subject. It would always stem from some little fit of temper on my part. Treating me like a small child, she insisted on calling these tantrums. Occasionally (very occasionally), and under provocation, I would have rages, which were completely natural. Everyone except Maman had two sides to their nature. Only she, with her addiction to the Church, insisted on having the character of a saint.

But no, every time I raised my voice or sent back an underdone potato, it was a 'tantrum'. She should have seen me in Canada. She had seen me at Claremont after Daddy died – those were tantrums, if you like. It amazed me that she could not see the difference between anger and grief. I think her knitting was beginning to unravel her brain.

'Kitty, Kitty, can't you see how dangerous your behaviour is?' she used to say in her level, deep voice with its measured words that sounded so pleasing to the ear, whatever she said.

'Don't you realise that the law will intervene? This has gone past spite. It is madness; and Kitty, I'm so worried that they will take you away if this gets out. My pittance cannot protect you, darling, not if they lock you up. Please try and control your tantrums, please. You must remember. You must.'

It used to make my scars ache when she spoke like that, because I realised that I had friends and connections, and she had no one except me. She must have felt the threads of her own mind going and she was afraid of winding up in an asylum. The very thought of my dear Maman having to suffer that ultimate indignity used to make the anger inside me shrivel up and turn instead to protect her. I tried to make her see that there was no danger of the law or her mysterious 'they' coming to get her. She would come the nearest she ever came to crying on those occasions, saying, 'Not me, Kitty, you. It's you they'll take away, don't you see?'

Her proud, patient mind could see no reason. She was convinced that there were doctors and enforcers of the law waiting outside for me. It was a strange predicament, knowing, as I did, that it was she whom they might take away when the time came if I didn't help her. So whenever the tension rose in our house, and Maman said 'remember', I did; I remembered that she was the victim of a paranoid obsession, and unless I managed to soothe her she might slip away from me to end her days in utter degradation. She transferred her fears, but that didn't make them any less real. She was battling with something she couldn't cope with. Her 'remember' was a warning that at any moment the misused network of her mind might go, and she was terrified because she sensed that she wouldn't have the strength to recover.

CHAPTER 17

I HAD a lot of beaux, as Maman called them, a lot of admirers. It was the only way I could stop myself feeling bored. They used to tell me they were in love, which was all right so long as they didn't say it too often. Some of them had served in the war, some of them were too young, but they all used to talk about dying. They'd pretend they would die if I didn't kiss them, die if I didn't see them, care for them, and die if I refused to accept their presents. I kept them at bay because I knew they became excited if I let them get too close to me. Maman liked the flowers and the gold-wrapped chocolate truffles they sent and the hampers and bric-a-brac, but I liked only gramophone records and emeralds. The boyfriends who failed to notice this didn't last very long.

I heard somewhere about a queen in Egypt who had been forced to marry against her will and had built a pavilion of precious stones to mark her infidelities during her husband's absence. She let the whole of her kingdom defile her body and then bought a jewel to mark the scorn she held her husband in, making what he had had as worthless as she could. It was a strange story, although I liked it. None of my lovers ever saw or touched my nakedness, but they did all bring me stones.

There was a jeweller in Golders Green who strung them for me. He became my friend, together with his sister, Elsa Müller, who could make any dress or suit look as though it came from one of the most exclusive Paris houses, when actually she lived and worked on our street. Maman disapproved of her; she was the only one of my friends whom she tried to exclude from my life. The Müllers were Jewish, and Maman, like most of my friends, had it in for the Jews. It didn't matter how charming they were, or even useful, Maman objected to having them in the house or near it. She minded if I so much as talked to them in the shop. She took it as another mark of our shame that I should even consider mixing with them socially. In her opinion, it was yet another twist of her penance that we should be reduced to living in the same street. Left to her own devices, she would probably have had them forcibly removed.

When it came to the redhead, although she admitted that the scarlet thatch itself was an undeniable blight and the grotesque size of the thing was what she called 'unfortunate' and the voracious appetite 'unladylike', she was always trying to make excuses for it, implying that its genetic defects were less accursed than they seemed. She claimed that Grandpapa had declared that Daddy's books and papers on hereditary flaws were often exaggerated and even wrong. Oh yes, she protected the redhead from the obvious verdict of criminal stigmata, but when it came to the Jews, she branded the whole race as evil, degenerate, repellent and practically every strong negative in her vocabulary. She tried to put me off the Müllers by assuring me that Daddy would never have spoken to them. When Elsa came to tea, bringing her cinnamon cake and huge *Pflaumentorte*, Maman either contrived to be out, or stayed in her room. Afterwards, she would invariably throw the remains of these delicious cakes to Rufus, her cringing little dog. Not surprisingly, the rich sweetness would make him ill. Maman, of course, interpreted this as a Jewish plot; while I liked Elsa all the more for it. I never could stand that dog.

Elsa had about a hundred cousins, and she had brothers and uncles scattered across the capital cities of Europe. She herself came from Vienna, and she could describe the place in such a way that it came to life with its wild music and its madness for dancing and balls and flirting and fun. All the men in her family were in what she called 'jewels', and she talked about precious stones and precious possessions quite unashamedly. Unlike most of my friends, who tended to be rather boringly modest about their things and therefore couldn't be brought into discussions about all the particularly lovely ones that used to fill Claremont, Elsa relished minute descriptions of vases and chandeliers and the thickly carved gilt frames of family portraits, and exotic treasures hauled and hoarded from all over the world. She truly admired my emeralds. She made me laugh with her quick cosmopolitan wit.

I enjoyed her infatuated stories about her cousin Dietrich getting lost at the Schönbrunn Palace and her cousin Josef waltzing in the street at midnight at the Graben and dancing so well that a crowd gathered and danced with him through the Viennese night. I almost loved her for so admiring what she had left. I cannot abide people who belittle their own past in their exile.

I am sure I would have liked Vienna, but I would probably have liked it best in the twenties. There were so many headlines and hoardings and talks about the Depression, it seemed to swallow up the whole of the thirties. If I stopped dancing for so much as a second, those years just became depressing. Everything was getting so serious; even one's friends were transformed into stodgy worried businessmen or politicians. Perpetual motion, that's the best remedy for boredom – or, rather, the best vaccination. I kept travelling, around the map of England from country house to country house, eliminating the weekends from Friday to Monday so that the weeks foreshortened and were easier to fill.

Considering that I've had half of Europe parading through my head, it shouldn't be so difficult to account for my own time. How can one lose the midweeks of twenty years? I can remember the beach at Selsey very clearly, though I can no longer remember which boyfriends did and didn't go there with me; but what else? I used to walk through the park sometimes, and sometimes we went boating. In summer there was tennis, and in winter, skating. I went to Paris several times, I enjoyed flying. I hated the cinema. I can't decide what was more depressing, the sight of a dole queue or the sight of a queue for the cinema. I went once, and I left halfway through. The whole idea of the darkness and sitting so close to people one doesn't know is quite horrid; as are the puppet movements on the screen with their endless oncoming black-and-whiteness. It reminded me of Canada. I enjoyed the opera and the odd concert, but I would often get restless and leave those too.

I don't know why all those middles have become so ephemeral. All I seem to remember are tunes.

*   *   *

183

And I remember that Maman finally relented and sent the redhead away. It was obviously the best thing to do. The thing was inflating under our eyes. Since it was quite clear that it was – literally – going to be a monster, it had to be better to train it. All we had left around us were fragments of Claremont. If we hadn't sent it packing when we did, there would have been nothing left at all.

Maman herself had taken a turn for the worse then. She took to sitting for long hours with the redhead, holding its huge freckled fist in her own delicate hand while staring out at the camellia bushes in the back garden and remembering Claremont in long sad monologues. It was awful to see Maman humiliating herself in front of a stranger like that. Sometimes I would separate them, and sit with Maman myself, but the shame of it all made her cry. It was worse for her to realise that she had been caught spilling her secrets to alien ears. On the one hand she was so paranoid about spies, and on the other she seemed to be genuinely unaware that the only dangerous one was in our house. The redhead was like an indestructible tapeworm in our midst.

The French convent to which it was eventually sent was far too lax for my liking, and too near, but it was better than nothing. One of the most sinister traits the redhead had was that its plainness was so severe that no one looked for anything else underneath. As soon as it mustered the strength, it became intent on destroying me. In fact, even before it was born it had been undermining and hurting not only me but Maman and our way of life, our beliefs, and even our Island.

It takes a great deal of cunning to take someone's country away from them. I, at least, could recognise my enemy. Poor Maman was duped, and ultimately infected. Just as the redhead had planted a cancer in our lives, as its father had planted one in mine, as it had filled the forty-five square miles of Jersey with the ineradicable seed of its destruction, so gradually it managed to plant its cancer in Maman's side.

I tried, God knows I tried, to keep its malice at bay. I quarantined myself from it, and I tried to save Maman from the insidious stranglehold of her freak grandchild. Yet by the time it went to the convent, the damage was done. At last we had the house in Hendon to ourselves. There were no more thefts in the kitchen, no more nights of whimpering. No more crocodile tears. No more infuriating sobs; and no more mocking stares from passers-by. Maman was free to visit Mrs de Gruchy without the embarrassment of the lumbering redhead in tow. She could go to Kew Gardens and enjoy it for once. She could finally lay down her crochet and put the ivory hooks back in their case. And yet, it was too late.

I struggled with her fears for nearly a year, then I realised that I would have to take a drastic step both to calm her down, and to protect her. I divorced Nelson, in the winter of '29. The court case, with its inevitable little ripple of scandal, reopened the old discussion about maintenance. Maman wanted help. The Stock Market had crashed in America, and several of her friends had suffered severe setbacks. There was much speculation of a financial crisis. Maman kept telling me over and over again, 'You have a right to his money, Kitty, and he has money, so please settle this whole unpleasant business properly.'

'You didn't want to live on the de Gruchys' charity, and they are your dear friends,' I reminded her. 'Why should I sink to taking so much as a penny from the man I hate?'

I was so determined not to give in that I felt quite sick some days just from arguing and standing firm. I was granted a decree nisi as a sort of early Christmas present, but nothing that happened that winter could do anything to lift Maman's spirits. She was having a fit of the doldrums; I could have found her nagging criticism of me tedious if she had not been so genuinely scared.

There we were, trapped in suburbia, she with her growing phobias and I with my newly acquired and potentially vulnerable spinsterhood. Ever since our arrival in the grey metropolis, I had been able to fend off would-be spouses with the insuperable barrier of my already being married. It is the only truly effective way to end, for ever, the whining proposals. My divorce coincided with – or perhaps produced – a state of panic in Maman. Nothing I could do or say would convince her of my sanity. I believe it is called an anxiety state or fit or something like that. In the course of it, Maman projected her own madness on to me. She even sacked the maid and refused to employ another, drudging away at her own menial chores on the grounds that we must not allow any strangers to see me.

I telegrammed to Agnes to come over from the Island and try to help soothe her. I took us away to Selsey to spend a windy Easter on the beach. I played patience with her until my own patience was virtually maimed for life. I even, as a last resort, allowed the redhead out of its cage to see if it could get through to her, but of course it made her worse – so much so that after the exeat, Maman peaked into a crisis.

That was when I decided to marry Peter. He had been chauffeuring me around for some months, and although I found his conversation hard to follow, at least it wasn't boring. And he was, in his way, the most eligible man I could marry at such short notice. He was eligible in Maman's eyes, not mine. But then, I was marrying him for Maman.

CHAPTER 18

ON the Island, when Harry and the other children came to play, we sat on the cliff and pulled the daisies and the clovers out of their leaves and tore them apart to find out who loved whom. The daisies were the best: 'He loves me, he loves me not, he loves me, he loves me not.' I dismembered daisies for Harry, and he for me, but when we were on our own he cheated and ripped his flower apart, calling out, 'She loves me, she loves me, and only me.' I loved Harry. I thought I loved Nelson when he first infatuated me, but I didn't, as it turned out. After him, I know I never loved anyone else. Flirting isn't love. It is a cure, a remedy.

When I married Peter, I didn't love him at all, but his feelings for me were enough for both of us – although they quickly cloyed and turned to something sour. That liaison always left a bitter taste, but it served its purpose. It showed Maman that I was normal. It proved to her that she had nothing to fear. Also, it lifted the air of scandal that had settled over our house in Hendon.

Peter was like the man in the pantomime, he insisted on seeing things his way, despite the shouting from the audience. The stalls and the circle were all calling, 'Behind you!' but Peter could only look ahead. I warned him to expect nothing from me. I told him I would give him nothing. I had nothing to give.

He said, 'Do you love me a little bit, Kitty?'

And I told him, 'No.'

But he didn't believe me. 'You're such a tease,' he'd laugh.

Life was a joke to him, the whole of it from morning until night. Yet his good humour didn't rise to a sense of humour. He had asked me many times to marry him. He was more stubborn than any of the others in that. So one day, I said 'Yes'. To marry is not to love. I did want to marry him, I wanted to set Maman's

187

mind at ease. I told him very clearly that I would never have another child, and that we would keep separate rooms. And that was fine. Everything was 'fine' before the wedding.

I don't know why I humoured him then as I did. I think I wanted to make sure there was no calling off. After years of being the refuser, I suddenly grew anxious about getting to the altar. I even went to the redhead's convent with him and pretended not to hate it for an afternoon. Yes, I kept my lip from curling as it came crawling towards us. Perhaps that was my mistake. Peter got the wrong impression. He actually invited it down to his place in the country.

Maman is not the only one to have her delusions. Perhaps from spending so much time with her, from listening to her wishful thinking and her nostalgia, I began to fantasise as well. I hoped that by marrying Peter we might, once again, have somewhere beautiful to live. I knew it would never be Claremont, but it might have been elegant and comfortable, and Maman could have back some of the attention she was pining for. Peter was like putty in my hands, he did as I wished, I could shape him into as many forms as I chose. I tested him during our courtship, inventing caprices just to see how he would respond. No whim was too bizarre or difficult for him to satisfy.

He seemed like the perfect guardian for Maman and me. He put his income at my disposal, he took over the redhead's fees and he bought me the loveliest emeralds I have ever owned, lovelier than the ones Daddy brought me and more beautiful than any of the single stones, rings and brooches that my other beaux had donated to the green fund.

My engagement cured Maman. It turned her back from the long squalid tunnel she had embarked down and led her out into the sunlight she so loved. She grew younger again, and began to notice the world around her and positively to enjoy it. When she talked of Jersey it was no longer with the air of a drowned sea captain feeling the waves lapping over his dead face on a foreign shore. She held her head a fraction higher as she strode down the High Street, and she pulled out some of her better clothes from their mothballs and wore them again, ready to take up her new position as mother-in-law. Maman had a weird fascination with the law. She talked about it as though it sat on the chimneypots of our squat little house, sword in hand, waiting to swoop down and chastise the Roberts of Claremont, singled out by their disgrace for the cat-o'-nine-tails, or a prison cell or transportation to the colonies. The law was under her pillow, and eavesdropping from the hard centre of her ball of silk. It was lurking in the kitchen and hiding behind the potted palm in the conservatory. It followed her into shops, and sat with her in the park. It had its eye on us. It had a gibbet marked out in an invisible design at our gate. The law and the Church, those were the two ends of the rack that tortured her.

The redhead murdered my dreams. It tried to break my heart, but I didn't let it. Maman could have come to live with us in Eaton Square, she could have spent her summers at Haddersly Hall, tending a real garden. That Yorkshire garden had few bushes in it, no proper shrubberies or long herbaceous borders clamouring at its walls. It had no lavender banks, or lilies on its ponds, no water hyacinths, no winter jasmine or dark camellias. She could have spent her old age happily pottering about a garden of her own creation. She could have had her own vines, and orchids too, had it not been for the redhead.

As it was, no sooner had we finished with the registrar, and placed the thin gold band beside my emerald engagement ring, than a battle began that was to end in the undoing of all my plans. Peter had already consented to the idea of Maman coming to live with us. I wouldn't have married him otherwise. But he insisted that the redhead come too. He even wanted to withdraw it from the convent so that it could act as a full-time pollution. He said he had always assumed that to be my design. The topic was like a fungus: it grew and spread and rotted away the tenuous threads of that one-sided *amour*. He claimed that the only reason he had accepted my stipulation of no children was because I already had one for him to adopt.

Our honeymoon was extremely tedious as a result of all this nonsense. I reached the point, within the first week, when I couldn't bear to have the subject broached. It seemed that the matter had dropped and fallen back into the pit it lived in when Peter completely changed towards me. I was making arrangements at Eaton Square to move Maman in with us (in the first-floor sitting-room, which was light and grand and nicer than any of the actual bedrooms) when my husband mutinied. He told me that Maman could come only if the redhead came too. And he was perfectly stubborn about it. I tried everything, I teased, cried, screamed and sulked, but he just ignored me. He said it was his house, and he was my husband, and he would tell me what to do.

I reminded him, of course, that until a few days before he had held none of these strictures. He looked at me, avoiding the direct gaze of my eyes, and he said in a stupid Yorkshire brogue, 'Where I come from, they say you don't run after a bus once you've caught it.'

So it was war. No, I think before the war it was just stalemate. The unpleasantness came later. I think Maman enjoyed her visit to Haddersly Hall. But that was even more cruel in a way. It reminded her of things she'd missed, only to take them away again. Yes, I think that was what finally unhinged her, because she was so well for that summer of 1930.

'Peter, Peter, pumpkin eater, had a wife and couldn't keep her.' He tried to frighten me, and he tried to hurt me. He wanted to take away what little I had left in the world. I married him so that he would give me more, so that Maman could settle, so that we would become honourable people once again. But instead he schemed and practised to destroy me. Just think how it hurt Maman to live on her own in Hendon without me to comfort her. That in itself was a cruelty. But he was a cruel man. Underneath all his smiles and his banality, he was a tyrant. As it became clear that I would not give in to him, he began to taunt me and get on my nerves.

I kept my temper with him for an inhumanly long time. I wanted to bring Maman away from Hendon permanently, so I ignored his wretched, nagging, stupid complaints, with only the odd lapse in my patience. He seemed to think that a short flash of my eyes and a few retorts in self-defence constituted some new kind of evil, and he became self-righteous and puritanical. One day he picked up his mother's Bible and, spreading his wide hand across the inlaid leather, he said, 'I swear by my mother's death that I'll never be a part of your cruelty to Joan.'

He looked so utterly ridiculous, with his upper lip quivering and the tears gathering in his eyes and the veins throbbing on the back of his outstretched hand, that I laughed. Who wouldn't have? People don't sit in their drawing-rooms vowing things on graves. We weren't in an Italian operetta, we were civilised people living in a civilised world. As I sat laughing in my chair, with my head tipped back to ease the stitch that was forming in my side from all his absurdities, Peter reached across and slapped my face.

I put the power back into my eyes. I summoned up the wrongs I had buried in the hopes of helping my maman, I ceased to tease him any more. Instead I told him all the things I knew about him that he didn't know. I showed him his own family. Introduced him to them, one by one. I told him all the thoughts that circled around the dinner table and remained unspoken. I told him my own thoughts of him. I made him shrink.

At first, he kept trying to apologise. But what is done is done. He came to my room that night and tried to kiss me. Then he kept to his own room for a day or two, healing the scratches. Kisses are for friends, not for enemies. Where was the kissing in the war? He had tricked me; used me for his own deranged schemes. The Honourable Robert Peel. From the time I had first decided to marry him, I called him Peter, because he was the rock on which I planned to build my Church, Maman's Church. Instead of rock, though, there was quicksand, and quicksands can kill. He cheated me, but he couldn't really hurt me, because I didn't love him at all. It wasn't like with Harry or Daddy or Maman, or myself where the weight of my emotion can cloud what I can see. All I had to do was look at Peter and I knew just what he was thinking, just what he was planning to do. I knew he'd come with his corny old ex-army gun and try to shoot me, and I knew he wouldn't have the nerve to do it if the redhead was there. So I beat him – I did the one thing he would never have guessed, I climbed into its bed and foiled his coup. It was there in the beginning and at the end.

After that fiasco, I wiped out the traces of Peter as best I could. Maman stopped voicing her fears, which seemed to return a little in the months after I left Yorkshire. I think she had learnt her lesson, although she was cheated of her prize: we were two normal people, two sane human beings, two women living together in the straitjacket of our penury, with no other scourge to fear but the vengeful machinations of the redhead.

From time to time, Maman would still have lapses. They were invariably provoked by the human giraffe. It could cause trouble even in its absence. It had become insolent and defiant. It feared me because I saw through it. It even dared to look at my boyfriends with lust. It was disgusting. Not that I hadn't always known it would be a slut. It was in its nature. Even as a small child it was forever pawing Agnes, and begging to be touched. Some of these things can be corrected. What use would education be if they could not? I tried. I never let it call me Mother, or wanted to be one, or liked the terrible burden of my lot. But I was a good mother to it in that. I tried as hard as any mother could to mend its ways. And but for Maman's weakness I might have succeeded, at least, in the basic decencies.

However, the strain was always there. The crack was visible and Maman, for all her resignation, still cried 'remember'. What else could I do? I loved her, I was her daughter, her only daughter. I was all she had. Whenever I could, I gave her the beach to soothe her. I gave her the sea. She used to ask for it. Maman could stare out at the sea for hours on end. And I held the skeins of her silk for her, and I listened to her memories of Jersey, hearing again and again the heartache she felt for our lost island. I went to Mass with her, and prayed with her, and tended her in her last long years. What else could I do? I was her daughter.

I didn't want her to go into the nursing home. Chislehurst was such a long way away. I would have nursed her at home. Her illness came very quickly when it came. It had always been a germ before, and a limp. Thank God she was spared the pain. I've heard that cancer can hurt quite terribly. But Maman just had her limp. Her pain came from her exile and the burden of the redhead dragging at her side, and her shame. She was afraid to die. She told me herself. She was afraid to leave me. I had protected her for so long, it must have felt very lonely having to make her last journey on her own. I told her I would be with her because she would be with me in my head, in her last days, but that made her more afraid. It was death itself that terrified her.

I had become so used to our being together, just the two of us.

We were so close. I missed her when she died. I missed her everywhere in the house. Sometimes I slept in her bed, trying to trace her presence there for me. Elsa Müller used to sit with me sometimes in the evening and play my records for me. She used to tidy the house up, too. The maids disintegrated after Maman died. They were the beginning of the end. The first step on a ladder that descended into brickdust and weeping.

I felt Maman's fears in my head long after she died. I felt them more than I ever had while she was alive. They stayed like a wedge in my brain, leaving a great gap exposed to the open air. The winter was cold. The fires kept going out, so I gave up the house. It was Maman who had chosen Hendon. I left it after she died. I moved into the West End, and lived in a hotel. That was when I realised how easily Maman could have done so too, had she not had the impediment of that demonic child. It wasn't a nice hotel. The people weren't nice. Maybe Maman would not have liked it after all. Except . . . she could have stayed on the Island. She would have liked that. She needed that.

It was the war that undid everything. It unpicked all the stitches in Maman's crochet. It scattered all my friends. The ones who were left became very boring, like people whose ideas have drained away. And they began to whisper. Not in the way people do, behind my back. They came to see me, and they whispered so that their voices were inaudible over my own thoughts. Perhaps they had nothing interesting left to say. Every night there was a blackout, and the darkness troubled me.

I remember, it was on July the 1st 1940 when the Germans occupied the Island. I heard it on the BBC. That was about the time the fighting started inside my head. Too many people were dying. They kept trying to get through to me, to go through me with their last moments. There were too many. They hurt my eyes. They would have killed me if they could. It was war. There was no respect for the civilians. No respect for anyone. Some people said the war would end. But it never did. They said the country had been riddled with spies for years before it started. We had one in our house. They say they don't all speak German, but there are telltale signs that give them away.

I've been a prisoner for years. They took me during the Blitz. I didn't see them coming because my head was already damaged by the other casualties. They took my emeralds away, stole them, and my clothes. It's very boring behind these bars. I keep wondering what the Germans will have done to Claremont. I keep remembering things, and remembering is what passes the hours, and talking – to myself, because there is no one else to hear. There are only spies, spies and spies. The walls have ears, loose talk costs lives. They stole my emeralds, but I still have my eyes.

PART III

Poor Florence

CHAPTER 19

I WAS born in Grantham in Lincolnshire in 1869, and my sister Violet was born two years later; Ivy was the youngest. Although I could remember Grantham very clearly after we moved to Jersey, my mother always told me I couldn't, that I was too young. All she wanted us to bring to the Island were our good manners, our names and surnames and an occasional mention of Berry Place, the house where she was born. My father was a doctor, the son of French Huguenots who had fled and settled in England. He was clever, kind and tolerant and he loved our mother very much. When she got cross with him, which was rather often, he used to twirl his moustache and say, 'I'm as proud as punch to have such a beautiful grumpy wife.'

Our mother was tall and had what were known as classical features, and her hair was strawberry blonde with white silken wisps around her forehead like a baby's hair. She too was very much in love, and sometimes, when Father solved a particularly difficult case or put up a particularly lovely Christmas decoration, she could be very proud of him, but she could never quite forget that she was a Berry, of Berry Place, who had married beneath her.

Once we moved to Jersey, people sought out the Huguenot link and found in it one of our highest recommendations. To Mother's chagrin, no one had heard of the Berrys there, but everyone had heard of — or was related to, however far back in their past — a Huguenot. The neighbours said it made us almost one of them, almost like born Islanders. So, right from the beginning, Jersey was good to us. We moved there because Father was dying. He had consumption, and the dank air of the Lincolnshire fens had brought him into a decline from which, contrary to his own and his colleagues' medical judgement, he partially recovered.

Although he was only in his mid forties at the time, he lost his strength, and decided that the only hope of prolonging his life and avoiding a recurrence of the fatal tuberculosis was to move into a perfect climate. The choice lay between Switzerland and the Channel Islands, and he chose Jersey because he had been at school with a boy who spent his holidays there and he himself had always wanted to live among palm trees.

Mother's family regarded our decampment to the Island as yet another sign of my father's foreignness and inferiority. They couldn't understand anyone wishing to move away from the edifying shadows of the gates of Berry Place. Nobody, not even the Berrys, I believe, ever denied Father's skills as a doctor, or his erudition in certain other fields, or his wonderful manners, but behind the backs of their hands, and behind his back, there was always a hint of an objection. It was not quite *comme il faut* to be French. There were scarcely any foreigners in Grantham.

There were a number of French people in Lincoln itself, nestling ostentatiously under the lovely cathedral with their second- and third-generation accents and their claims to lands and titles seized from them during the Revolution. Father had friends there. He had been to school there, to the cathedral school, and he had sung in the cathedral choir. Grantham was a small town, though, and it seemed a long way from Lincoln, and foreigners were regarded with suspicion. People talked about them, and watched them – a little less closely than the wandering gypsies, but with something of the same misgiving. It was foreign to have been born far from Berry Place, and unforgivably so not to be able to weave your heritage into its history, whether by descent or service.

Beyond the parish boundaries of Grantham lay the county of Lincolnshire, and beyond the borders of Lincolnshire lay the sprawling, less fortunate but still friendly neighbouring counties of England, protected, by God's foresight, by the sea. Anyone who came from across that water was at a severe disadvantage, despite any anthropological interest such immigrants might arouse. The miscegenation had been carefully mapped out and recorded. There was an Italian mason living in Sleaford, and in between Sleaford and Grantham, in a small farmstead along that bleak, raised fenland road, there was a Negro who had married a local girl and tended her sheep with her, and their own brood of gingery-skinned woolly-haired children. Then there were the Royalists of Lincoln, and within bugling distance of the moss-stained and stately Berry Place there was Dr Martin, my father, who had increased his gossip value by at least a hundredfold when he carried off the Berrys' youngest daughter.

Our life completely changed once we moved to Jersey, and all the changes were for the better. It was, for Violet and me, like moving to paradise. Contrary to Mother's wishes, I remembered our life in Grantham and I used to describe our house there, our nursery, and the town itself to my sisters. It was Violet who took the greatest interest in our birthplace. She didn't really remember it except for certain images that needed my help to make sense to her. So I would tell her of the shape and size of our mid-terrace house with its stone windowframes and its slate and pammet floors and its steep staircase turning up through three storeys, and its narrowness and the smells of food that rose up from the kitchen and the smells of snuffed candles that clung to the curtains and the overriding smell of dampness that was the hallmark of the Fens.

Lincoln has remained in my memory like a county of black and green, like a bruise on its first day of healing. The fields around Grantham were black, because the earth was black and muddy and the mud seemed to encroach into the town. The smoke from all the chimneys was black, and the smoke from the brickworks was black, and although the bricks themselves were a bright, dusty orange when they were new and stood in stacks beside the kilns, the smoke from their making blackened the bricks of all the houses and made them look very old. In winter, it was black and shadowy in our attic nursery with its small windows and its long nights that fell and wrapped the town in darkness hours before our bedtime. The gates of Berry Place, where we were taken to visit once a month, were black, and the moss and ivy clung together in between black and green, darkened by the cedar trees and the tall pines, laurels and hollies that dripped their dank shadows over the drive and round the square, uncompromising, ageless house.

Then there was the green. There was the summer green of elders and hawthorns that grew on the common on the edge of the town, and the green of front gardens and the green of the new wheat growing in the fields. In winter there was more green than in summer, because there was the green of mould that grew over everything inside the house and over every wall and tree trunk and piece of iron. Our shoes and clothes and windowsills were green, as were the backs of wardrobes and the insides of drawers.

I used to think the whole world was covered with mildew, just as all people were covered with skin. The only place that was any different was the beach at California, where Father took us once in our last summer there, to show us the sea so that we would not be afraid of it when we made the crossing to the Channel Islands. I can still remember that first sight of it, stretching out to the horizon in the most wondrous pattern of shifting greys – Just as I can still remember our crossing to the Island in the half-empty packet from Weymouth harbour that tossed and rolled all the way to St Helier.

We settled in the manor of St John, in the north; renting first one house, then another. Father had done his homework: the doctor who had lived at St John until the winter before had gone senile and was confined to his house and unable to deal with any of his former patients. Because the old man was still alive, though, no one had dared to replace him – that is, until we moved in, transformed by some cross-Channel osmosis from lesser Berry of Berry Place, to the Martins from England. Father was, indeed, a clever man. He didn't move to St John as a doctor, one who hoped to make a good living out of his skills. Instead, he moved as a man of slender means who was himself convalescing.

We didn't, of course, mention the consumption in so many words; his recent malady was known as 'lung trouble brought on by the damp'. So he sat in a high chaise longue in the window of the pretty study that gave on to the street with a book in his hand and a telescope tucked almost, but not quite, out of sight behind him. Every morning he took a ride through the village and the outlying hamlets, stopping to pass the time of day with everyone. He let it be known by all and sundry that he was a doctor, a medical man who had come to Jersey to take the air, and what excellent air it was.

Within weeks the burns and the cuts, the births and the deaths, the oyster poisoning and the gout of St John's parish were being brought plaintively to his door.

'Excuse me, Ma'am, but could Dr Martin possibly come out to Mrs Dauvergne up at the Hall?' It was an emergency, and there wasn't time to call in the doctor from Ville à l'Évêque. Or it was 'Is your father at home? Could we call on him, do you think? The baby has fallen ill and we don't know where else to take him.' And Father always made his 'sacrifice' and pulled himself out of his premature and pretended retirement until gradually he became established as the doctor, with patients in three parishes and a great many friends. And he prospered, as he had never been able to under the belittling patronage of his in-laws.

Violet and I attended the dame school run by the Misses Grandin. We learnt French and English reading and writing, and we learnt the names of all the flowers on the Island, and we learnt plain sewing and crochet and the bits of the history of the Channel Islands that reflected best on Jersey. When Ivy was old enough she joined us there, and became a great favourite with the younger Miss Grandin. But of all the children in the school, no one was more popular than my sister Violet. She was my parents' pride as well. Father called her 'his darling', and Mother called her 'a Berry through and through'.

Violet had light-brown hair that gathered on its own into silken ringlets and she had inherited, more than either of us other two, Mother's classical features, with the high forehead and the straight nose and chin. She also had an extraordinarily pale skin. Whenever the summer came, and we made our treks to school and further afield to the beaches at St John and Bonne Nuit Bay, I used to tan to a most unladylike brown all over my face, no matter how large or tight a bonnet I wore. And if I removed my gloves – which I was not allowed to do, but sometimes did – the backs of my hands would become gilded in an afternoon. Violet, however, was never affected by the weather. She had a complexion as fair as a guillemot's breast, whose startling loveliness was capped by very clear, very large green eyes. She was a beautiful child – so beautiful that neighbours seeing us on our way to school would pause to admire her and, seeing my own pretty, but far more ordinary looks, would murmur, 'Poor Florence'.

At home, Father would pet Violet, and lift her to his knee and cover her hair with kisses, and then, looking down at me, he too would say, 'Poor Florence, we mustn't make you jealous.'

And so it was at school and everywhere, this misapprehension of my poverty. Nobody understood how happy I was, and content, and as proud as any of them of my sister's beauty. I loved Violet. I loved being with her and basking in the reflection of her glory. I loved the bright funny things she said, and the pages and pages of drawn flowers she gave me. She had a passion for sketching that none of us others shared. Father said his maternal grandfather had been a painter until the Revolution, and had been the master of a fine studio with students and visitors from all over Europe. Soldiers had gone one day to close down his atelier and arrest him, but he had been warned and managed to escape. He sent word to his family that he had fled to Lyons, after which he was never heard of again; although a stranger in a brown cape had stopped my grandmother in the fruit market of Les Halles and whispered that he was dead. When we were children, we liked to think that Madame La Guillotine had cut off his head. We often played a rather gruesome game of trying our rag dolls and sentencing them, before wheeling them through a clearing behind the shrubbery and re-enacting their death. We even devised a way of unstitching a doll's head, so that at the drop of a plank of wood it would loll off.

Sometimes, later, when anyone asked me if I didn't think my own Kitty was too spiteful, I would remember that game and realise how all children can be cruel. Its memory veiled for me, for a long time, the fact that Kitty, my daughter, who was Violet incarnate, was actually different from the rest. Yet she had so many kindnesses about her, and so many ways that came straight from my dear sister, that I loved her the more for it, or despite it. Kitty was a victim of circumstance, a beautiful flower transplanted into the wrong soil.

Back in the eighties, though, in my childhood, I can remember no hardships at all. I lived a life without trials. At weekends and on holidays, I would sometimes help my father to prepare his surgery. He was very meticulous, and he liked to do everything himself.

'How can I keep it clean if Marie passes over everything with her dirty mop and duster every day? If I ask her to keep it extra clean, she spreads the rest of the household dirt over my instruments twice a day. Twice as dirty. What do you say?'

Father believed in salt. He said the Romans had used it to bathe all their wounds in after battles, and that it could stay the course of gangrene, so it could do only good to his cases of instruments with their spikes and hooks, lancing knives, scalpels and even saws. He also had beautiful books, mostly in Latin and in French, with diagrams of bones and veins. I have never known anyone love their work so well – except, perhaps, for Violet herself, when she became a painter and moved to London and made the miniatures that looked as lovely as the ones we saw in Italy.

Around our house, Father planted a hedge of rosemary. It was never as trim as the box and privet and tall Portuguese laurel hedges of our neighbours, with its unruly spikes and its aromatic flowers. Mother would have preferred something more traditional, but the rosemary was popular with passers-by who picked it for their dinners, and Father said it was very healthy to be surrounded by its healing powers.

I never understood why I was referred to as 'poor Florence'. I wasn't poor at all. In Grantham, at the far end of the town, there was a road that muddied into a track along which we sometimes drove, and the families who lived in the crumbling piles of bricks on either side were poor. Their children were barefoot, even in winter. And their clothes were ragged and much much uglier than ours, and they were all very thin and dirty and they scarcely ever brushed their hair. At the end of the track, looking out across the great flatness of the Berry fields through the thick black bars of its railings, there was a poorhouse, which was much larger than any of the other cottages. On Sunday afternoons, after our dinner, Father and his friends used to discuss what they called 'the dreadful state of the Poor Laws', which I could tell must be very dear to them, particularly to Father, since we ourselves were poor in-laws; a fact I had gleaned from Berry Place.

On the Island there were no such streets and no such houses, yet my nickname followed me all the way from Lincolnshire. I didn't mind it, I just didn't understand it. I felt like the most privileged child in the world, living as I did with my family so near to the sea, in that place of bright colours and warm days and long evenings, with Violet beside me, and the mildew of my earliest memories raised like new flags into palm trees.

Later, when Dickie died and I became a widow, and Kitty came home from Canada on her own, the name I had lost through most of the middle years of my life returned, settled and stayed. It was Emily de Gruchy who recoined it, and I realised I had probably been called it as a child so that I would get used to it, and find a certain familiarity in its sound, and feel not so much the pity but the sympathy. For I was never poor. Even during the worst years, I always had Joan to sustain me, and Kitty to care for. Father used to say, 'There is no time to feel sorry for yourself, so long as there are others who need you more.'

CHAPTER 20

FATHER had not expected to live for more than a few years after we moved to the Island, so when he did, he saw this prolongation as a gift from God. He had always been a devout man, but he became more so with each new year. St John itself was a devout parish. At least a third of the parishioners were Methodists, who worshipped in their own chapel and were far stricter in their observances than anybody else. A number of my friends were Methodists, and although I was fond of them I found their tastes and houses too plain for my liking. They seemed to worship all that was simple in a way that reminded me too much of the bare flatness of the Fens. There also, the low, brick, Wesleyan chapels had abounded. But I believe it was more of a stigma to be a Methodist in Lincolnshire, where the boundaries were drawn more firmly than on the Island.

Most of us were Anglicans, and worshipped in the big granite church that stood in its garden of yew trees at the crossroads, with its rectory on one side and its cemetery over the road. There were three Catholic families in the village but they all lived on the outskirts, in big houses, and were rather grand. Father attended them professionally, and as soon as we girls became eligible to attend their soirées and dances, the 'Miss Martins were asked to attend'. We were known everywhere as the Miss Martins, even before Violet and Ivy were of an age to be called that. So at first it was just me, with Violet allowed to accompany me sometimes as a treat for both of us. We were all very close. When one of us went shopping for ribbons, the other two always went along, and when one of us had a secret, the other two were told. I couldn't help being closer to Violet, though, because she was so lovely, and her nature was so sweet, it drew me to her, just as it did everyone else. At dances, Violet's card would be full of partners before the evening really began.

When Violet was first ill, Father kept hoping that whatever ailment it was would pass with dieting and exercise. He told me later that he should have recognised the symptoms of his own disease, but he could not bear to see them reproduced in his own daughter. He didn't say favourite daughter, but of course she was. Her illness seemed very gradual, as though it were sucking her from the upstairs of our house, with its row of bedrooms, to the day bed in the sitting-room and then out of the door, and away across the Channel.

By the time she was eighteen, she bore some of the marks of her consumption: the red flush on her pale cheeks at night, the slight pain in her side, and the coughing fits, but there were no telltale spots of blood on her handkerchiefs. So her initial weakness was treated as many things. It was hoped to be growing pains and feared to be anaemia; it was said to be a weakness of a kidney and the aftermath of a chill caught dancing on a neighbour's lawn when the dew was particularly heavy. Father dosed her with all his salts and patent remedies, the tonic wines and liver oils, the beef teas and the calf's-foot jellies that were customary then.

Some days Violet would feel better, and sometimes she would actually seem to recover, and get up, and sit in the garden under our favourite apple tree, and the malady would appear to be beaten. But then there would follow the inevitable relapse. Father continued to follow the course of her daily graph; and Mother continued to fuss around her angelic daughter, inventing her own regimen in a less scientific and more random way. One day she would insist that Violet remain on the day bed and read, and she would go to St Helier and bring back the latest instalment of Charles Dickens for her, to ensure that Violet's interest was held and she would stay put. The next day she would confiscate the half-finished episode, claiming that reading was tiring and bad for her.

After Mother had tried all the contradictory cures she could think of, she swallowed her pride and wrote to the Berrys to ask their advice. The Berrys of Berry Place, who had felt purposely slighted when we moved, wrote twice, through the pen of our grandmaman, to say that the only conceivable chance of forgiveness and a reconciliation would be our immediate return to Lincolnshire. Our failure to comply resulted in a rift that had lasted at least ten years. Mother had continued to send Christmas greetings, and to remember her family from time to time and send them letters that kept them up to date with our good fortune, good health and prosperity. These letters – whether to her mother, her father, or any of her numerous brothers and sisters – remained pointedly unanswered.

Had Mother been even the tiniest bit less proud of her ancestry, she would have stopped writing on the receipt of these regular silent snubs. But she had been bred a Berry, and she believed there wasn't a finer family in the world, and any amount of rebuff was worth suffering so long as it was at the aristocratic hands of her own mother and not the infinitely more plebeian hands of anybody else. She had fallen in love with Father as a girl, when he had splinted her broken arm after a fall and left it, after seven weeks of treatment, as beautifully formed as ever a Berry elbow could be. She had been bred to be headstrong, and when she insisted on marrying Father, after failing to forget him throughout a year-long separation, she had been shown just how chilly an ancient family can be. They showed her that a fall from a horse and a broken arm were as nothing compared to the fall from grace that inevitably followed when a Berry married beneath her.

I think, as well, that Mother kept writing her letters because she genuinely wanted to show how well-to-do and grand we were becoming as a family, and how well received we were in all the big houses, and how Father was no longer just the doctor, he was Dr Martin, and always used the front door. However, this was obviously not the sort of news her offended family wanted to hear. Perhaps the news of Violet's illness had a sweeter ring to their ears. There was a chance to write back and say 'I told you so'. There was a chance to show how a careless move could damage a young girl's health.

After a decade of silence, the Berrys replied. The postman brought my grandmaman's black-stamped letter to the door. Mother was so surprised when the letter was carried up to her that she had to use her smelling salts. I always associate Grandmother Berry with the sharp unpleasant shock of sal volatile. She wrote, under the embossed heading of her letter,

Dear Charlotte,

It is obvious that what your daughter needs is a change of air. Send her to Berry Place on the first of next month. Edgar will meet her at the station. She must catch the train that arrives at noon, which will give her time to change for luncheon. If the child is as Berry as you say she is, she will be welcome. It is to her credit that she does not thrive on foreign soil.

You may spare us the details of the preposterous dot that you have so wilfully chosen to move to.

I remain,

Your Mama

Mother interpreted this letter as a full welcome back into the fold. She told us, 'Mamma hides her feelings. She always did. But she's very particular about who she invites to stay. We were only allowed to spend afternoons there when we were in Grantham.'

I felt my heart shrink when that distant invitation was read to us. I hoped Father would never let little Violet go. I didn't know, then, that the mould I remembered would actually hasten Violet's death, but I sensed that the coldness of the family, and the coldness I remembered in my bones, would hurt her, because they would hurt me. It would be unbearable to be away from my sister. But Father had been worrying about his child and about the confusing pattern of her symptoms. He had called in another doctor, an eminent colleague from St Helier who had examined her and prescribed 'a change of air'. He mistook her lethargy and pallor as signs of boredom and, with a typical disregard of one doctor for another, he pooh-poohed Father's worries about anything more spectacular.

Father never forgave himself for letting Violet go. He blamed himself for failing to chart the signals of her decline accurately enough to have known that a spell in the Fens would be the last thing she needed. His own decline dated from the time when Violet returned, wasted and branded by the vermilion spots on her cheeks. As to Violet herself, she had always been curious about the Berrys, and she wanted to see them, so although she was sorry to leave us, she was excited about the journey.

Father accompanied her on her travels, all the way to Grantham station, where he saw her safely into the care of the waiting Edgar.

She stayed at Berry Place all through August, writing almost every day with letters full of sketches of her cousins, aunts and uncles and our monosyllabic grandfather who was a mumbling martyr to his gout, and the vociferous ageing matriarch who was our grandmother. It seemed that Violet made a hit in Lincolnshire. The family proclaimed her to be 'all Berry' which, as she wrote, 'was all berry well, but isn't there something more to life?'

By the end of August her letters became tinged with homesickness, and by September they were trickling through at the rate of no more than two a week – posted, as she told us, by a local girl named Rumsey who worked as maid and skivvy and general scapegoat among a formidable hierarchy of dour staff. It was Rumsey, so she told us, who eased some of the spartan household rules for her, and kept her abreast of the current state of the family feuds which, apparently, were constant and petty. When Violet's letters ceased, abruptly, in mid September, both Mother and Father wrote to enquire after her. For three weeks their escalating worries were met by polite but firm rebuffs from Grandmamma herself: 'Violet is doing well, she has taken a slight chill but has quite recovered.'...'Violet is too engrossed in her cousins to write for herself, but she sends her regards.'...'Violet has promised to write' – yet there was no sign from Violet herself. Nor would there have been, had not Rumsey sent a misspelt message to 'the Iland of Jersy' saying 'Vilet will die if you do not come for her.'

Both Mother and Father left on the next sailing. I remember the day because it was October the 5th, my birthday. I was twenty years old and I promised myself, and I promised God, and I promised the rough waves on the sea, that if Violet lived I would give all the rest of my own silly life in gratitude and praise for that mercy. The three days they were gone seemed the longest I had ever known. All the happiness and safety of our lives was suddenly eaten away. We all of us changed after that, the whole family. Ivy, who was sixteen and almost as scared as I, clung to me. We wept for three days, as though our sister had already died, and then, on the third day, a strange carriage brought her back to me.

It was the Island that saved her, even though the turning chestnut leaves were showing signs of winter. The weather was mild, and stayed mild for the weeks that were needed to bring her back from her wrecked and wretched condition to something approaching her former self.

Then the tide turned, and now it was time for Grandmother Berry to write to her daughter and ask her forgiveness. Grandmother said she loved Violet more than any of her other granddaughters, and when she took ill, with what was only a chill, she thought she would cure her before telling us. When the chill turned into bronchitis, and Violet's fever rose, she had been afraid to admit it. When the illness increased, and Violet refused to break through the crisis, Grandmother hadn't known how to admit to being in the wrong. She had hoped and prayed and nursed her grandchild herself, sitting up with her to the exclusion of the nurse she had called.

Father blamed himself as much as his arrogant mother-in-law, and Mother lost the backbone of her pride. She had never detected a flaw in a Berry before, but with the neglect of her favourite daughter she suddenly seemed to find the whole basket of her blindly proud family rotten. She never forgave my grandmother, not even during the thirty-six months of respite that lasted from the time of their return to Jersey to the time Violet died.

As the Island air began to revive her, Violet began to pester for a prize. At first the idea was mixed into her delirious wanderings, but soon it emerged as a plea. If she got better, she wanted to go to Italy with me. Father would have promised her anything in the state she was in. She could have gone to Greenland or Patagonia, or to the Grand Canyon, or Timbuktoo. If it helped to calm her, and eased her fever, then Violet could have been granted any wish under the sun.

'If I live, Father, let me go to Italy, to Italy, please.'

And Father would rub her brow with a cloth dipped in pure alcohol, and with the tears in his eyes he'd say, 'Of course you shall go to Italy, darling, of course you shall.'

Then Violet, like Father before her, recovered from her illness, and she grew strong again on the mild sea breezes. By the spring of 1890 she was well, or so it seemed. Father had suffered from the same disease and lived for fifteen years, so far, as a healthy man. We none of us knew, not even Violet herself, that she was destined to die young. Meanwhile, her disordered longing to go to Italy had turned into a proper plan, aided by one of our neighbours who had loved Violet since she was a small child. She had agreed to chaperone the two of us for three months on the Continent, travelling through the South of France and on to Italy.

CHAPTER 21

FOR months before the trip began, we spent our winter practising and preparing for it. We had gathered together a handful of words and phrases, to which we added all the musical terms we knew, and thus produced a hotchpotch of fluency depending almost entirely on adverbs. Our life seemed to fill out proportionately, and swell with energy. We tried to behave as we thought Italians must. We had heard of their operatic qualities, and we exaggerated all we did to conform to this preconception. We no longer 'went' downstairs, we crept down *pianissimo*. Simple queries at the breakfast table would be met, not by a shake of the head or a smile, but by a negative *fortissimo*. One day, we tried to translate our feelings into entirely musical phrasing. Each day the *allegro* was *crescendo* to such a degree that by the time we finally set sail for France, the quieter members of our village and family must have been glad to see the back of our high spirits.

The excitement was unavoidable. We were going to Italy, the Queen of the Mediterranean, the home of the Romans and opera and beauty, the crowned monarch of painting. It was Violet who wanted to see the paintings; I was happy to accompany her. For me, the thrill of travelling with her, of having her to myself, of seeing her happy and (apparently) healthy, in the lovely surroundings of Liguria and Tuscany, were more than enough to satisfy my needs and even my wildest dreams.

Our chaperone was a widow called Mrs Travis-Clemmons. She had very thin hair at the top, which she covered with her bun and a twist of artificial hair that gave her more problems than any we encountered on our tour until the disaster struck. She was also plump, and suffered from the heat, and had what must have amounted to an addiction to lemon drops. An entire portmanteau of her luggage was reserved for carrying these sharp boiled sweets. It was always the first piece of baggage to be checked on arrival, and its loading was most lovingly supervised by Mrs Travis-Clemmons in person.

In a way, I owe everything to those lemon drops, for had not the case that held them gone astray somewhere between Pisa and Florence, Mrs Travis-Clemmons would not have retired to our *pension* to mourn them so deeply that Violet and I were left on our own. For the first three days, we felt it our duty to remain within earshot of our chaperone. It was impossible to stay by her side for more than a few minutes at a time, though, because her grief was so vocal on the one hand, and so impenetrable on the other, that it seemed totally to exclude us.

Through the lonely years of her widowhood, Mrs Travis-Clemmons had consoled herself with her boiled sweets, getting to know the exact taste and tang of each one. They had their own vintages, just as the lemons used for them had their own harvests. One of the reasons, it seemed, that Mrs Travis-Clemmons travelled was to seek out and bring back new strains and variations of the lemon and the bitter lemon drop. Although in past years she had ferreted out all the available species in the sweet shops of France, Switzerland and Germany, and sampled them on the spot and shipped back more for careful comparison, the St Helier brand remained unbeaten. Despite this pride in being so close to the champion sweet, she hankered after some as yet undiscovered brand that would yield up the ultimate ecstasy in the line of boiled sweets.

Our chaperone's weakness for lemon drops was well known to us before ever we embarked. Her predilection was noticed with indulgence for many miles around our village. There was hardly a neighbour who had not, at one time or another, been stopped in their carriage or cart and asked, if they were going to St Helier, to 'bring back another half a pound of the best lemon drops from Lemprière Street'. Mrs Travis-Clemmons was also one of the prime organisers at the annual parish fête, and she grew some of her chrysanthemums specially for the harvest festival. When anyone in the village was ill, she made the best beef tea in St John, and her rosehip syrup was a byword in cold cures. So her obsession with lemon drops seemed harmless enough. It would certainly never have occurred to either of our parents as a reason for debarring her as a suitable travelling companion.

And yet, although all of us had seen her offering, saving, or sucking a lemon drop, and knew her character as it was when thus appeased, none of us had ever seen her deprived of her lifeline. From the amiable, easy-going guide, with one hand toying on the handle of her parasol and the other permanently dipped into the brocade bag that hung round her not inconsiderable waist, fingering her talismans, her mascots, her loves, the precious lemon drops, she became a wailing virago.

When the offending portmanteau failed to arrive, Mrs Travis-Clemmons immediately lost her self-control and began to shout not only at the carriers but also at curious passers-by. She pinched and pulled so at their clothes and persons that by the end of half an hour quite a crowd had gathered around the patch of the Lungarno that lay immediately outside our quiet hotel, and our gentle chaperone was purple in the face and clutching wisps of hair and bits of torn clothing, and although recognisable words no longer issued from her mouth, she continued to gasp out a garbled stream of protest. Mrs Travis-Clemmons was still muttering in her sleep that night after an English doctor had been summoned by the distressed landlady to sedate her.

By the end of the next morning, despite the alluring view of the Ponte delle Grazie arching across the river, our chaperone was lying inconsolably in her room, which invited one to cross and sit and contemplate the Arno and the city beyond it, with its mottled red domes and its enormous marble doorways a mere hundred yards from our hotel door. But Mrs Travis-Clemmons' condition ruled out any sightseeing or even simple musing. Between her fits of weeping, she would rise up and wring her hands or thump her breast in a way that looked quite painful.

'What can you girls know of grief?' she would complain. 'How can you understand what it is to lose that which is dearest in the world? First it was Mr Travis-Clemmons, and that seemed like the hardest blow a member of the gentler sex should ever have to bear. But now ... now ...' she wailed, smiting her corsets dramatically, 'my darlings have been taken from me, stolen, robbed by brigands. Oh Violet, Florence, where can they be?'

She would sit and stand and sit again, made restless by the

combined weights of her emotion and her tortured flesh. The last of her surviving lemon drops had been sucked and eaten as an antidote to the shock of the loss of their companions. The contents of her suitcases and trunk and travelling bag were tipped out on to the bed and carpet in a series of disordered heaps.

'Girls, girls, think of the little ones, the yellow diamonds that I found in Munich, think of them in the unwashed hands of a ploughboy. Think of them, Violet, scattered across his field, imagine them trampled under his bare feet and then – no, no, it is too much. Florence, my smelling salts, and the plump sugary sweeties that I save for the evenings. Where are they? Was ever a Christian plagued like me?'

From sinking into these fits of pessimistic depression, our grief-stricken friend would suddenly round on us.

'Why didn't you notice what was happening? You have much sharper eyes than me. You should have seen. It is disgraceful that I have brought you two all the way from my source to this torture chamber, and this is how you thank me. I have never come across such ingratitude . . . My little ones, my bitter ones . . . Violet, run downstairs and see if there is any news. Florence, you must send back to the station. Both of you, you must go back and hunt through the luggage. What can these natives understand of life's fineries? Yes, you must order a carriage and bring my darling treasures back to me.'

Neither of us knew how to respond to her mercurial authority. One minute we would be rising to do as she bade, the next she would be pressing us back into our seats to enlarge on the merits of her culinary jewels.

Eventually, as Mrs Travis-Clemmons' energy ebbed away, and her rage subsided accordingly, her insistence that the railway station be searched and the offending parties brought back to her for interrogation prevailed. Violet and I were despatched, unchaperoned, across the city. The figure which (we had been told as we crossed from the French Riviera into Italy) had once been the toast of St Helier was rapidly returning to its former glory. Mrs Travis-Clemmons refused to eat. She said she would die rather than touch another morsel of food unflavoured by her customary delight.

After a confusing and unsuccessful trip to the station, Violet and I left our one-horse cab outside the pillars of the Uffizi gallery, and entered the city on foot, not meaning to fall in love so much as to ease our chaperone's broken heart by locating an Italian equivalent to the lemon drop. We found tiny mint drops, and sugared jellies and assorted nut toffees and what were definitely pineapple cubes, and almond meringue bars, and dozens of wine bars and stalls and lemon stalls, but no bitter lemon candies. It was the landlady who finally suggested that our good lady descend into the kitchens and supervise the making of a new batch of these sweets. It was by no means her first suggestion. Several times she had begged us to leave, to return home, to silence (if need be, with laudanum) our protesting chaperone. The other guests were complaining, she told us, and although she had explained that Mrs Travis-Clemmons was newly bereaved, her behaviour was considered excessive even for a widow, even in Italy.

For the next ten days, a precarious calm was restored to the Pensione Grande Bretagne while experiments took place in the kitchens. Pounds of sugar and lemons were boiled and tested, tasted and discarded, as gradually an acceptable replacement was found. Despite the turmoil that this produced below stairs, the landlady obviously preferred it to the wailing and pacing of the previous stage, and she encouraged our chaperone to remain over her labours for the best part of each day.

Meanwhile, we girls had the run of the city. It was hot, but not unbearably so, and from under our parasols we drank iced tea in the Piazza della Signoria, and strolled through the Boboli Gardens and the high vaulted salons of the Palazzo Pitti, and the dark alleyways that led from one square to another, stopping for hours to admire the cool churches with their clusters of thin candles and their darkly luminous murals.

Day after day we returned to the Uffizi, hurrying through the lovely corridors that were as wide as whole rooms and painted from floor to ceiling, in search of the Botticellis. Violet was in love with Botticelli. She worshipped his work in such a way that her own appetite for anything as mundane as food waned along with that of our once fat friend. Violet loved 'The Birth of Venus'. She stood in front of it for hours on end, staring into the sea and the whitecapped waves in a kind of ecstasy.

I confess that I used to grow restless, trying to adore the work as much as she. I loved the gentle face and the pale graceful body; they reminded me of Violet herself. I wondered if she noticed this, but it seemed almost sacrilegious to ask her. Whenever I think of Violet, I think of the sea, and vice versa. If I stare hard enough at the waves, I can almost fancy that I see her pale body rising up to keep the storms at bay on her ethereal shell.

I loved Violet so much, and missed her so, it was my greatest blessing to be given Kitty, as I was, born in her image. Mother thought it was quite uncanny when Kitty was born, looking so identical to her own lost daughter. She told me what I knew for myself: there had to be a connection. No one else I have ever seen or heard of had such emerald eyes. It made Mother cry once, because she said she feared that little Kitty's eyes came from beyond the grave. I remember it made me cross; at the time, Kitty was only three or four. Yet Mother was right.

Of course, I didn't know any of that then, when I was in Florence entranced by its beauty to such a degree that my feet never seemed to touch the cobbles and my neck locked into a stiff position from staring up at so many angels and frescoes. When we returned to Jersey, we were questioned very closely about our tour. No one could understand how we had left as two devout and happy members of the Church of England, and only a few months later returned, the two of us, as would-be Catholics. Had the Roman Church accepted us then and there, we would have embraced it on the spot – the delay was theirs, not ours. For even the Catholic Father at St Mary's and St Peter's Church in Vauxhall Street near the pier was wary of our sudden and unprecedented change of faith. 'Unprecedented' was Mother's word, drawn from the saddle of the high Berry horse which she mounted temporarily to try and dissuade her dissenting daughters.

Later, when anyone asked me how and why I changed from the religion of my childhood to the Papist faith, I say that it was caused by the beauty of Santa Croce, because it is simpler to attribute such a great change to a single cause. It is like being late for school: it is more believable to give just the one excuse. So I never mentioned my love of Violet and her beauty, and how much more moving than any painting in itself was the vision of Violet in love with 'The Birth of Venus', and the loveliness of Botticelli's goddess reflected in my sister, and the two enshrined by the strange yellowing Tuscan light that bathed the whole of Florence during our stay there.

Nor did I mention the disturbing subplot of our chaperone's hysterics and their course. For it may seem trivial with hindsight, but had Mrs Travis-Clemmons not lost her lemon drops, Violet and I would never have been free to roam, or free to stay and drink in the intoxication of either the Botticellis or the churches. But somehow it doesn't sound sufficiently serious to attribute one's revelations and visions to a boiled sweet.

Something happened in Italy, and I still don't know exactly what it was. I know it began with the flowers and the sweet, heady scents of wisteria and the banks and avenues of cascading acacia. When I die, I would like to be buried on a mattress of wisteria, or maybe just under a gnarled and drooping wisteria tree. It would be a shame to cut the flowers, though. Maybe I should be buried with violets, because violets are always cut into posies anyway, cut down in their prime, as my own Violet was when she was scarcely twenty.

CHAPTER 22

I LEFT the Island three times in my life. Once, and for the first time, to go to Italy; once to travel the sad trail to London with Mother and Father and Ivy, to see Violet buried in the Catholic cemetery of St Joseph's in Hampstead; and once, for the last time, for my exile. Each time, though I travelled for what I thought to be my own purpose, I was learning another facet of God's will. In Florence He showed me His glory; in London I learnt that He was, indeed, a jealous God; and later, for all the long years of my loneliness, I learnt to serve Him and to see that my own suffering was as nothing compared to that of others. I was placed in the uneasy Trinity of my own family to do His will.

Violet was called to paint, and taken from her calling. But I was called to protect and nurse. Kitty never understood the world as it presented itself to her. There were too many changes. Emily de Gruchy couldn't understand it either. I am sure that is why she took to her bed. It was the only safe place. She could control the sick room and pretend that when she got better everything would be the same outside. If she didn't look at it, she could pretend nothing had changed, she could believe that her Harry hadn't died, nor her other son suffered so much in the war that nothing his mother said or did could break through his barriers any more.

And Kitty? She was never like the rest of us, she fitted more into the fairy tales I read her. She put her dancing shoes on and she was dancing herself to death, nothing else seemed real to her. Her favourite story, though, was the one about the Snow Queen who smote her victims with a sliver of ice and bound them to her for ever. I'm sure Kitty thought that by flashing her eyes she could send out those cold burning splinters from her story book. She never realised it was love, not fear, that others felt for her. I was never afraid of her. I was afraid for her. I am afraid for her. What will become of her Antarctic gaze after I am no longer alive to help her?

And Joan? Joan was like my own child. Even her size, which so offended Kitty, and hurt her, was like a miracle sometimes. I lost five babies of my own. Five children that formed and floated in my womb and were born with the same pains as Kitty was. Each time, Agnes prepared the linen cloth, the winding sheet to shroud my tiny sons and daughters in. I embroidered the edges of those linen cloths so that the burial would be less forlorn. So my tiny, weightless babies were all lost, and in their place Joan was given to me like the combined size of all.

I so much wanted another child, someone to keep Kitty company. She always said, even when she was a little girl, that she was happy on her own, but I felt, even then, that she needed somebody. When she came back from Canada, so wild and angry, I didn't realise that the child she was bearing would be for me. I know I saw her suffer so much, and I know she blamed me. She screamed at me through her ordeal, accusing me of wilfully making her suffer. But it wasn't so. I have never come so near to wanting to die myself as I did on that night of Joan's birth. I loved Kitty, more even than I loved Violet, perhaps because Kitty was weak, and needed me, while my sister had been strong. No one could have known that she would undergo such agony. No one could have wished that on her.

I have heard say that the road to hell is paved with good intentions. I don't think Kitty ever understood my own. She never recovered from that night. No matter what Joan did or said or was, her mother was unable to love her. Having witnessed the cruelness of Kitty's pain, I cannot blame her for the way she is. It would be wrong to judge her. I have tried to explain it so many times to Joan. We were given to each other, she and I.

Right from the moment she was born, and the doctor handed her to me, we were our mutual consolation. She had heavy bones. She was born hungry, and she cried as I have heard no other baby cry. I think she was hungry for her mother. Five days passed, and still she had no name. I tried to approach Kitty about it, but she wouldn't tolerate any mention of the child that had so nearly killed her.

'But Kitty, she must have a name, she must be christened.'

Kitty never wanted Joan to live, not before or after the birth. She hated her. I have seen feuds and dislikes and preferences, and I know it is true that not all mothers love their children, and when they do, it is not a love that is shared equally. My own mother loved Violet best and I suppose, if I had had another child, a child who hadn't died, I would have still loved Kitty best. But Kitty hated Joan. It wasn't even the passing furious hatred of the war, when we all learnt to hate the Germans and then to let that sudden hatred fade and disappear, so that the killing fields were soon forgotten. Not even Emily de Gruchy hated the Germans, she hated war. And the other Emily, Dickie's cousin, who had lost her husband out in France and tried to fill the boredom of her widowhood with travel, she couldn't bear to visit France, but she spent many seasons in Baden-Baden. What Kitty felt for Joan was different from all that, though. It was like poison.

I chose the name. It was the year of St Joan, and many of the babies born that year were named after the Maid of Orleans. I thought the name would help her, and give her strength. I hope it didn't help to make her a martyr. Dickie said that names were very important. When Kitty was born, I had already decided that if it was a girl, I would like to call her Violet. Dickie thought it was morbid to name a child after someone who had died so recently. When we saw her, and saw her green eyes opened wide, and not closed as the eyes of other babies were, and she stared out of the lace of her cradle, lovelier than any baby I had ever seen, I said, 'Please let her be called Violet, Dickie, look at her. She *is* Violet. You've seen the miniature. Please.'

It seemed to frighten him to see Kitty there so very much a person. I think he thought babies were a woman's task, something a man could not understand until they grew and became able to lean on a knee and ask questions. It unnerved him to see this first-born girl stare up at him with such apparent understanding. I remember that the door blew open and he shuddered with the draught.

'No, Florence, no, you mustn't. It's uncanny. I don't want her mixed up with the dead. Choose another name, any other name, but not Violet.'

So I chose Kathleen, which came from Dickie's family, and also for a friend of my girlhood in St John and also for Kathleen Pitsligo, who had sent me Agnes to cradle me through my days. It seemed like a good name when I chose it, but it became Kitty before the first month was through, and Kitty it has remained. There is a kind of magic in names, a hidden power. Take my name, Florence, for instance. Even before we moved to the Island, I knew I was bound to Italy. I dreamt of Florence and I loved it before ever I went there. I was terribly disappointed when I discovered that in Italian they call it Firenze. It felt like a betrayal. I sympathised with Mrs Travis-Clemmons in her first full day of grief, and I confess that it wasn't so much for the loss of her sweets as for the drop in my own misplaced pride. Firenze. I still don't like it. It's the only thing about Italy that I don't like. Florence sounds much nicer.

So Joan was called and anglicised for Jeanne d'Arc, with Mary for her middle name – a name of grace, an offering. Kitty told me to choose a name. She said she didn't care what we called it so long as she didn't have to see it. It, always 'it', that was how Kitty insisted on referring to our baby. Sometimes she called Joan 'the thing', which was even worse. I don't think she ever used Joan's name. In eighteen years she contrived not to mention it, not to say it, skirting round a subject for any length of time just to avoid saying 'Joan'.

Kitty never liked babies. When I was pregnant, for the five times of my miscarriages, Cook told Agnes she thought it was Kitty who was causing the pains to come. I remember, when Agnes told me that, I called Cook up to me, up to my room, and I asked her, 'What have you said to Agnes about Miss Kitty?'

Cook went very red in the face, and she looked at Agnes as though she would have liked to slap her, and she shuffled her flat feet in the doorway and mumbled, 'Nothing, Ma'am.'

I could tell she was covering up, and I was angry at her spitefulness. Kitty was only seven at the time, and it seemed quite terrible that someone in a position of trust, as Cook was, should be gossiping about our child in our own kitchens.

'Is it true that you think Miss Kitty's presence has a bad effect on my health?'

Cook continued to shuffle, and then, quite suddenly, she stopped and looked me squarely in the face and said, almost defiantly, 'Yes, Ma'am . . . She does it to puppies too. You ask the groom. The setters all come stillborn when Miss Kitty goes near them.'

I gave Cook a month's pay in lieu of notice, and we had a dreadful week trying to replace her. Dickie complained that the new cook was never as good. He would have been quite cross about it, had it not been for my delicate condition. I never told him my reason for sacking her, of course, but I have often felt a little guilty about my harshness to the poor woman since we moved to Hendon. For really, all she had done was to notice something I hadn't. Kitty was a good child, better than any, I think, but she did have very disturbed thoughts at times, and it would be possible for such inward troubles to upset a pregnancy.

Kitty's life was so full of 'if onlys' after the war. I am sure, though, there was but the one that would have made the greatest difference to her life. If only we had not lost Claremont. Claremont meant more to her than anyone. She loved that house. She loved it as a tiny child, and she never recovered from the move. Why, even Joan could have been more acceptable to her there. Joan could have grown up in the nurseries, and Kitty need hardly have seen her. There would have been no need for the convents, no need to hide her. Claremont was big enough to swallow up a child. With a proper nanny and enough maids, Kitty could have lived her life so differently there. The scale of our troubles grew directly in proportion to the size of our house. We were too cramped in Hendon – far too cramped to disguise the tension of all Kitty's bitterness.

I tried to give them back as much of Claremont as I could, by remembering it. It was Kitty's house. She had no brothers to inherit over her head. It would have been hers by right, and later it would have been Joan's. I wanted them both to have that legacy, if only as a memory. I missed Claremont so much myself, I knew it must have been unbearable for Kitty. That was why it was good to have the cottage at Selsey. Kitty was like me, she loved the sea. I suggested that we move to the South Coast somewhere when we moved to England, but Kitty said she would die of boredom.

She wanted to live in London. If she couldn't have her house, she didn't want the Island either. She was ashamed. After Dickie died, she shunned her friends and pretended they were laughing at her for all her misfortunes. While she was with child, she locked herself away from everyone. Only Agnes and I were allowed to see her. And later, she latched on to Joan's red hair and made it a further cause for her dislike. She insisted that no one should see the child. At first we kept the baby in the attic, to distance her inconsolable crying from Kitty's tired ears. She had suffered enough without being driven wild by those screams.

Agnes and I did everything we could to calm Joan when she was a baby. We hired a nurse and then another and another. They couldn't bear the screams, though. No matter how many times the doctor was called to her, nothing seemed to be wrong and nothing seemed able to quieten her cries. I carried her in my arms for hours on end, feeding her bottle after glass bottle of milk. She sucked voraciously and then wailed again. It was the most difficult time. The doctor and nurses and neighbours all said Joan needed her mother. They all tried, barging in on Kitty with the screaming Joan, but the mere sound, let alone the sight, of her distraught baby made her wild, and she would scream as well, and then the whole house would shake with the cacophony.

It took six months for Joan to realise where her love could come from, and to accept the attentions of Agnes and me. After that, Kitty's paranoia just grew alongside her unwanted child. She interpreted the critical stares she sometimes met as aimed directly against Joan, whereas it was not pity for Kitty for having to bear what she described as the monstrous redhead, it was pity for Joan for having to suffer her mother's indifference.

Joan was a sweet and clever child, she went out of her way to be kind and obliging. I could not have wished her to be more devout or dutiful. She brought me a solace I thought I would never know again. She was affectionate and witty, and I loved her as much as a mother or a grandmother could. It would be wrong for me to have been blind to certain things, though. Joan was a plain baby, and she grew into an even plainer child. Kitty despised her for her size, and although the rate of her growth was, I admit, unfortunate, it was not in itself a handicap. Kitty herself was so very small that she bore an innate prejudice against size. I, on the other hand, was tall, as were all the women of my family with the exception of Violet, who was three inches shorter than I. Mother said it was a Berry trait to be tall. I don't know if even Grandmother Berry, in her Lincolnshire pride, would have rejoiced to see my Joan, who measured six foot at the age of thirteen.

Kitty had watched Joan grow with sheer disgust from the time she first came into the world as a very oversized baby. Not even tall boys were six foot tall at her age. Joan had been shooting up. Every time she came back from the convent, she would have put on another few inches and another few pounds. We didn't know that she would stop growing at thirteen. It looked as if she was all set to keep going indefinitely. Joan herself was horrified by it. I even caught her smoking and drinking gin at Selsey because, she claimed, her Uncle Frank had told her it stunted people's growth. It was alarming. I was worried about it myself. But she stopped at six foot, which I think was actually five foot eleven and a half, but it sounded a little pernickety to say it like that. And it was still eleven and a half inches taller than Kitty and a good two and a half taller than I.

Worse, though, than her height, her freckles, her big bones or her grey eyes (which were very beautiful eyes, but reminded Kitty of Nelson) was the colour of her hair. Of course one would have preferred any other colour. Red hair is, inevitably, a vulgar colour to have. Kathleen Pitsligo wrote to me that many of the Irish girls have red hair, and indeed I had noticed myself that a couple of the girls she sent across, over the years, were redheads. Kathleen Pitsligo, I'm sure, meant well when she mentioned all the Irish girls with red hair, and even went into the details of her cousins (all distantly related to Dickie) who had trailed their red tresses through the family tree. But of course, one was not overly anxious to be Irish. Not that there are not some excellent families over there, and undoubtedly the best of maids, but we were Jersey and a prey, I fear, to the prevailing anti-Irish snobbery. Her letters merely confirmed what I already knew: red hair was a bit of a calamity.

But once it is there, what can one do? It is like buck teeth, or a club foot, one cannot disinherit one's children for their defects. Dickie himself had found it difficult to accept Kitty's lack of growth. He so loved measuring things, particularly people, and he was terribly disappointed that Kitty was so petite. Joan could have been much worse, she could have been ugly, which she definitely was not. She was plain. Kitty insisted on calling her ugly, but really she was just plain. Then again, her hair could have been carroty, brick red and glaringly orange, but it wasn't, it was a deeper red, a blood red. In fact, when she was born I thought her hair was stained with blood, and I washed her poor battered scalp too hard. There was a distinct unusualness about Joan's hair. It was impossibly thick, and refused to curl, but its colour was not as offensive as Kitty tried to pretend.

Now Joan has grown up, and got engaged to her Dickie, I watch her when she comes to visit me here in the nursing home, and I actually quite admire her hair. It has a glow like the conkers on the grass outside. It has a hint of the intense dark of copper beech leaves at Claremont in the late spring. I love copper beech. Were it not for the stigma of its vulgarity, others might rather like her hair as well. I've never seen another head like it. I can't abide ginger hair, of course, but Joan's is different. It has something quite unique about it, like Kitty's and Violet's eyes.

CHAPTER 23

THERE is a very thin line, like an invisible tightrope, between the acceptable and the unacceptable. Kitty lives on that line. It is nearly twenty years now since she sought it out, and she has been living on it ever since. She thinks that because she has friends, and an endless supply of dancing partners and young infatuees, she is safe. She doesn't realise that it is her very friends who put her at risk. All it would take would be for one of them to see her other side, to catch her in a tantrum, actually to witness how she tortures her daughter, for people to start talking and turning on her.

We are at least anonymous in Hendon. We have lived there for so long that we have become a part of its dreary background. There has always been gossip there, and no doubt some of it is harmless and some malicious, but we are too far out of their circle to be tampered with. Mercifully, my pittance keeps us untouchable even though we are hanging by our teeth on to the fringe of that elite. Because we have never been obliged to work, we can keep ourselves relatively secret. The maids, I'm afraid, have always been a problem. Only one of them went so far as to sue for assault, and I managed to settle out of court. In fact, the matter went no further than the girl's father.

I really don't know what got into Kitty. She never used to be violent. As a child she was always a tease, and I know she could be spiteful. She used to make some of the other children cry. She used to say things that upset them. Twice, I remember, she pinched a little boy until he fainted, but he was bigger than she was. Kitty never used to be dangerous, whereas since Joan was born I have lost count of the number of times I have had to drag that child away from Kitty's temper. If Father hadn't been a doctor, and taught me how to stop blood and suture wounds and set sprains and dislocations, the family would have been broken up long ago.

I have asked Joan to be kind to her mother and to try and protect her after I die. I have asked her, but I know that it is probably too much to ask. That girl can sit down on her bed at night and count her scars as other children might count stars. If it weren't for her freckles and the thickness of her hair, they would show up more. Her poor head has been split open along almost every parting. Who knows, perhaps it's for the best if they don't see each other any more. Perhaps it would be tempting fate to interfere with Joan now that they are apart. I have spent all of her short life separating them to protect her from her mother's battery. It is a kind of miracle that Joan has grown to womanhood.

It pleases me that Joan is nursing. It keeps her busy and it keeps her away from home. I was so anxious for her to grow up. The last two years I have wanted to catapult her into her maturity. First of all we wanted to shrink her and keep her small, then Agnes and I wanted her to grow quickly. I felt myself ailing, and the illness accelerating, and for once I knew without Kitty telling me that someone was going to die. It's a strange feeling to sense one's own demise. Kitty and Joan both saw me limping, but they didn't either of them realise that it was cancer. I didn't want them to know. It was easier to bear without that. But I did want Joan to grow up and escape before my tumour grew, as it has now.

All through the Hendon years I wanted Joan to stay with me. It was dreadful when she was away at school and I couldn't even see her at weekends. She was my crutch, I suppose; as Kitty's temper worsened, she was my one support. I could have kept Agnes with me. I know she would have stayed. She offered to come, to give up her house and the Island, everything. Despite our difference in station, we had grown to be very close friends. She would have come as my companion. But Agnes had done so much for us. She sheltered us when everything else seemed lost. She helped me to nurse Joan, she nursed Kitty through her pregnancy, and afterwards it was Agnes who dressed her wounds. I have missed Agnes. I think I have missed her even more than I have missed Dickie.

I do not regret making her stay on the Island, though. With

everything I have had to bear and witness with my daughter, I have managed, and managed to keep my faith. I don't know if I could have done that if Kitty had gone for Agnes. Even in Jersey, when we were in St Aubin in Agnes's own house, Kitty had begun to attack her.

I sutured Agnes's head once. I couldn't bear to have to do that again. The other maids all left before the damage got too extreme – except poor Susannah and the dress. But the others just ran away. Agnes would have stayed. I managed to protect Joan. I saved her by sending her away. Agnes would have stayed.

Since I became a Catholic, not a day has passed when I haven't gone to Mass, except when there was danger in the house that might have erupted if I left. But every day, with or without St Joseph's, I have said my creed, and I have believed it. My faith has sustained me, just as it sustained Violet through her last years and the days of her death. It was our faith. We embraced it together and I swore, in my last letter that reached her on the day she died, that I would never leave it. It has kept us together. It has even kept Kitty and Joan and me together through decades of domestic warfare.

The nurses here say there is another war started. They say it is with the Germans again. Cousin Emily will have to stop going to Baden-Baden, and Emily de Gruchy has written to say that she has been asked to vacate her rooms at Tommy's, so it must be true. My neighbour here listens to the BBC; she tells me every day what is happening with the war. I don't think I really want to know. It is a relief that nothing does seem to happen from day to day, although last week she told me a German submarine torpedoed the *Royal Oak* at Scapa Flow, and now there are as many dead as all the men from Jersey who died in France those many years ago.

Agnes writes to me every day. There is an air-mail service now, which means that letters take no time at all. I almost feel as though I were back on the Island. If it were not that Violet is waiting for me at St Joseph's, I would like to be buried on the Island, beside Mother and Father and Ivy.

Mother was so pleased when Ivy married. Ivy became the favourite after Violet died. Ivy had not denied her faith, and she married a very nice young man who not only had a pretty house and a reasonable income but had travelled abroad and knew our part of Lincolnshire and had heard of Berry Place. Mother never forgave the Berrys for letting Violet get so ill, but neither could she quite forget her lineage. It crept out almost against her will. When I married Dickie, she was so proud that I was marrying into the 'Roberts of Claremont' that she resuscitated all her old friends and neighbours from Grantham just so that she could write and tell them – hoping, I know, that the news would seep back into Berry Place.

She used to visit me there every Friday, staying over until Saturday afternoon before being driven back by Dickie's groom. I think her main thrill came not from seeing me or Kitty or even the Roberts (of Claremont) but from being handed down from the carriage with its pair of white horses and its crest on the door. I invited her to come and live with us – Dickie was very generous when it came to family – but Mother said, at Claremont she would merely be a lesser relative, while at St John she got all the cachet of having her daughter placed so high and everybody knowing – besides which Mother always treated her widowhood with an element of disbelief, as though Father had merely teased her by dying, and would return if she waited long enough. Her capacity to tolerate death was very limited. She treated Violet's as a tragedy, and up until her own she wept for her. Ivy's – in childbirth, barely a year after she married – she treated as carelessness, and her grief was one of scolding disapproval. Father's death, though, which came only two years later, in 1896, she regarded as a form of treachery. He had no business leaving her. She complained constantly of jobs he had left undone, and papers he had stashed away.

Father went into a decline which dated, I suppose, from way back in 1890, and then tricked its chart, as Violet's had done, navigating him through all the usual symptoms of consumption and then pulling him back again. He developed certain fixed routines and ideas about his disease, which he transferred to life in general. After Violet died he decided it was virtual suicide to leave the Island, and from there he shrunk his horizons to the parish of St John. He never went to St Helier again. He became quite obsessive, too, about smaller things. He monitored the health and progress of the sprawling rosemary hedge and his fever peaked and fell, he swore, according to the daily state of those bushes. He drank rosemary tea, and bathed himself in the thin aromatic leaves. Since he drew such a great many twigs from the bush, it began to suffer from its random pruning, and he then confined himself to the house, convinced that to venture outside would destroy him.

Mother was very impatient with his whims. She felt that if *she* could withstand the loss of her daughter with such fortitude and without copying her illness, the least Father could do was follow suit. 'And you a doctor!' she would tell him, trying to rouse him from what she swore to be his hypochondriac's bed. Then Ivy died, and although Father did attend the funeral, he returned to his study and his invalid's bed and remained there for the next eighteen months.

Mother's lack of sympathy continued long after Father should have been dead. He was coughing his lungs out, and still Mother insisted that her husband was malingering. It was only in his last month, when he was already wasted to a shadow, with the bones glowing through his cheeks and wrists, that mother realised he was actually going to die. Even then, her tears were mixed with resentment. Why had he cried wolf? Why had he made her be so hard to him, why didn't he stop haemorrhaging so that she could nurse him properly? Wasn't he her husband, after all, and how could he know that she loved him and had chided him for his own good? What would people say if he just died?

Meanwhile, after all my months of vigil with him, I actually wanted him to die. He had suffered so much. By some mysterious means known only to himself he had stayed alive for longer than the years that had been allotted him. He had beaten the tuberculosis in his lungs for so long and at such a cost to him in pain. I wanted him to rest.

I asked him how he had outwitted his illness for so many years and he whispered, with a smile, 'Willpower, poor Florence, that's all I have. Willpower.'

When my own illness began, I knew I had blood from my parents on both sides, and not just the traces of the Berry blood that Mother sometimes detected in me, because I too found the willpower to survive. I knew it was the only way to keep dear Joan alive. Now Joan is marrying for herself, she says. She brought me her young man, a naval officer. Now he will look after her, but who will look after Kitty? Who will hide her from the prying eyes?

Last night I dreamt all my cinerarias had died. I woke up feeling so unhappy, and then I found myself thinking and unable to get back to sleep. I thought the curtains in my room were too yellow, and I thought my crochet had all come undone. It hadn't, though, it was still in the basket by my bed, and I took it up and crocheted until morning to calm my nerves. As soon as it was light, I read from my missal to ward away the bad thoughts that kept coming into my head.

I made my confession again today, although it is only Wednesday. I told the chaplain I had wished that Kitty had died before me, which was to wish her dead. I punished Kitty for that same mortal sin. She has always wanted to kill Joan and I have never understood her. Maybe, too, I have been hard on her in certain ways, because I never could forgive her for wishing her own child dead. And now, when I am so near to dying, I have done it myself. Kitty's own sin is mine. I lay in bed, and I wished she had preceded me to the grave, so that I didn't have to fear what would become of her. The chaplain tells me it is my illness that has made my mind wander. He says it is the drugs the nurses give me to dull the pain that make me think strange things. He has told me not to worry, to say three Hail Marys and be absolved.

He doesn't understand. My mind isn't wandering, it is quite clear. I shall have to talk to that chaplain again. I don't want to die in sin. I have tried so hard to do right ever since Violet came home from Lincolnshire. I made a vow, two, four. I must be sounding like Dickie with his eternal numbers. And yet, I was confirmed into the Church of England, and then I made my own vow, and then I became a Catholic, and then married, but I also vowed to keep my grandchild alive and to keep Agnes safe from Kitty. That is a great many vows for a thin lady. Perhaps I have been presumptuous; and maybe Kitty takes her whims from me. She thinks she can control the world as well.

I would so like to ask the chaplain to clarify my thoughts. 'Poor Florence' was what my parents called me, 'poor Florence' is what my old friends call me now. I have been 'poor Florence' to the world since Dickie died. Yet I have never been poor. There was always my pittance, Mother's legacy, the Berry inheritance. It wasn't much, but since I outlived all the rest of my family it reverted to me. So I was never poor like the end lanes of Grantham. Hendon was often a hard house, but never poor.

It is only now that I am truly poor Florence. I feel it myself. I haven't enough to leave Kitty to protect her. I know one cannot buy sanity, but one can buy the privacy that keeps its presence hidden from the law. Now that Joan is to marry, and I see from *Burke's Landed Gentry* that she is marrying well, she will be safe. Not as safe as I would like her to be. A woman needs to have her own money. It is the only real independence there is. We have the franchise now, but that has not made us free. Freedom is to be found in one's own purse. My freedom was my pittance, ultimately. I would like to leave what I have to Joan to help her in her life and to repay her in some way for the years of confusion and pain she has had to live through.

Whatever debts I feel I owe to her, though, must be in some way repaid. The very fact that she has grown to be eighteen years old is proof of that. I gave her her life. I am her surrogate mother. It is an act of God that I do not understand (though I have tried, I cannot understand) why *her* birth had to be at the cost of her real mother. Whatever Kitty has done, she was provoked. She should not have had to suffer as she did. Even before those long hours of labour, something perverse had tortured her. I cried when I saw her scars. They were terrible scars and badly healed. They all broke open when Joan was born, and ripped and tore even further.

What was natural became unnatural for her. What every woman does to conceive a child, or just for pleasure, was made perverse for her. My first reaction when I saw how hurt my daughter was in her sex was to track Nelson Allen down and make him pay for what he had done. I wanted to prosecute him, but of course the scandal would have been more harmful to Kitty. She wrote and told me she had been hurt and I was stupid enough to interpret her outrage as prudery. I didn't realise that she had actually been injured. I told her what I thought was true: it was just a part of marriage that she had to get used to, a natural thing which she could grow to like. She must have thought I was mad or cruel.

Kitty is different from other girls. Her skin is not like other skin. Maybe that is what the whiteness means, a weakness of some kind. It is obvious that her body was not made for marriage or childbirth. I questioned her many times about the consummation of her marriage, and I cannot blame Nelson now for what occurred. For any man to have held back for five months with his own wife is a mark of delicacy. Kitty hated Nelson second only to his child, she really hated him, but it was her description of his acts which cleared his name for me. I know that if he knew about our altered circumstances he would support both Kitty and their child. It seems wrong to have kept him in the dark for so long.

Nelson loved Kitty, but then so many people did. Her other husband loved her too. I was pleased when she married Peter. She had reached a point when I could no longer control her even enough to stop her from hurting herself. She came so near to killing Joan that I sent the girl away and warned the nuns to keep her back through all her coming holidays. I paid off the last maid. Twenty-five guineas for two black eyes and a broken arm. I don't know if that is what a human arm is worth, but it was more than I could afford. I did the housework myself, living in Hendon with only my dear old Rufus terrier for company, and Kitty storming in from time to time.

Rufus had come with me from Claremont; he was still almost a puppy then, and he had stuck by me through my sojourn at Agnes's and he had been my friend in St Aubin, and made the crossing with us from the Island. He was older than I, I suppose, by the time Kitty remarried. He was deaf and his joints had become arthritic and he had begun to smell a bit, I'm afraid. I made him up a basket in the kitchen and I always carried him up to my room. Rufus was not allowed on the stairs. Kitty used to check the runner for stray hairs, and when she found them she would get very angry indeed. Rufus and Joan were good friends. They lived under the same cloud. They were permanently in the doghouse. Kitty was determined to have Rufus put down. She lobbied for it weekly. In the end, even little Rufus defied her; he lived to be fourteen, despite her sly and her not so sly kicks.

I don't know what I would have done if Kitty hadn't married

Peter. However bad that marriage turned out to be, it did save her from herself for long enough to give her another lease of time. I have tried talking to Kitty about her health and her behaviour, but I don't know whether she understands the risks that are involved for her or the edge she's walking along. She ought to know, she grew up balancing on La Corbière's cliff. I hope she can still recognise a precipice. But I don't know. Sometimes she seems so strange. When she grows violent, I can usually drag her back to some form of normality by reminding her that the asylum is never far away. Yet she just lets a little time pass and then flies into another rage.

Had it not been for all the provocation and the disappointments in her life, Kitty might have been a good girl. She still is in her own odd way. She tries to be very kind to me. When she thinks about me, she is most attentive. It is just that she forgets not only me but the whole world in her tantrums. I have worried about her temper ever since she came back from Canada. I don't know what to do about it except hide it away. I have never come across such an accumulation of anger and bitterness. She was not such a spiteful child; she has become more spiteful since she returned. I worry about Kitty's temper more than I worry about anything else. It makes me forget my hip, it makes me forget everything except my own name, poor Florence. That is what I am, I am too poor to protect her.

I fancy that I see the bars of the Grantham poorhouse looking sinister and sad as we ride by in our battered carriage. There was an asylum in St Helier, and it too had bars. The workhouse, the poorhouse and the asylum, they are all waiting at the end of the lane. My pittance is not enough to keep Kitty from them. My pittance has kept us all for nineteen years, but it will not be enough to pay whatever it costs to keep my Kitty free. Nine years ago, it cost twenty-five guineas for a broken arm. I haven't the strength or the will or whatever it takes to stay alive any more, and I haven't enough money to save her. Maybe her emeralds will save her. She must have hundreds and hundreds of them by now.

CHAPTER 24

I HAVE always been needed, and that has made my life seem full. Kitty talks of boredom. She is afraid of it, she says it is the only thing she fears. She and her friends talk about freedom. They discuss it as though it were a real possibility. I had a bit of a discussion once with one of her beaux, I remember; I told him that only entirely selfish people can be free. He was very polite, but I know he didn't agree with me. He thought he was free, yet he was in love with Kitty and behaved like her slave. The drudgery of love is inescapable. Perhaps if Kitty had given her own heart more she would not have been so bored. I think, perhaps, that I spoilt my daughter. If I had seen how deep the tyranny of her temper ran when she was a child, maybe she would have more of a chance now.

I have always mixed the past up with my present, just as Kitty always mixes in the future. I treated Kitty as though she were Violet reincarnated in my womb. Violet had such a sweet nature, I couldn't believe that Kitty, who was so twinned in her looks, could be any different in her character. When Violet and I were children, we were rarely punished at home. Everyone told me I was such a competent nurse, such a good entertainer, such a fine mother, that I never questioned whether I really was any of these things. When our world started to fall apart, I did feel very uneasy sometimes, but it was nothing specifically about my own behaviour. I worried about Kitty. It was as Father had said, I had no time to worry about myself while others needed me more.

I never had time to stop and think if I was doing the right thing. I followed my instinct as women do, but it all seems different now. My time has become elastic. It has stretched and stretched until every day and hour seems too long. I know it will continue to do so until the elastic snaps. This is my last autumn. I can feel it.

Every morning the nurses wheel my chair into the bay window and leave me here with a hot-water bottle and a tartan rug over my knees. It is cold here, particularly cold by the window, but I can see the gardens and the trees. All the leaves are turning now, even the oaks, and they have begun to fall. Soon they will take on their winter transparency and make skeletons. This winter, I shall share in their frailty.

Kitty can tell when her friends will die. She can even predict it for strangers, but she is blinder than ordinary people when it comes to her family. Or rather, she was blind to Harry and Dickie, and she is to me. When she was hardly more than a baby, she felt her grandfather's death. And when Emily St Aubin's husband was killed in the war, Kitty told poor Cousin Emily a week before it happened while she was at Claremont for tea. It was quite embarrassing for both of us, although Kitty finds it so natural she really doesn't see why she shouldn't mention people if she gets them 'on her mind'.

She doesn't come often to see me here. She has a new beau, and they are both anxious to enjoy themselves before this new war begins in earnest. He is a soldier, and he's worried about being sent away. Kitty says that if I'm not home by the spring she will come and see me more regularly. She isn't feeling herself at the moment, as I can tell when she does come to visit. She is terribly pale, and her eyes are shining too brightly. She says she feels disturbed by the war. She complains of headaches and bad insomnia. Last time she came, she said, 'How can I sleep, Maman, with armies marching through my head? I feel as though the whole world were being invaded and my brain is the tunnel they all march through. I just have to keep busy to take my mind off it.'

I used to think Kitty was exaggerating and pretending with her premonitions. I used to think it was a bit like showing off or trying to shock. But over the years, she has seen too many deaths to be mistaken. I don't know why it happens, but it does. Emily de Gruchy says clairvoyance runs in families. I used to think that was just one of Emily's silly notions, but now I see my own dreams in the day. I feel this war coming as surely as the winter;

and I feel the people dying just like Kitty says. I feel a sense of hopelessness when I look out of the window. My neighbour here keeps reading extracts from *The Times* to me. There are rumours everywhere that the fighting will be over by Christmas. The fighting has hardly begun. They call it the phoney war, and scoff at its future.

I know I have lived for ten years with this cancer, but I held it off to stay with my family. All my pleasure in my garden has gone. I cannot rejoice at the falling of the leaves any more. I have my dreams now, and my heart shrinks at what I see. I don't want to live through this war, I don't even want to live after it. God has given me my release, He gave me a season ticket, and I'm ready to go. I had a good innings, as Dickie would have said. I no longer recognise the world, it has become a strange place to me. This must be a bit how Kitty sees life, with the chaos of the future stirred into each day. No wonder the whole business of living is so disturbing to her.

Agnes tells me to go back to the Island. She says she will come and fetch me. I told her a little of what I have dreamt in one of my letters. She assures me that Jersey will be safe whatever happens. It is too small to be in danger. Why would Hitler want to bother with an island that is only nine miles by five? Jersey has always been safe in my mind. Even when we left it, I preferred to take our troubles away and leave it intact and unharmed in my memory. I dreamt about Claremont the other day. It was full of grey soldiers. There was barbed wire around its railings and the soldiers in my garden were making the funny salutes that Joan and her school friends used to make.

They say in the papers that Hitler is persecuting the Jews. I never liked the Jews, but then again, I never liked the Germans. It was Kitty who wanted the German convent. She thought the French nuns were far too lax, and I know she hated having Joan nearby. She used to claim that she could feel Joan's presence at Les Filles de la Croix, and in a way, so could I. I liked having her close to me. It felt less lonely for both of us when she was just a walk away. It was Joan herself who forced the move. Kitty was always angling to shift her, but I didn't let her. In some things I did defy Kitty, and that was one.

Once, I caught Joan brawling in the park like a common

guttersnipe, and then I had to move her. Kitty had been waiting for a chance to catch Joan. She had been looking for a chance really to hurt her. Joan was never naughty, though, and that foiled the violence that was always hovering. Kitty used to pounce on all her little faults. I think the worst Joan ever did was break the china. She is, without a doubt, the clumsiest person I know. I used to mend things to keep her out of trouble, but Kitty could always tell. She could read her daughter's thoughts. I panicked when I found Joan in the park. I thought if Kitty saw her she would know what Joan had done, and for once I would be unable to defend her, because she was in the wrong. So I sent her away. I hoped that by my agreeing to the German nuns, Kitty would get sidetracked, and feel her battle won, and fail to see what had gone on.

I tell myself I'm not afraid of Kitty, but I am – or was. I was afraid of what she'd do to Joan. I want to see the chaplain. I want to tell him all the things I have done wrong. I never noticed before, confessing all my weaknesses as I went along, that despite the Hail Marys they still accumulate like dead leaves on the lawn. The future looks too bleak to contemplate, and the past is falling apart. If it weren't for the photographs I keep with me, I would hardly be able to recognise us, three women and their awkward love. I thought I had done my best, but I no longer think I have.

'Forgive me, Father, for I have sinned.'

My fingers are stiff, very stiff, but I must keep knitting. Isn't that what one does in times of war? I should be knitting all the white feathers that should be my lot. Violet and I used to gather seagulls' feathers from the beach at Bonne Nuit Bay. The white feathers were the most prized, but the grey ones were commonest. I used to climb the rocks to collect the white ones. I haven't needed to go so far out of my way of late in search of my cowardice. I have shirked my duties, and I shirk them still.

When I close my eyes to sleep, I can see my lovely baby staring out at me with terror in her eyes, and I can see Joan, my plain baby, given to me so late in my life, staring too with the uncertain, lost look of her grey eyes. I know they both still need me in their different ways, and I am deserting them.

* * *

It was Emily de Gruchy who started me knitting. It made her nervous having her boys away. People kept telling her that she must be so proud to have three sons, and all of them officers, all serving in France. But Emily wasn't proud at all – she never has been, and she wasn't then. She was terribly unhappy worrying about what would happen to her boys. When Philip, the eldest, was sent to convalesce at Osborne House on the Isle of Wight, she was quite pleased. Nobody really knew about shell shock in those days, we thought it was a lucky release, a sort of condoned skiving. A man could go home without too much dishonour, and with all his fingers and both his feet, with shell shock.

Philip never quite recovered. It used to make me so sad to see him wandering around his house as though it too were a giant shell that might explode at any moment. Some of the other de Gruchy boys – that is, the other branch of de Gruchys – suffered in the same way, jumping whenever anyone tried to speak to them. But I think Harry made her more nervous than any of them, because he was there on the Island for the first three years of the war, and he was so impatient to go and join his brothers that it frightened Emily. He brought the war to Jersey, I suppose, talking about it all the time.

Later, when he didn't come home, it killed something in Emily. She took to her bed when the telegram arrived, but it was Harry's letter that really made her ill. The letter arrived at St Brelade a week after the news of his death. I believe letters always had to pass through the censors, and that was what delayed them. He wrote to his mother about coming home; and he broached to her, for the first time, his wish to marry Kitty, and live at Claremont and never be away from Emily again. I have seen that letter so many times and its faded words sear through me. It is life as it could have been, as it should have been, were it not for the war.

Nothing was ever the same afterwards, not us, not anyone. Yet while the fighting was going on, we saw the soldiers leave for France. We saw them off, Emily and Kitty and I. It was something to do, a day out to St Helier, and to the port, and then lunch or tea in the Old London Hotel, and a lovely drive back along the coast.

And we saw the Lists sometimes, with the casualties. Emily, of course, watched those more than I, although there were boys from

Claremont who had gone overseas with the Jersey Contingent, but they all came home. They were changed, too, but they all survived. There was a little rationing as well, but that didn't really affect us. Some of the girls joined the Red Cross, but most of us just knitted; we made scarves and socks for unknown soldiers in the trenches. Yards and yards of scarves.

Emily said she felt closer to her boys while she was knitting. She used to say that if one of her scarves should happen to fall into the hands of one of her sons, they would know, somehow, that it was she who had knitted it, thinking of them as her needles clicked: knit one, purl one; knit one, purl one. Emily de Gruchy was never practical with her hands. She learnt to knit as part of the Red Cross effort, but it didn't come naturally to her. Even after we had been knitting for three years and our output could almost have stretched to the port on its own, Emily's efforts were very noticeably hers. Some of the scarves were four feet wide in the middle, tapering into bizarre shapes at either end, while her socks were the most extraordinary sizes. In solidarity, I gave up socks when she did, and we just knitted mufflers – knit one, purl one, row after row, every day until the war ended.

It became addictive. It was our only way to do something constructive. After Harry died, Emily never picked up her needles again, but I had grown used to transposing my emotions into the mechanical click, so I kept knitting. At first it was blankets and coverlets for the servants, then it was rugs for the dogs. The setters had a pile of my handiwork so big that it became absurd. Rufus was like a pampered baby, with so many blankets for his wicker basket that he could not chew through them fast enough or soil them.

Then Dickie and Kitty went to London, and I felt lonely on my own. That was when I took up crochet. It is so much prettier than knitting, and the lace that comes from the single hook is usable and nice. Dickie told me the trips to London were for Kitty, to help her forget that Harry would not be coming home. I had wanted her to marry a Catholic. I didn't realise that Harry and she had been engaged. They always seemed like brother and sister. Emily and I were so very close, it seemed only natural that our children should love each other. I suppose I should have been able to tell the difference between the different kinds of love, but friendship, for me, has always been so important that no amount of closeness has ever seemed unnatural.

I felt guilty when I saw Harry's letter. I had thought I was so close to my daughter, and then I found I wasn't close at all. I didn't even know where her heart was tied. She had often said she would never leave Claremont but I imagined that to be just an idea. It turned out she had made her plans, years before, while sitting on La Corbière cliff. I hoped that by going to London she would forget her childhood Love, and fall for someone new and find another kind of happiness.

I should have known better. Father always said it was as good as suicide to leave the Island. Emily often asks me what I think of Dickie's gambling, and it makes her cross when I reply that I don't think anything of it. I don't think about it. I cannot blame Dickie for what he did, he was a good husband to me, and a good friend. It was the war that made him change. He told me he felt impotent knowing that men not so much younger than he were playing Russian roulette with their lives not fourteen miles from our shore. He wept when Harry died. He often wept in his last days. It was the only hint I had that something really bad was wrong. He never told me about our debts. I expect he was ashamed.

He used to get up in the night and stand on the upper terrace looking out to sea, whispering things. I followed him once or twice, and saw him there, but I left him. I thought it was better to leave him on his own. I didn't realise the weight he was carrying then, or the secrets. He walked round Claremont sometimes, just before the end, touching things, the carved door frames, the windowsills, the banisters, stroking them with tears in his eyes.

During his illness, he asked me to sit with him day and night. He seemed terrified of being on his own. He held my hand so tightly that the blood drained from it and bruises came in a bracelet on my wrist.

'Florence, poor Florence,' was all he could say, and 'Forgive me, will you ever forgive me?'

I tried to calm him and I kissed him and smoothed his hot, troubled brow. I told him over and over again there was nothing to forgive. It seemed to make him worse, though. He became distressingly restless when I tried to soothe him, and he would start mumbling again, 'Florence, my poor Florence.'

I wish I could have known about the debts, and that we were to lose Claremont, before he died, so I could have told him, and he could have known there was truly nothing to forgive. He gave me nearly twenty years of happiness and love. He made me the mistress of Claremont, he gave me my daughter to heal the wound of Violet's loss, he gave me so much. He gave me the finest camellias on Jersey, the most beautiful cinerarias, and his family ship anchored in the calm waters of the ornamental trees. He would never have hurt me deliberately, he was a kind man. I could never measure his kindness. He measured and counted everything, it was his way. He counted the war dead, he kept a tally of the casualties. There were, I remember, eight hundred and sixty-two Jersey men slain in the war. For me, Dickie was another casualty, there were eight hundred and sixty-three. Had he lived, he could have counted all the others, the ones like Kitty and Harry's brother, the so-called survivors. He would have known how to equate the losses.

I wanted to go to Italy after the auction. I tried to persuade Kitty to come with me, but she wouldn't hear of it. I don't think she ever believed that Joan would be born at all. She knew I had miscarried, five times between my fifth and sixth month, and she was banking on a similar fate. She hid her pregnancy from me, poor child, she was so scared, she mutilated herself trying to force Joan out of her. God wanted Joan to live, He must have done, for no other child could have clung as tenaciously to such an unloving mother.

I still kept thinking about Italy. Kitty couldn't have travelled in the last months, but I hoped that after the birth we might make a new start, somewhere warm and beautiful where the pittance would stretch to make us really comfortable. We could have lived well if we had gone abroad. We could have regained a little of the style we had lost. We could have had a villa somewhere by the sea. I had been through Rapallo and Genova and places like that with Violet, and I knew that we could have rented a huge rambling house with pillars and gardens and cascades of wisteria on the Italian Riviera. We could have had mimosas and bougainvilleas. We could have kept almost as many servants as at Claremont, and entertained, and had our friends from Jersey come to stay in style. Joan could have grown up with nuns who didn't mind how plain she was. Maybe, even, Agnes could have come.

But Kitty hated the idea of Italy. She said she could think of nothing more boring than being surrounded by foreign peasants. She told me her only friends were in London. No matter how much I described the terraces and the stone walls and the butterflies and the long Mediterranean beaches, she said she couldn't dance along a wall, and she'd been abroad, and hated it. In London, there were friends who knew her before the fall; it was always important to her to belong. She told me that since she had been cheated of her birthright, and tricked into childbirth, the only place we could go would be London.

'If you want to be an exile, that's where we'll go,' she said. 'You talk about the sea as though one could be substituted for another. Our sea is at La Corbière, our beaches are here, on the Island at Petit Port and La Rosière. You need the sea, Maman, I need the lighthouse; can you give that to me?'

Joan had lovely eyes, grey eyes like her father's that reminded one of the sea. In certain lights they could look almost green, as though a tide were washing over them. When we moved to Hendon, it was true, I did miss the sea. I used to look into Joan's eyes sometimes, when she wasn't looking, and she seemed to give me back a little of the winter seas. Eyes are so vulnerable; they say things that words themselves can't say. I used to feel sad and lost looking into the greyness of Joan's gaze. It was almost a relief when her eyes weakened and she had to wear glasses. It shielded me from all her unspoken reproaches and all the unanswerable questions that lay there.

Kitty was very proud of her own eyes, quite rightly, they were her finest feature. Now that we have both grown older they show not only her beauty, but the darker untouchable side of her character as well. Her skin has remained as smooth as when she was a little girl, so she thinks that age has not touched her, but it has gathered in her eyes, and the depth of her bitterness is quite frightening. I see people shy away from her gaze more and more. It hurts them. I'm afraid it is her eyes that will give her away in the end. That is where the focus of her madness lies.

I remember, once, sitting on a bus with Joan and seeing a crowd of jobless men grouping themselves to march. We were on our way to Tommy's to see Emily, so it must have been a Sunday afternoon. One of the marchers pressed his face against the window of the standing bus, and his eyes stared in at us with a terrible violence in them. He looked quite crazed, desperate. I thought of Kitty then, going hungry on the streets with all the violence that she holds in, let out. It made me feel dizzy, it was a horrible feeling. It was the first time I sensed what I now know: a time will come when I cannot protect her. There is one law for the poor, and another for the rich, and my pittance will never be enough to keep her within the bounds of the privileged.

After I die, will anyone understand that Kitty's cruelty is not her own doing? There are soldiers who suffered in their heads, heroes and veterans. They should have been cared for, but nobody wants to know about victims, particularly not the walking wounded. Scars are embarrassing. It is easier to sweep people aside once they cease to be useful, or normal. The man at the bus window was a veteran, it hadn't kept him from going hungry. I wish I could knit a wall around Kitty to keep her safe, to hide her eyes, to camouflage her difference from the world. I wish I were strong enough to stand by her. That is all a mother can do once the threads have broken. I wish I had the courage to leave this wheelchair. I wish; but I know I won't do it.

I have reached the end of my last skein. I have crocheted all the silk that I had inside me. It is November the 22nd – Saint Cecilia the Virgin's Day. These are the last days of the year. Yesterday a bomb fell in the city, and today my neighbour tells me her nephew has been sent to Caithness for training. Where will it end? I wonder if there will be soldiers at Selsey.

There are only seven Saints' days left until Christmas, but I shall not see Christmas this year. I shan't be sending any cards, gilding names on watered silk any more, or putting presents under the tree. I have had some sweet Christmases with Joan, times when there were just the two of us. So it was usually Boxing Day – the Feast of Saint Stephen, when Kitty would have already gone away with friends.

Joan tells me she has changed her name. She says she calls herself Joanna now. Names stick like burs, but they stay like scars. Being called Joanna cannot alter Joan's past. It may distance her, but her past will always be there, if only in photographs.

The holly berries have set their weather vane to frost. My hot-water bottle has grown cold. I feel a chill inside my blood. Outside, the oaks have all grown bare. It will be a hard winter this year. The war is bringing scoops of the beaches back into this Southern greyness.

Even here, in Chislehurst, which is known only for having sheltered Napoleon's son in exile, and for its nursing homes, there are sandbags. There are sandbags in the garden: some of them have burst.

I used to love looking out to sea, any sea. There are pictures of us every year that we sat on the beach at Selsey: snapshots of the three of us locked together in a frame. Joan would always be looking down, trying not to offend, sifting sand through her hands, as though to hurry time. I would be in my deckchair with my crochet, and my eyes on the sea, and keeping them apart. Them: my two poor darlings. Joan would always be on one side, and Kitty on the other. Dear Kitty always looked lovely in her summer clothes.

Those photographs should have been mere holiday souvenirs, snaps of a family on a beach. But the camera seems to have its own power, its own eyes. It has captured us as we really were. It has caught the trap, even down to Joan's uncertainty, even down to Kitty's unyielding stare.

PART IV

Joanna

CHAPTER 25

IT took me two months to find her. By April, I knew she was an inmate of a lunatic asylum on the outskirts of London. I explained, over the telephone, that I was Kathleen Allen's daughter, and I wanted to visit her.

'I wouldn't bother if I were you. She won't thank you for the visit, and you can't get anything out of it, her estate was forfeited to the Crown for her upkeep after she first came in.'

'I don't want anything from her,' I said, 'I just want to see her.'

There was a long unhelpful silence at the other end of the phone.

'How long has Mother been there?'

'Oooh! Years!'

I didn't tell anyone what I had learnt. I didn't tell my lover, who was tormenting me with his infidelities. Or the husband I had left for him, or had left me for someone else. It was always hard to see how that particular knot unravelled itself. I didn't tell my friends – not even my best friend, Barbara, who had seen me through my own spell in a mental hospital, when my depression got the better of me one year, and she brought me pomegranates and paperbacks to read and all the gossip from the French Pub until I was well enough to take my place there again. I wasn't ashamed of Mother's madness. I was afraid of my own feelings, of the pull back towards her. As though, at the mere mention of her name on a register, all my life, all that I had, receded into nothing and turned to ashes, leaving only the old bloodstained cord, hand over fist, dragging me back to the bitterness of her womb.

I took the bus from Paddington, across the river and into South London. The magnolias were coming into flower, and the squares and gardens looked pretty with their gaudy forsythias and straggling tulips topped by the occasional feathery tamarisk. Once in a while I'd catch glimpses of wisteria, my favourite flower, but I couldn't smell it as the bus glided past. I was thirty-two years old, just two days past my birthday, and I felt the weight of presents on my body. I was wearing the dangling jade earrings with their silver mounts and the gold ring on my finger that my lover had given me as a symbol of the for-everness of our union, and I could feel the reassuring warmth of a new baby growing in my womb. I wasn't large enough to show my pregnancy, but I was large enough to feel the comfort of its company. My body was flowering as surely as the waxy magnolia, and I basked in that knowledge, catching the afternoon sun in my window seat as I knitted and speculated on how Mother would receive me after all these years.

I had to change twice to get to the asylum, and the waiting made me nervous. I had been irritable now for three weeks, ever since I discovered her whereabouts. I had been bracing myself for this day. There had been rows at home, bad rows that had ended in so much unresolved anger that my family was scattered in the rancorous aftermath. The children were all away, temporarily, and I was alone with the eight-week-old fetus inside me. The last words I had said to my departing lover, two days before, were,
• 'Get out and I hope I never see you again, ever!'

They had been screamed rather than spoken, and he had left, not for the first time. I wasn't unduly worried by the outcome of our fight. I had said much worse before, and so had he, and we still came back together like iron filings and a magnet. We were both helplessly caught in a field of attraction beyond our control.

I had just passed the stage of my romance, however, when 'for ever's' concrete interpretation was lost in a pleasurable mist, and reached the point where the pattern of repetition in my loves was becoming apparent. I wasn't particularly interested in my affair; for once, I had something far more intriguing on my mind. I have often tried to remember exactly what happened that afternoon. I know I sat on the three buses, feeling the coming of spring and the baby inside me. And I know I felt in a strangely receptive mood: overemotional. The sight of many little things made me want to cry. Watching the children playing in their suburban gardens reminded me of forgotten incidents from my own childhood. They were snatches of sound and colour that had drowned under the weight of stronger things. But they all flooded back to me as I sat on the red bus with its tattered tartan seats.

I remembered rolling marbles along corridors and being able to beat even the senior girls at my French convent with one particular green and yellow wonder. The French skipping which always required a level of agility beyond my own, and the humiliation of untangling myself in the playground of my first school. I remembered Granny's first camellias of each year and the radiance of her face each time she cut that precocious waxy bloom with her secateurs. I remembered too the walk across the sands at low tide at St Aubin's Bay. But most of all, I remembered sitting in Agnes's garden keeping out of the way, pushing ants and bits of gravel across the back doorstep while the sunlight warmed the crown of my head. I was often happy sitting there, wrapped in the hovering scent of wisteria.

I felt so safe on the bus that I didn't want to leave it, but I had asked the conductor to tell me my stop, and he was waiting for me to get off.

The hospital looked huge and forlorn. I hadn't realised there were so many mad people. I found my way to her ward, and I kept thinking, 'Mother wouldn't like it here'. She had always been so fastidious, so clean and dainty in her ways. She had always kept her filigree, silver-lidded jars in exactly the same order on her dressing-table. When she went out, I would spy on them from her doorway. They were polished and clean. Even her gramophone records were arranged alphabetically in a box made of tropical woods with numbered ivory keys inside that released the records when pressed. Mother liked her things. She liked her clothes, her tortoiseshell combs, her emeralds. I began to wonder what they meant by 'forfeited to the Crown'. Did it mean they had taken her income away to pay for her costs, or did it mean they had confiscated her emeralds and her tiny crocodile-skin shoes? And then, 'certified' – what exactly did they mean by that? If it was that Mother was mad, Granny and I knew that, we had known it years before, so why had they taken her things away?

The corridor seemed to last for ever, with tread after tread across the rising smells of creosote on urine. There were strange noises coming from behind some of the doors. People were weeping, and the sound of their muffled tears made me want to cry. My head shrank at the thought of so many people locked away. I felt the hot sand in my skull shrivel my scalp, I became a tribal trophy, a walking head of hair ashamed of being there. I was in limbo, between the two worlds, wearing down my sensible shoes on the long corridor. Before I ever reached Mother's ward, I felt both guilt and grief for her having to be there. I hoped, beyond hope, that at the end of my walk there would be a suite of rooms like Mrs de Gruchy's with all Mother's things arranged stylishly around, and music playing tangos and charlestons, while Mother held her customary court of young admirers.

Passing as a voyeur through that public concentration of private purgatories, I began to feel afraid, knowing how it would destroy me to have to spend so much as a day there. My own hospital had not been like this. It had been more of a halfway house than a terminal. I realised suddenly that when the young doctor with the buck teeth who had treated me the most urged me to recover, it was this he was keeping me from. And it made me wonder if I would have got better without the help of Barbara and her pomegranates, and Louis's rambling letters and a place to step into in the world outside. Circumstances seemed to control so much. No wonder my grandfather had gambled, life itself was like a game of roulette in which one picked one's chips out of a tombola.

The worse that place seemed, the more I wanted to see Mother, to tell her I cared for her, I would help her all I could to get out. I felt the words tumble in my mind, tussling to get out first, to say I loved her and I needed her, I always had, and I had only ever been so difficult because I wanted her to forgive me. It all seemed so stupid in my mind to think of the way I used to be to her, hating her because she disliked my ugliness. I couldn't wait for her to see me as I was, so famous for my looks now, so renowned for the deep red of my hair.

She was in the big ward at the end. I recognised the name 'Faraday' over the doorway, but there was no one there among the inmates whom I could recognise as Mother. I realised that she would be changed, possibly beyond any easy recognition, so I looked carefully at every one of the twenty women in there. They seemed to divide into pale zombies lying motionless in their metal beds and a number of forlorn figures with staring faces, wandering listlessly around the narrow spaces allotted to each one. In the far corner, an ancient pile of spindly bones was brushing her hair, muttering her tally of strokes along the inflamed scalp of her long bald head. Beside her, a very large, much younger woman was twitching inside a regulation straitjacket. Her face was like a specimen from the geological museum, with striated bruises demarcating their volcanic progress through her flesh.

There was an acrid rancid smell. It was a smell of neglect, and picked scabs and fear and sweat. I began to resort to childhood tricks. I began to count the stained squares of the floor, and the iron bars of the beds. There was a window, a small rectangle of light and hope directly ahead of me. I moved towards it, not wanting to pass back through the gauntlet of stares. Voices were calling to me. Voices were driving me away, shouting abuse, taunting, pleading, ordering, but they all sank into the synchronised banging of beds. The cot sides were rattling. Even the zombies, it seemed, had woken from their stupor enough to bang their rusting bars. The baby inside me was safe and hidden from their disintegration. I was leading it up to the light. I became an androgynous Orpheus determined not to look back.

When I reached the window, it too was barred. I clung to it, staring down the four floors of its height into the littered patch of ground below. An elder tree was growing from a wall. Strips of white gowns like bandages were clinging to the drainpipes. There were heaps of them on the ground: soiled dressings that would cushion my fall. I wanted to glide down. The vertigo in my head wrapped itself around my knees and turned my legs to a boneless jelly. Strange hands were clawing at my elbows, stroking my hair. I felt them reach into the baby inside me. I felt them trying to bind me to that ward. And then a bell rang loudly by my ear, my mastoid ear that ached at any shrillness. My head was scooped out there, dented on the bone with heavy-handed wartime surgery.

At the sound of the bell all the hands but one withdrew. The ward returned to its former silence, with only the whispered numbers of the old lady at her hair.

'I'm sorry, you'll have to come away,' a young nurse told me, lisping slightly and rolling down the mauve and white stripes of her sleeves. 'It just excites the patients to see a visitor, you shouldn't have come in here.'

She steered me back towards the corridor. I wanted to tell her that I'd come to see Mother, that I couldn't find her. I wanted to ask her so many things, but my voice jammed in my throat like an enormous Adam's apple and I couldn't speak. The sentences formed in my mind but refused to translate themselves into sounds. I had begun to fall inside my head and I needed to keep falling, to hit the ground. I pretended to be Granny. I imagined myself standing as erect as she with her charcoal jacket with its oyster buttons done up right under her chin and the Carrara grey marble of her hands clenched into each other, as they were whenever she asked for assistance.

'Please take me to Mrs Allen, Kathleen Allen. I believe she is here on the ward.'

The nurse kept walking as I spoke, accustomed no doubt to disregarding every kind of female raving. But as the words sank in, she paused and turned to me, nearly tripping me over.

'She's on the side. She doesn't have visitors. I'm sorry.'

'I want to see her. I've come to see her.' I tried to add, 'I'm her daughter,' but the words shrivelled in my mouth.

'Look,' the nurse said, not unkindly, 'it's better not to disturb her. I don't know who you are, but it won't do either of you any good.'

I opened my mouth to speak, and she hurried on: 'I don't even know if she's in her jacket today. Sometimes we just strap her to the bed to give her arms a rest.'

I had been struggling to draw my trump, and I blurted it out, reversed into a more appropriate relationship: 'She's my mother.'

'Then go home,' she told me. 'Please, go home.'

The demon of my fall was pushing me. 'I insist on seeing her. You've no right to keep her chained to her bed. No right at all.'

'Strapped,' the nurse said, with a hint of curtness in her voice which softened as she explained, 'It's the only way any of us can get near her, and to be honest, it's the only way we can stop her from going for the other patients.'

'I want to see her. She's my mother, don't you understand?'

'When she first came,' the nurse told me, ignoring what I said and speaking more to the pale-green, grubby walls than to me, 'we had so many suicides in here, we had to put her on the side. Even now, most of the nurses can't go into her room. We've tried sedating her. We kept her down for two years like that, on drugs, but there's something about her, it's not like with the others. Nowhere else will take her. We have tried.'

I can remember the day up to there quite clearly. And I can remember seeing Mother on her bed, as small as a child, with her feet reaching only to a bump in the middle under the hospital coverlet. All her face had changed, her thick brown hair was cropped, almost shaved and grey, her face was marked with strange lines as though a child had scribbled them in with an unsteady hand. She was Mother by her eyes, though. They had remained the same deep green, but they were locked into a flash crueller and angrier than any I had ever seen. Searching for some sign of fellow-feeling in those green orbs, all I found was a hint of surprise that any rage could last so long – a hint, perhaps, of boredom at the emotional vitriol that came flooding out of her presence.

I knew she recognised me straight away, and I knew she spoke to me, and she sounded like someone else, a sort of underwater voice. And I know that even as she spoke, I tried not to hear what she was saying because it sounded too terrible. I remember I backed away from her and the wall behind me seemed solid with no door to let me out until the nurse came and took me in my blindness to a lavatory caked with urine and I was sick and it seemed that the child inside me puked out of my mouth and was lost. Everything was lost. Fourteen years of my life, all my escape, obliterated. I don't suppose I'll ever know what it was Mother said to me, because my memory still curls away from it as fire. Ice burns.

They say a thousand people were shipped away from Jersey and only one came out alive from Belsen. They say the Nazis threw their prisoners over the cliffs at Alderney. Our soldiers brought back photographs from Poland and Germany. There were piles of shoes there, and mountains of teeth. Nelson said we did worse things to some of their cities than they did in the Blitz. He said we had to. Sometimes we have to do things. Sometimes we have to.

After I saw Mother there, I had to go home and die. I had to. I turned the radio on, because I knew then that I was weak and I might cry. It was Dickie Murdoch talking. I liked Dickie Murdoch. I put my head in the huge womb of the gas oven, and I lay there until his voice faded away. For once I was doing what Mother wanted.

The rest was like Jersey talk: second-hand recollections. I don't recall the next six months at all. I don't recall coming round in hospital, or fighting with the nurses and the doctors for the next three days. Nor my refusal to recover; my five months of paralysis, the 'inversion hysteria' of my file. They moved me from the clinic to a mental hospital in the Fens. The windows looked out over flat black mud. The nurses wheeled me to sit by those bleak views, hoping that something would stir in me and give me back the will to live. The psychiatrist came and went, pressing my secrets from me like buried splinters, but I never told them of my trip to Mother. That was my secret. I never told anyone, so that what she had said died even though my own robust life had refused to capitulate to her need for death. I kept what she had said so closely guarded that I lost it myself. I pretended so hard that I hadn't been to see her that I almost believed it.

It was only when my own child threatened to find her, twenty years on, that I relented. Because Mother might still be there, driving the weak and the restless into their graves. She might still have been there then, and I was afraid. For this was the child who had survived my own visit, survived the gassing and the drugs, and grown inside my womb as I lay in the Fens until her stirring drove me back to life.

Sometimes I feel that I have picked up Granny's crochet and tried to do it, copying her stitches, and done it wrong and made mistakes which have so altered the tension that they can never be put right or be disguised. So I unravel, and try again, adding unsatisfactory loops to the already complex mesh. That's how it's been since I tried to die. I find myself trapped in lies. If only I could remember what she said, I might be able to straighten it all out now. It has taken up so many years of my life.

When I look back, I know there must be so much more. What about my career? What about the twenty years I spent dealing with the maladjusted in my job, running concurrently with the other minor delinquencies of my four daughters? What about them, the girls? Why must it always be Mother and Mother? I was a mother too! If this rambling is to be my memoir, where are the secrets of all the men who used me as a repository for their own hopes and misgivings? Where are my recollections of their thoughts; and my own memories of their transient use of my body? I knew so many people then, yet it seems that the only ones who really knew me were the other two corners of my first reluctant triangle.

I have thought of Granny a lot recently, and I seem to be almost near enough to touch her. If I can untangle what I feel about Mother, I can lie back and die.

My own life is fading as surely as the copper beech leaves in my childhood winters. And at last I want to understand her, to know what forces drove her to be as she was. I feel a need to get close to her, not by pestering with my physical presence but by knowing what it must have felt like to be her: to be the reluctant keeper of so much power and the focus of so much unwanted attention. I only ever saw her at her worst. I want to see her as other people did, not as the lunatic she came to be but as the bewitching girl she began as.

There was always an intrinsic problem between us. It prevented any progress in the way we felt. The only way, before, that I could avoid her disapproval was by not existing. I had to be a nonperson. Since I did exist, I was forever in her way. I shifted from wanting to die so that I could be forgiven, to wanting to live just to spite her. To be, or not to be . . . the choice is now out of my hands. My own years have run out like so much sand through my fingers; all I have left is the hot sensation in the palm of my hands and my memories. Everything seems different.

'Bits of you are feeding into me, Mother, I am being drip-fed my absolution. Bits of you that I never saw before are oozing through my veins. I kept cutting you out of my life with the same well-meaning ruthlessness with which the doctors here have cut the tumours from my breasts. Your rivals, Mother, that double bill that drew in so many admirers, can only tout tickets now for this hushed cancer ward. Here are the scars, but the cancer is still inside me; it is lining my spine.'

I always envied Mrs de Gruchy for living as she did with such ease in the hospital. I used to dream that one day, I too would have my own room there, overlooking the Thames, with the five bays of St Thomas' Hospital dropping their shadows into the passing tides. And here I am, with a smaller space than those two lavish rooms, but still with my own bed and locker, and the chair for my own daughters to take turns in. Two of the wide bays have gone now, bombed in the war, and in their place there are high modern blocks. But it is still St Thomas', the Tommy's of my childhood with its view across the river to the Houses of Parliament and Big Ben.

I have come full circle from those days, and here I am, seeded with Granny's cancer, which I have tended as carefully as her own suburban garden, watering the cinerarias and the pink camellias so that they can flourish in the London sun. Every time the clock strikes from across the water, it seems to strike off a part of my life. It has chimed all my lovers away, and left only my hovering daughters. It has knocked me off the Embankment wall where I used to sit on summer nights and watch the people hurrying across Waterloo Bridge while I had all their urgency combined: waiting for my darling to honour his tryst. The clock has annihilated the darlings and broadcast all my old kisses to the muddy waves. It takes me back over and over to the place of least endearment. It takes me back to Mother. Even its precision seems to be synchronised by the ruthless mechanism of her eyes.

Sometimes, she used to hover and stare with that alarming emerald laser, and she'd say, 'I can't get so-and-so off my mind.' Then, within the week, so-and-so would die. It was infallible. It annoyed her, that trick of people clinging to her when they died, particularly strangers. It annoyed her because once someone had fixed inside her mind in this way, she would feel their feelings, intermittently, until they sighed or choked their last breath. Granny said it made her brain ache to know someone that well. Mother felt the world was using her to funnel its excess emotions through.

In Hendon, it used to make me jealous when I saw her pause in the way she had and comment that 'someone was on her mind'. I wanted to be on her mind. I wanted to be the one to pucker her pale forehead with worry. I can feel her near me, not as the bitter caprice of her silhouette portrait but as the tormented ferry that she used to be, guiding the dying across that anxious causeway into death.

'I used to have all the beach to sift, and all the time in the world. Now that it's running out, though, and all that is left is the bandaged ceiling of this hourglass and the last few bottles of my drip, I need to add your pieces to me, to puzzle it all out, I suppose. I keep forgetting what you looked like. All I can remember are your cold, Antarctic eyes. I always knew that there was more behind them than your anger, but I was afraid to admit it. Afraid too, perhaps, to see myself mirrored in their flawless glint. You had to be wrong, so that I could be right. It was black and white only, mediated by Granny's charcoal grey. I couldn't deal in green before, I was too jealous of my sanity.

'Who were you? I've always called you "Mother" in my mind, and now, at last, I feel you here with me, mothering me into the darkness with the brightness of your emerald light.'

The nurses will be coming round soon with their trolley. I have become a junkie in my respectable old age, they have made me into a morphine addict here. It helps conceal my distress. I suppose it does help the pain as well, but it can't stop it. Nothing can stop it now, it's on a home run. It has curdled my blood. If the drip came out of my hand now, I would die. But they can't do that. They have to keep it in. They have to. And despite all their efforts I have to die now, any day. I hear them say that even a horse couldn't last another week in my condition.

This horse doesn't want any morphine yet. She wants to think, and be an old mare exorcising her nightmares, exercising them on their way to the knacker's yard.

The ward has reverted to numbers. Big Ben is dividing the darkness into fractions. The ward clock is copying it. Beside me, the old lady with the white brittle hands is brushing her hair, counting. She counts all the time, brushing her ancient baldness with an imaginary brush.

'Seventy-eight, seventy-nine, ninety.'

She loses count and picks up again and carries on, brushing her hair a hundred times a day just as Granny taught me to, and, no doubt, as her mother taught her to, a hundred times a day.

'Ninety-two, ninety-three, sixty' – she never gets to a hundred, her numbers have disintegrated with her years.

I don't want to hear her any more. I don't want to hear anything but my own mother's voice, her thoughts.

'Am I on your mind at last, Mother? Can you feel my thoughts, like you used to feel those other premonitions of death? Do you see that I was quite like you? I had my madness too.

'You can climb down from your potential pyre, and I stop torching it with the embers of my hair. It is all clinker now. You can climb out of the ducking pool of my myopia. Your malign clairvoyance doesn't have to withstand the battering ram of my affection any more. You no longer need to be my own vain parcel of guilt. *Mea culpa* was my creed; but I think I'll have another epitaph.

'I imagine the cold in my spine to be a perfect emerald that will shatter when I go, and lie in my coffin in tiny pieces. What would my whole life have been like if I could have seen you as a glittering jewel and that only, a flawless precious stone? Gems have no meaning. You had no gardens, no traces of cracks or flaws in the pure brilliance of your eyes. There was nothing for Granny to hoe or prune.'

One, two, three . . .

The night is nagging, and after all that hatred, we are much the same. Emeralds and glass look much the same in this darkness.